A BUNCH

OF

WILD

ROSES

also by Edward Forde Hickey

The Early Morning Light
A New Day Dawning
Footsteps in The Dew

A BUNCH OF WILD ROSES

EDWARD FORDE HICKEY

Copyright © 2020 Edward Forde Hickey

The moral right of the author has been asserted.

Apart from any fair dealing for the purposes of research or private study, or criticism or review, as permitted under the Copyright, Designs and Patents Act 1988, this publication may only be reproduced, stored or transmitted, in any form or by any means, with the prior permission in writing of the publishers, or in the case of reprographic reproduction in accordance with the terms of licences issued by the Copyright Licensing Agency. Enquiries concerning reproduction outside those terms should be sent to the publishers.

Matador
9 Priory Business Park,
Wistow Road, Kibworth Beauchamp,
Leicestershire. LE8 0RX
Tel: 0116 279 2299
Email: books@troubador.co.uk
Web: www.troubador.co.uk/matador
Twitter: @matadorbooks

ISBN 978 1838592 486

British Library Cataloguing in Publication Data.
A catalogue record for this book is available from the British Library.

Printed and bound by CPI Group (UK) Ltd, Croydon, CR0 4YY
Typeset in 11pt Aldine401 BT by Troubador Publishing Ltd, Leicester, UK

Matador is an imprint of Troubador Publishing Ltd

www.edwardfordehickey.co.uk

Frontispiece Days in Olde Tipp'rary

in memory of Biddy and Jack

Contents

Author's Note	ix
The Arrival of Dandy	1
Darkie's ups and downs	30
Fandango from Galway	94
Days of Laughter, Days of Tears	141
Cousin Daisy	190
Stylish and his merry soul	224
How Stylish Redeemed Himself	268
Sammy-Joe's sorrow	366
Deelyah, the little saint	419
Fingers-Jack	455
Little Nell's journey	482

Author's Note

There was a man called Dandy and he lived in Galway, not far from Portmantle, the far side of the Mighty Shannon River. It was at a time not long after the famine. His father and his father before that were from the race of Spallidagh and some said that their pedigree went back to the days of the Ribbonmen, who a century or two earlier were the blight of certain absentee-landlords in parts of north Tipperary. Rumour had it that some of these Ribbonmen, the Spallidaghs among them, had come by their property by putting a burning branch down on the chest of a gallant bailiff, whose ruffians had previously burnt down the thatch from some of the nearby cabins, sending families out onto the roadside to die.

    Such idle chatter might well have been a romantic fireside tale to while away the long beer-drenched evenings in the drinking-shop of Dancing-Jack, who himself was a descendant from a family of Tipperary exiles that had landed in Galway many years earlier. But a story such as this did not explain why Dandy's people or the ancestors of Dancing-Jack were living in Galway and not Tipperary at the time this tale begins.

Children had been taught at home and at school a truer and more accurate version of history and it went much further back – back to the evil rogueries of Cromwell's soldiers and his henchman, Ireton, under whose orders the native Irish, peasants and clerics alike, had been driven from the fertile fields of Tipperary and banished to the western counties to see what they could do with land that was often much less fertile. *To Hell or to Connaught* had been the cry of the invading forces, the echo of which would last for generations to come. The thinking of the foreigner was simple enough: give the natives the rocky stones to plough and they'll soon find themselves starving, eventually dying on the side of the road.

This was the more likely reason why Dandy was led to believe that the fertile fields of north Tipperary were his ancestors' rightful homeland and that the spot, long held sacred in the minds of past generations of Spallidaghs, was the hillslopes at the foot of the Mighty Mountain – the brown foothills of windy Mureeny.

ADDISON & COLE

A BUNCH OF WILD ROSES

EDWARD FORDE HICKEY

I thoroughly enjoyed working on this last novel in your Rookery Rally series, which I found as completely beguiling as your previous manuscripts. All the familiar attributes – the effortless evocation of an almost-forgotten world, the wonderfully personable narration, the endlessly charming characterisation – were again present and correct in this fourth book. Life and death in Rookery Rally were again treated with simplicity, profundity and a lightness of touch. Every individual story within the narrative was undoubtedly very strong. It is another wonderful collection of tales.

feedback by Ben Evans, Senior Editor

Days of Laughter, Days of Tears: a tale of olde Tipp'rarie

ONE

The Arrival of Dandy

The ancestors of Dandy had the good fortune to be labelled the trusted servants of Lord Allsworthy, a distant cousin of the queen. He treated the Spallidaghs with the greatest of kindness – to such an extent that he gave Dandy's father the position of butler over his household, a task that eventually saw him raised further aloft to become keeper of the estate's accounting-books with the title *Head Steward* bestowed on him.

A year or two later Dandy was born, the one and only offspring, his mother *(Betsy)* having died in childbirth.

Good fortune smiled on this growing child when Lord Allsworthy saw fit to allow him a place in the daily schoolroom of the Big House alongside his own sons and daughters. From that day forth he was to acquire the same skills of book-and-pencil as the gentry themselves – absorb the same lessons in music and dancing and even gain the use of the embroidery needles that they themselves were using.

His father quickly realised that his son's pathway to grandeur lay in the pages of books and in the understanding of lofty subjects such as poetry and Euclid and he was daily seen at his son's shoulder, making sure that he applied himself most studiously throughout his schooldays. Over the next few years, therefore, young Dandy grew in wisdom and strength.

He Left the Big House

The day came when he had to stand on his own two feet and, armed with the blessings of the kindly lord, leave the Big House. Good fortune followed him once more and he arrived in the town of Portmantle on the edge of the Mighty Shannon River where, thanks to the lord's high recommendations, he found himself in the enviable position of the town's schoolmaster. It would seem that his future was firmly secured and his fame and fortune assuredly made.

It should have been the start and end of a pretty little story but fate can sometimes bring bad news round the unseen corners of life and can trip a man up when he least expects it. For it was the long-established custom in that particular town for a former pupil, who had previously shown scholastic excellence in that self-same schoolhouse, to come back to the classroom one day and throw down a challenge to his previous tutor as to who should be running the school – the established master or the youth himself.

The Challenge

In a flurry of agitation a batch of school records and reports were brought down from the attic and carefully scrutinised. The priest and the managers were called into the schoolyard for the challenge to be formally written down and for Dandy to be summoned to account. You can imagine the panic settling into his poor head and the many prayers he said to the Blessed Virgin and any other saint that he could think of on the morning of this great event.

The contest between himself and his former scholar started off slowly enough around ten in the morning. By late afternoon it had built up a fine head of steam, the subjects varying from the realms of bog-Latin and advanced arithmetic to reciting lengthy stanzas from *the Rhyme of the Ancient Mariner* and *the Lady of Shallot* – as well as some sophisticated understanding of the ancient Egyptians.

Dandy tried his level best to hold back the ecstatic onslaught of young Foxylocks, who had brought with him a bag of long-winded facts, figures and ideas that he proceeded to hammer out at the table-front. The mesmerised townie onlookers, mainly the gossipy women (*'Aren't these two almighty windbags the very wonder-of-God?'*) stood agog outside the railings and enjoyed the contest powerfully. It was a long time since any of them had had so much fun and amusement.

By the evening the mental tussle began to wane and the judgement was finally written down in favour of the proud youth. For once in his life Dandy had fallen short of the mark in front of the witnessing bigwigs of the town. The young lad's uncle was the diocesan archbishop and had more than a fair share of influence, which was quickly pointed out by the local cynics. However, destiny was to have its way and the two sporting combatants spat on their fist and shook hands like a pair of gentlemen. It had been a very sad day for poor Dandy.

For the next month Foxylocks became apprenticed to the minister of a small church in a nearby village. Thereafter he returned to Portmantle amid rapturous applause, wearing a suit of black clothing to match his new image and was installed as the new schoolmaster. The town's old turncoats drank his health from dusk till dawn. They spared not a moment's thought for Dandy.

It seemed that the priest, unlike the archbishop, was a man to be trusted for he gave Dandy an excellent written testament as to his fine character and his studious industry with the pen-and-ink. Then he sent him away without ceremony or reward, his tail between his legs, his two eyes full of salty tears and his heart as heavy as an old corncrake's. No more would he enjoy the wonders of the classroom – no more would he march his pupils up and down the yard with the military rhythm of his Irish poems or teach them the art of cultivating the new carrots, tomatoes and lettuces in his garden – no more would he fill them with the honest-to-goodness hatred of all forms of injustice and enrich their growing character with all that he deemed good.

The Tipperary Road

Sprung from proud stock, Dandy soon learnt to wipe his tears away and hide his heavy heart. He was no fool and had expected no sad farewell or grateful salute from his townie neighbours – nobody to see him off down the road or wave the red handkerchief after him. Nor was he disappointed. The next day he started to make his preparations for the long haul back to Tipperary. He gathered together his little satchel of schoolbooks. He paired his ash-plant and polished his hobnailed boots, which (to give his mare an occasional rest) would be needed on the trudging road now beckoning him towards Mureeny.

Monday came along and the yellow awakening of dawn slowly turned into the sunny beauty of a new day's light. He washed and shaved by the light of the candlestick and put on his corduroy britches and the new hobnailed boots. He wrapped himself up against the cold air and brought his mare (*Sunlight*) from the stable, all the time whispering words of encouragement into her excited ears. He blessed himself with the holy-water from the font at the half-door and then he slammed the door shut for the last time.

Sunlight zig-zagged her hooves along the town's quiet cobblestones. Then, as if to cheer the soul of her master, she stepped with a determinedly brisk clip-clop towards the winding road that led on towards Tipperary and the heather and gorse that patched the hills above

Mureeny. Not once did Dandy look back. Galway had faded forever behind him like an old-fashioned dream and soon the day's sun was streaming down on top of himself and Sunlight.

He found himself crossing the Mighty Shannon River's bridge when he saw a forlorn tinker-woman bemoaning her plight at the side of the road.

'Gimmee a copper! Gwan, do!'

How often had he heard this same cry on previous market-days and had given it not a moment's thought. But something urged him to lean down towards the twisted face of the tinker-woman and look her in the eye. He gave her the honest smile that was always on his lips and fumbled in his pocket. He placed a few bits of silver in the palm of her outstretched hands whereupon she raised her face to heaven and gave him her blessing. She blessed his future children and she blessed his children's children. Dandy believed in the goodness of her prophecy and he headed on towards Tipperary with an ever more joyful heart.

He Reached Mureeny And Began To Teach

A day later – just as the last shoots of sunlight were pointing their glassy rays across the hills round Mureeny – he reached the doors of the little church that stood in the centre of the village. He slipped down from his mare – to be greeted by a rosy-faced young priest (*Father Magnanimus*) with a warmth befitting the return of a prodigal son and as if the Galwayman had just stepped down from the moon. In front of Dandy was a warm fire to toast his weary legs. Sunlight was given enough hay to feed a famine and shortly afterwards he himself was given a fine bowl of hare-soup, followed up with a brimming plateful of mutton, spuds and cabbage. Restored to life, he found himself once more in powerful shape and before the astonished eyes of the young priest he started to unwrap his shoulder-load of schoolbooks: the poetry, the books of the almost-forgotten Irish language and a good few more.

From that day on the young priest offered Dandy not only his sympathetic support and understanding but gave him all the encouragement a man could wish for. It wasn't long before The Galwayman was able to settle back into his customary ways of teaching the young and obliterating from his mind all traces of the recent sad interlude with that crafty little Foxylocks back in the schoolyard.

With no permanent schoolhouse to call his own, he took to the local lanes and went further afield to the remote pathways as directed by the priest. With the clanging sound of his stout brogues and a second pair laced around his neck he was a strange marvel in the eyes of the peasants, many of whom were still barefooted. He also had the greatcoat of the priest wrapped close round his shoulders in the face of the permanent wind and rain and he travelled from dawn till dusk the length and breadth of Mureeny. When too far away from the clergyman's house he was always given a jovial welcome for the price of his knowledge and teaching and was provided with shelter abroad in the turf-shed. There were times when he got a warm bed inside in the house itself, always with enough to eat and drink and fatten his belly and legs.

He was soon teaching in hedge-schools – teaching the shy boys and girls a full programme of learning: stories from the penny-books: copperplate writing: weights and measures to help their fathers at cattle-sales: teaching them their Christian faith with well-chosen biblical stories. That's when the generous priest, feeling that Dandy might be destined for higher realms, found him a permanent place in the schoolhouse below in Saddleback village. Henceforth he'd be warm and dry with a comfortable roof over his head. Fair play to you, Father Magnanimus. If ever there was a guardian angel, it was you.

The Name 'Dandy'

You must have wondered about the name *Dandy*. For all we know he may have been christened Jack or Tim or Ned like the rest of the world. Another year hadn't gone by, however, before he was able to hold back a few pound-notes in his hip-pocket and take off his old Galway shirt and his corduroys. In their place he donned the three quarter-length leggings with the silver buttons down the side. He began to wear the swallowtail coat with the emerald waistcoat underneath it. He acquired a half-Caroline hat and, to polish things off, he slipped onto his legs some delicate fine hose above a pair of shiny buckled shoes. He now outshone even the proudest sons of the rich farmers, who lived on the far side of Mureeny and these prime buckos were forced to acknowledge him as the dandiest dandy they'd ever laid eyes on. From that day till the day he died he was referred to as *Dandy-the-Galwayman.*

There was a reason for this stylish turn of events and it lay in the maidenly shape of Sadie-from-the-Well. She was the shy and only daughter of Sam Pickett, the principal master in the Saddleback schoolhouse. Poor fretful Dandy! On her he cast his great big calf-eyes. To her he gave his heart and soul. For she had the magic in her – with her long flowing hair and her slender legs like a crane. Hers was a beauty that the songs of street-singers paraded before market-day crowds: her smile was a present from heaven's gate: her cheeks were the pink of the rose: her teeth were like little pearls of whiteness and those laurel-berry eyes of her were as soft as a bog.

Dandy was not alone with these thoughts for the neighbours would stop and stare at her when going to the well to fetch back their buckets of water. They'd heave a little sigh and they'd shake their heads: 'Wouldn't ye give yeer two eyes to be looking at the likes of Sadie and to see her walk the green fields and watch her pick the little wildflowers.'

It was summertime and the days were growing longer. They were getting hotter too. As soon as his scholars had run off home, Dandy took to moping round the gate in front of the Pickett front door. Any excuse would do him. Maybe he'd lost his pocket-watch. And as he stalked his damsel, it wasn't long before those weary old gossips (*the Weeping Mollys*) gave their tongues a good airing and said he had the appearance of a young weasel that steadfastly chases a stray rabbit. It was true for them, until finally – *SNAP!* – he got hold of Sadie's childish heart, what with his winning ways and his bunches of stray poppies and his armfuls of blue cornflowers.

Realising the force of the love that was freshening between them, Sadie's parents gave them their blessing and the two of them started walking hand-in-hand through the dreamy cornfields up around Sheep's Cross, the oats brushing their sides. From there they would walk out over the hilly slopes above the Valley-of-the-Pig, two gentle souls as innocent as the day they were born and always looking for a shady spot to put down their coats and stay a while.

Before a single leaf had fallen from a tree there came a Sunday afternoon when they took the pony-and-trap (the politest way of travelling) across to the churchyard to meet up with their new priest (*Father Solemnity*) and tell him of their love. With his consent and with the blessing of Mother Church they got married in the little church in Saddleback village. Gladsome was the day and the style and pomp of it would take your breath away – to see the guests growing richer in heart and the sweet music of the dances and songs blaring out across the hills – the voracious devouring of the numberless roasted hens and skinned rabbits and pig slices (lashings of it) and the soda-bread doorsteps stacked like bricks and the pans of puddings frying away like blazes. Everyone was full-bloated for days to come for it had been better than a priest's wake. And then the sun went off in the last of its pink afterglow and the world became silent once more. Dandy and Sadie closed the front door and, tired and worn, they lay in each other's arms until the dawn came in the window. It had been a wonderful day.

The Laneway At Sheep's Cross

Himself and Sadie bought themselves a horse-and-cart and came down the mountains to a tiny thatched cabin in a winding laneway near Sheep's Cross, less than a stones-throw above Rookery Rally. It had once been the home of a band of roguish sheep-stealers (*The Burgundians*). The two of them purchased a tiny field (the *haggart*) at the very boundary of Lord Fashionable's estates and before the next year was out they got hold of a second haggart a few yards further down the lane.

The seasons rolled by and Dandy started using his two haggarts for the wheat to make their weekly bread and for the spuds and cabbages for their dinner. It wasn't long before he bought a pig and two goats. He kept a small corner for a short-horned red cow (*Suzy*) to be milked and he bought a dozen hens for Sadie. These hens were always following her down the yard as though she was their mother. But before all that he bought a big four-poster bed and a well-sprung mattress to enable himself and Sadie to get themselves merry from time to time.

Early each morning Sadie rubbed the mists of sleep from her eyes, her thoughts punctured by the new shy song of the birds. This was the signal for her to stretch her hot legs out from under the blankets. She was always first to get herself out of bed, to unbar the shutters and unlatch the front door before busying herself lighting her fire with the crushed brown papers and the sticks of kindling.

But Dandy wasn't far behind her in greeting the new day. He left their little thatched house, saddled up Sunlight and, while the fields were still smoking with dew and the grass covered with cobwebs, took the two-mile trail up to Saddleback schoolhouse. He had already done a fine morning's work in the two haggarts. He had dug a bucket of spuds for Sadie and had cut and brought back the sack of cabbages to fill her skillet-pot, the leftovers going to the hens or mixed with mash for the pig. And while he was away at the school, Sadie was seen to keep pace with him: sweeping the floor, the hearth and the yard until they were spotlessly clean: making her new loaves of bread and marking them with the cross before putting them in the burner to bake: churning her butter as fast as she could from the cream in her sweet-gallon, shaking it rhythmically till the arms ached off of her.

As soon as Dandy came home in the evening, he went back to inspect his haggarts and give them his last look-back before closing the gate. Then he cut Sadie a pile of logs and took an armful into the cabin. He watched her as she darned his socks for him, the light from the lamp touching her nimble fingers before airing his shirt on the crane that she'd pulled out from the fire. The two-of-them were as contented as two young cats and they placed their chairs in front of the hearth and looked into the fire's merriment. With the strength of his love for her and the strength of her love for him they began to turn their little abode into a snug residence that was fit enough for a king and his queen.

The Neighbours

Well, the sky is not always full of the yellow gleam and the odd dark cloud can come speeding in. And so, much to the surprise of the two young lovers, the neighbours on seeing the rapid improvements in their daily lives now proved themselves to be a little bit grouchier than before – a little bit more miserable than before. It was always the same when a new couple came in amongst them and were seen to be happy in themselves. Jealousy and snobbery started to spread among them and they began to label Sadie and Dandy with the derisory name of *blow-ins* from over the hill.

It wasn't long before their sour shifty faces had a genuine reason to sneer at Dandy and his bride for the thatched roof on their cabin was worn down to a sad state of green after years of constant rain. Even the rafters were a maze of swallows' nests. Dandy worked hard to repair the roof but was forced at last to give up. Then a sudden idea came into his head: instead of putting on some new thatch, it'd be better to tear it off altogether and replace it with grey slates from the nearby Yellowstone Quarry.

In the eyes of the neighbours this proposed venture was nothing short of a sacrilege and they spent the day and night spitting on the ground and throwing their hands up in the air in mock horror. No other cabin had ever been seen (they said) to have posh slates for a roof – apart from the priest's small church over in Copperstone Hollow. Seeing the new and almighty Dandy taking on this task and feeling that it would put him a step or two higher than the rest of them, they began to gather in the dusk abroad in his yard, protesting in frustration at the sight of the new slates replacing the thatch. It wasn't long before they began adding to their unkind vocabulary, calling Dandy and Sadie *the two outsiders living in the little flea-nest beyond the bounds* and accompanying this sort of talk with gales of foul laughter.

Yes, their little thatched house wasn't big enough to swing a cat in but it was nothing like a nest of fleas. If water will wear away a stone it wasn't long before this constant unfriendliness caused the old burning sorrow from the time he was outmatched by his former pupil in the schoolhouse contest to resurrect itself inside Dandy's chest. The result was that himself and Sadie began to look sadder than the alder-trees on the ditch round their door. The mischievous talk, however, wasn't strong enough to stop our Galwayman from spitting on his fists, putting his hands to the plough and tilling his garden right up to the edge of the ditch so that by the following spring he was able to produce a fine garden of vegetables – one that even Lord Allsworthy would have been proud to call his own. Fair play to you, Dandy.

The days rolled on. The months followed after them. Storms will come and then they go away again and there are times when there's no explanation at all for it. In the end the passersby were tempted to occasionally rise up in their horse's stirrups and when no-one else was looking peer in at the gardening handiwork of the merry-faced Dandy and the rows of vegetables that he'd planted – neat as a pin and right upto the ditch with not a weed to be seen.

They would stop for a while and listen to him whistling at his work. 'As good as any thrush or nightingale,' they had to admit. One by one they started admiring the strange fernlike carrots – the red tomatoes and the beetroots (*bigger than yer fist*) and the lettuce-leaves, glistening with water that he'd liberally given them and everything shining out at them from inside the ditch. Even a fool could see how Dandy's good-nature was winning them over and how he was always willing to impart his knowledge of gardening to each and everyone that he came across. 'Give them plenty of manure,' he'd say with a warning finger.

It wasn't long before the neighbours' bitterness, like any miserable toothache, disappeared from view as if it had never been there in the first place. Their natural warmth and goodness came flooding back into their hearts and they were forced to smile. They began to vie with Dandy as to who would produce the best armfuls of spuds – who would field the largest cabbages. The women weren't slow either in coming forward and they began to compete with Sadie as to who would grow the finest flowers for the dresser and the front-table. Soft-hearted laughter had finally replaced tears.

Sadie's Gentle Sunlight

In the following days Sadie's gentle sunlight filled every moment of Dandy's life. Her cheery smiles filled his bed, his fireside, his yard and the bit of meadow that he was scything in the last days of that summer. As in a fairyland book of poems, they merrily dreamed the next few years along. See the two glowing hearts gazing into the firelight as the evening draws in and out at the new gooseberry bushes at the bottom of their haggart – bushes which Dandy had brought home from the Roaring Town. See the two of them wrapped in uninterrupted contemplation, listening to the birds twittering in the ivy-clad trees that surrounded their cabin: the little birds and the rosy-cheeked Sadie and Dandy all in harmony, a-sighing and a-carolling most tunefully and not a wrinkle on their brow. A painter in oils could paint it all for you from start to finish.

The Children

Dandy was never a man to leave his toes roasting in the ashes of his fire. There was a swagger growing in him and over the next decade in that snug feather bed behind the chimney-hob he fathered eight children – a small enough family for the time. There were seven boys and then there was Kate, the only girl.

Like many others they listened to those wonderful tales of the great wealth that lay in store for them in far-off Van Diemen's Land and the gold that lay in the streets of Baltimore in the Land of The Silver Dollar across the ocean. Sadly, in less time than Dandy and Sadie would have wished, the two sad souls found themselves waving their sodden handkerchiefs to six of their seven sons as they hit the road towards glory – all on the self-same day – in the jaunting cart borrowed from Ned-the-Herd's father (*Hoppity*). It rolled down the hillslopes like a goddamn funeral, disappearing forever and leaving behind just the one son, the youngest lad (*Handsome Johnnie*) to help his heartbroken father plough and till the two haggarts in the days that were to come.

Kate

All this was after his daughter (*Kate*) had disappeared from view the year before. A strange and memorable day it was that sent her away for she was still but a child of eleven.

The morning had started out cold and drizzly and Sadie found herself abroad in the yard. The lazy sky was soon getting itself flushed with the glitter of the sun that was to replenish the rest of the day and she began washing out the small milk-churn that was needed for saving the day's milk from Suzy-the-cow. Kate, now as good as any young housewife, was giving her a hand with the wiry brush and scrubbing off the dead flies from inside the churn when a clattering of wheels and a jaunting-cart came shuddering down the lane. There was a crowd of screaming women and children running along behind the cart. It was so unbearable – you'd think it was the keeners arriving, those black-clad hired mourners that cried at wakes and bawled behind the clanging of a hearse bell.

'Don't go! Don't go! Please come back!' wailed some.

'We'll never see you or your lovely faces again,' mourned others.

'For the love of sweet Jesus-on-his-cross, don't go away with the children,' they cried out with one voice. It was a common enough scene, a mixture of curses and blessings. The departure of loved ones would leave the rest of the hills mourning after them and the countryside round Sheep's Cross often seemed to lose its heart and soul for the rest of the summer. In the haunting silence of the woods and rivers big men would be heard bawling shamelessly, remembering the faces now gone from their sight – gone away as far as the blessed moon. It was as good as seeing their old friends buried alive below in Abbey Graveyard.

On the day of Kate's sudden departure the cart stopped at the haggart-stick and Sadie looked up from her creamery tank. Kate looked up too.

Sadie suddenly caught a hold of her daughter's arm. 'Kate, my dearest child,' she whispered, 'it's the Jugpussers and they bound for Van Diemen's Land and the making of a new life. Look at the seven of them above on the cart. Good-God-in-heaven, there's surely room for them to take another small child like yeerself along with them.'

Kate looked at the creamery-tank and the scrub-brush in her hand. She thought of the many jobs she'd have to do this morning. She glanced at the cart and the eager faces of her neighbours and they on their way to make their fortune in a far happier land across the seas.

'Wipe yer hands and make yeerself decent,' said Sadie. 'A fine chance this bright May morning – one ye'll never see coming yeer way again. Forget the cleaning of the wretched tank. Forget the heartbreak ye'll be feeling on leaving yer mother behind. Had I the chance, I'd be off with ye in a flash – faith 'n' I would.'

It all happened so quickly – a sad and happy scene: Kate, a growing child and Sadie with a mixture of a desperate mother's cruelty and kindliness that even in those times seemed harsh and unusual. A painter could paint it for you – the sight of Kate helping to clean out the creamery-tank (the good girl that she was) and the very next minute seated high on the cart of the Jugpussers and the tartan rug wrapped round her feet and bound far away for Van Diemen's Land, a place she'd never heard tell of.

It was a stranger sight than if a young sow had begun to talk to them for before anyone could blink an eye Kate with not a penny to her name was beyond the bend of the Open Road, the crowds of neighbours on their tiptoes and craning their necks to get a last fond glimpse of her, their tearful handkerchiefs waving behind her and poor Dandy running dementedly down the road in an effort to whisper his goodbyes to her and offer her his religious medals to protect her or to bring her back home if he could. It was the last he'd ever see of his daughter as the road bent round by the Kill and the child looked back for the last time at him. It was time for the crowds of mourners, their sighs and their tears still audible, to fade away home, each to their own tasks. Kate had gone. It was a death: the child's death: the father's death.

The afternoon daylight was rapidly fading and the sun had already plunged down in the bushes. Sadie left Dandy standing speechless in the yard, a look of horror on his face. She came into her cabin and threw the contents of her piss-pot into the briars. She sat by the fireside, her mind full of mixed thoughts.

Dandy would come in later on and join her at the dying fire, gazing silently into the darkness, the faint rain clattering against the front window on the two of them. All they could hear was the gurgling of their yard stream. There was not even a whispering prayer out of them for their daughter sailing off into the four winds.

When Sadie had risen from her bed that morning and offered up her prayers to God she would never have thought of this good chance, a daughter going off to make her fortune. Not a tear had she shed. It was one less mouth to feed – a chance of money coming back to the cabin one day and for Kate to better herself away from this lonesome place where money and riches never saw the light of day. She assured herself that when times came for loved ones to leave the nest, hunger-pains in the belly were even more troublesome than pains in the heart of a mother and father.

Handsome Johnnie

With seven of them gone from him and only his youngest son (Handsome Johnnie) left to fend for him in his older years and look after the two fine haggarts – and with Sadie, now a plump little woman of forty-four and growing old before his eyes – Dandy spent more and more time with his pipe-of-tobacco and his books of poetry.

After a lengthy period of working for Lord Fashionable and learning how to plough his wide acres, his son was appointed chief steward to the Big House and became a man of some importance, just like Dandy's own father had been. Together with his handsome looks he also became the blight of many a young girl's heart, what with his homespun songs and his battered concertina that whiled away the evenings – as well as the rest of the merriment that came with him. There were times when this man was like a child that hadn't grown up, always looking for fun and amusement.

As fortune would have it, he laid his eyes on a comely young servant-girl while she was peeling her spuds in the lord's back-kitchen. She came from the Valley-of-the-Black-Cattle and, though she'd been christened Bedelia, she was to be known hereafter as Dowager. She was a marvel of ladylike grace and style and in the height of her bloom, with apples for cheeks as well as those dark eyes of hers. From the first day he met her this admiring suitor of hers would wait at the hall door after her day's work was done Then he'd help her out across the gates and stiles and carry her across the muddy gaps, ever careful lest she'd get her foot wet or catch her long flowing dress on a bramble-bush. And then the two of them – she in her Sunday boater hat (which was all the fashion) and her pretty violet dress – he in his best brown suit that the Two Little Tailoresses had made for him – would take their evening walk across the fields and on by the side of the chattering river that flowed through the pine-trees up around Lisnagorna.

These were days without sunset. Theirs was a match made from the heart rather than the handshake of the two families and was to cause a long-lasting bout of uncharitable feuding when the day came for their wedding. In spite of the hitherto love-match of Dandy and Sadie above in Saddleback village, it was a thing almost unheard of for two young wobbledy-heads to go off and get married for the sake of fluttery *Love*: everyone since kingdom come had married for the sake of *Land* and the security that came with it. After all (said the Weeping Mollys), what on earth were the credentials of Handsome Johnnie Spallidagh? He was the mere heir to Dandy's two miserable scrawny haggarts, thrown up against the side of the lane at Sheep's Cross. The fact that he wasn't a farmer of a good few grassy acres was enough for them to sour his good name and they refused to talk to him. His manly girth and handsome looks meant nothing to these old gossips and when the next year's harvest dance came on inside in the Big Balloon's barn and the women met the men in that part of the dance called *the ladies' chain around the circle,* Dowager's own sisters refused to touch her young man's hand. Oh, the beauty of a comely sneer and a cocked-up nose! Oh, the miserable blight of petty ignorance! He may as well have been a leper from outside the gates of Jerusalem.

The Forty Acres

But nothing stopped the marriage taking place and (like Dandy's own wedding) it was to be a most powerful day – almost royal. Everybody was let drink their fill and one or two lads, new to strong drink, were seen falling in the fire and getting a hole in their best britches the size of a colander. With the many platefuls of food, you'd think it was a slaughter-house with the eight hens plucked and dressed and a few satin-soft geese roasted over an open fire and a woodcock and a snipe – and after that, all the sweet stuffs thrown in.

That year was a good one for the young couple. The times were beginning to change and the dark skies to lighten for them and others like them. The dividing of large estates saw Handsome Johnnie given a forty-acre parcel of land below in Rookery Rally, not a mile below Sheep's Cross. From that day forth he worked with an ever-increasing gusto, his new land stretching out before him – *his* to plough and till and trim, in which to sow his potatoes, mangolds, turnips and cabbages. Ah, the immensity of his work. He was the stamp of his father. See Dandy smiling gently at him from the field-gate.

He bought himself seven short-horn cows and a shy mare (*Sandy*) from Tipperary Town. He kept hold of his father's two haggarts above at Sheep's Cross and used them for the immediate needs of his dinner-table and (I swear to God) there was now a vigorous leap in his step – much to the sourness and the outrage of his sisters-in-law and those same old Weeping Mollys. And in time there followed a batch of children to himself and Dowager. Old or young alike, she protected each one of them from the day they were born – as fiercely as any goose or gander caring for their little yellow goslings.

Hot-blooded Boys

History often repeats itself and around the hills in the heat of that summer there was many a lively step taken beyond field-gates and among steamy groves. These were hidden places where hot-blooded boys with just a touch of a moustache above their lip and where blossoming damsels with the damp odour of youthful love in them went looking for the source of Love – places of stillness where the peaceful sky went around and around above them – places where they could entangle themselves in the feathery-heeled pleasures of their awakening bodies and free themselves from the ache that had been recently growing inside in them.

One of Dowager's older sons, Warbling Will, had reached an age when his natural instincts led him unfailingly up to the Valley-of-the-Pig and to the haunts of Mary-the-one, known by the rest of the young buckos as *Come-and-give-me-a-test*. During this hot summer he found it far better sport to go chasing after the supple-limbed Mary than hurling a slither-ball abroad in the field or vying with friends at cardplaying for the prize of a goose. Many a pleasant evening he spent in her charmed company, far away from the roads and lanes where the notorious flash-lamp of the forbidding priest was unable to spy on him and his youthful Mary.

In all, there were half-a-dozen young rascals who held this resplendent beauty in their arms at one time or another on those dizzy evenings and we will not spy on them or the besotted Warbling Will – only to say that Come-and-give-me-a-test reduced all their knees to water with the murdering looks that she gave each of them.

No one knew which of the youths was the father of the child that came to be born out of a series of clumsy jostles and tumbles with the little heathen. But people love to crow and they love to turn their noses up and so, ugly rumour began to insinuate its way the length and breadth of Rookery Rally. Dowager herself, whilst hanging out her sheets on the Monday bushes, got to hear of it – how her lovely son was stamping his boots up the hill for a bit more than tea and soda-cake. Her fears and apprehension almost brought her to her knees for the first time in her life.

Her Rage

She was raging fit to burst and, though every mother was in dread of her life for fear the new priest (*Father Laudable*) might curse their sons from his high place on the altar, she was now far beyond fear and she vowed she'd go and look the holy man in the eye. She hit her table a savage belt of her ashplant and to the surprise of Handsome Johnnie swore an unprintable oath. She put on her dove-coloured stockings, her best navy coat, her blue-basket hat, not forgetting her wedding gloves. She tackled her ass (*the Lightning Whoor*) to the ass-and-car and stormed over to the little wooden church in Copperstone Hollow where she damn near kicked the door in with a belt of her boots.

Without so much as *good-day-mee-young-man* she shook her little fist at the priest and demanded that he put a stop to the gossiping and the lip-curling – that he use his position to honour the name of her son and the rest of the Spallidagh household. There had to be an end to the sniggering and finger-pointing at her lovely son (she said). Nothing would do but a public recognition of her family's good name – of the name of her ancestors (she said) and by the living God, if he didn't act the Christian, Bishop High-Hat himself and even the saintly Pope on his throne in Rome would hear tell of her. After this lengthy tirade she was out of breath. Ah, the love and anguish of a delirious mother for her son.

In spite of himself Father Laudable had to make an excuse to leave the room and unload a fit of spluttering laughter before he could return from his sacristy with a degree of priestly pomp and dignity. And then the teapot and biscuits were introduced into the conversation and there were promises and kindly handshakes made and received between Dowager and the priest. Warbling Will's good name (guilty or otherwise, only God would ever know) was thus saved and he found himself so chastised and chastened that for the rest of his life – and to avoid the wrath of his mother – he never so much as cast an eye at the sight of a woman's bare leg.

The Penance

Dowager was not a pure fool and she knew it would cause her soul and that of her son to fry in hell if she continued to allow him to go off unchecked on his evening rambles, exploring the realms of fleshly temptation. As soon as she had untackled the Lightning Whoor and let him off down into the Bull-Paddock, she did what any sound-minded mother would have done: she waited till Warbling Will was sound asleep. She placed her fingers on the lips of his brothers, Blue-eyed Jack and Lofty, who were lying awake next to Warbling Will in the settlebed on the Welcoming Room floor. Cursing her supposedly black-sheep-of-the-family and the devil-that-was-in-him – cursing the wayward life that she presumed he'd been living unknownst to her – she tiptoed over to the stool and took hold of the bucket of spring-water. She cleared the other boys out of the way and, raising the bucket aloft in what looked like some sacrificial ritual, she ceremoniously lashed its freezing contents down on top of Warbling Will's terrified head. 'Yuh little shitty-arse from hell! I'll nourish yer heathen hide for yuh!'

Like all his brothers, a shirt was all that the poor lad was wearing. You'd grieve to see the sight of him as he fairly lept out the half-door. Himself and his soaked linen was seen by several startled men on their way home from drinking their pints of stout at Curl 'n Stripes' drinking-shop – seen running like fair hell out across the yard and the stream, stumbling dementedly out across the Easy Stile and through the ghostly fields of Simple Simon and on up towards the hidden ruins of Fort Dangerous and the Danes' Hill.

For once in their lives the gossipy Weeping Mollys and their tossed curls were knocked sideways when they saw the state of the poor lad. They asked one another had Warbling Will been out in Bog Boundless for a sally-hole swim at such an unearthly hour of the night? Could it be possible? Surely not. And then their cackling explosion of laughter echoed behind his unhappy heels – all the way up towards the hills where the whirlpool of sleep finally overwhelmed him. His only companion was the sad clouds round an even sadder moon and a fox barking sharply in the woods of Lisnagorna. And he lay there, dreaming how best to fathom the next steps to take so as to secure his mother's previous unbounded love towards him.

TWO

Darkie's ups and downs

It was a time when Handsome Johnnie's three older sons (Blue-eyed Jack, Warbling Will and Lofty) were still young. It was the day before the christening of Dowager's fifth child, the newborn Celia, to be known hereafter as Darkie. The little girl was a month old and, unlike her sister Cathleen, who had died shortly after birth, she was unlikely to die in the near future and therefore had not needed the hurried dash of holy-water at her birth to save her from an eternal life in Limbo.

Handsome Johnnie took Dowager into town on the horse-and-cart to visit his cousin, Lena. She was a lace-maker and lived in the Lanes. She had given him the loan of a beautiful white gown-and-shawl for the christening of each of his previous babies and once more there was no way she was going to let him make a show of himself with a shabby gown opposite the neighbours. Lending him the gown was a mere formality to enrich the morning when Darkie would be taken out on display.

Because it wasn't a Fair Day there was no thought of Handsome Johnnie making his excuses and stopping off to visit his usual drinking-shop haunts in Jinnet Street after the sale of a prime beast, getting his back slapped and his pockets emptied by his townie cousins when they'd know very well that he had the price of several whiskeys in his back pocket with which to fill their bellies. After all, a christening was a christening and a very precious moment in the lives of everyone. But in case there might be any little slip-up, Dowager walked down the lane beside her man to make sure he was as meek as a lamb and that he brought home Darkie's baptismal gown-and-shawl in a state fitting for a man whose newborn child was going to be made a Christian and a saint-of-God by Father Laudable at the holy-water font.

The Christening

The night before the christening, Dowager was hard at it, making up a few extra carrot-cakes and a rack of ham sandwiches. Next day Cheerful Nan was first to enter the Welcoming Room and bring down a few niceties with her. There was a half-bottle of port and in addition there were two dozen bottles of the black-doctor stout from Curl 'n' Stripes' drinking-shop (on tick, of course). Moll-the-Shuffler sneaked down a bottle of the rawgut potheen from her brother's secret potato-still so that everyone (she said) could have the fine old time of it. Wasn't a christening of all days a day worthy of celebrating with a few stiff drinks – even more than a wedding? For it was not often that we had the chance to thank God for coming down into the soul of one so young as this newborn child.

We will not dwell on the holy and memorable event itself, which took place with a great deal of pomp and ceremony. Nor will we mention the fine howling chorus that Darkie beguiled the gathering with, the minute she was hit in the forehead with a blast of the freezing holywater from the font. An hour later Handsome Johnnie drove the cantankerous ass back home at the speed of light. Dowager brought the baby saint out into the Welcoming Room and laid her in her cot next to the fire. With her satiny gown and the lovely shawl wrapped around her, she was fit to be a queen. And indeed, said everyone present, she was just that.

The Celebrations Began

The celebrations then began. Leaving the women inside, the men took the chairs from the four rooms out into the yard. They placed them in a formal circle next to a few additional chairs borrowed from Cheerful Nan, who found herself again in the enviable role of godmother to yet another of Dowager's newborns. For a moment they stood around awkwardly in the yard, eyeing the bushes with the new flowers in them, as if unsure what to do. The inquisitive hens, ducks and geese, seeing the men and their chairs, cleared a path for them and made a quick getaway down the yard and in underneath the ass-and-car. The men sat down and began to delve silently into the bucket and reach for the cold bottles of booze. They meant to enjoy every minute of this day's christening and they spent the next hour or two at the fine eating and drinking, inhaling their woodbine fags, filling the yard with smoke and coughing chestily like old sheep. Needless to say, it was too early in the afternoon to be seen whaling into the heavy stuff opposite the cautious women; it'd be much later when they'd make a raid on the whiskey. Once the women's backs were turned, they promised themselves that they'd burn their bellies wonderfully with an applied mixture of those two deadly drinks (the whiskey and the rawgut potheen) rattling around merrily inside in them – and to hell with the next day's sore heads.

As for the women, they had turned themselves in towards the fire. They let their tongues get loose and were soon as busy as a missioner with all their chatter. Dowager heaped the blaze higher than ever with a barrow-load of turf and some added hawthorn bushes to give it a blast. You'd think she was going to scald the hairs off of a slaughtered pig's back. She had swept and scrubbed the Welcoming Room floor the previous night and before the crack of dawn she'd been down on her knees, making sure there wasn't a single drop of chicken-shite anywhere to be seen. You know the way those cheeky little hens can ruin your floor in their efforts to steal the spuds from the skillet when your back is turned.

And now, with the men out of the way, these saintly dears delved into the carrot-cakes and the plates of ham sandwiches and the china cups of tea and the odd coy little thimbleful of port. As they sipped their tea and emptied their glasses of drink, they cocked their little finger daintily – just like Lady Elegance herself. Around their feet the older children tugged at their skirts (their betters) and they made sheep's eyes up at them (the young puppies) – all the time looking for a crumb or two to drop down their way from the plates of lovely cakes.

Before the evening came on, the men and women were given one last chance to come and take a look at the newborn child as she was paraded round the circle of chairs in the yard – to admire her swaddling clothes and her fine satin christening robes. There was a moment of pure quietness and of gentleness creeping softly among them in the fading sunlight of the yard. And as the men took a last little peek at the newly-christened saint, a kindly glaze crept into their eyes. Seemingly Darkie had steeped herself into their hearts. Dowager's own breast heaved with the natural pride of a mother. Praises for Darkie went on and on and turned into something like a church aria: what she looked like: whom she resembled: how she'd turn out: what rich prince she might marry one day.

The christening day had ended. It had all been quiet and orderly – almost prim – with none of the usual high antics or those bouts of raucous singing – not even a rowdy fight after the consumption of so much whiskey and potheen. And then, with the little summer breezes ruffling their hair, they all took a stroll out across the Bluebutton Field, the women with folded arms, careful to gather up their long skirts when they were too near the mud or the briars – the men admiring the surrounding hills and the changing colours of the evening sky. And when at last the red sun waved goodbye to them, they and their celebrating hearts went home to their various nests as happy as a tree laden down with song-thrushes.

Next year everything would happen all over again when the sixth baby would arrive on the scene and when Lena's baptismal gown-and-shawl would be borrowed once more. That baby would be Little Nell – a frail little waif, whom (like Cathleen) Dowager was to think might not live passed her first few weeks on earth. But when this sixth baby arrived, she would prove to be a plucky little soul and, though the tiniest speck imaginable, would have a heart as big as a boulder and as stout as a gander. A baby every year was the norm in Rookery Rally. I ask you, weren't our mothers the almighty women to be seen replenishing Ireland with the Lord's good works!?

The Arduous Years Ahead

The name Darkie suited the newly-baptised Celia down to a tee for she had lots of black hair – as black as the rich sods of turf in the turf-shed, even on her christening day. It matched her two beautiful eyes, which were as jet as a couple of laurel-berries. Before she'd reach the age of seven it would be long and wavy, reaching the lower end of her back like some flowing inky river.

But let's not sing a song about those earlier years. For as quick as a jig-step it came to the time when Darkie's young sister, Little Nell, was six years-of-age and, it being the beginning of September, she was ready to be sent off on the daily three-mile trek to the schoolhouse of Dang-the-skin-of-it. As for Darkie, although by now she had become a big stump of a child and had reached seven – what the church called the age of reason when children were judged ready to acknowledge their mortal sins – she had never yet spent so much as a day in the schoolhouse. But now it was time for her since Doctor Glasses had at last given her the go-ahead to step out alongside Little Nell on the long haul that led to school: down the Open Road: up to High Straits and on to the Two Goats Hill. She'd be in the safe company of her three older brothers, all of whom were still young enough to be going to school at the time.

The Hole-In-The-Heart

There had to be a reason for Darkie staying at home a year later than the other children. The doctors in the Limerick hospital had spotted a small bit of trouble and had insisted that she stay one more year with her mother before her uncertain body could be depended on to take such a long journey every day. These wise men had informed the startled Dowager and Handsome Johnnie that poor Darkie, not long after her birth, had been seen to have what they called a *hole-in-her-heart* and that this was why she had the odd bout of fainting-fits. Would you credit it, by the time the news of her bad heart reached the Open Road this same hole was as big as a crow's nest and once more we had to thank the gossipy Weeping Mollys for this gross piece of exaggeration.

As the next few years of the child's life unfolded, this prime little madam did nothing to stop the rumours about her bad heart: 'I can't be asked to do jobs like the rest of ye – I have a hole in mee heart,' she'd say and she'd grip her chest and run her agonising hand round and round it. What a performance! The little actress should have been tossed up onto the Dublin stage. And as the months rolled by and whenever her mother and father were gone to town, she got into the habit of this sort of playacting. The rest of the children could see what was happening and how she was growing more and more like those two ugly sisters of Cinderella – the two old miscreants in the storybook that they took down from the bacon-box underneath the hob's chimney tapestry.

'It's as big as a pig's bladder,' she'd say at every imaginable opportunity. By this time her big brothers were afraid to confront her and fully believed every bit of these damned silly lies of hers. For nowhere else was the likes of this hole-in-the-heart heard tell of in Rookery Rally. Her soppy soft-hearted father, in whose eyes she shone – saying she was destined to become a lady – was by far the most serious offender in utterly ruining the likes of her, all the time nuzzling at her ear and rubbing his whiskery old jaw against her mischievous cheek with an affection that made her brothers and Little Nell as sick as a pack of distempered dogs.

A Pure Slave

While Darkie was monotonously using the hole-in-the-heart excuse like a broken gramophone record for being bone-idle and warming her little arse in the ashes at the fireplace, Little Nell was turning into a pure slave. Each day she dust-sprinkled the floor from the saucepan of water and swept it as clean as a pin and (with her brothers) went to fetch the heavy buckets of water from the well and filled the sack with spuds above in the Seventh Field.

'Will ye look at Darkie, lording it over us and not doing a hand's tap and a smirk on her jaw and she polishing her shiny nails,' moaned the frustrated Blue-eyed Jack.

'Will ye look at Darkie, wrinkling up her nose in that broken bit of looking-glass and singing *tra-la-la! tra-la-la* the livelong day,' sighed the envious Lofty.

By now they had begun to dislike their young sister – almost to hate her. And who could have blamed them? But their hatred was not entirely unmixed for they were also forced to pity her. They knew (because their mother kept on telling them) that there was some truth in the *hole-in-the-heart* argument. Doctor Glasses had explained it in detail and he had never told a lie in all his life. That's where the pity came in: they could see that some sort of sentence had been passed on her and that, though she towered above Little Nell by a foot, she was always going to be a delicate blossom. But the extent of the hole – the crow's nest and the pig's bladder description – was always somewhat in doubt in their minds. One thing was certain: much to their annoyance, they would have to put up with her overbearing antics and so would Little Nell for the rest of their natural lives.

She Couldn't Run A Step

With the neighbours it was the very same thing: pity for Darkie wasn't hard for them to understand. Whereas the brothers could run races from one end of the Bluebutton Field to the other and even as far as the Rotten Tree, she couldn't run a single step after them. Nor could she join in their splashing games below in River Laughter or in robbing Old Stroller's orchard. All she wanted was to sit on Handsome Johnnie's knees when he came home from the bog and gaze out at the others and their funmaking from the loneliness of the haggart-gap at the henhouse-stick.

There was another thing – something that her brothers and Little Nell, being but children, couldn't yet understand: the fact that their rowdy playfulness was already causing Darkie to seethe with a deeprooted frustration inside her – something akin to anger, so tormented was she at not being able to join in their games. It was the beginning of a storm brewing up in her chest – a sort of jealous rage that one day was going to burst forth in a fierce torrent and attack the likes of frail Little Nell or anyone else that stood in her path.

Her Lovely Dark Eyes

Given her dark raven beauty, you might want to mix her brothers' pity for her with a little bit of envy for if her heart wasn't in the best of health, the rest of her body most certainly was. Doctor Glasses had only to take one look in her direction after Sunday Mass and he'd say, 'This little missy of yours, Dowager, is as spirited as a mule. Can't you see the fine sheen a-glinting in her lovely dark eyes?' He spoke as true as the venerable pope for even before she had reached the age of seven the rest of the household had learnt all about the wild fire established in her heart. Already it had developed into a temper that could rock the bowels of hell, said Dowager with those long-winded words of hers.

Admittedly her daughter was sly enough to give vent to these spasms only on those occasions that suited herself. Not everyone had the privilege of seeing this fierce temper in her. You can be sure that the little mischief-maker always charmed the trousers off of her father, in whose eyes she was nothing short of a saint. Not once had he witnessed her fearful fits. All he ever saw (the poor simple man that he was) were those dark eyes of her, their uncanny dark beauty and their immense charm. Given time (thought Dowager) he would learn that this little minx could spit fire quicker than a red-eyed rat in a henhouse.

Her Choice Of Breakfast

There was another unusual thing that made Darkie the object of everyone's curiosity. As soon as she had said her morning prayers on the bit of sacking beside the bed, she came hopping out into the Welcoming Room to warm herself by the blazing fire, placing herself on the wobbly three-legged stool beneath the oil-lamp. Before Dowager had boiled her own two eggs in the tin canister on the fire twigs, Darkie started in on her own peculiar breakfast by scratching away the lime from the hob and eating it by the handful. So well-used were her brothers and Little Nell to the sight of her unusual breakfast that in the end they paid no heed to it. She told them it tasted better than buttermilk. All she was doing (as usual, they felt) was looking for as much attention as she could get – even to the point of eating away half the lime from the wretched hob. And soon she got into another little habit – feasting on the cinders around the fire once they were cool enough. The only use the other children had for the fireplace was the soot behind the circular chimney-lid, with which they cleaned their teeth on Sundays before heading off for Mass.

Standing at Our Lady's grotto before Sunday Mass, Doctor Glasses would ruffle Darkie's lovely hair and say, 'Ah, my brave little fireside-eater!' And turning to Dowager, he'd add, 'There's something lacking in this little girl's growing body – some sort of deficiency in her system that makes her prefer eating lime and cinders rather than bacon and cabbage – something that is making up for certain losses in her nature. Take it from me, Dowager, there's not a drop of harm in it'. And with that he would turn on his heel and, smiling to himself, walk away at a smart pace up the street towards Mass.

Time To Start School

By September Darkie was at last ready for the road to school. Dowager could picture it all: Darkie and Little Nell starting off on their exciting journey together, straggling behind their three big brothers who had already told them all about the new trip they'd be venturing upon – down to the metal bridge and across the Easy Stile that would lead to Red Buckles' Meadow – then on up to the Difficult Stile that led to High Straits and the remaining two-and-a-half mile pull along the gentle hillslope in the direction of Tipperary Town. The wild eyes of the two little girls were full of excitement and expectation. They could hardly wait to explore all the new mysteries that were about to unfold before their eyes. They had never walked so far before. It'd be enough exercise and adventure for any young child to boast about for the next week-and-a-half when they got back home each evening.

Like them the schoolmaster (*Dang-the-skin-of-it*) was also full of expectation. He knew that the three Spallidagh boys walked by far the longest distance to school, setting off each morning before eight o'clock.

He also knew that, in spite of all this, they were among the brightest sparks in the schoolhouse and he put this down to their long walk, coupled with the mountainy breezes hitting them full in the face and clearing the sleepy mists from their otherwise dull skulls. It was the answer (he felt) to many a scholar's difficulties with the sums, dictation and reading. If only God could have given the likes of his slower pupils a right good walk like the Spallidaghs every blessed morning (he said) and at a time when the grey and black haze was still hanging down over everything – could have given them a chance to fill their lungs and brains for an hour-and-a-half with the healthy winds – it would surely have awakened the little dreamers and sharpened their wits for them.

Dowager Prepared Them

Before Darkie and Little Nell set out on this new escapade, Dowager spent half the previous night, preparing for them. Instead of being married to her candle at the front table and giving up her time to her sock-darning and reading *The Messenger* with its stories of the black heathens in Africa who needed saving (there'd be other evenings to read such stories to herself), she got herself busy with the clothes-brush, the boot-brushes too, polishing the five sets of boots till they shone like glass (the heels especially) and laying them out in a row next to the press. This was not going to be a day for the bare feet.

And then there was another item: the school satchels packed with writing copybooks that she'd recently bought for them. She had a bottle of cold tea for each of them and also a bottle of milk, wrapped up in one of her old stockings. Before that – and even before they had got out from under the blankets – she had lit a good fire with her kippens and the twisted newspapers, using the sweet-gallon lid to bring the flames bursting to life so that she could warm their coats on the fireside chairs. The shirts she had placed on the out-turned crane, as close to the blaze as she could. They'd be cosy and snug little souls, well wrapped up against the wind and rain and ready for the road that would lead them on to Education.

Oh! Celebration Day

The morning was here. Oh, Celebration Day! Dowager fed the little school-trippers with eggs, soda-bread and a few mugs of milk, almost smothering them with her attention. She parcelled up a final bit in their satchels – two extra cuts of bread with a little smear of blackcurrant jam on them to go with the school's midday mugs of hot cocoa. She made sure they said one prayer each for the souls of their new teachers – for Big Screech with the harsh red eyes of a gander that could strike you dead on the spot and for Dang-the-skin-of-it, her kindly husband, with his gentle coaxing smiles and his waxed handlebar moustaches.

They were almost ready. She hated to see them getting to school late on their first day and she warned them not to stop on the way, picking blackberries or those shy wild strawberries that'd make their bit of bread taste even better when mixed with it.

She hit the table a rap of her brush to summon all five children to the holy-water font at the half-door. The three older boys left their coloured court cards behind them in the Big Cave Room. They came and stood behind Darkie and Little Nell and gave them each an encouraging smile. Dowager gave the five of them her blessing, marking them with the sign-of-the-cross on their forehead and sibilating a silent prayer to Saint Anthony (who always finds lost things) so that he might come and give Little Nell and Darkie a helping hand to find their lost brains. Then she whispered another little prayer to Saint Jude (the patron saint of lost causes) so that he might disentangle the brains of the two little girls from out of their sleepiness and turn them into successful scholars on this most important day – the very first day of their school life.

Off They Went

Off they went, wiping the remains of the holy-water from the bridge of their nose. It was still very early in the day, the sky a tangle of dark slate and foggy light above the fields and just a few clouds overrunning the pine-trees in Old Sam's Grove. The three older boys had been warned by Handsome Johnnie to guard Darkie (his little pet lamb) and take the journey at a fairly steady pace in case she and her bad heart fell down and died on them before they even got to school. In the weeks that lay ahead it would not be uncommon for her to keel over on her way home.

Armed with their makeshift ashplants, the brothers had no fear when they reached Galloping Gret's hayshed and saw her two big sows parading the length and breadth of the Open Road. Nor did they fear her fierce geese, hissing and gabbling (a sure sign that a storm was brewing), as they tried to bar their way and guard the good woman's turkeys and guinea-hens from these supposed child-marauders. If the sows or the geese were to make a run at them, Handsome Johnnie had instructed Blue-eyed Jack not only to chastise the sows' snouts with his switch but to cut the legs from under the geese. These animals needed a bit of education as well as his own children (that's what he said) and the five school-trotters passed safely by Galloping Gret's hayshed and continued on their long journey, making their way across Red Buckles' Meadow. In the corner of the field was the spot where grandfather Dandy in earlier days had taught children of all shapes and sizes, sitting on their logs on the sheltered side of the ditch. Dowager had drummed it into their heads how well those children had listened to Dandy's wise words and for her two young daughters to take it to heart – how those children had learnt to chant their tables and recite their poetry so that before they headed out into the big wide world they were able also to recount the romantic and warlike legends of old, all of which they'd remember for years to come. Wasn't Dandy a mighty-mighty man?

The five children trudged up the incline in Red Buckles' Meadow. At this time of the year the ferns and thistles were four-feet-high and a good ass was needed to chastise the entire field. In spite of the few drops of misty dew rising up, Blue-eyed Jack took off his coat and shivered in his shirtsleeves. The earlier storm clouds had made the ferns and thistles wet to the point of saturation. He held his coat out in front of him like a bullfighter's cloak and then he made his brothers and two little sisters fall in behind him like a flock of ducklings running after their mother and he marched them dry and safe up to the Difficult Stile, which would lead them out onto High Straits.

Unbeknownst to Little Nell, Darkie's snack-box had a small additional nourishment to the two cuts of bread – a layer of Lady Elegance's icing sugar on top of the jam. This was a special treat for her and her hole-in-the-heart for she'd need the energy from the icing sugar if she was to make it all the way to the schoolhouse and back home again the same day. A very thoughtful woman was Lady Elegance.

Led by Blue-eyed Jack (coated again) the brothers climbed over the stile. They lifted their little sisters out after them and handed them down gently onto the road. The five of them found themselves (something new to Darkie and Little Nell) in a shelterless spot – up on the winding slopes leading to Polly's Hill. They buried their chins in their coats to hide from the black monster of the wind that came shrieking down the road towards them as if to hold them back. It had already searched out the surrounding chestnut trees, rocking them fiercely enough to bring the first few prickly seed-shucks drifting down and bursting open with smooth brown conkers spilling out of them. This was a prediction of what was to follow – the oncoming rain that would lash down on their heads and drench them to the skin unless they quickly dragged Darkie by the hand and urged her weak feet to keep pace with them. Looking at the dark clouds, there wasn't a minute to spare and the boys glanced at each other knowingly. Other children were aware of the storm's threat and a bunch of them soon passed the Spallidaghs out and belted up the road ahead of them. These were the late arisers, anxious not to arrive after the school bell and get a birching of the sallyswitch from Big Screech.

Full Of Confidence – At First

With the cheerful encouragement of their big brothers the two little girls soon forgot their worries about the unreliable weather and they threw out their chests proudly. They were full of confidence, having learnt at least a dozen prayers at the knee of their mother during the past twelve months. They had learnt heaps of poems and nursery rhymes too. But Darkie was about to recall a little obstacle, one that she'd recently heard tell of – that there was to be an unheard-of lesson known as *Sums-on-a-slate* and she was none too sure what this great mystery was. However, clever little minx that she was, she'd be sure to have a handy answer for this or for any other problem facing her. For if she failed to succeed with the Sums-on-a-slate, she could always roll around on the floor and summon up a few tears on account of her hole-in-the-heart. Surely that'd be good enough reason for not performing as well as the other children. Wasn't she the devil's own?

They Arrived

By now there was a crowd of children gathered at the school-gate where the master and mistress had come out to greet them. Breathlessly all the scholars stormed in the doorway – a flock of geese about to lose their freedom and be caged inside for the day. They were only too grateful that they had got there before the first bell and without a drop of rain on them.

And then, what a sight! – to see a bunch of older boys from the Gap-of-The-Two-Goats (some of them had been out poaching rabbits all night) storming down the hill at such an unnatural speed in case they'd be late. Their heads were held high and in Darkie's eyes it seemed as though their minds must be full of all sorts of jumbled learning, including the Sums-on-a-slate. They were led by the tallest boy Darkie and Little Nell had ever laid eyes on. He was known as Mick-the-Walking-Hayshed. Each morning this huge child had to duck down so as to get in through the school-door or else his head would have been left behind him whilst the rest of his body went in to take its place on the bench.

More often than not he was left at home to help his father plant a few firtrees at the top end of their haggart where he would experience a far different type of education than the school had to offer – positioning the stronger tree-roots on the south-west side of the trench and keeping the young trees firmly upright as his father pelted in the clay and firmed it down with his boot. Like the other mountainy lads, he was wearing no shoes: they were tied behind his back with a wad of string. Himself and the others wouldn't put them on until they had entered the school gate so as to save the leather. Some of them (Darkie noticed) were reciting strange words (their times-tables and spellings) in a doggerel singalong sort of way, which had always helped them shorten their journey. They each had a bit of soda-cake in their bag and a raw onion or turnip to sustain them, stolen from a nearby farmer – as well as another little theft, the sod-of-turf to throw on the fire and help warm the teacher's bum.

If a thunderstorm had caught them, there'd be a busy little scene for the next half-hour. For as soon as they entered the classroom Big Screech would make a run at them and remove their soaking jackets that were pasted to their skin. She'd take the wiry towel from the mantelpiece and give their necks and hair a good rub down. Then she'd line them up in a row and stuff several sheaves of newspaper down between their sodden shirt and skin (they wore no undergarments) so as to mop up the wet. They'd be freezing icebergs for the rest of the day and when it came to home-time they'd put on the same wet coats. It was plain to see that they were as hardy as animals and never got so much as a cough or a sneeze.

Magnetism and Hairy-Puss

In previous years the school had been taught by Hairy-Puss and his coy little wife, Cacky-Eye. This same gentleman was known to have a taste for rawgut whiskey. Each day he chewed a piece of cork that was pierced with a needle – to prevent (he said) the magnetism from getting out of his body. His mother too had been a teacher of some sort and went by the charming name of the Belter since with stick or fist – even with the toe of her dainty boot – she could belt Ignorance (she said) out of even the tallest boys and for this they hated the sight of her.

Cacky-Eye was the daughter of Hawk-Eye, a notorious villain, who lived beyond the Mighty Mountain in a place called the Rocky Field where he made dispairing efforts to plough round the rough rocks. This same rascal (said the Weeping Mollys) would steal the eye out of your head if you let him.

Cacky-Eye was Hawk-Eye's only child and she terrified the life out of her pupils (*My Contemptibles*) by shouting abuse at them: 'Aren't ye the bould pussahauns to be troubling the life outa me?' From time to time she'd mesmerise a recalcitrant pupil by leaning in towards him, her tongue spitting fire into the lad's ear – before putting that same ear almost out through the side of his jaw with a belt of her hand that would rattle his poor senses for the next week-and-a-half. Those sad old gossips (the Weeping Mollys) never got tired of spreading the fame of her fists (*'she should have been a boxer'*) the length and breadth of the countryside and how she beat her pupils to within an inch of their lives.

Enough was enough said the priest at the time (*Father Adamantine*) and he called for the town doctor (*Old Sawbones*) to come and take a look at what he suspected was a child's broken jaw. To Cacky-Eye's dying shame a full apology was forced out of the old vixen. Then the holy man made her kneel down for his Words-of-Absolution in front of the packed school as though she was a bold child. He gave her the strictest of Penances so that satisfaction was restored to children and parents alike. To everyone's astonishment Cacky-Eye became a changed woman and at home-time she'd have a few small gifts lying in the corner of her classroom – maybe a box of apples for the children to delve into. Miracle-of-miracles, wasn't the power of the priesthood a wonder-of-God?

Dang-the-skin-of-it

Summer came and then it went away again and the two old teachers moved off west, heralding in a new era for the children. Parents prayed that the incoming master would turn out to be a gift from heaven. Their prayers were quickly answered for with the arrival of Dang-the-skin-of-it happy days were to lie ahead – days in that springtime when he would lead the children out into the school field to sit in a ring with their reading-books – days when he'd take them out to help create a precious bit of garden and show them how to measure out the rows, using the easel-ruler. The children zealously carried out his instructions, planting the seeds at regular intervals. In the scorching summer they took turns with the watering-cans and sprinkled the burgeoning crops, making them look silky and glistening. How they loved his garden – *their* garden! There'd now be fernlike carrots and cabbages as big as a pig's head. There'd be onions, rhubarb and peas too. See the children marching up and down through the vegetable drills and trying to whistle with their tongue behind their teeth the way that Dang-the-skin-of-it did. See them reciting their times-tables after him (the younger ones) and chanting their poetry (the older ones) as they stamped their feet in rhythm up and down the furrows to keep down the weeds and all the time tanning themselves with the sun and the wind. Ah, blissful days!

This New Man

Dang-the-skin-of-it was a man who liked his pinch of snuff. The children liked watching the way he'd daintily sneeze into his handkerchief. He was a man who also took his tea-drinking very seriously. Not for him the cup-of-tea or the mug-of-tea. On her first day at school Darkie saw him reaching behind the blackboard for a pint-glass instead. Ah, the first drink of the day is always the best drink (that's what he said) and he filled the glass to the top with tea that looked as black as soot. Then he dipped his nose into the glass and sipped and sipped at it for a few minutes before gazing down at his scholars to start off the first lesson.

"If ye're to drink yeer tea, ye must do it correctly," said he, relishing the last few swallows out of the bottom of his glass.

The School Itself

The school was beside a river at the bottom of Polly's Hill. It was almost hidden from the road by the dark foliage of chestnut trees and their creamy flowers. It was the biggest building that Darkie and Little Nell had ever seen – bigger than their wooden church in Copperstone Hollow and bigger than Din-Din-Dinny-the-Stammerer's long-house where the harvest-time dancers had recently been shaking the life out of the rafters.

A turf-fire blazed at either end, the master standing at one end and his wife, Big Screech, at the other end and they warming their gable-ends. The windows and door rattled threateningly with the wind moaning and wailing like an old banshee and breaking up the silence of the classroom. Blue columns of smoke drifted dreamily here and there. The air was sweetly perfumed by the logs that blazed heartily, tincturing the room with a soft brightness and cheering what would otherwise have been a dreary day.

During the summertime the little ones were left near the door so as to get the better air and the middle of the room with its stifling air was reserved for the older stockier children. During the winter the little ones were huddled together like cows in the middle of the room to get the warmth from one another's bodies and the big children were left out near the door. There was the odd disruptive skirmish when a winter's rat, blue with the cold and desperate for the heat of the fire, brought in the remains of a turnip or a stick of rhubarb, stolen from the master's new garden, and started nibbling it by the fire until the children's screams echoed off of the walls.

On the side-wall Dang-the-skin-of-it hung the picture of Wolfe-at-Quebec, fighting his battle for the freedom of Canada – a picture that was later to inspire some of the older boys to carry rifles on their shoulders in an effort to fight for the freedom of Ireland. Next to this picture was another battle scene with that other great warrior, Nelson, lying close to his death on board his ship *(The Victory)* at The Battle of Trafalgar.

Pupils of different sizes and different ages – all with similar abilities or the lack of them – sat next to each other – big lads of school-leaving age next to six-year-old children on the lowest bench under the indomitable gaze of Big Screech. Among them were two big girls *(The Sillies)*, who ruined the serious image of the first day by disrupting the lessons with their sudden bursts of foolish laughter.

Satchel

The teachers' one and only son was Satchel – so called by the children because of his beautiful leather satchel, which stood out against their own hand-me-down bags. In the weeks to come he'd receive a thrashing at least once a day from his mother to show the rest of the children that she was not allowing herself to spoil or favour her precious son. On this first day, however, the children saw something else – how Satchel's snack contained several fistfuls of cracked oats wrapped up in newspaper and how Big Screech mixed these oats with cold water to make him his stirabout. It was enough (thought the lad's father) to put a knot in a child's stomach and he promptly boiled up a kettle of hot water for Satchel. As a result of this little incident with Satchel's snack the children's pity for him and the way in which he would be thrashed gave way to a growing resentment against him and his lovely stirabout – him and his leather satchel and his emerald green jersey and his lovely head of wavy red hair, so unlike their own jet-black hair.

A Little Bit Timid

As soon as they were inside the door Darkie and Little Nell timidly held onto their big brothers' hands and hid themselves behind their coats and peered out shyly at Dang-the-skin-of-it. He'd have a devil-of-a-job getting their names down in his book, so tongue-tied were they. Even Darkie had lost her well-known bravado and her customary snootiness. They sat on the back bench, not far from the doorway, the sun shining on their backs. They tried to size up their new situation, wondering where on earth they had found themselves and what strange events would now come freshly into their lives to make or break them. They weren't too sure. There were so many older children all round them, all rudely staring at them and the two of them were getting more and more frightened. They'd remind you of a newly-dropped calf, staggering to its feet and wondering which way to go and what to do next with their legs – whether to stay still or make a run for the gate and the homeward road to Dowager.

All the children were now penned safely inside, the rain from previous days still freezing the toes off of the older children in their soaked boots. Like Darkie and Little Nell there were one or two other small children (shy little mice) and they too were quick to make a beeline for the back bench, afraid almost to breathe.

'*Shoov oop! Shoov oop, can't ye – get into the corner*' they whispered, trying to bury themselves from the rest of the world. See them there, squirming together closer than fleas on an old dog's back.

Sitting between Darkie and Little Nell was tiny Pinfeather with one brown eye and one blue eye on him and next to him sat poor Hobble-Foot and a double-growth of hair on him. In years to come he'd often have to wear the dunce's cap. Ah, Hobble-Foot indeed

– hobbled since birth and never to dance a step hereafter at wedding or wake. At the end of the row sat Tommy-never-say-a-word. Wasn't he the cute one? All five newcomers had their view of the master almost blocked out by the huge shape of Mick-the-Walking-Hayshed in the front row. In the middle row in front of them were the Leather Fists, all four of them. They always sat next to one another. 'Stick together while ye're at school,' warned their mother, 'and let no-one bate ye.' These four undaunted souls took to heart their mother's advice and were good scrappers with their knuckles for the rest of their lives. There wasn't a row or a ruction that they couldn't handle victoriously at future Fair Days.

An Air Of Command

Dang-the-skin-of-it stood before his class. His white collar was shiny and stiff, the colour of new snow, and his hair was well-oiled with brilliantine. He put on his spectacles and fidgeted with his waxy moustache. Darkie and Little Nell had never before seen a man of such importance – not even Doctor Glasses. They couldn't put it into words but there was about him a certain sagacity – a clear air of command – as he paraded majestically up and down amongst his scholars.

The other children hung their heads down low while he tried to work some sort of miracle on them and drum knowledge into their sleepy heads. A few drops of sweat lay on one or two crinkled foreheads.

Well-practised eyes were screwed up uncomfortably in concentration as some of the slower children (*The Strugglers*) tried to grasp the faraway answer to one of his questions. However, the kindly master rarely cast a threatening eye in their direction for he had the patience of an old spider. During the first lesson (Point-to-the-map) he spent most of the time bouncing on his toes good-humouredly, his coat-flaps in his fist behind him. He threw a large map onto the easel and began pointing out the hills and valleys – the rivers and seas – the great countries of the world and their capital cities. He selected one or two of his quick-minded scholars (*The Improvers*) and handed them the red-and-white barber's stick to see if they had remembered the list. 'Point to the map,' said he in that tinkling little voice of his. The sugar-candy jar was behind him and a bit of candy was in his fist, a reward for the most successful answers to this Quiz-of-the-day.

Meanwhile…

Meanwhile, at the other end of the room his wife (the indomitable Big Screech) was conducting the singing-lesson. She could sing like a bird and before school started she had already practised her scales and arpeggios in the school-shed, thrilling the nearby thrushes in their nests. She could play the school piano like crystal and now she introduced her five newcomers to her old favourites, *Clementine* and *The Gypsy Rover,* in an effort to warm up the start of their new life at school – but not before those fierce eyes of hers had caused Tommy-never-say-a-word to wet the floor on her.

Unlike Tommy, Darkie and Little Nell had no such fears of the mistress for Dowager had almost smothered them in prayers and holy-water for the success of their brains in the hope that they'd come home in the evening with a sackful of praises from the mistress. And now they made a valiant attempt to swim in the new and mysterious pools of Learning.

Big Screech closed the piano and handed out the slates and the coloured chalks. Darkie and Little Nell began following her instructions – drawing out shapely letters, repeating their names and their sounds (a lesson known as Repeat-after-me). This was quickly followed by Sums-on-a-slate. They took their slates and copied down a few simple sums, which they could rub out with their spit and start afresh with more advanced ones. So successful were the newcomers at these early attempts (Darkie too) that even the slower learners, the Strugglers, ended up with a smile on their face –especially when it came to the singing of the elementary times-tables, their voices echoing pleasantly round the walls.

It Was Recess Time

Recess-Time came and brought with it a well-earned break from the two little girls' lessons. The teachers went out and took a morning walk up the length of the avenue, Big Screech dangling on her husband's arm and both of them smiling at one another. The nosy children peered out the window at them. They could see that the mistress was the apple-of-his-eye. This was the half-hour when the older boys boiled the kettles of water for the children's mugs of cocoa. It'd bring the warmth back into them all.

'Blasht yer hide, yuh bleddy ould featherhead. Can't ye hold yeer hand steady till I pour,' snapped Blue-eyed Jack to Lofty. The master was just returning from his walk and he shook his head and smiled at Blue-eyed Jack as he passed him by.

Raggy And Little Nell

By now the early shyness and uncertainty of Darkie and Little Nell had ebbed and they had settled down like any fretful ass in a new field of clover. The master's hungry terrier (*Raggy*) had been sunning himself abroad in the school field. He was now standing at the classroom door and, being an inquisitive young dog, appeared to be taking the greatest of interest in the next lesson (Any-News-from-Home?).

Suddenly he spotted Little Nell's snack-box lying at her feet and before she could blink an eye the little devil had it stuck in his ravenous jaws.

'He has run away with mee feckin bread-and-jam,' cried the tearful Little Nell, using the language of all grown-ups in Rookery Rally and the one bad word which every child used when they were vexed or needed to emphasise a point. What was she to do now but starve for the rest of the day? Raggy ran off and hid himself under the bridge at the river to escape a kicking. Guilt was a fine thing, even in dogs.

For once in her pampered life this was the day when Darkie was to take second place, unable to be cock-of-the-walk or the centre of everybody's life. The howls of Little Nell could be heard above at the priest's house, worse than a cow about to calve. There was no consoling her. It was a sad state-of-affairs for any poor child to be in.

Dang-the-skin-of-it and Big Screech felt responsible for their blasted thief-of-a-dog and had only one course of action they could think of – extend Snack-Time (something never heard tell of before) for a further half-hour. They led Little Nell up to their fine mansion (*The Palace* it was known as) where they gave her a fine feed of meat, the likes of which she had never even known existed – not even in the dreamy storybooks in the bacon box under the hob. This was followed up with a spoonful of sugar. When Darkie heard of this, she was utterly put out of her stride – agitated beyond belief.

Next Day

Next day came sailing in poetically. Behold Dang-the-skin-of-it drinking his serious tea all over again. It was then that those old slyboots, *the Foxy Fairies,* came sailing in the doorway. At the commencement of the first lesson ('Which of ye have the Norman names, the Saxon names or the old Irish names?') the wily Darkie decided it was time for her to enter the *snackbox game* and get herself a big dinner like the one Little Nell ate the previous day. Before she fell asleep at night, she had taught herself a crafty little trick for this coming morning.

The lessons had hardly started when she saw Raggy standing at the door and licking his lips a second time. She placed her snack-box temptingly at the leg of her desk for the dog to feast his drooling eyes on. With her dainty toe she slyly nudged it nearer and nearer to him. The eyes of Darkie and the eyes of Raggy were now locked together. A painter would like to paint it.

This was Raggy's moment and he was about to make a dash for her snack. At the same time the wily Dang-the-skin-of-it had been parting his coat-tails in front of the fire and watching this playful little scene between dog and child. He smiled to himself. 'Ah-ha, the crafty brains inside these Spallidagh children's heads – doesn't it beat the band?' Quick as a wink he raced between the desks and beat the yelping terrier out the door with a well-aimed kick in under its tail. The teeth of a very crestfallen Raggy were never meant to reach their intended feast.

The master had to go behind the blackboard and hide his merry old face for now as always during these little interludes a fit of laughter was bursting to escape from his throat. '*Dang-the-skin-of-it,*' he whispered, shaking his head and twirling his waxed moustache, 'isn't Darkie the cutest little devil on earth?' How well she had spotted the way Little Nell got herself the fine feed of meat. However, neither Dang-the-skin-of-it or Big Screech could allow this sort of thing to happen a second time. There was to be no favourites in their schoolhouse, not even a small child with a hole-in-her-heart. Kind though the master was, he would not let himself be outwitted by the wiles of a seven-year-old girl – not even Darkie. 'Clever Darkie,' sang one or two of *the Hillside Fairies* lurking in the bushes outside the door. 'Even cleverer Dang-the-skin-of-it,' sang the other hillside spirits.

With the rage boiling up in her, there now arose a new and pitiful song inside Darkie. It started to work its way down into her heart and then into her soul. The name of this song was *Jealousy*. Her sister (*'blasht her into hell!'*) and the tearful howls she had made had been good enough the day before to get her the fine feed of meat above at the palatial mansion. But what of today – what of Darkie herself? She found she had nothing to show for all her clever planning and all her mischievous scheming. Oh, the frustration! She had been taught her first abrupt lesson – that she and the hole-in-her-heart did not bear fruit at the click of her madamy fingers. And if ever she felt the need to put Little Nell in her place, this was the day – the second day of their joint adventure into school life.

What Followed...

It was now the end of the school day and sulphur-fringed clouds began to hug the hills all round about. The classroom was empty and fast asleep, free at last from the children's ghostly voices. As soon as they ran out the door, the morning's lesson (Who has the Norman names, the Anglo-Saxon names or the old Irish names?) was still ringing in their heads. It was to have consequences other than what Dang-the-skin-of-it had intended.

Children in groups sauntered down as far as Moll Black-Cap's Shack where some of the boys began putting on a bit of a performance in front of the girls, climbing up the hill and chasing Sando's wild ass, trying to jump on his back and ride him round the field. Others got into the Yellowstone Quarry where Bill-the-bee's-knee had once chased Blue-eyed Jack in an effort to steal his stolen turnip. The latter (fair play to him) was in no way afraid but lifted his snagging-knife and made a run at him. With a superb pair of heels the intrepid Bill-the-bee's-knee, puffing and panting like an old train, ran back to the safety of the schoolhouse before Blue-eyed Jack got a chance to give him a swollen nose to take home.

Men had recently been working in the quarry, blasting gelignite into the side of the hill so as to make a new road out as far as Bog Boundless. Each evening the boys would stop and stare at the bit of hillside that had been blown to bits. If only they could get into the workmen's hut – if only they could steal some of the gelignite (they said) and give it a bit-of-a-test. The girls kept laughing for they knew that such talk was mere gallantry and that the boys were only giving themselves airs – that they weren't brave enough for such a mad idea to take hold.

Some of the girls had reached Moll-Black-Cap's Shack and Moll's beautiful apple-trees, which would be laden to the ground with red apples in a fortnight's time – red apples to feast on – red apples to rot their stomachs. They inspected the scarlet rosehips and the ripe blackberries and began sucking the juices out of them until they were in danger of getting the gripe and belching for the rest of the way home. Their young faces would soon be slobbered from ear to ear and their dresses dirty and black with berry-pips. When boys and girls alike reached home their parents would shake their heads good-humouredly and sigh: 'Ye went off to school this morning with yeer boots black and yeer shirts white. Ye came home this evening the opposite – yeer boots white and yeer shirts black.' And then everybody would laugh and laugh.

The Row And The Battle

The children weren't much further down the road when the usual row rose up between some of the bigger boys as Slogger Hogan confronted Tearaway Butler:

'Come here, *Daybuclaire*,' (his Norman name for Butler) 'and tell me this – who or what are ye and yeer likes?

This was a stout enough challenge and there was no answer from Tearaway Butler. Slogger Hogan gave him his own roughly-worded answer: 'A pack of fools – that's what ye are and that's what ye always were – nothing but the breed of the bleddy ould Normans in ye.' And with a snort and a spit this cocky young upstart looked around him for a bit of support from the rest of the lads.

It was now his turn to face the same sour music: 'Hymph, yuh bleddy ould eejit,' snapped Tearaway, 'what are the likes of ye? A bunch of ould *meeyaws* with nothing in ye but the breed of the bleddy ould Saxons'

Thick and fast the insults came tumbling out of the other boys too, some cursing the Norman names and some cursing the Saxon names. The children with the old Irish names sat on the ditch and watched the start of this petty warfare. Some of their own names, including the Spallidaghs, went back to the days of that great warrior, Brian Boru.

The boys' cheeks were now rosy and aglow, all itching to put on a bit-of-a-show opposite the girls. Fists were seen flying as they lept around the road, roaring like a pack of rampant wolves in an attempt to box each other's ears off. But tongues and fists weren't enough for them to do the talking with and they ran into the Yellowstone Quarry where they picked up stones to pelt at each other. The Norman faction and the Saxon faction stood at opposite ends of the quarry. The children of the old Irish stock (weren't they the wise ones?) kept themselves safe and at a sensible distance.

Seeing how enthralled some of the girls were at their proposed warfare, the boys roared all the more:

'Bleddy ould Normans! Bleddy ould Normans!'

'Bleddy ould Saxons! Bleddy ould Saxons!'

Then they let fly with their stones: Normans and Saxons at war, yet careful to sling the stones high in the air so that no-one was about to get hurt by a stray stone. This was the way (at least for The Strugglers) of getting rid of the pent-up anger which they were unable to vent on their enforced enslavers back in the schoolhouse.

It all came to an end quickly with the clip-clop arrival of Dang-he-skin-of-it's pony-and-trap. Children scurried off in all directions, each trudging over stiles and streams and eventually back into their own weary yards for their jug-of-milk and cold spuds.

Soon this little melee between Normans and Saxons would be blown up into an out-and-out war where imagination would see the downright lies pouring out of the children's mouths – especially the younger children. A pebble would become a stone and a stone would become a rock and a rock would be as big as the rock that the devil on Devil's-Bit Mountain once hurled into the sea to turn itself into the Isle-of-Man. Some of the young rascals would go still further and try to convince their mothers that this same rock was bigger than the Rock-of-Cashel itself. For heaven's sake, whom were they trying to cod, the little schemesters?

And then their fathers would shake their heads and they'd smile and wipe the laughing tears from their eyes, recalling how they themselves had done the very same thing – told whopping big lies in the days of their childhood so as to impress their mothers. They knew that life continued as it always had and always would – boys forever at war with each other, one day blowing cold and another day blowing hot and fervid, according to their whim. It was this (said their mothers) that had caused wars all round the world. They knew it only too well. After all, it wasn't the women who went to war.

Little Nell's Pluckiness

Though frail and low in height, Little Nell was soon called upon to demonstrate that pluckiness which was in her bone and marrow ever since the early struggling hours of her birth. Each afternoon, as soon as they headed out the school-door, her three older brothers, Blue-eyed Jack, Warbling Will and Lofty, ran on ahead down along High Straits and forgot their father's order to keep a sharp lookout on Darkie in case she keeled over in one of her fainting-fits and died on the way home. They might have already raced as far as the metal bridge where you'd find them sitting among the trees, looking for the sour sloes that were in their first blue bloom or for the ripe hazelnuts or blackberries hiding in the copses. You'd find them midst the prickly brambles trying to discover a deserted blackbird's nest to bring home and show Handsome Johnnie, he being the lover of all things connected with Nature.

The following days were unusually warm for September and the sun was shining gaily, almost too hot for this time of the year. Little Nell, her head full of all the strange new learning, was melting from the heat and the lack of air getting into her lungs and she was dragging her weary feet behind Darkie. You could see she was worn to a thread these days.

From the time she'd received the delicious dinner at the master and mistress's house she'd been roundly tormented by her jealous sister. Being bigger and older, Darkie was well able to get her own back and each afternoon she forced Little Nell to carry home her schoolbag of books and her snack-box and coat as well as her own bag and coat. None of the children wore their shoes till they got within spitting distance of the school-gate and it was the same thing coming home since they preferred the freedom of walking in their bare feet. Their battered shoes, therefore, were laced round the back of their necks and so, to add to her load, Little Nell had to carry Darkie's shoes as well as her own. She wasn't sure if she had enough energy left in her to carry so much. You should have seen the smirky look on her big sister's face!

By the time they reached the Difficult Stile her own bit of childish anger – like her outburst in the previous fight with Raggy – had risen to fever-pitch. She was no longer galvanised with fear of her sister and an unknown river was about to burst its banks. She gave herself a little thought: 'It's not only Darkie that has the great big temper in her. I too have some of that metal inside in meeself.'

She went on like this, muttering to herself: 'Even poor sad Jesus didn't have to walk as far as I'm walking – the day he carried his heavy cross up the hill to Calvary – and then he had someone to give him a bit-of-a-hand with it.' She had been the soul of patience up until now and had put up with this sorry state of affairs for the first week or two as she wasn't sure what Doctor Glasses had meant by a hole-in-the-heart and she didn't want Darkie (mean as she was) to die on the spot in front of her.

Then she had another little thought: it wasn't going to be Darkie, who might die on the way home: it was her own good self when her heart would be torn asunder from the sheer weight of what she was forcibly carrying on her back. She knew that even horses had died from too heavy a load and she also knew what a little voice in her head was urging her to do.

She threw Darkie's coat down on the road: 'I'm not yer feckin donkey, Darkie,' she shouted, again emphasising her anger with the harsh language of the grown-ups. Then she threw her sister's shoes and bag into the ditch: "Pick up yer own bleddy belongings and carry them home yerself from now on.'

If lightning had struck Darkie full in the face she couldn't have been more stunned. It was one thing to be lectured at by a teacher during the day but to be treated in this way by a mere strip-of-paper like Little

Nell was beyond endurance. You could see the thunder rumbling in mee-damsel and the hatefulness flickering in her eyes.

The two-of-them were once more passing the entrance to the same Yellowstone Quarry where they had witnessed the warring games of the boys in the *Battle-of-The-Names*. Being only seven Darkie hadn't been discreet enough to see that the boys had fired their stones aimlessly into the air or that their little war had been a mere show of strength and defiance rather than an act of malice or wickedness.

She ran to the ditch and ferreted out a stone – the first one she could lay her hands on. It wasn't a pebble and it wasn't a rock but a handy-sized stone that fitted into the palm of her hand like a glove. Then, to the astonishment of the girls striding along behind them, she let fly her stone. By chance rather than by skill her aim was direct and it nailed Little Nell in the forehead, almost blinding her. The startled child fell down in a heap on the roadway, the blood oozing down her face from the fierce gash above her eyes. And now for once in its life the daylight seemed cold and miserly, hiding itself away from the children.

You would think that Darkie might have realised her error and that she would have run to the aid of her little sister. For it was a fact known to every child that blood is thicker than water – especially when it came to defending kith and kin against wrong or injury. But Darkie stood her ground, leaping round the road in triumph.

The older girls gathered round her: 'Look what ye've done, yuh heathen! Ye're a limb-of-Satan, that's what ye are!'

Darkie picked up two rocks, one for each hand. 'If ye know what's good for ye, ye'll shut yeer gobs or else feel the weight of these rocks into yeer own heads!'

'We'll tell! We'll tell!' they shrieked. They didn't know what else to say or do. They could have leathered her there on the spot with their fists – and it might be as well if they had – but by now they all knew about the hole-in-her-heart. Nevertheless, they couldn't let it rest: 'We'll tell the master. We'll tell the mistress. We'll tell yeer mother too and she'll flail the arse off of ye.'

They ran back towards the schoolhouse. The younger ones had already fled in panic, climbing in over the ditch into Red Buckles' Meadow. They couldn't wait to tell the news to their parents – how Darkie had half-killed poor Little Nell with a pelt of a rock.

Hearing the screams and the ruction, the three big brothers ran back up the road. They could see the damage. There wasn't a moment to spare. They ignored Darkie altogether and took Little Nell by the hand. They led her half-staggeringly to the infant stream that fed into River Laughter where they wiped the blood from her face. Although the wound was ugly, it wasn't as bad as they had at first thought. There was something else, however, that no-one knew – not until much later – that Little Nell would have the mark of Darkie's rock printed on her forehead till the day she died.

By now the other children had time to whisper to one another and to ponder it late into the evening. They couldn't believe what they had seen – the wickedness in Darkie. Had the bold sook not an ounce of shame in her – not a crumb of comfort in her? Unbeknown to them, the hole-in-the-heart had long left Darkie an embittered and resentful child – and a vengeful one too. On this sad day of her life she was paying back the world for the wrong done to her at birth – a wrong that would end her life (she believed) before she had a chance to grow up naturally the same as her brothers and sisters.

Lady Muck

In the days that followed, never forgetting the way Little Nell had been pampered and fed with the master's colossal dinner, Darkie's chastisement of her little sister with the rock was to be the mere beginning of a long line of bad days. With her hole-in-the-heart and her dark eyes constantly taunting the rest of the children to gainsay her, she was seen as Lady Muck around the house, never allowed to do a hand's tap of work. She was always preening herself like a young turkey as she skipped and danced round the yard among the hens and geese, cackling with cruel laughter from one day to the next, and, much to her brothers' and little sister's annoyance, lording it over them – especially when Dowager and Handsome Johnnie were gone shopping to town:

'Blue-eyed Jack, let you go and chop the wood.'

'Lofty, let you go and polish the shoes.'

'Warbling Will, let you go and clean out the ash-hole.'

And when her father and mother came home and saw how neat and immaculately trim everything looked, Darkie (the little blackguard) took all the credit for these jobs, never explaining that it had been the rest of them hard at work, down on their knees with the goose's wing and getting the four corners of the Welcoming Room spick and span and sweeping away the scuthery shite left by the two pigs and the fowl in the yard after the rainstorm.

Frustration was now boiling not only in her but in the rest of them and they began to side-step away from her. You should have heard the litany of curses they poured down on her head after her crime against Little Nell:

'Darkie has been spoilt-to-death and now she's turned herself into the feckin Queen of Sheba,' said Blue-eyed Jack.

'She has become the feckin Lady of Shallot,' said Warbling Will.

'I'll tell ye what she is,' said a sour-faced Lofty. 'She's a right royal pain in the arse.' It was true for them and not one of them bothered to laugh.

Home At Last

But back to this late afternoon. The children were home at last. The sun had mellowed to a pink blush and Dowager lit the two candles on the front and back tables so as to block out the shadows and shed some light on her children when they'd start filling out their copybooks.

'We can't coom out to play," they'd shout to the other children passing by. 'We're doing the *booooks*.' They said this with a half-hearted sneer and emphasis on the word *books*. To encourage them, their mother sat by the window and took out her pen and ink to write one of her long-winded letters to her two cousins in Yonkers across the sea. Her children couldn't miss seeing the way she was busying herself – the assiduity with which she wrote as her thoughts freely flowed across the double pages. Now and then she'd pause like a crow having a break from eating a bit of dead meat. Then, inspired once more, she'd write on and on till she had completed four sides of her own post-office copybook and she'd end up with *I have scribbled enough*. The children would laugh at the word *scribbled* for she was a powerful letter-writer. After that she came back to the children to inspect the progress they were making in their school copybooks, clicking her boots in and out between each of the two tables, her lighted candle in her fist like a latter-day Florence Nightingale to see if there was any need for correction.

When each had completed their work, she blew the candles out ceremoniously and lit the oil-lamp. Its light flickered across the walls, bringing cheer to the Welcoming Room for the remainder of the afternoon. And (I was wondering when you'd ask) not a single word had the children said about how Darkie had tried to kill Little Nell with a pelt of a stone. The child's fringe had been long enough to hide the mark on her forehead and Dowager's wrath would be held back – at least for another day.

Dowager Fingered Her Rosary-beads

Next morning, when Dowager heard the news, she was scandalised beyond belief at the wicked stone-pelting of Darkie and, after inspecting it, the sad state of Little Nell's forehead. However, she was hog-tied as always for she didn't want to fall out with her beloved Handsome Johnnie.

What was she to do? She began fingering her rosary-beads. She could see that her sound man was spoiling his little lamb to death and that the hole-in-the-heart was the best bit of news that had ever happened to Darkie, the great big actress that she had become with her feigned fainting-fits, each one performed with one eye closed as though she were about to die and the other eye winking at her brothers behind her father's back and she all the time laughing up her sleeve.

Blue-eyed Jack spat contemptuously into the fire when he saw the hopelessness of their case for there was to be no punishment for Darkie's crime – not even a slap on the leg from Dowager. Nor did she get the expected tap on the jaw from Handsome Johnnie when he heard the bad news after milking-time. If it had been any of the rest of them, they would have been thrashed to within an inch of their lives; that was the sorry bit. The hole-in-the-heart was the little demon's trump card with her father and, like her guardian angel, it kept her safe from any sort of retribution.

Dowager's Prayers Are Answered

That evening – the evening after the crime with the rock – a light shone brightly in the door and Dowager's prayers were finally answered. God sent down one of his more sympathetic angels to her as she was saying her prayers. He whispered a little message into her ear, telling her that the monstrous child that Handsome Johnnie had been encouraging – with one law for Darkie and another law for the rest of the children – was now out of control and that matters must no longer go on the way they were – that the child would have to be stopped.

Up until now Dowager had prided herself on being a noble mother and the best of women when it came to the religious and educational upbringing of her children. But now she listened to the voice of the angel. She would obey the call. She would bring matters to a head.

The Inevitable Battle

She set out the scene for the inevitable battle with her daughter. 'Coom here Darkie, I want you,' she casually said as she continued to darn one of Handsome Johnnie's socks. 'Ye're to go down to the well and help Little Nell bring back the heavy buckets of water.' This was nothing short of a declaration of war.

Dowager knew how Darkie would react when she heard such an unheard-of command. For her daughter believed that she was assured of her father's protection and could hide behind his coat-flaps at every twist and turn – that she could give her mother whatever back-answered impudence she felt like. What did her mother think she could do to her? She was smart enough, however, to make sure she was standing at a safe distance from Dowager – a few inches outside the half-door where she could scuttle away in case her mother had the temerity to run after her and break her skull like an egg.

When Dowager again ordered her, this time with a bit more severity, to go to the well and *be quick about it*, Darkie (Brazenness being her middle name) stamped her angry foot: 'I will in mee arse!' she said, feeling bold enough to treat her mother with the daily language that men used when passing by on the road.

Dowager reached for her famed walking-stick (*Wattle*) with which to chastise her headstrong daughter:

'You dare touch me and I'll tell father.'

With that the little madam stormed out across the yard-stream. She could hear the big boots of her mother following behind her. In spite of her heart's weakness she was too nimble to be caught and she led her mother a merry dance down as far as the well – all the time looking back, taunting her and cursing her in a way that no child in Rookery Rally's memory had ever been allowed to curse their own mother.

With head held low Dowager (the crafty woman) turned back home, a look on her face that showed she was dejected and defeated. Darkie reached the well and saw Little Nell labouring away as usual with the heavy buckets. She sat herself down on the slab by the well-hole, looking on at her frail little sister and singing her *tra-la-la-tra-la-la* song to annoy the daylights out of her. The smirk never left her lips. Her mother was no match for her.

But Dowager had other thoughts. She had tiptoed across the road, her whispering skirts scarcely rustling. She took the hidden shortcut through Old Sam's Grove and hurried her boots down passed the spiderwebs, knocking the thorny bushes out of her way with her angry walking-stick till she was near the well. Her face was as black as a thundercloud.

Darkie stooped down to get herself a drink of water when suddenly her mother's gnarled hand appeared from out of the sky. Her eyes blazing with anger, with a powerful blow she sent her impudent daughter crashing to the ground. She grabbed a fistful of Darkie's hair in her hands and dragged her – yelling, swearing, howling like a pig about to die – all the way from the well-hole and up through the dirty puddles of the road and in across the yard in front of the startled hens and geese:

'Father! Father! Father! Mee feckin hair – mee lovely black hair – is torn from mee head!'

'It's no use ye yelling for yeer father. He can't help ye anymore,' snarled Dowager. It was a miracle Darkie wasn't completely scalped for her mother was left with rolls of black hair in her fists. She didn't care a fig if there'd be an unholy row when Handsome Johnnie got back from mending the gap where Old Sam's bull had gotten in and mounted one of their unsuspecting cows. Hadn't she heard the voice of the angel?

They Couldn't Believe Their Eyes

When they peered in the half-door and saw the bedraggled state of Darkie, her brothers and Little Nell couldn't believe their eyes. Incredibly their mother had done what she'd never have dared to do before this day – laid her hands on the sacred head of Darkie. With her hole-in-the-heart perhaps this was the day that she'd drop down and die in front of them. Wouldn't that be a sight to see? They almost clapped their hands when they saw the way Dowager was showing her metal and chastising Darkie. Justice was showing its honest face at last and the punishment had happened not a day too soon. The walls and windowpanes must have rattled in fright.

Dowager swung the little heathen round and round the Welcoming Room before finally pelting her towards the dresser where she stumbled and fell in a heap:

'Lie there with yer impudence till yer father comes home and sees his choice pet, his spoilt lamb!' snapped Dowager and the angel skipped back up into the clouds, well pleased with the performance of a mother in earnest.

The Sourest Of Music

For a second or two Darkie lay mesmerised and motionless on the floor. But then came the sourest of music you ever did hear as she began howling like a wolf, the temper flying from her mouth in a river of spits. She was like an overflowing kettle on top of the fire and it was a miracle that the house didn't fall down on top of them all.

'No! No! No!' she roared. She would not be quelled. She would not lie down quietly and die on them. Her angry heels began to rattle off of the floor. She kept the music up for the next hour. What energy she had with her hole-in-the-heart! Where did she get her savage strength from? The Weeping Mollys could hear the roars, croaks and curses of her as far away as the crossroads at Shy Dennis's Shack.

'Do ye think that Dowager has at last killed her altogether?' they said as they filled their buckets at Red Scissors' spring-well.

Crime And Punishment

Chastisements such as this (the scalping antics of Dowager) were the accepted way in Rookery Rally with which any mother worth her salt would treat an abusive child – even a child similar to Darkie, forever throwing her hands up in the air and using the hole-in-the-heart as a reason for her intolerable impudence. With houses full of children, mothers had to be the sternest of lawgivers. Fathers (wouldn't you known it) took on the pathetic role of Pontius Pilate and washed their hands of it all instead of leathering out punishment on their children. Enough said.

Children had seen it all before with their own eyes. On the ditch beside River Laughter sat Limping Tim and his wooden crutches. As a child he had been the only one blind enough to warrant a pair of reading-glasses – expensive items. During play and in order to avoid the rough and tumble of the clattering hurleysticks he had lost these glasses deliberately – and for the third time in a year. His patient mother (*Sanctity*) was out of her mind with anger when she heard that he'd lost them yet again. Where was she to afford another pair?

For once in her life she forgot her rosary-beads and she drove Tim into a corner of the yard as if he were a goose about to be killed. Then she gave him a repeated kicking into his two shins – far better than she would a milking-cow hitting her in the face with its shitty tail. His leg was in absolute ruins from the savagery of his mother and he never recovered. On their way to school each day the children witnessed him gazing down into the on-rushing current of River Laughter, the perfect image of mournfulness. There'd no longer be any hurling games for him – even had he wanted the rough and tumble of the sport. There'd be no-one to play with – no-one to talk to but his two crutches and the two little robins winking down at him from the ditch nearby.

And another thing – in contrast to Dang-the-skin-of-it, who was the kindest of schoolmasters, the Weeping Mollys remembered Hawk-Eye (the previous incumbent before Hairy-Puss) with his regular bouts of savagery whenever a misfortunate lad like Nipper came in late for school after travelling a long distance.

'Here's the knife. Go down to the river and cut yerself a sally-switch.' And when Nipper returned from the river and handed the master the stick, old Hawk-Eye – his head full of drink from the night before – beat him till the boy's eyes were a pleading river of salt-water.

You remember poor Muddlesome Tom and the hidings he got from Hairy-Puss for not being able to read or write his own name. When the heathen died and was lying in his coffin in the grave, Tom stood above the grave when everyone was gone and he whispered these sweet words down into the hole to the old teacher's shade: 'If I had but one wish granted from heaven, it's this: that I might leap down on yer coffin and dance a fine jig on yer head.' And then he pissed into the grave.

Handsome Johnnie's Bad Humour

Handsome Johnnie, unlike his usual cheery self, was not in the best of humour. Old Sam's bull had broken through the fence under the bridge yet again and had performed on one or two more of his unsuspecting cows. Getting the exhausted bull down into the river and in under the bridge – out across the wire fence and the three borderline sticks – had proved a tedious task. He had wasted a precious hour or two when he should have been tending to the weeding in his haggart in case any fearless weed was foolhardy enough to show its head above the ground. Thanks to the wretched bull he had also neglected the rest of his other plans this day – the preparation of his vegetable-plot for next year's spring cabbages and lettuces – the cartloads of dung and the spreading of it. If the ghost of his father, Dandy, had been looking down on him, what on earth would he be saying to himself? Is this the good-for-nothing son that I once reared?

He was coming in across the yard to get himself a mug of water before getting on with the real work of the day when suddenly he heard the roars of defiance and (worst still) the foulest of curses come pouring out of Darkie's mouth – from her, his beloved pet, who in his eyes had been the model of politeness all the days of her life.

He stood at the half-door with his hat in his hands. Was it a dream? He couldn't believe his ears. Unaware of his presence, Darkie had the appearance of a colourful peacock as her two heels (a wonder they didn't break her legs) kept belting the fiercest of rhythms off of the Welcoming Room floor.

'There's your fine daughter,' barked Dowager as soon as she saw him enter the half-door. 'She's been whaling the life out of the floor this last hour or so.'

For once in her life Darkie's temper was nothing to her mother's rage – thanks to the angel. If his wife had hit him with a rock to the head Handsome Johnnie couldn't have been more bewildered.

'Your pet indeed,' snarled Dowager, her tongue acid, triumphant at last in being able to portray Darkie in a light that her husband had never imagined. 'Yes, your sulky lamb and the temper flying out of her. The devil is alive and well inside in her heart.'

He stood there a moment, bewildered. Suddenly it dawned on him. It was all his own soppy doing, the misguided old fool that he'd been all these years. There was a single moment (just a moment, mind you) when he thought:

'What will I throw at her? Will it be the mug of water? Will it be the full bucket-load?'

'What's this, mee pretty missy?' he roared, raising his voice a solid octave and stopping her dead in her tracks. His eyes flickered with black light and his voice sounded strangely harsh and sour. An ungodly fit of temper had not been what he'd ever expected to see from his little treasure. There was no time to question his daughter – no time to converse with Dowager. He knew what he must do and he reached for the bucket of water:

'Yuh sulky little pussahaun,' he screamed, 'I'll teach ye the Irish language!'

Furiously he lashed the freezing contents of the bucket over his startled pet, unmercifully drenching her to the skin and leaving her in a crumbled snivelling heap on the floor. He stormed out the door, his head buried in his coat as if to hide his feelings. His boots rang out across the stream's flagstones as he headed for the drinking-shop to calm his nerves and wash the thoughts of his unruly daughter out of his mouth with a few good pints of the black-doctor stout. There'd be no prayers said by him this evening.

The Finest Piece Of Education

What a miserable baptism it had been for Darkie – the finest piece of education that had been seen in a long time and it was to be the turning-point in her life. As Father Laudable said a week later: it was Darkie's Road to Damascus.

The rest of the children now felt vindicated. The cruel double-punishment of Darkie – dragged by the hair of her head along the length of the road – drenched to the skin by her father's bucket of water – was the most appropriate penalty in the laws of the household for a child as bold as this, hole-in-the-heart or not. And for a good while thereafter there wasn't a murmur out of her There'd be no more Miss Madamy: no more Lady Muck: no more Queen of Sheba: no more Lady of The Manor: no more sulks or insolence. She had lost the protection of her father and was now as good as gold, if not a canonised saint.

Her Rosy Days Of Glory Were Over

But that is not quiet the end of Darkie's tale. The following few days were dreary for our wild child. She seemed incredibly small and shivering, dangling her feet on the lace of the ass-and-car and looking at the wobbling tails of the playful ducks at the edge of the stream. Now that she no longer held sway over her brothers and Little Nell, she was all the time restless and unsure of her path. She knew her rosy days of glory were over. She was itching to get back to those good old days and regain her father's friendship and favour – to savour the love and friendship in his whiskery caresses. But she didn't know how.

Handsome Johnnie was shoeing his stallion (*Foldoon*) at the henhouse stick. He went in the half-door to fetch his pipe and tobacco. In an effort to please him the estranged Darkie made her way down the yard among the hissing geese and got down in front of Foldoon's back heels. She tried to lift his foot like her father did and to cobble his shoes with the hammer and nails like he did. This was a dangerous piece of folly and all for to show what a good and cooperative child she had become.

The stallion (wasn't he the quiet one?) could have reared into the air at any moment and dented her head with a kick from his hooves. However, alarmed by the child's awkward touch on his hooves, the good-tempered Foldoon did what was unexpected and unleashed a shower of hot poolie from underneath his belly – straight down on Darkie's lovely tendrils of hair, illuminating them with the green colour of piss. Little Nell and her brothers had to hold their sides from the laughing fit that they took at the sight of Darkie's lovely hair getting drenched in piss. They lay on the ground kicking their heels deliriously to the heavens.

Her Vengeance

Life thereafter was to remain even more thorny for Darkie. There'd be not a moment's peace for her. So, true to the anger that was always inside her, she made up her mind to take out her vengeance on all of them: on the stallion: on her mother: on her father. She took the hammer to the flagstones where she killed the entire nest of red ants at the oak-tree. After that she killed the two beautiful caterpillars, precious furry ones, Little Nell's recent pets.

Then she jumped over the singletree and headed down through Old Sam's Grove. She saw the discarded hurleystick belonging to Blue-eyed Jack. She picked it up and wielded it over her head, striking out at all the bushes, cutting them to shreds and breaking up the lovely gossamer patterns of the dewy spiderwebs that Little Nell loved so well.

Further down the grove there was a secret fairyland where the ducks could cluster for their afternoon matinee, escaping from the sow and the gander back in the yard. Darkie saw them dozing in the heat of the day after feasting on some adventurous post-rain snails.

Suddenly she spotted the finest of her mother's drakes. She looked at the drake. The drake looked back at her. How self-satisfied he was (she thought). And, sending the rest of the ducks bouncing into one another, she trapped this noble-fine creature by the ditch. Then, puffing herself up with another bout of her rages, she charged at it as if she was in pursuit of the whole world. She flailed the hurleystick into its back, beating it unflaggingly till the poor drake was nothing but a frightful heap of feathers, bleeding and broken and dead – never again to groom its beautiful dazzling colours. A sombre moment if ever was this. Black were the clouds that whipped their way across the sky – as though some devilish serpent had crossed through the heavens. And after this bout of killing Darkie shed not a tear of guilt.

Dowager's Sorrow

Ever since the row with her daughter, the joy had gone out of Dowager's life. It was late that same evening when she was counting her hens, geese and ducks and putting them to bed in the henhouse – for fear of the fox. But something was wrong: she missed her favourite drake and (where was Darkie?) she ran out in search of her wayward daughter.

'Yer precious drake is dead in the grove,' said Darkie, humming a mocking tune to herself – a tune that was filled with gloat and glory.

'Dead is it?' groaned her mother, hurrying across to the grove to see for herself.

When she looked down at the bloodied body of the drake it was as though lightning had scorched the sky above her and she went away sadly and sat on top of the ash-pit behind the pig-house where she soaked her bib with her tears. She knew (of course she did) that the malicious

Darkie had killed the drake. She retreated silently to the Welcoming Room and from that moment on she stored bitter thoughts deep in her soul. It's the devil's own fault (she thought) – surely it is – getting inside the heart of a child.

That night Blue-eyed Jack, Warbling Will and Lofty knelt down and said a few extra prayers in front of the Sacred Heart picture. They prayed fervently that Darkie would grow up and meet a man that would marry her – a man with as fierce a temper and as much of the devil in him as there was in their sister.

Her Brothers' Prayers Were Answered

But their prayers were answered in a way that none of them could ever have imagined. It was fifteen years later when Darkie found herself a man: she found Tom, a boat-builder from the Shannon side of Clare. She had met him at the Windy-Windy Dance-in-the-Fields – him and his shy tender glances – him in his suit of grey and his shirt of cream. She had washed her face in the stream and was coyly perfumed with a few stolen drops of her mother's lavender-water. They married their way across the dance-floor, whaling breathlessly into the wooden boards and before the night had fled away, the shy lad had taken the liberty of planting a fretful kiss on the dome of her head, thereby catching her in his web forever.

From that day forth his heart was as soft as a bog for her and he came courting her unceasingly in his pony-

and-trap with the dancing legs of his stallion (*Dancer*) leading him ever onwards to her half-door. Couldn't any fool see (he thought) what a fine young woman she was and she all the time smiling up at him with the magic and wonder in those dark lucid eyes of hers.

Damn the bit (thought her brothers when they saw him): Tom was as quiet as a church mouse.

'He's a real ould sheep,' said Dowager when she laid eyes on him. In no way was he the bulky bully-boy that her brothers had hoped and prayed for her – a man that might put Darkie across his knee and leather her arse for her.

This tale, however, ends gloriously for (bless my soul) it wasn't long before Tom received the blessing of Dowager and Handsome Johnnie and went off carrying Darkie across the Shannon Bridge to a new life of joy beyond in Clare. Away from home, she became a new woman – forever acting daft and combing out his hair for him. The marriage was a good one, producing ten sterling children and it lasted till the end of their days. Never again was there a stage on which her anger might flair up. And as the years rolled on so did those old storm clouds of temper decrease until they ran out the door and fizzled away silently, astonishing her brothers – and all this, under the compelling influences of her sound man, Tom from Clare. There was never a cross word between the two of them – not with a gentle soul like her boat-builder, who was always reluctant to dispute with her – a man who knew not the meaning of confrontation and warfare. Her anger had nowhere to deliver itself and with its departure she forgot the reason why it had ever existed in the first place, namely the hole-in-the-heart.

Tom and herself were often seen walking spritely along, hand-in-hand on their way to the town's Market Cross to buy a few shrubs or young trees. Hand-holding was something you'd never see or hear tell of in the countryside.

Darkie's brothers and sisters laughed at their own stupidity. As he looked at Warbling Will and Lofty across the fireplace Blue-eyed Jack was left rubbing his jaw – to think of Darkie and Tom: 'Who the hell would have thought it'd work out the way it did,' said he. 'Salt and sugar and they mixed together – a recipe for life-lasting joy.' And then they all laughed and laughed and they thanked their Blessed Saviour for what they knew was an unbelievable aftermath – a miracle brought about by *the Queen of All The Fairies*, namely *Love herself.*

THREE

Fandango from Galway

Over the coming years, as if her unruly daughter, Darkie, wasn't enough to worry her, Dowager would be faced with yet another shock to her system. The day came when their stallion, Foldoon, failed to get up on his hind legs and he closed his eyes for the last time and went to his eternal-resting place in a burial spot behind the monkey-puzzle tree. A sad-eyed Handsome Johnnie laid him reverently in the ground, wrapped in the tarpaulin sheet left to him by Mikey-from-the-well (Dandy's ancient brother-in-law). Then he said a silent prayer of gratitude for this great horse before traipsing back across the haggart with his pick and shovel.

Blue-eyed Jack and Fatty-Matty

These days Handsome Johnnie was slowly ailing. It was not just his sorrow over the way Darkie had let him down: his liver was now in a very poor state and bit-by-bit he was forced to let Blue-eyed Jack, with the help of Warbling Will and Lofty, take over the reins of farming the forty acres. With Fuldoon's death and the springtime ploughing near at hand his son now had an urgent need to go and buy a replacement plough-horse. There wasn't a moment to spare. So, together with Fatty-Matty, the friend of his bosom, Blue-eyed Jack decided to head off for Galway and get a horse to match up with Fatty-Matty's great horse (*Shout*), who had previously worked in close harmony with Fuldoon. The two men knew that Galway was the best place to go to – where plough-horses like Foldoon were known for their self-discipline and good-nature and were famed not only in Galway but the length and breadth of Clare and Tipperary.

They Went Off Riding Their Chestnut Mares

They set off early one morning when the hens were still in their roost. One or two ghostly stars still spattered the dark sky but the sun was already beginning to appear between the patchy clouds above the pine-trees in nearby Lisnagorna.

The road (they knew) was going to be long and slow. Neither of them had ever travelled such a long distance before and it was bitterly cold at first. Nevertheless, they were in holiday mood as they sailed away on two chestnut mares borrowed from Rambling Jack. They would be taking the northern road that led to Galway and the Shannon Bridge at Portmantle.

Their mood began to alter as they travelled on. You could see by the cut of them that they had given themselves time to reflect and a mixed feeling of joy and anxiety had now come over them – joy for the grand and unusual adventure they'd be having – darkness, ready to match it, in case they failed in their quest to bring back a plough-horse – one that'd be a reliable companion for Shout – one that'd last them as long as Fuldoon (poor soul) had done. And another thing (there was no getting away from it) – Dowager had sent them off with her sharp tongue ringing in their ears: 'Be sure not to come back here and darken the door without a spanking new Clydesdale stallion trotting at yeer heels.' And to back this up she had showered them and the two mares with the best part of a gallon of holy-water.

They Rode The Grassy Edges

The sky round about was fringed with orange clouds that hugged the surrounding hills and the day in front of them was beginning to be hot and thirsty work. Well-trained in their use of horses and asses, they kept the mares on the grassy edge at the side of the road wherever possible so as not to wear out their shoes or get pebbles lodged in their hooves.

The previous night they had made sound preparations for this great venture. Like all farmers in Rookery Rally they had learnt not to mollycoddle their mares before setting out. However, they made sure that their hocks and hooves were treated with as much comfort as possible for a journey as long as this one was going to be. They had given the two comely creatures a thorough rub down with the Cindy-powders so as to increase their speed if the need arose for who could tell what might lie ahead of them on this strange and memorable day? They might get themselves ambushed by the rascally Galway men as soon as they reached Portmantle and the bridge at the Mighty Shannon River. They had already made up their minds to give the mares another dose of the foot-powder when they reached the halfway stage of the journey where they'd cool them in the river outside Borrisogandery. If they were going to be waylaid, that's when their mares would need the legs of an absolute racehorse on them.

The Halfway Stage

It was near nightfall when they came to Prodigal Hill. The moon was already drifting languorously over the ditches and the first few stars had newly-appeared by the time they passed Twin Rivers and rode into Borrisogandery. They hopped down and tied the mares inside what looked like a friendly haggart-gate so as not to lose sight of them.

'Where there's a need there's a way,' said Fatty-Matty as they crept stealthily across the haggart and took a few armfuls of turf from a good woman's barn. They climbed into the top of her hayshed. They shook out a few sops of hay so as to make a tidy little nest for themselves and they placed the turf in a ring round it to shelter them from the wind and keep in the warmth of their body-heat. Was ever a bed so grand? There they slept soundly for the rest of the night and felt as snug as any two bugs.

Church Bells

Next day was Sunday and they were awakened by the tune of church bells – woke up also with the hunger of a poor widow in Lent on them. However, unlike that little bantam-cock, Fatty-Matty's uncle (*Pon-mee-sowl*), they were not heathens enough to go dirtying their copybook by stooping as low as that rascal had done some years earlier, here on this very spot in Borrisogandery. It was enough to destroy his immortal soul – the time he traipsed into the foreign chapel behind those he called the *black Protestants* and drank freely from their Communion cup. After that little sin he ate the Protestant wafer-host before sneaking into the dark corners of the sacristy for a raid on a sackful of other hosts at a time when the foreign service was at its height. Even now they crossed themselves at such an unheard-of act of sinfulness on the part of Pon-mee-sowl and the glorified way he told the drinkers in Curl 'n' Stripes' drinking-shop his tale when he came back home, recounting his many adventurous escapades on the road to Galway. 'Why, 'twas only the house of the black Protestants – a mere few sops of stale bread and a drop or two of their pagan wine that I was swallying.'

The devil that was in Pon-mee-sowl – he couldn't leave his tale alone. Glad of an audience, he went a step too far in adding how he'd traipsed up to the foreign altar-rails four times in all to get his lips at the wine and the wafer. This account was met, however, not with buffoon-like laughter but with silence and a shaking of heads in disbelief at the sheer insolence of him. If there was a shred of truth in Pon-mee-sowl's words Blue-eyed Jack and Fatty-Matty were left wondering whether a shocked Saint Peter would be kind enough ever to let such a sacrilegious fellow inside the gates of heaven when he died. No, that was not going to be the unholy route for our two adventurers if they were to be blessed by God in their search for a sound plough-horse.

However, there were other ways (they told themselves) of staving off hunger than desecrating a poor Protestant chapel and they went and found themselves a little farm on the outskirts of the village where they were sure to get themselves enough food to keep the wolf from the door. Though they were not up to the standard of Pon-mee-sowl and his wicked blasphemy, they had not suddenly turned themselves into two politely-canonised saints and they thought that a bit of innocent thievery wouldn't damn their souls everlastingly. They stole half-a-dozen mangolds and turnips from the field of a very good farmer and began to eat them raw. They stole four duck-eggs from a good woman's henhouse to nourish them on their way. With the hatpins from the collars of their greatcoats they'd pinprick the gable-ends of the eggs and suck out the fine medicine inside.

Furthermore, they were well-armed with a package of biscuits from Curl 'n Stripes' shop but these they had paid for with sound money, or so they said.

They'd Need Their Wits About Them

What with the fine night's lodging in the hayshed and the fine feed of vegetables and the package of biscuits, they felt like two young princes on a magical carpet as they strolled round the early-morning deserted streets of Borrisogandery, waiting for next day's Horse-Fair to beckon them on towards Galway. They knew that when they got to the Shannon Bridge buying a suitable stallion for the plough would be a job requiring a scrupulous knowledge of horse-flesh, backed up by a bit of foxy cunning in the give-and-take of bargaining. They'd been told that the Galway jobbers were the devil's own when it came to buying and selling horses. But they were as determined as hell to get the right horse for their necessity and, fearful of the threats of Dowager to brain them with the tongs if they came home empty-handed, they felt sure that success would not be denied them.

Hammer-the-Smith

Two years previously the jovial Hammer-the-Smith, like many a Tipperary man before him, had made this self-same journey but the poor soul had come home empty-handed. For when the Galway Horse-Fair was wearing away and the horse-traders were fading off into the evening dusk, he found himself woefully fidgety and desperate and began rushing up and down the streets in a last-minute attempt to get himself a horse.

Blue-eyed Jack and Fatty-Matty had listened to him a number of times as he told them his dismal tale and were now about to benefit from the hindsight he had accumulated. The night before they set sail he had given them a dose of his fatherly advice – describing every little detail of that dark and dismal day that had let him down so dreadfully. He told how he spent the afternoon investigating every blessed horse along the town's main street – even up and down the backyards and alleys – testing their hooves and fetlocks, their teeth and their temperament to such an extent that in the end he couldn't make up his mind which horse was best to his liking. They were all such fine-looking animals.

There had been an added factor to all this that had troubled him. Like the rest of Rookery Rally he had heeded his mother's warning to be more than careful before foolishly handing over his few hard-earned banknotes to a few Galway unknowns. Lo and behold (and before he knew it) the daylight had crept away and gone on him. Would he ever forget the sorrow he felt when he finally got home after his fruitless search for a horse?

For the rest of that week he kept to his bed and was as sick as an old corncrake. There he lay, cursing the two sides of his mother for her over-anxious warnings to him. It was a holy show opposite the neighbours: no fine plough-horse to bring him joy after his forty-mile trip or to boast about to his close friends who had waited in the yard to greet him on his return. And (worse still) a week later he was forced to head off yet again – this time to Tipperary Town – to make do with what proved to be a second-rate animal.

Poor Hammer-the-Smith! After all this, it was easy (said he) to understand how the likes of him was sore and heavy-hearted – especially as he had been as good as gold the livelong day amongst those strange Galway men and hadn't treated himself to a single glass of stout or a drop of whiskey poured down his throat. He had made a vow to himself that he'd never set a bleddy foot inside Galway hereafter and told them that the homeward trek had made him as miserable as an old woman driving home her bad-tempered ass in the rain. Neither of them laughed.

Up With The Cockerel, On To Portmantle

After their stop-over in Borrisogandery the new day came in sprightly enough. They were up with the cockerels and heading north at a fairly lively pace. They passed through Monks' Vale and it wasn't long before they reached the Mighty Shannon River itself. While they were waiting to cross over the bridge they saw what looked like a lively commotion going on at the far turn of the river. They stopped and listened to the strange-sounding talk going on among the buyers and sellers – hotly arguing over a particular roan stallion.

In the middle of the throng stood a well-known tinker *(The Ranger)* and he no bigger than a child. With his two hefty sons he was gamely struggling to hold onto the stallion by its head and the blinkers. At the side of the road they had placed an upturned felt hat with a fine fist of money in it. This was to befuddle and cod any Tipperary fools, who might be tempted into an early-morning challenge when they crossed over the bridge. With these wily tinkers it was always the same old singsong at one Horse-Fair or another. They were renowned for their love of roguery when it came to wild horses.

The Jinker's Challenge

'Coom on, blasht ye, who is man enough to step out here with the bridle and bit?' cried The Ranger, marking a spot in the road with his toe.

'Coom on, lads,' echoed his sons, 'which of ye is able to cart this fine stallion beneath the shafts?'

The cautious crowds stood back in silence. They didn't need brains to see that this stallion was a wild young devil if ever there was one.

'Ah lads, coom on, let ye. Spit on yeer fists just this once in yeer miserable lives and lay down yeer pound-notes. We'll match them with five of our own and we'll throw in the ould cart as well. Ye'll never get a bargain like this?

It was indeed a fair offer. But there were no takers and after all the fuss and hubbub the crowd began to lose interest. Some of them had already drawn away and were looking down the street where the sport and merrymaking might be better.

Into Town Galloped The Tipperary Men

That's when the tinkers saw the two Tipperary mares and Blue-eyed Jack and Fatty-Matty hopping up and down on their saddles like a pair of cowboys out of the west.

As soon as they saw the hat and the shiny heaps of money and heard the offer that was on hand they lept down and threw two pounds apiece into The Ranger's hat. The crowd turned on its heel and quickly hurried back to watch the sport and see the Tipperary men outwitted. There wouldn't be a drop of drink for the newcomers for the rest of the day unless they won the challenged wager.

The Ranger and his sons eyed Blue-eyed Jack and Fatty-Matty up and down and then up and down again: 'Huh, two prime boys from the mountains of Tipperary,' they gloated, 'and they bringing us their fine drinking-money.'

This was a noble chance – and so early in the morning – for them to horde in a bit of sound money and get themselves a few pints of stout at the expense of these two foreign simpletons. They spit on their hands and rubbed them gleefully together at the thought of their young stallion kicking the cart round the road and leaving it in pure splinters.

The Gift Of Horse-language

However, they didn't know half as much as they thought they knew. No-one at the bridge knew that in the stables of Lord Elegance at home in Rookery Rally both Blue-eyed Jack and Fatty-Matty had worked and gained experience with horses of all shapes and sizes and that, after mixing with one or two of the English trainers, they had long been acquainted with the gift of horse-language, the ear-whispering and nose-blowing – as well as a few other handy skills handed down to them from the likes of Dandy and Handsome Johnnie.

'We'll cart this stallion beneath the shafts this very day for ye. We'll save the three of ye the labour and we'll drive her back to Tipperary,' shouted the two prime boys and they stamped their boots in a show of mock-defiance.

'True for ye, we know ye will,' sighed the tinkers, shaking their heads in well-trained mockery.

By now more crowds had flocked back to the bridge to see the carry-on and they started to smile. It was the same as a cattle-fair-day and it was time for the insults to start flowing with regards to the stamp and breed of these two Tipperary upstarts.

'Ye were always good for nothing except wiping yeer arse,' shouted the tinkers. This was a good start and it raised a laugh from the onlookers – even the children.

'Is it to cart this horse that ye've coom all this way from Tipperary? What have ye to offer? We'll tell ye what ye have to offer – nothing but yeer shite, that's what ye have!'

The tinkers turned back to the crowd and they held their sides laughing. That wasn't enough. Full of himself, The Ranger went on to cast doubts on the workings of the bodily parts of the Tipperary men's mothers and fathers, who had had the misfortune (said he) to have put these two manly specimens on the earth in the first place. There was more of this banter as the three tinkers threw in one or two more quaint curses and oaths, which only a tinker from Galway could have invented and none of the rest of us could even spell. But time and time again it was met by the smiles from the two good-natured Tipperary men. This sort of nonsense had simply spurred Blue-eyed Jack and Fatty-Matty on to even greater bravery.

'If it's the shirts from off our backs that ye want we'll throw them into the hat as well,' shouted Fatty-Matty, spitting at the tinkers' feet and narrowly missing the hat and their bare feet.

The Hollybush

Meanwhile Blue-eyed Jack had disappeared from the crowd. He had lept in across the ditch and with his tobacco-knife had cut himself a prickly hollybush three or four feet in length. Back he came, waving it over his head. Meanwhile, Fatty-Matty had gathered into a heap each of the tinkers' articles: the reins: the bit and bridle: the blinkers, saddle and chains. The crowd were now standing on tiptoe and craning their necks to get themselves a proper view. From now on their eyes would be riveted on the antics of the Tipperary men – to see what would happen next. They began to sigh and murmur at this unheard-of sight – a strange Tipperary man and he rushing among them with his arms waving a hollybush wildly in the air.

Quickly, in case the Tipperary men might change their minds, the tinkers pulled the cart out from the wheelwright's yard next to the church and left it standing in the middle of the road. All was now set up and they were ready for the fray to start between the prized stallion and the two simple strangers.

Avarice has always been a fine thing and they were beside themselves with what could only be called *money-lust* as they waited for the expected bouts of fireworks when the wild stallion would start kicking his hind legs out from under him like a wild jack-donkey and break the cart into matchsticks. In their head they were doing their sums and adding together the extra bit of money they'd get from the two Tipperary upstarts – the price of their broken cart as well as the poor scholars losing their bet.

All was as still as a picture and an awed silence took over and darkened the bridge. The game was on and the black-winged crows stopped circling round the treetops and the cows in the nearby fields stopped bawling to be milked. There was no need for Blue-eyed Jack and Fatty-Matty to make a mad rush at the stallion and in order to prove this they turned themselves into two ancient snails and began their work with the hollybush.

Slowly… ever so slowly… and slower still. That was the art of it – a little bit of a Tipperary man's patience and not a single harsh word out of their mouths. Fatty-Matty had a smile on his jaw – a smile that would light up an angel's face as he began to talk in a mellifluous language that any stallion would love to hear:

'Mee noble beauty, is it you that's in it? I'd have given mee two eyes to behold so beautiful a creature as yeer own good self.'

And he went on: 'Can I believe mee eyes? I've been dying to meet ye these past long years – been dying to behold a creature as noble as yeerself.'

Blue-eyed Jack chimed in too: 'I give ye mee oath, there's no horse in Ireland a patch on ye. Ye're the wonder of all wonders – that's what ye are.'

Fatty-Matty then took over. On and on he went. Oh, the mesmerizing old charmer that he was and he all the time edging gently round the horse's head in a nearer and nearer circle. The crowd sighed and they waited.

Meanwhile Blue-eyed Jack got to work with the prickly hollybush. This left everyone scratching their heads as he slowly began waving it back and forth as though he were charming a snake. Like a cat with a dainty feather, he began to apply it, tickling the stallion's mane with its sharpness. The onlookers were flummoxed. Not one of them knew the secret of the hollybush.

Patience. Patience. That's the way of it.

He started tickling the stallion's sides with the itchiness of the hollybush. His fingers had a stealth in them that only a fox or a weasel could muster when marking out their favourite hen or rabbit.

Bit by bit. Bit by bit. Caressingly.

The stallion's chest started to palpitate like fresh dung. It cocked its ears back in apprehension.

Blue-eyed Jack drew the hollybush down the stallion's flanks, nearer and nearer to its tail. The crowd marvelled at the changing features of the stallion as though it were hypnotised. Just like the lion is tamed before the circus-master's whip, the fate of this wild beast (they didn't know it yet) was doomed from the start. What the blazes was this strange Tipperary man doing to The Ranger's stallion? He was tickling its belly underneath.

Gently. Gently. Gently.

Cripes, byze! Could it be true? He was tickling the rubbery private particles of the stallion, using the exquisite hands of a fiddle-player.

The stallion was entranced by this new romance between himself and Blue-eyed Jack's hollybush. May this wondrous feeling go on and on for all eternity (he must have thought) as his rubbery mechanics were seen to enlarge. The Galway men were as bemused as the horse by these strange antics – seeing the two Tipperary men and the way they were using a hollybush to caress the private machinery of the tinkers' prized stallion.

At last even a fool could see the truth and they were roused to anger: 'The dirty filthy whoors,' they roared and some of the women fell over themselves in fits of crude laughter. Was anything like this ever seen in any Christian country?

Mesmerism

Blue-eyed Jack and Fatty-Matty put their fingers on their lips to silence the roars of the crowd. The dazed stallion began to tremble. He bowed himself to the reins. Then he bowed himself to the bit – and finally to the bridle, the blinkers, the haymes and saddle and chains.

All the while Blue-eyed Jack continued to apply the magic potion of his hollybush to the bemused stallion's private particles. At the same time (slowly, ever so slowly) Fatty-Matty encircled the chains and shafts of the cart round the stallion's rump. It was like walking a tightrope at the Daffy-Duck Circus. Breathlessly he lowered the harness onto the stallion's back whilst Blue-eyed Jack went on distracting the poor beast, his hollybush moving on to caress its testicles.

For the first time in its life the wild horse had been chastised and like a bird in a cage had been carted beneath the shafts. The bargain had been made and won and the stallion and cart was there's for the asking. Realizing the magic that they'd just witnessed, the crowd's ungrudging applause rang out and echoed off of the bridge.

Blue-eyed Jack and Fatty-Matty snatched up their winnings from the tinkers' hat before anyone could blink an eye. Then they lept up onto the cart, their two mares following along behind them, and slipped away, raising the hollybush aloft in triumph. If a bolt of lightning had struck The Ranger dumb, there could have been no more astonished man than he in the whole of the Galway Horse-Fair this blessed day.

That same evening as the darkness was settling in, the two happy horsemen (*success to yeer elbow – ye're the two best men in Ireland*) drank as much black stout as any hurling-team put together. Then they sailed off into the sunset, their beautiful stallion dragging them forth in the cart and the two mares following along behind them, this time roped to the back of the cart. What with all the fine day's drinking, our heroes hadn't had time yet to consider christening their prize with a name.

By now the dark clouds were patching the sky's rafters and soon they were well out on the Tipperary Road and out passed Twin Rivers. They knew what would be in the tinkers' minds and were anxious to make a start before nightfall so as to avoid the previous owners following them and getting their hands on their prized possession and stealing it back. They weren't thoroughbred eejits and they knew the dangers of being robbed of the five-pound-notes that they'd won. They were so eager to get home that the thought of stopping in Borrisogandery or Prodigal Hill for a sleep in a hayshed was the furthest thing from their minds. Besides, they wanted to show off this fine animal as soon as possible to the expectant neighbours in Rookery Rally and tell them the hilarious tale of the hollybush and its magical prickly powers that had ensured the grand purchase of the stallion.

A New Dance In Fashion

Around this time there was a dance in fashion both in the Roaring Town Institute and at the Platform Dances-in-The-Fields. It was known as the tango and came from Argentina. It required more than a drop of twists and turns in it and it was far better than any of the lazy slow waltzes. Dancing its mazy steps gave the hairy old men a chance to lace on their Sunday boots and come out of hiding and attack the dance-floor. For once in their ancient lives these happy old rascals could catch a grip of a comely young woman and press their bellies up against her. One or two of the merry souls got more than one firm uppercut to the jaw for placing his hands firmly on an innocent damsel's arse rather than round her waist – as though the wily old devil was ignorant of the proper dance graces and procedures of the new dance. Would Life ever change?

'What sort of a fandango-of-a-dance is this new tango?' said some of the older women, who had no interest whatsoever in going off with their men to try out a few foreign dance-steps. These old beldames had to laugh when their weary men came home after their dance and showed them what they'd been missing and did a few fancy currywhibble steps for them round the Welcoming Room, their heads full of the twists and turns of the new crazy dancing.

And now the name *Fandango* took hold of the imagination of Blue-eyed Jack and Fatty-Matty and they fandangoed their lovely horse all the way from Portmantle towards their own purple hills. The stallion soon got used to his new name.

The road passed by as quick as a jig-step. They made a grand procession: the two cautious mares and the reins that tied them to the back of the cart in case the stallion got himself into too amorous a fit after his recent antics with the hollybush. They had seen enough of that tomfoolery already. Blue-eyed Jack and Fatty-Matty ran the cart along the grassy verges of the road the same as before so as to keep the sharp stones out of Fandango's hooves and, wherever they could, they took the shortcut across the velvet fields. It had been a glorious adventure from start to finish and the two heroes were more than satisfied with themselves and their stallion and with all the fine day's drinking still rattling around in their bellies.

At Sunset

It was not till next morning that they got back to Rookery Rally and glided up the Open Road. By which time the cocks were crowing and the cows were well and truly milked and the sun was a red blur gleaming in the sky. To see them – they were as proud as two turkey-cocks. The Spallidagh children, led by Warbling Will and Lofty, skipped out expectantly and lined the roadway to greet the great adventurers. How astonished was the look in their eyes as they beheld the high-stepping Fandango and welcomed him into their midst, none the worse for wear after his long journey. You would think he'd come down to them from the moon.

The Men Got Busy

At Hammer-the-Smith's forge the two men got busy, examining Fandango's hooves and his hocks and especially his shoes, to make sure that no particular damage had been done to him. With his delicate pen-knife the smith removed one or two tiny pebbles from his front hooves.

They then took their prize down to River Laughter with the rest of the Spallidagh children following along behind them, it being a Saturday and not a school-day. They were inquisitiveness itself. The men led Fandango into the river and soaked him in the waters of the sally-hole to cool any ache that might still be in him. They knew he was finding himself (like Darkie and Little Nell their first day at school) in a very strange place and they continued to whisper those bits of encouragement and endearment into his ears that any stallion wold love to hear.

An hour later their new prize was reluctant to leave the coolness of the river. Once more they made use of the Cindy-powder mixture and gave his legs a good rub of it. After that they gave him a feed of oats and water from the trough – just a light feed and not too much in case he got the wind and cholic trapped in his stomach. With the back of his coat Blue-eyed Jack wiped away the surplus water from Fandango's back.

Handsome Johnnie came down to watch and he placed a warm blanket on his stallion before taking him up the road and crossing the yard where he proudly presented him to Dowager. She took out a bottle of holy-water and shivered the stallion all over with its contents, making the sign-of-the-cross on his eyes, his ears and nose. And though the two men had returned tired and weary and with a full growth of beard on them and their coats were that bit dirtier and shabbier than before, the smile on her face now told it all: she was as happy as a queen on her throne. It was clear she was not going to be stopped from expressing her happiness and she invited all the well-wishers to come in and see the razzle-dazzle of her fine new beast. They were chockful of joy. She cut them several thick slices from the ham that she'd prepared in celebration of this great day. Everyone whaled into the meat as well as the fat onions that she'd thrown in to make up a juice and soon they were all scraping their plates clean – even the ailing Handsome Johnnie.

Fingers Jack

That evening Blue-eyed Jack and Fatty-Matty sent for Fingers Jack, the bonesetter, whose knowledge of asses, jinnits, ponies, mules or horses was renowned the length of north Tipperary. He came at once and gave Fandango a right good scrutiny before passing his judgement:

Said he, 'I sin meeself if this isn't the finest horse to ever grace the fields of Tipp'rary.' From his back-pocket he took out a bottle of his mother's holy-water and Fandango was blessed (if not canonized) all over again – even his belly and privacies, so that he might sire a fine foal the following spring when coupled with Red Scissors' giddy young mare (*Hot-Lips*).

There was still a deal of money left in the two horsemen's pockets after their victorious Portmantle exchange. Along with Fingers Jack and Hammer-the-Smith they decided to celebrate with a proper carousel. At Curl 'n' Stripes' drinking-shop they bought an indescribable amount of whiskey and coupled it with what they labelled *the medicine*, the rawgut potheen which had been hidden in the base of Handsome Johnnie's press cupboard. It still had the corn-seed in it.

In the twilight the four of them sat on the singletree across in Old Sam's Grove where they proceeded with great reluctance to throw the whiskey down their throats and smack their lips – a toast (they vowed) in praise of recent times and the acquirement of their noble Fandango. It proved to be a long and powerful drink and the rooks in the rookery did not get a wink of sleep from all the singing they were forced to endure this blessed night. Eventually all four of them staggered home and collapsed in their beds where they slept far into the next day, dreaming no doubt of Galway and the successful Horse-Fair and what everyone in Rookery Rally thereafter remembered as a *rale full booze*.

Treated Like A Royal Prince

From that day on there never was a stallion treated with so much kindness as Fandango. This contrasted with many other animals (ranging from cat to dog, goat, cow and horse) that felt nothing other than savage curses and a kick from the wellingtons of many a man or (worse still) the ashplant down on top of his back or across his head. If a swish of a cow's shitty tail hit them in the jaw while they were milking, these fine fellows belted into the cow's ribs with whatever implement was nearer their fist – the stool or the rake. It was not unknown for a brute with a Monday's sore head on him after a previous night's feed of strong drink to whale into his horse with such ferocity that he killed the misfortunate beast outright. That was always the way with men and their animals: it was one thing or the other and no in-between – pure pain or pure affection. If we live to be a hundred none of us will ever forget the good care that was taken of Fandango. His heart must have been dancing a jig-step and he turned out to be the most good-natured of creatures and responded with what can only be termed a dog's own loyalty. If the sheepdog

(*Blue*) was Fatty-Matty's best friend, then Fandango and Blue-eyed Jack became closer to one another than the two sides of a dinner-plate.

The Lightning Whoor

For the next four years Fandango's life continued in this heavenly way below in the Bull-Paddock where he spent many days in the shelter of the solitary oak-tree with Fatty-Matty's horse, Shout. There was, however, always a cloud hanging close by them. For, after Handsome Johnnie's ancient ass (*Lazybones*) had gone to his home in the pastures of death, Fandango had to spend his days in the self-same field as he newly-purchased ass (*the Lightning Whoor* – so named by his previous bad-tempered owner, Sikey). This ass was to prove himself as cantankerous an old devil as Sikey himself. Whenever he was in one of his foul moods, Fandango made insistent attempts to express his goodwill towards him, nuzzling his backbone and endeavouring to draw him back from the brink of despair. But the unusually sour ass remained a stranger to any such efforts of kindness towards him.

Said Handsome Johnnie, 'I give ye mee oath, this poor ass was turned bitter and mean long ago, after years of wretched treatment from Sikey – ye can be sure of that.'

'True for ye,' said Dowager. 'It's the same thing with a badly-treated child. It's only natural that he'd now turn out to be as cranky as hell and carry on biting the hand that feeds him.'

There were times when they were both sorely tempted to put the switch to the Lightning Whoor's back but both Handsome Johnnie and Blue-eyed Jack continued to bring the spirit of kindness to him and never laid a hand on him.

His sickness of spirit had increased more and more as the months rolled by. The children on their way home from school would peer in over the ditch and give him a smile but all they could see in return was his cantankerous outer skin. They were too young to know why such heaviness had grown in his heart, though Dowager could have told them the whole story – how recent events with a nearby ass (*Sleeping Beauty*) had simply added to the previous load of the misery that he'd brought with him when Handsome Johnnie bought him from Sikey.

It Was the Beginning Of Springtime

It was the beginning of springtime – a time fresh and green – and the blackbirds were at their finest. Herald-the-Post came storming into the yard with the news that Dowager's younger brother (*the Little Yellowhammer* – he could whistle as good as any yellow-hammer) had been taken to his bed with a dose of double-pneumonia. The whole world knew what a killer this was and that it might put a finishing touch to both his lungs, poor man.

When she heard the news of his illness Dowager was agitated beyond belief and pushed Handsome Johnnie out the door to go down and fetch the ass so that she might tackle him up to the ass-and-car. Unbelievably this was a day when the Lightning Whoor found himself in the best of possible humours and was already at the field gate, his heart rustling inside in him. There were times like this when boredom set in and he was glad to escape from the confines of the Bull-Paddock and get himself out onto the road. After all, this was springtime – and springtime can bring out the best in all of us, even in sulky asses.

Handsome Johnnie led him back up the road and into the yard where, much to the children's surprise, he took to the tackling and chains at once – to the carting in the shafts and Dowager's gentle encouragement.

Off They Went

They set sail down towards Old Sam's Stile and, knowing his regular forlorn spirits, Dowager put the whip soft-and-easy to his back as they tripped their merry way to the Little Yellowhammer's sick-bed in the cottage he was renting from Baggy-Britches, a lofty farmer over near Sammy-in-the-fields. This prized lodging had long been the Little Yellow-Hammer's home in return for looking after this sporty old fellow's Cheltenham racehorses and keeping them in fine fettle.

The Lightning Whoor soon worked himself into a steady rhythm, prancing gaily passed the pump outside Merrymouth's drinking-shop. See those swanky ladylike legs of his and the chains and tackling swinging and swaying in harmony with his hooves. All this — the swanky stepping and the shifting of his arse and tail — would cause any lady-ass to fall helplessly in love with him.

Pat-the-Bear's Ass

Lo and behold, it was at this moment that Pat-the-Bear's snow-white ass (the aforementioned Sleeping Beauty – a fleshy young she-ass that had recently replaced the good man's own dead ass) escaped from the gate at Murty's Meadow and burst down the lane and out onto Travellers Rest where she finally entered the gateway of High-Hands at the Slippery Gap.

That's when the two asses met up. They began neighing heartily to each other from inside and outside the ditch and giving each other the winking eye with more than a passing interest. And just as a garden flower yearns for water, so had the Lightning Whoor reached an age where he yearned for a she-ass's companionship.

'*Neigh-neigh-neigh*,' went the two of them, melodiously braying in one and the same accord. There was so much ass-talking to be done.

Pat-the-Bear's she-ass was a rare ass indeed – a true beauty, equal in stature to Dowager's own rough-diamond-of-an-ass. There were none of the usual bloodstains round her eyes or her ears or on her private regalia where the bloodthirsty flies had left her alone (thank God). The two asses were at once completely captivated by one another and were not to be moved from their joy. Nothing could shake them and they stuck their hooves into the ground – one ass inside the ditch and the other outside on the road. Clearly the arch woodland fairy (*True Love*) had moved in on the scene and overpowered the pair of them.

Ah, what merry sport they would have one fine day!

Oh, what noble young asses they'd produce if given half a chance!

They continued to speak to each other in an ass-language that Dowager, for all her years' experience, didn't understand:

'Bless my soul, I haven't seen ye these past ages,' the Lightning Whoor seemed to say.

'And how has that master of yeers been treating ye this last while?' Pat-the-Bear's ass seemed to say.

On and on went the charming discourse of their ass-talk, as if they had the livelong day to converse with one another. Who knew when these two handsome creatures might set eyes on each other again. It had become an ass's love-tale – the tale of Sleeping Beauty and the Lightning Whoor. Ah, Love herself, the sweetest of all virtucs!

Dowager's Concern

'What on earth's to be done now?' cried Dowager, seeing her ass's hooves stuck so firmly into the ground. The minutes were ticking by and she started working herself up into a fine old fit of stormy temper for at this rate she'd never get to see the Little Yellowhammer. He might even be dead before the evening was out. No jab of her reins could do the trick. No swift snap of the bit. Not even the famed curses of Dowager ('Coom on, blasht you, yuh ould shitty-arse!') could work the miracle on this wretched eejit-of-an-ass.

Pat-the-Bear came out across the road to size up the situation and give a helping hand with a few sound kicks of his boot into the ass's belly. the Lightning Whoor wouldn't budge. Dowager took out her infamous hatpin from the side of her blue-basket hat and she fixed it into the heel of her ashplant. To stick the hat-pin up into the ass's arse was always her last resort but she may as well have tried counting a shower of moonbeams as move the Lightning Whoor.

Madge Roundabout

Madge Roundabout, the Ballad-Boy's wife (he never seemed able to get out of bed), had been digging her spuds and was pelting them into the bucket. And now, with that little light laugh of hers, she stopped and leant on her fork. She had been watched this charming little spectacle. She was a well-known lady of great intuition when it came to farm-animals, especially asses, and she wiped the clay from off of her hands and stepped tidily out the gate.

'God spare ye the health – I've the very thing ye've been looking for,' said she, just as poor hapless Dowager was about to untackle her ass and pull him the length of the road with her two good arms. This old fool-of-an-ass (she thought) would think nothing of kneeling down on the road as though he was saying his prayers and staying there till the Guards came along and carried him off on a stretcher to Nackers' Yard – or else shot him there on the spot.

A minute or two later she saw Madge running back from the house with an old stocking and the steam rising up out of it. Inside it she had a boiling beetroot. She now took over and waved everyone aside and took up her stance – as close as she could to the Lightning Whoor's tail and the cart. She clutched the stocking in her gloved fist and gingerly tied it round the unexpected tail of the Lightning Whoor – as far away from him as she could so that he wouldn't feel the heat coming out of the beetroot. Then delicately and ladylike (almost elegantly) she rammed the stocking-with-the-boiling-beetroot in under the ass's tail, as close up to his arse as she could.

With eyes of the purest fire the startled creature – and he on the verge of a memorable courtship with Pat-the-Bear's Sleeping Beauty – thrust his two fine legs out into space and took off with the speed of an express bullet, dragging the mystified Dowager and the cart after him and at the same time kicking lumps out of the road and almost throwing the poor woman and her hat into the dyke.

Ah, Fame at last.

It was said in several drinking-shops during the course of the evening that this misfortunate beast shot out passed the red sports-car of the Bearded Vet, who was on his way home from Limerick. It was reported also that Dowager and the Lightning Whoor spent a day-and-a-half getting back their shattered senses.

Fame too for Madge Roundabout and her boiled beetroot-in-a-stocking. It had done the trick that no-one else could do and this became true in more senses than one. For when the Little Yellowhammer heard tell of her famous exploit with the beetroot, he damn near wet his bedsheets and fell out onto the floor from the fits of spluttery laughter he took. His whistling-skills came back to him in no time at all and he entirely forgot about his double pneumonia. In future (thought Dowager) Doctor Glasses would have a handy way of treating anyone with the double pneumonia: mention Madge Roundabout and her stocking-with-the-boiled-beetroot that was shoved up the Lightning Whoor's arse. That'd be medicine enough for anyone.

Ploughing Now Took On A New Edge

Going to fetch Fandango and Shout from their respective stables was never a hard job: no need for coaxing – no need for the whip or the foul curse: no need for administering the wellington boot or the shortness of temper or the brutish chastisement that some other horses endured and expected every day of their lives. The two horses were the most honest workers and were never reluctant to start a day – and now more than ever since it was the start of Ploughing-Time.

The kindliness and the whisperings into the horses' ears by Fatty-Matty and Blue-eyed Jack inspired the pair of horses to the very height of horsemanship and the ploughing took on a new edge. There was no horse-fly or horse-bee, out looking for the sweet smells of ammonia underneath a horse's tail, that could stop them whaling their way across the early-morning ploughing-field. See the flashing blades of the ploughshare silvering its way above the dark clay – turning the grass from frosty green to brown clay time and time again – trimming it as neatly as a man's beard after making friends with the well-stropped razor of the town's barber (*Tom Slappity*).

At John's Gate

Handsome Johnnie came down to John's Gate to inspect the work. He could see the power in the horses and the sweat hopping off of the two farmers' jaws as they took it in turn to steer the speedy plough. He laughed to himself, seeing the men struggling like blazes to keep up for they hadn't time to light their pipe or give so much as a cough as the two gallant beasts opened up the straightest of furrows, the ploughshare cutting deep and regular drills.

What a magnificent sight (he thought). Flawless the teamwork, one horse stepping on the soft grass and the other one keeping pace on the hard-pulling sweaty clay: one horse always on the right side and the other on the left as they strove up towards the headland, the ditches answering them back when they drew themselves back-back-back in perfect harmony at the turnabout – one in the bigger circle and the other in the lesser circle, scarcely pausing to draw a breath.

There was no need for words of guidance (*coom oop! careful now! steady! whoa!*) as they stamped their hooves and pushed on firmly down the field towards the lower turnabout before Handsome Johnnie could even blink his dreamy eye. He was tired these days and it wasn't long before he had seen enough. He shook his head and headed up the road, a happy man, leaving behind him this precious bit of the day when the hearts of Fandango and Shout beat as one. He took with him their memory – the fire in their legs and the steam on their backs spiralling its way to the heavens – out over Simple Simon's ditch and into the blue sky beyond Corcoran's Well.

Dinnertime Tea

Blue-eyed Jack had almost forgotten to look at his pocket-watch to see if it was time for Dowager to bring out the tea and sandwiches. Suddenly he saw his mother appearing at the gate as though she was a visiting angel with wings on her back. She stood for a moment with her hands on her hips, her sweet-gallon of tea at her feet and the doorstep sandwiches wrapped in newspapers. She gazed in wonder and admiration at the two ploughing beauties. It was an even better sight to her wise old eyes than the little birds and the bellflowers all over the sunny ditches.

Later on, in the cooler and fading light of afternoon, when ploughing-time came to a halt all over the fields of Rookery Rally, Blue-eyed Jack and Fatty-Matty inspected the one-and-a-half acres of noble new ploughland. They stowed the plough away in the ferns by the ditch after scraping its share clean with their sharp flinty stones. And now the legs of Fandango and Shout called out for their scrutiny – legs that were aching like the legs of our mighty Tipperary hurlers after the fray. The two men took them down to River Laughter, scattering the cows that had been peacefully sheltering from the flies in under the metal bridge.

Now was the most important part of the day – the time for precious silence – the time for peace. And those woodland fairies (*the Springtime Maidens*) could only stare out from the Bog Wood and admire the two great horses and their stout-hearted masters. *Slurp-slurp-slurp!* Fandango and Shout mopped up the cool river water – for ten minutes and not a minute more, since too much water would damage the wind in their lungs. It was time at last for sport and the horses rolled over in the sally-hole and kicked their restored legs into the air. The men had to smile and they sang the honest praises of their horses.

'Could any men in Ireland have a better pair of horses than ye?' said Blue-eyed Jack.

"Where did ye get yeer legs from?' said Fatty-Matty.

They bathed and soothed their horses' burning hooves and hocks all over again, tending to any swelling that might have appeared on their limbs – up as far as the fetlocks. After all the playfulness they took them out of the river and up onto the grass.

It was time at last for them to tend to their own needs and they took off their wellingtons and cooled their feet and the aching fire that was in their ankles. Underneath the bridge where no women could lay eyes on them they took off their shirts and britches and swam bare-arsed around and around in the cool of the river. They were like little children all over again. Heaven (they thought) must surely be a moment like this.

In The Fifth Year Of His Life

Life is never a fairy-tale for the faint-hearted to glow and gloat upon. For what next befell Fandango was nothing but pure sorrow. It was the next year – the fifth year of his life and ploughing-time was here again. The morning was cold and a wind sprang up and tried to howl like a grown-up wind. The banshee, who as everyone knows sits inside the ditch at Easy-does-it's Stile, was combing out her long golden hair. Some (like Jack Fart) had the gift of hearing her weeping wails but the Spallidagh household was not so fortunate. Her haunting cry now told others that Sergeant Death was lurking round the corner and about to herald in an imminent death.

The evening came on and the fields were shining. The Spallidagh children were in jovial mood and the cows and their calves were getting along famously. The day's ploughing was over and Fandango and Shout were standing in the cool of the river waters, absorbed as usual in their horse-conversation. Blue-eyed Jack and Fatty-Matty were washing down their flanks and letting them drink the delicious mouthfuls of freezing water, this time to their heart's content, the day's reward for neatly trimming so much grass from that day's field. They gave them the customary Cindy-powder rub-down and let them spend the next half-hour underneath the fresh blanketing to get the warmth flowing back into them limbs.

Full of the day's happy spirits, the two horses returned with Fatty-Matty, both of them into his yard, for Blue-eyed Jack was hurrying off to the Hills-of-the-Past to inspect a recently-discovered ash-tree that would make a fine hurleystick for his younger brother, Stylish.

The evening was quieter than usual. Shout was feeling tired and went into the shed where he was soon sleeping like a baby.

Fatty-Matty was left alone with Fandango. He took the reins and blinkers off of him, all the time speaking softly into his ear. He tapped his hind quarters ('*Off with ye, mee beauty*') and sent him across the Bull-Paddock towards the Lightning Whoor, who had been hiding himself in the ferns and nursing his burnt gable-end from the surprised meeting he'd recently had with the boiling beetroot-in-the-stocking.

Free at last from the afternoon's cosseting of Blue-eyed Jack and Fatty-Matty, the Galway stallion was as free as the birds in the sky and for the next half-hour he cantered round the Bull-Paddock, the last sunbeams of daylight caressing his shoulders. See him – mad as a March hare and striking his hooves out defiantly towards the failing red sun above Bog Wood and the plantations of Lisnagorna. His evening was bliss – like music to his ears. Could life ever get better than this?

Fandango! Oh, Fandango!

Fandango! Oh, Fandango! Alone in the Bull-Paddock for the first time in your life and without the support of your good friend, Shout, what ringing devil suddenly worked its way into your head? Why (*blasht it*) did you gallop over to the dark corner of the field where the orange ragwort grew most tall and strong? What was the great force that distracted you?

Was it the thought of later harvest-days and the merriment amongst the hayfield farmers?

Were you yearning for the nose-nudging of your noble friend, Shout?

Were you listening to the echoes of the ploughshare clashing with the clay and the afternoon song of the fairies (*the River Nymphs*), who live in the depths of River Laughter?

Why did you forget yourself and eat the poisonous flower that you'd never touched from the day that you left Galway?

Why did you go and eat the deadly root that you'd steadfastly avoided up until now?

Too Late!

Yes, Fandango, the noblest of beasts, ate the poisonous ragwort. Too late! Too late! He knew he had done wrong and soon he realized that something terrible was about to happen to him. His legs became frail. He felt as weak as crumbled powder.

He managed to stagger to the lower gate and into Fatty Matty's yard. By now the sweat was rolling down his sides like rain splashing off of a hayreek and the faintest of whinnying arose from his gaping nostrils and a rasping, wheezing sound from the depths of his belly. I ask you, was this what so fine an animal as himself deserved?

You'd have to be there in the yard to witness the grief written on Fatty-Matty's face – the appalling pain in him as though he'd fallen into a thousand thorn-bushes. And yet he had the presence of mind to send Warbling Will and Lofty racing to the doors of the Bearded Vet to tell him that the life of the precious stallion was in ruins if he didn't get back quicker than a falling star.

The sad news had quickly spread across the fields and a crowd of men, women and children came running into the yard.

A minute later the Bearded Vet was seen leaping out of his car. He saw the exhausted Fandango lying on his side and the demented Fatty-Matty kneeling in front of him, gently stroking him. The poor man's tearful voice was no use to poor Fandango now. No amount of *coom on, mee beauty – you're the best little horse in Ireland* would work the magic for him. Fandango's eyes were livid and burning in his head and his despairing whinnying came from far away, scarcer and scarcer by the second.

The crowd groaned – to see how Fandango's eyes never left Fatty-Matty. The stallion couldn't even lick Fatty-Matty's trembling palm – the trembling palm with a few grains of oats now held out on it – the palm from which he had so often eaten the icing sugar at the end of a hard day's labour. Pitifully he strove to talk to Fatty-Matty in that horse-voice of his that only Shout could ever recognise – a voice over which he was soon to lose control. Vainly he tried to rise but he was too weak to pull even a feather let alone pull a plough. He rolled onto his back, his feet kicking feebly at empty air as though it were some sort of living thing.

The Bearded Vet knelt down and shone his torch into Fandango's eyes. He lifted apart his dry lips and examined his gums. He shone the torch into his ears. Then he grabbed a sack and began violently rubbing his legs, his chest and withers. Fandango didn't even move a muscle.

He had one last resort. He told the fastest runners to hurry to the barrel in the barn and bring back as many buckets of water as they could. Lofty, Stylish and Sammy-Joe hurried back with the buckets and the vet unleashed their freezing contents all over Fandango's sides and onto his head in a last effort to restore him. Little good it did him.

News Had Spread Like Fire

Nothing so dreadful had ever before been seen in Rookery Rally. The crowd were cloaked in sickening silence as they listened to the faint hollow sounds coming from Fandango's throat, his whole body shaking and constricting as he gamely tried to convey to all of them his heartfelt sadness. They saw his eyes half-closing, the lids thick and dry – saw the thin stream of fluid running from his nostrils – heard the ghostly whistling sounds fighting their way against the nasal obstructions as the poor stallion snorted to clear a vent in his nose. The Bearded Vet had witnessed something like it before – but only in his textbooks. Fandango's coat had now started to turn unkempt and lustreless.

And Then Came Blue-eyed Jack

Blue-eyed Jack was still absent, searching in the hills for his hurleystick-makings when he heard the heart-breaking news. Like a wild racehorse he came galloping along the road, the rest of the young Spallidaghs struggling to keep up with him.

He entered the yard, fingering the rosary-beads in his pocket. He pushed the crowd aside and ran towards his horse.

From across the yard Fandango raised his ears, hearing the well-known footfall of his master and feeling his presence. The big man knelt down alongside Fatty-Matty, the air stifled in his throat so that he could scarcely breathe.

Fandango turned his head towards him, his doglike eyes flickering – eyes longing for the daylight he'd soon be seeing no more. He then turned his head away and little sob-like sniffles quivered out of him as though he were ashamed to be seen dying, no longer serving his master.

Blue-eyed Jack stroked Fandango's jaw for the last time. He put his arms round his neck and nuzzled him for the last time. Then he threw his body across him and let loose his tears.

For a second or two Fandango felt a delicate strength flowing back into his thighs from the body-touch of Blue-eyed Jack. It was only for a second – just that split second – and then it vanished.

Demented from crying, Blue-eyed Jack left the yard. He sat himself down on the house-step outside Fatty-Matty's half-door, knowing that he'd hear Fandango's cheery notes no more.

The after-world of olden-day horses would now be calling him:

'Come home, Fandango, come home!'

'Come and join us in the green pastures that lie hidden from the eyes of men, beyond the clouds and the Mighty Mountain.'

A Vision Never Seen Before

There was one more labour for this great animal – one more determined task before leaving Rookery Rally for ever. He lifted his shivering head. He staggered to his feet. The spellbound crowd couldn't bear to look at this vision – this spectre – and the birds in the groaning trees were silent.

He wobbled and stumbled round the yard. Was it a dream? Was he trying to reach the field? They stood back to give him a space.

'Keep back, lads! Keep back!' they whispered.

But Fandango, hearing the sobs of his master, lurched drunkenly towards the house and the half-door where Fatty-Matty now sat next to Blue-eyed Jack, his comforting arms around his good friend, his own tears mingling silently with the ants on the doorstep.

Fandango finally reached the doorstep.

Could it be possible? It was as if he was trying to say something to his master: 'Don't cry! Don't cry! Come now, Jack – dry your eyes!'

Blue-eyed Jack raised his head. The look of astonishment on his face – would anyone ever forget it? The crowd saw Fandango standing beside his master there in front of the house. It was something he himself would never forget. In all his life he had never owned a horse so loyal and true as the noble Fandango, who even at this moment of death was compelled to offer him this final act of devotion.

Then came the last act, as Fandango took a step passed Blue-eyed Jack and leaned in over Fatty-Matty's half-door where the house-fire blazed lively. From deep in his belly he gave a last sad note to the house-fire – a whispering whinny of goodbye – a last secret voice between himself and the house before falling on his knees on the doorstep.

He had paid his homage to Blue-eyed Jack, to Fatty-Matty – to Life itself.

Sergeant Death drew near and Fandango's head drooped low. His tongue hung out dryly and traces of black blood oozed from his mouth.

That's when he died, his spirit flying off over the hills. The birds flapped their wings and sped away in terror as though knowing the ghostly spirit of Death.

Blue-eyed Jack, Fatty-Matty and the Bearded Vet took the tarpaulin from the barn and they reverently covered Fandango's naked shame – his death – from the eyes of the crowd. An orchestra of flies began to surround his corpse.

All That Toil

All that toil – all that service to Man – all gone. The crowds snivelled in sorrow and wiped their eyes guiltily. They walked over to the half-door and said goodbye to the dead stallion – the stallion they all knew had come to Rookery Rally only a few years earlier.

The two men now wanted to be alone with their dead horse.

A short while later Blue-eyed Jack left Fatty-Matty and took the shortcut across Lord Elegance's estate. He fingered his rosary-beads and knelt beside the grave of his grandfather, Dandy, to tell him of his sorrow over Fandango – the horse that (like Dandy himself) had come to Tipperary on that long journey from faraway Galway. The day was getting cold and he rose to go home. The bats and owls slipped by him and the swans idled and cruised their careless way along the surface of Lord Elegance's lake as if nothing unusual had happened of late.

For days to come it'd feel like the end of Blue-eyed Jack's life.

No more would Fandango have those visions of green pastures or of creamery roads – no more those dreams of Galway and that wily old tinker, The Ranger – no more would the Spallidagh children see their stallion rolling round, deliciously tickling his back on the grass below in the Bull-Paddock in the reddening sunset of evening – no more would they see him good-humouredly teasing the Lightning Whoor, the cantankerous ass – no more would they watch their great horse ploughing the fields or cavorting with Shout as the two of them raced the length of the Bull-Paddock – no more would Fandango bawl out his heartache when the Lightning Whoor was tackled for his run to the creamery or the forge, leaving him alone – no more would he run and look out over John's Gate to greet the young Spallidaghs when they called out his name on their return from Dang-the-skin-of-it's schoolhouse.

Up At Dusk

Next morning the men were up at dusk – even before the cockerel had started his impudent crowing. They took their shovels and pickaxes across the haggart. Blue-eyed Jack, along with Fatty-Matty and Red Scissors, buried Fandango in a big black hole in the depths of the Callow Field. He'd not be going to Nackers' Yard and they drowned him in their tears yet again.

The following Monday, as the children headed off to the schoolhouse, they saw Fatty-Matty passing by with Shout. He was heading for Hammer-the-Smith's forge to get him his new horseshoes. A strange thing – stranger than all that they learnt in school each day – was happening in front of their eyes. For, as soon as Shout reached the gates of the Callow Field, he fixed his hooves steadfastly into the ground and set up a mighty din – a terrible din that they'd never heard before. His yellow teeth grimaced in an angry snarl and he raised his front legs in the air in an effort to leap out over an imaginary ditch.

Fatty-Matty was no fool and he opened the gate. He had sensed what was in the mind of his noble beast. Although Shout hadn't the slightest notion where the men had buried his good friend, he nevertheless raced across the Callow Field towards the precise spot where Fandango lay cold in the grave. It was as though from somewhere far away – beyond the Rookery Rally skies – the dead Fandango was calling to him. He could feel the ghost of him close at hand. One thing was clear: Hammer-the-Smith would have to wait a good while yet before putting on his new shoes for him.

Round and around the grave-site tramped the sorrowful Shout – like a priest that ceremoniously walks round a coffin with his incense and thurifer. Then he whinnied for all the world to hear. He whinnied and he whinnied and he went on whinnying. It seemed as though his own heart and the dead soul of Fandango were (and always would be) as one – as when once they ploughed together the fields in springtime – as though their spirits would stay locked together for ever.

Fatty-Matty instinctively took off his cap, as if in reverence, and he scratched his puzzled head. Who would have believed it? The whinnying voice of Shout told him a tale that no human heart could ever supplant, could ever equal. For, there in the Callow Field – there, in front of the children – in something akin to majesty – Tipperary had witnessed the innermost heart of Shout – had witnessed his own final toast to the very best of Rookery Rally horses, our truly-beloved Fandango, the tinkers' stallion that came from Galway. Enough said.

FOUR

Days of Laughter, Days of Tears

After the wretched death of Fandango everyone was left in shreds of grief. But life had to go on and every day brought back anew the living breath into the people of Rookery Rally so that the memory of the stallion's death would gradually fade away just like the morning dew.

Meanwhile, lurking in the dreams of the younger Spallidagh children (Stylish and Sammy-Joe) and taking the place of their sorrow over Fandango, there stepped in a new feeling. It was Fear – a fear that their arch enemy (*the Boodeeman*) would rise up from his sleeping-quarters in the hen-house and make his unwelcome entrance through the bedroom-wall and snatch them away from their mother's skirts. There was another fear to back this one up – a fear that their old enemy, *the Wreck of The Hesperus*, might go back on his word and put them into his wicked sack as soon as Dowager and Handsome Johnnie were abroad in the cowshed, milking – that he might carry them off and drown them in River Laughter's sally-hole where that terrible old witch, Slipperslapper, had once drowned a tinker's puppy.

It was not only the children's dreams about ogres that was upsetting the Spallidagh household. There was the real threat from Dowager's recently-acquired cockerel, the multi-coloured Delancy, a gift from Moll-the-Shuffler. You should have seen the cocky strut of the rascal round about the farmyard – the impudence of him from his half-hidden perch in the noonday hollybush – his imperious look of distain over the hens, the ducks and geese, even over the harmless passersby.

Poor Fandango was hardly a day in his grave when this malicious villain flew out over the yard stream and pecked the blood from Red Scissors' neck whilst he was coming home from taking his cows to the river for a drink. That same afternoon the braggart pecked the blood out of Herald-the-Post's neck the minute he hopped off of his bike to bring Dowager a letter from her sisters across the ocean. Bolder and bolder did the wicked devil grow so that Dowager had to run the length of the yard and give him a few sharp belts of her walking-stick (*Wattle*) to chastise his ugly gob for him.

However, that wasn't punishment enough to curb his intent. For, now that he had discovered how much he liked the sight and taste of human blood, Delancy was out early next day and starting to eye his latest victims, this time the necks of Dowager's young children as they were about to set off for school and on a day when they were just beginning to wipe away their tears over poor Fandango. It was too much to bear. Maybe their big brother, Blue-eyed Jack, would cut the legs from under him with the heel of his hurleystick. Maybe he'd kill him outright with the blade of Handsome Johnnie's hatchet before the week was out. It'd be good enough for the likes of him.

Delancy, however, was no fool, and was well aware of human cunning. Far from repentant, he flew out over the henhouse roof and hid himself behind the dung-heap to escape a further dose of retribution. He was safe and sound for a little while and in that high-pitched squawk of his he went on raucously crowing out bursts of defiance and showing the rest of the world that he was the farmyard's cock-of-the-walk and afraid of no-one on earth.

Lo and behold, if that wasn't enough to keep the Spallidaghs on their tippy-toes, dancing up the road came Galloping Gret's two great big sows. They were forever taking control over the road, chewing the tasty briars from off of the ditches. And now they took it into their heads to come suddenly striding in over Dowager's flagstones and chase her trembling sow round the yard before driving her in a near-faint out through the pig-house gap.

With all these worries constantly plaguing the life out of old and young alike, was it any wonder that Fandango's cruel and untimely death was scarcely given a mention?

Little Dan

But it wasn't all bad news. Little Dan was the baby chick of the Spallidagh brood and a few years younger that Deelyah and Tiny Jim, who in their turn were a few years younger than Sammy-Joe and Stylish.

The little fellow's start to each day was nothing but joy. Once Stylish and Sammy-Joe were off down the road to Dang-the-skin-of-it's school-house, there was little for him to do but lie there, snug and warm under the blankets, wipe the sleep from his eyes and look round the dark recesses of the room or peer at the luminous shafts of sunlight swarming in at him through the window.

He had oceans of precious time and he spent it listening to the gentle breezes rushing across the floor towards him – listening to the noise of Dowager's fowl abroad in the yard and to the fierce battle-cries between the sow and Delancy and the braying of the crotchety old ass, who had just recovered from his fight with a beetroot and was trying to stick his head in through the broken-glass back window and give the little fellow a proper greeting – to the gabble of the geese and ducks showing off their metal by the side of the yard stream. So many sounds that it was nothing short of an orchestra, as though the big world was calling the little sleepy-head to get his two fine legs out of bed and come and join up with Life.

But not yet a while (thought Little Dan). Trembling with excitement, he waited until he heard the metallic footfall of his father's hobnailed-boots. Handsome Johnnie came gingerly in the door and stamped across the bedroom floor. His big moist eyes gazed down lovingly at his youngest son. He was a shy sort of man and, as no-one was looking, he leaned down and he breathed his warm breath into the child's ear, causing him to laugh giddily. Then he rubbed his beardy jaw against Little Dan's pink cheek, just as he did the day before and the day before that.

He showed the little fellow the egg that Dowager had brought in (or so he said, the rascal) from under the Little Speckled Hen's feathery bum. And to prove it, he pointed out the fresh bit of hen-shite staining the egg's shell and the small white feather cutely stuck onto its side to show that it had just fallen hotly from you-know-where.

Little Dan lept from his nest and followed the big man out into the Welcoming Room and to the front table. He dived into his egg, freshly oozing with butter and salt, and he attacked the three cuts of soda-bread. After that he washed the whole thing down with a huge mug of milk from the jug. This was a daily ritual for him and it lasted a long time. He was as contented as the calves abroad in the cow-shed.

As soon as Handsome Johnnie went out to cut the day's logs for the fire, Little Dan knelt on the chair and looked out over the geraniums on the windowsill. From there he had the finest of views across the yard and the stream. He could see the Open Road where huge men and their horse-and-carts were streaming along their way, the odd one gaily singing to himself, as they carried their tank-loads of milk to Abbey Cross and the gates of the creamery. He could hear the merry jingle of the harness and the rattle of the cartwheels accompanied by the odd bout of horse-farts. He could see how some of these dazed specimens were still wiping the sleep from their eyes while others were sneezing and snorting out long spits onto the road – could see how the air was full of pipe-tobacco-smoke, climbing in wraiths from their pipes and pleasantly filling the men's nostrils, themselves half-hidden under its cloak. The road was full (though Little Dan had no way yet of knowing it) of the smells from the men's wet greatcoats and the previous night's drinking in Curl 'n' Stripes' drinking-shop after the death of Fandango.

And then (before he could blink an eye) their carts had sailed out of view, down passed Old Sam's Stile, and all the sounds and sights and smells were dead and gone and nothing was left for the little dreamer to peer out at and witness.

Contentment And The Men

Happiness and contentment weren't a domain reserved for Little Dan alone. Now that the days were growing longer and getting brighter and the springtime daffodils were bursting forth all over Rookery Rally – now that Galloping Gret's fierce sows and the cockerel, Delancy, were but a distant memory – these were the days of light-hearted joy, each day as colourful as the last one – days of purest fantasy when the men and their war-whoops were seen running out to play games with the children. The women (as you'd expect) were far too coy and never able to demean themselves in such bouts of play and abandonment.

It was as if these beardy old fellows had a relic locked irremovably inside in their hearts, left over from their early childhood. For, as soon as they had milked their few cows and were back home from the creamery, they pretended they were tired from their long journey and they left the women to make their way over the fields to bring back the sack of spuds and turnips for next day's dinner.

Once the women's backs were turned these lively fellows quenched their thirst with a mug-of-tea and a few cuts of soda-bread and then skedaddled out the door to while away a few pleasant hours before the late afternoon's milking – playing skittles on the flagstones and enjoying the quiet afternoon light.

At these times of the day there was nothing to do (they felt) but purify their souls in bouts of playfulness alongside the children and (they said with a laugh) wait for the hay to mature and the corn to ripen. They felt as free as the untackled ass or the horse, both of whom, when freed from the jambs of the carts and led away to the fresh green fields, could be seen twisting hysterically round on their backs and kicking their fine legs into the air joyfully.

On these occasions the afternoon sun, too roasting for any energetic work to be done, was simply a noble excuse for these men to set off on new escapades such as climbing the trees surrounding their yard stream. See Rambling Jack, Red Scissors and Blue-eyed Jack scrambling up the lower limbs. See them straddling themselves across the overhanging branches above the stream, looking down into the astonished eyes of the children from what seemed to their innocent eyes a very great height. See them towering up there in the sky, turning themselves slowly upside-down – twisting their knees one around the other – stretching their aching arms down low (down, down, down) to see if they could touch the surface of the stream. Listen to the shouts of encouragement from the older lads, Lofty and Warbling Will among them, all the time urging these wild men on to newer achievements. Witness the heart of Little Dan going pitta-patta at such a rate that he thought he'd burst asunder with joy in the hushed silence that accompanied the big men's feats of bravery.

There came a moment of breathless anticipation before Blue-eyed Jack's hands (he was always at the forefront in these games) reached down and finally touched the surface of the yard stream. It was better than the Daffy-Duck Circus and all the children jumped up and down ecstatically and clapped and clapped their hands – as though the glory of the world had come home to them in this moment of triumph.

After a short break and a drink of water from the bucket the games would start all over again. Down through the slippery gap between the pig-house and the half-door came the heavy hobnail-boots of Simple Simon and the roars out of him as he chased after Little Nell, hoping to catch a hold of the squealing child (and she a mere seven years old) and get a hug out of her before she'd reach the stump of the tree at the flagstones and cry out '*Home!*'

For an hour or two the children were kept on their tippy-toes (some with wet knickers) as the men raced after them – round through the back of the hen-house – the pig-house – the haggart (hear the alarm of Dowager's sow and her six little piggies) and tried to catch any child they could get hold of before their little legs made a last joyful dash for Home.

What with the screeches of the men and the screams of the children, Dowager had no time to sit with her candle and read her holy-books. Nor had Handsome Johnnie time to bury his nose in the gramophone and listen to the voice-in-the-box. She and her flour-stained apron (and Handsome Johnnie by her side) stood at the half-door, laughing heartily at the antics of the men and the children. Was she imagining things? Were these real men or were they not? Would the pack of simpletons ever grow up (she thought)? And she prayed that in some way they would not, for these were unreal moments of pure innocence and a delight for herself and her sound man to behold.

The Sinister Side Of Devilment

That was the joy-of-life and all children welcomed the fun and the games between men and children. It was sometimes followed, however, by the sinister-side-of-life when *the Sorrowful Fairies* left their home in Bog Wood, bringing their tears along with them, and paid a most unwelcome visit with the gift of *Pure Devilment*.

It was a Monday morning and a week since the men's tree-climbing and merrymaking escapades. A slight misty rain (just the sweat off of the clouds) had covered the fields of Rookery Rally, glistening the springtime leaves on all the trees as though little elves had been polishing them overnight. Below at John's Gate, not a stone-throw from the metal bridge, came Yellow Patsy – with his yellow hat and his heavy yellow coat and his long mane of flaming yellow hair combed aimlessly back on his poll. He was clip-clopping his mare (*Hefty*) up along the slope towards Old Sam's Stile. Patsy was a remote hillsman and he lived out beyond Halting Cross, a stone-throw from Moll-the-Barracks' place, in a shack tucked into the side of the hill and no bigger than a hen-house. He was a silent sort of man but in no way a misanthrope. It was six months to the day since he had last come down the hill and he was making the seven-mile journey back home from Liam Purple's Mill where he had gone to get his half-yearly supply of flour and that of his neighbour (*Rosary-beads*). Though he was as skinny as a scarecrow, his father, old Short-Britches, had been a giant-of-a-man and well able to lift a forty-stone bag of oatmeal. But this morning, thanks to the help of Ned Shufflalong's son (*Blathery*), Patsy had been able to load up the six eight-stone sacks of flour onto his horse-and-cart from outside the door of the mill. The two-of-them stowed the sacks in the centre of his cart, in under the latboard, in a neatly secured pile so as to give the load a bit of balance. That was always Patsy's way of distributing the unnatural weight of so much flour and he was more than satisfied with the trouble and patience he and Blathery had taken. He'd have enough flour now for himself and for holy Rosary-beads to bake their batches of bread for the next few months.

However, in spite of all his care there was an unmistakable quandary that he'd have to deal with again this time. For, as soon as Hefty reached the bridge and started pulling against the steep slope of the hill, there'd be the same old predicament for himself and his sacks and he'd be forced to keep looking back over his shoulder to see if they were still in their place under the latboard or were they slipping away from him and edging back towards the heel of the cart.

Alas, he was again stricken with horror when he saw the heavy sacks slipping back down the length of the cart. For, with six miles yet to go before he reached home, he was in danger of losing all his flour. This sort of thing left everyone scratching their heads: why on earth couldn't Yellow Patsy have a stem of sense like the rest of the hillsmen (said some)? Why couldn't he be a bit more cautious and bring home one sack of flour at a time (said others) and come down to the mill more frequently? There'd be less flour then to lose, should there be a mishap and the cart topple over. It was an easy puzzle for him to solve: none of the other hillsmen had to travel half the seven-mile distance that he and Hefty had to in order to reach the mill. It was common sense (he'd tell them) to come half as often and take home three times as much flour each time, saving himself both time and energy.

Good Neighbours As Always

Whenever they saw Yellow Patsy on these missions for flour, Dowager and Handsome Johnnie made sure to hurry their children down the hill and help him get his sacks of flour safely up the slope and onto the level plain. Neither Lofty, Stylish or Sammy-Joe needed to be pushed out the door in order to run down the hill to support Patsy and add their own extra bit of weight to his cart so as to stop the sacks sliding off onto the road. This day was the same and as soon as they reached Old Sam's Stile they saw the frightened aspect of the old hillsman, his face yellower than ever, and poor Hefty puffing and wheezing her heart out as she struggled up the slope.

Without so much as a *good-day, sir* the three children surrounded the back of the cart and gave Patsy a hand pushing the sacks back under the latboard so as to ensure that the flour was again balanced nicely. Then they mounted up beside him – Lofty sitting on the lace of the cart so as to weigh it down in favour of the front and his younger brothers balancing themselves bravely next to the mare's tail and ready to run out along the jambs if needs be. Patsy settled himself back on the latboard behind them. With the arrival of these three heroes he could see that his load would be safe and sound – that there'd be no fear of his flour tipping back onto the road. Spare a thought, however, for poor Hefty. She was now so overloaded with the children's added weight that she was left gasping for air. But she was a willing mare and no-one had ever yet seen Patsy put a stroke of his ashplant to her back. Nor would there be a need of the whip this time as she forced her way up towards the top of the slope near Shy Dennis's Shack.

It wouldn't be long before the cart arrived at Sheep's Cross where the road would start to level out. With Patsy's *thankyou, byze – fair play to the lot of y*e ringing in their ears, the brothers waved him a hearty Godspeed and scampered home to tell their mother of the successful journey of the old hillsman's flour and that the cart had levelled itself out at Sheep's Cross.

Tom Foolery

Meanwhile, inside the ditch lurked that ugly-faced galoot (*Tom Foolery* – the son of *Mick Crackawlee*). He stamped out onto the road from his hidey-hole in the bushes behind Shy Dennis's Shack – himself and his sparkling eyes – himself and his laceless boots – himself and his beaky nose. Like all our countrymen the young charmer was well able to put on airs when it suited him and he stepped forward and bade Yellow Patsy a *hearty-good-day, sir* and saluted him with the usual greeting: *may there be a bed in heaven for you, Patsy*. Then he followed along behind the cart, chatting gaily, as it twisted its way on and up towards the Valley-of-the-Pig.

This was the time for the *Wicked Fairies* to enter the scene and for this sly little weasel to liven up his day and put on a bit of a show. So, what did he do? He stooped down low and out of sight behind Patsy's cart. Without a word of warning he pressed his entire weight down on the back-heels of the cart, causing the front jambs to lift straight up into the air.

Woe and alas, the poor misfortunate Patsy (his shrieks can be heard to this day) suddenly toppled backwards and lay in a littered heap on the roadway – himself and his six sacks of flour.

Good humour and bad humour had always been easy to separate but not in the raw mind of a heathen like Tom Foolery. His rosy face was a picture of merriment – to think how he'd played such a fine trick on Yellow Patsy. He had to hold his sides from the pain of his laughter at the sight of Patsy waving his arms about listlessly. He thought he'd see him getting up from his ridiculous position midst the spilt flour – hear him exploding – hear a brand of undiscovered curses raining down on his head – see him (if luck prevailed and the sport proved good) getting up and chasing after him so as to beat him black-and-blue or shatter his skull like an egg. Only such a response would satisfy the devil that had gripped Tom Foolery's pagan heart.

His childish laughter, however, was met with something new. His skull was not to be shattered like an egg. His ears were not to be deafened by Yellow Patsy's fierce curses. The *Wicked Fairies* had done their work only too well this time. The world had turned into a dark and eerie place and the angels wept – to think that poor Patsy's days had come to this and he a man that had worked hard all the days of his life.

Patsy Was Silent

Patsy lay helplessly rooted in a frozen patch of sadness – there in the middle of the road – himself and his sunken yellow cheeks – himself and his spilt flour – himself and his twisted ankle – himself and his rusting tears running down the sides of his nostrils with only the horseflies in the dung to comfort him. This was a new one on Tom Foolery. He had never seen a man in tears before and his indisputable joy and his hitherto self-confidence had vanished. Like Adam, he now realised the seriousness of his crime – a lesson learnt too late – and he felt the first pangs of remorse as he scuttled away through the bushes behind Shy Dennis's Shack.

They Heard The Commotion

Lofty, Stylish and Sammy-Joe were carrying their buckets of water from the well when they heard the commotion. They stopped what they were doing and sure-footed their way up to Sheep's Cross. There was no sign of Tom Foolery but they saw the flour all over the road and the miserable Patsy stranded in the middle of it. They quickly calmed the startled Hefty and then got Patsy unsteadily up onto his feet. They soothed him as best they could and then ladled him and his twisted ankle back up onto the cart where they sat him gently on the latboard. Were ever children so prodigious or industrious? They gathered up the flour and reloaded most of it as best they could and tidied the sacks back underneath the latboard.

They accompanied the cart as far as the Valley-of-the-Pig before running on ahead to give Moll-the-Shuffler the news of Tom Foolery's treachery. Good woman that she was, she forgot her hens, ducks and geese and ran out the door to meet the poor man. Though he was as frail and quavery as a reed, Moll rekindled his spirits by pouring a full mug of her best rawgut whiskey down his throat as fast as she could throw it into him.

For the rest of the summer the miscreant Tom Foolery decided to keep himself hidden from the people of Rookery Rally. The anger of the children was so great, however, that they swore if ever they caught up with him in his self-imposed exile, they would get a shovel and make mincemeat of his arse or they would hang him (said some) on the yardbeam outside the town jail. They might go further (said others, growing into the theme) and nail him to a tree and leave him there to rot and for the carrion crows and foxes to chastise the wickedness in him. Ah, the young poets that they were at times!

Summer Days Blazed On

As the hot season of summer blazed on, so did the time for more and more merriment and devilment. And a week or two after the sadness of Yellow Patsy, the older sons of Moll-the-Shuffler, namely Zippity and Punch, were seen sailing cheerily down the road.

At Old Sam's Stile they saw Old Hayload leaning back on his own small patch of ditch – what he called his *lolling post*. It was the very same patch where his father and his father's father had lolled. He had the livelong day to sit there and think of nothing else but the grandeur of life (a pleasant enough pastime) and spend his mornings gazing at the grass growing on the ditch and waiting for the first creamery carts to reach his stile on their way home from the creamery and give him the most recent news: who was sick: who had tragically died: who had accidentally hanged himself with the ass's reins: which cow had since calved and to know whether Madge Roundabout's sow had *pup*ped.

Beside him was his long-handled four-grain pitchfork and a huge load of hay, which he was about to take up to his outfield in the Valley-of-the-Pig where he had a spoilt mare waiting to be foddered.

As soon as they saw him Zippity and Punch's excitement rose rapidly, knowing that their day was about to improve.

Old Hayload's hat was slouched low over his eyes against the flies. The boys were saddened to see this as they always liked to see the old man *in his hair*. They knew that the dye from the sweaty green-and-yellow innards of his ancient hat had long since turned his grey hair into a startling green-and-yellow similar to the colours of the Kerry football team – a mixture unlikely to be seen anywhere else on earth other than on the head of the Giddy Juggler at the annual Daffy-Duck Circus and a colour that always mesmerised them.

When they were a short step away from him they pretended they hadn't seen him and they turned in over the ditch and waited.

Old Hayload rose up from his comfortable perch and with his huge fork-load of hay on his bony old shoulder he strode on purposefully towards Shy Dennis's Shack and Sheep's Cross.

Peeping out from their hidey-hole the boys could see what looked like half-a-tram of hay balanced on his upturned pitchfork as he challenged the hill.

The old man was deep in thought and by now his head was lowered down to his knees from the sheer weight of the hay. To give his spirits a bit of a lift he was humming the latest of his own homemade songs:

> *'Tim Noodle, out one morning,*
> *Was taking the airs awhile*
> *He saw a German airyplane*
> *Whilst seated on his stile.*

He had spent a sleepless night worrying whether the word *seated* or the word *sitting* was best suited to his new song – until it dawned on him that *seated* was a politer rendering and one that would charm the ears off of his future listeners.

The children had to stop themselves from laughing, knowing, like everyone else, how unmusical the old fellow's voice was – a voice that he employed when milking his cows to amuse them when firing the milk into the bucket – a voice that caused his cows to occasionally curse him and kick the bucket over.

Out From Their Hidey-hole

Out from their hidey-hole in the ditch crept Zippity and Punch. They were armed with their mother's box-of-matches for lighting her fire – the matches that they used each day for smoking their grandmother's stolen half-smoked fag-butts.

Zippity greeted Old Hayload with a courteous bow (*fine warm day, sir*) whilst Punch crept up unseen behind him and his forkful of hay.

The little procession strode on pleasantly – Zippity all the time engaging the old man with the usual degree of conversational bantering (there was always some outrageous news being whispered round Rookery Rally) and keeping his curiosity alive by informing him, among other things, how a recent bumble-bee had visited the inside of the Big Y'Hoo's britches and had stung him on the tip of his privacies whilst he was making his poolie.

Meanwhile Punch (that other little snake-in-the-grass) was busily setting fire to the old man's hay.

As soon as they reached the crossroads Zippity waved Old Hayload a hearty goodbye and the old fellow went off on his way, singing the same long-drawn-out song to himself.

The two villains watched him plod on: 'Tis a fine warm day – a very warm day indeed (they thought, mimicking their earlier greeting to Old Hayload). It was about to get warmer still and they ran down the hill, looking for further pleasant pastimes.

Old Hayload wasn't much further up the slope when they heard the roars thundering out of him. This time he was singing a far filthier song: 'Jaysus, the scuthery young feckers have set mee arse on fire. Wait'll I catch hold of them – I'll humble them – I'll drive mee pitchfork up into their shitty little arses.'

He realised not only was his fork-of-hay a mass of fire but that the back of his hat was turning into a fine blaze too and he himself was rapidly disappearing inside a ring of smoke.

Half-an-hour later he could still hear their roars of laughter from way below John's Gate. Oh, what merry old times Rookery Rally's children were having during these fine summer days!

The Following Morning

The following morning – the day after the fire of Old Hayload's hat and hay – Glorious Glory-oh (himself and his red hair) was asleep on the ditch at the Easy Stile and blissfully dreaming of the green fields of Canada where his brothers were thriving like young nettles.

He had just come from his sister's haggart with a fine sackful of turnips.

Down the road (*who have we in it?*) stamped the big boots of that impudent rascal, Red Scissors and he a man and not a child, although you wouldn't have believed it. He had his trademark scissors with him to cut Handsome Johnnie's hair and turn him completely bald if he got the chance. His sharp eyes beheld the sleeping Glorious Glory-oh on the ditch. With nothing else on his mind but sheer devilment and with the patience of a cat that stalks a sparrow he stole up behind the old fellow and cut a tidy hole in the corner of the sack.

He moved quietly back inside the ditch and stayed there, waiting till Glorious Glory-oh should wake up from his dreamland. He spent his time studying Fandango's burial spot at the far side of the Callow Field where a crow was turning over a dried-out piece of cow-dung so as to get at the juicy pile of worms underneath it.

Glorious Glory-oh woke up, fully replenished from his ditch-side nap, and went off home to his cabin on the hill.

Plop-plop-plop! The turnips dropped out haplessly, one by one.

Feeling the increasing lightness of his load, he realised that there must be a hole in his sack and he retraced his boots to collect his lost store of turnips.

By this time Dowager's children had heard the news of the lost turnips from the lips of Red Scissors himself:

'I hear, my young friends, that there's a tribe of runaway turnips marching this way. I saw them meeself just a minute ago – and they all tearing down the hill in this direction. Be good children, let ye, and go forth and arrest them and take them off to the Guards!'

Ah, the unforgivable and unforgettable Red Scissors!

When Glorious Glory-oh reached the bend of the road there wasn't a single turnip to be seen. The ripe ones lay firmly inside in the bellies of Sammy-Joe and Stylish or would do by the end of the week. The small unripe ones were being used as hurling-balls by the rest of the children, even by Little Dan, belting them round and around in the Bluebutton Field.

Tuesday Came Along Nicely

Time was moving along nicely. It was the following Tuesday and the summer sun had again come scurrying in over Rookery Rally, transfiguring every yard and stream as it glided across the treetops. It would stay that way for the whole of the day.

Nance-the-Smith rose up with the lark's song and was lugging home her heavy oil-tank from Curl 'n' Stripes' drinking-shop. Always an arch-planner, she would have enough oil to fill her lamp for the rest of the year.

The previous evening saw Clever Jack (and he, like Red Scissors, being a man and not a child) making a hole with a nail in the bottom of Nance's tank. When she was making her way home from the shop the oil began to drip-drip-drip slowly behind her onto the road.

At the behest of Clever Jack, one or two of Dowager's children (Stylish and Sammy-Joe again – Dowager's very latest scientists) tried to light the trail of oil with a match. They wanted to see if Nance would catch fire. It must have been one of those sad days when *Mister Boredom* was raising his head a little too high in the air. For what of interest could any child see in watching Nance dancing a jig-step round the road and trying to put herself and the fire out? Surely the little devils could have thought of a more harmless novelty? But there was always, even within the confines of Rookery Rally, a greater pleasure in watching another's fight for survival rather than one's own.

The Snowman

The following Wednesday came on and Old Stroller (son of the ancient Sam) was out early. He lived a stone-throw away from the Spallidaghs and was now well into his seventh decade. He was a man who always seemed to have the wind in his face – with his sharply-pointed blue nose and his lilac-coloured cheeks.

He was not at his ease this morning. Perhaps it was due to a change in the weather or maybe it was the liveliness of *the Woodland Fairies*, who were invisibly exercising their sway over Rookery Rally. Maybe his own guardian angel had forsaken him and was fast asleep inside the ditch.

He didn't need a calendar to remind him of the trick the children (may God forgive them) had played on him the previous February when the harsh snows were luminating the fields all around Rookery Rally. On that cold winter's morning Dowager's children, including the older ones, Lofty and Warbling Will – together with Moll-the-Shuffler's Punch and Zippity – had come down to his back yard whilst he was abroad in the outhouse, busily sawing his timber into logs in an effort to keep himself warm. He was singing away like an old peacock in a voice that would ache your ears off.

In previous years these children had entered his yard with a barrowload of snowballs to belt the head off of him. This time, however, they were bent on giving him a little present to ease the pain they had caused him in those bad old days and doing something a bit more creative. They had stolen a number of shovels and yardbrushes from one yard or another. The housewives everywhere would be sure to leather the hides of the next tinker they met since it was a well-known fact that these rogues were the thieves of all their shovels and yardbrushes.

With Lofty in charge of operations the little army got to work and brushed the snow off of Old Stroller's yard. They made it into heaps (another act-of-charity) and finally swept the heaps into a great big mass outside the linhay, which ran the length of the house and led in the back door to Old Stroller's Welcoming Room.

Then they crept into the Welcoming Room and dislodged the table and chairs from the middle of the room, arranging them tidily around the walls. This left them a good space in the centre of the concrete floor.

The happy young souls rolled up their sleeves and prepared to give Old Stroller the welcome of his life when he returned from the outhouse. They spent half-an-hour firing piles of snow in through the back door until they had a huge amount of it on the floor.

And now they got to work in earnest, building a ramshackle snowman that would (they felt) make a fine adornment to Old Stroller's room. When they had finished, they arranged the old man's hat on top of this charming snowman and stuck a long twig in the corner of its mouth. To liven things up a bit and as an addition to their art they stood a pitchfork up against its side at a nonchalant angle and then they ran like fair hell out the back door before Old Stroller came back and caught them and pelted them all into the dyke.

Back To This Wednesday

But the gift of last February's snowman was a long way back in their history – an almost forgotten (if not quite forgiven) memory on this bright Wednesday morning. And now Old Stroller was seen picking his way out over the wire fence that bordered his ditch from the Thistle Field. With him he had his billhook for searching the dyke near the spring-well where Stylish had recently lost his hurling-ball. The children could always depend on the old fellow for an everlasting supply of patience and he began to hack his way through the briars and nettles where he finally found the ball – the fifth one the children had lost.

Taking the awl and wax from his pocket, he made good the stitching that had come loose and he threw the ball out amongst the young hurlers. Then he sat down on the bank to watch them start hurling their ball in and out mid the ragwort bouhilauns with the broken bits of hurleysticks left over after the recent senior hurling-match in Abbey Acres. Before they could start, however, they had to turn their britches inside-out, the whites showing so as to make themselves a hurling-britches in imitation of Tipperary's famed hurlers

Elated by his success on finding and repairing their ball, the old man strode across the field, his billhook resting importantly on his shoulder. He then called a halt to the children's play and settled them in a ring around his feet. He could feel a moment of inspiration coming on and he decided to give them their first hurling-lesson – the result (he said) of his own famous hurling-exploits in the days of his youth.

'Be good children and gather round me. Listen carefully to what I tell ye.'

'Ye're great little hurlers entirely. There's no doubt about it – if only ye were taught properly.'

He then set the other children aside (*step back, let the rest of ye*) and he stood next to Stylish and Sammy-Joe. It was time for the hurly-burly to begin.

'When I say pull on the ball, I want ye to be quickness itself so that one of ye gets his strike at the ball in first and drives it up the field. Ye must let fly fiercely, the pair of ye – no holding back – one stick clashing bravely against the other stick. Whatever ye do, remember yeer manly forefathers – that's all I'm asking ye. We'll soon see what kind of stuff the two of ye are made of and who's the clever little fellow that'll get his strike in first.'

A New Possibility

Like many children, Stylish and Sammy-Joe were quick learners and could see in this, their first hurling-lesson, a new possibility for fun and entertainment.

Stylish (the devil that he was) gave his younger brother a sly little wink and placed the ball an inch or two away from a freshly-dropped lump of cow-shite.

Old Stroller didn't seem to notice the ruse lying in wait for him or the danger he had let himself in for:

'One, two and three! Pull-on-the-ball!' he roared, his face a rosy-red and he leaping like a madman round the two protagonists and waving them on enthusiastically. The cows above on Smiling Bab's Heights looking down bemusedly on it all.

A minute later the hurling-master was seen leaping a far different leap when the two rascally specimens missed the ball completely and belted the wet cow-shite up into his gob, drenching him in dung. Yellow, green and gold were his new features, the smell from which would last for days to come.

Time after time (*To blazes with ye, ye pair of little feckers. Stop, stop, will ye!*) the young heathens whaled the juicy dung into him. You'd have paid good money to see such a fine bout of amusement for it had the makings of an unprecedented comedy. The rest of the children clapped and clapped.

Old Stroller sank to his knees and he cursed the pack of them into the four corners of hell – them and the mothers that had brought them onto the earth. Then, as mournful as poor Jesus on his cross, he sloped sadly home across the wire fence.

At the sight of Old Stroller and the artistry of their handiwork, Stylish and Sammy-Joe (like Zippity and Punch before them – and Old Hayload's burnt hat and hay) were doubled in two from their fits of delirious laughter. Their hearts would be content for the at least the next week-and-a-half.

Daylight was now quickly passing and the tree-shadows were beginning to spear their way out across the Thistle Field and the blue of the evening was wasting away and growing dark. Stylish and Sammy-Joe took themselves off home with the other children, the echoes of their merry voices ringing in poor Old Stroller's ears as he crossed into his yard.

If Only They Could Have Heard

If only they could have heard his grief-stricken voice ringing back at them – especially since it was he, the recipient of a gobful of cow-shite for his pains, who had spent time looking for their lost hurling-ball.

However, before he was finished with them he would have his own bout of merriment and would add a few retaliatory ramifications to their childish devilment. For he was as cross and as vengeful as a Turk and he swore he'd chastise their little arses the same way he chastised his ass. There was a new smile on his face and in his mind's eye he was already reaching for the cartridge-box and his fierce double-barrel gun.

For the rest of the summer, however, the story continued to circulate – how the young devils had drenched Old Stroller's clothes and stained his face with dung and how he and his scalded heart had retreated defeated to his yard. It didn't need a mind-reader to see that the day would shortly come when he would wage his own particular war of attrition on the little heathens – a day for his own particular moment of glory.

All Was Forgotten

The weeks and months kept moving on and it wasn't long before all those escapades seemed to have taken place a long time ago. For in Rookery Rally the sins of everyone were always forgotten (if not forgiven) and children and adults were quick to resume peace and truces by the day – if not by the hour.

There appeared to be a renewal of friendship between Old Stroller and the children. Then, as soon as the days of harvesting were over, the old man seemed to have completely forgotten their previous boldness and the crudity that had ended the comical hurling-lesson. However, if you had been able to look inside his head, the damage to his dignity and pride was still lodged there and in spite of all his efforts he was finding it hard to get back into his stride. There was a certain nervousness about him, a certain fidgetiness in him – like a hen waiting to lay an egg – and everyone waited to see what might happen next.

Welcome to Candlelight Tales

September went by peacefully enough and the next bout of roguery hadn't yet raised its head. Then an evening arrived when the children had taken the cows back to the field and had counted the hens, ducks and geese and housed them all inside in the henhouse and had finished all their other jobs.

Old Stroller summoned them down to hear his storytelling, for which (like Old Hayload and his homemade songs) he was well famed. Dressed in their best clothes for such a grand occasion – especially Warbling Will in his recent brown Confirmation suit – they rushed down to his Welcoming Room

'Tell us some of your stories about the Rookery Rally heroes of old and the fierce battles they fought with pitchforks and shovels against The Burgundians when these wild men came to steal their horses while they were at Mass behind the hedge.

'Tell us your stories about the ghosts inside Fort Dangerous and how the fairy-folk came out and stole young wives from their wizened old husbands.'

'Tell us your own favourite ones – the olden-day pissing contests and the ones with grisly murders in them.' The list went on and on. Excitement was rife and they pulled in their chairs and sat round the long table. An hour earlier Old Stroller had banked up the fire as high as he could with turf and logs. He now placed himself at the head of the table – himself and he wrapped in his two coats, for he was always complaining of the cold, even though by now his fire was roasting hot.

He solemnised the event by lighting his two brass candlesticks. The light shone and glittered on the children's heads. He lit his pipe and the smoke dizzied its way up to the rafters. The mood was all set for the tales to begin.

The Children Were Enthralled

He started his stories with a right good will and the children, enthralled by each new tale, were quickly engrossed in his finely-toned delivery and they clapped their hands and asked for more.

But as the minutes drew on and the dusk started to settle in, the old man began to lower the tenor of his voice – especially when it came to the misfortunate tale about Poesy's Ghost, the ghost that had manifested itself to more than one night-rambler as he tried to find his way home across the Pool Field. The room had taken on an almost supernatural hush and it was getting late. A worried Dowager was out at the flagstones with her flash-lamp and she was heard banging her tea-tray to call her children home.

Old Stroller made a little bow as a signal that it was the end of his tales. With his thumb and fore-finger he ceremoniously quenched the two candles and left the children in complete darkness. Then an eerie silence filled the room.

Suddenly it felt as though a thunderclap had struck the house as the old man put an end to the calmness of his recent storytelling and, stamping his fist on the table, smashed the candlesticks off of the table and onto the floor. The darkness in his soul had taken over and fear had come rushing in. The children heard the metallic scrape of his hobnail-boots crossing the floor and one or two of them (especially Stylish and Sammy-Joe) began to be sore afraid, realising that he had turned into a raging bull.

'Becripes – the basthard is going for the bucket,' they whispered. It was too late for them to be expressing their alarm for – *whoosh! whoosh! whoosh!* – with military precision several saucepans of water were fired at them in the darkness, drenching their shirts and good clothes from top to toe. You could have heard the screams of them above in the Hills-of-the-Past and the curses out of them ('the dirty ould pisser!') as they ran for the back door like an army of scalded rats in front of a thrashing-machine. They had never anticipated such wicked treachery.

In their scramble to get out the door they could hear his angry roars ringing behind their heels. The tongue in his mouth wouldn't keep still: 'I'll get rid of yeer devilment – I'll thorn yeer arses for ye – I'll teach ye young skitteries a new language on the back of yeer polls.'

Crying and gasping for breath and some of the younger ones wetting their britches, they retreated out passed the hayshed, leaving Old Stroller and his fits of heinous laughter standing at the door, the floor all to himself. For the rest of the month there were no more stories from the old serpent and none of the children appeared within a mile of him. So much for the days of renewed love and forgiveness.

The Orchard

By now they knew it – they knew it only too well. Old Stroller was the craftiest rogue on God's earth if not an out-and-out heathen with the devil's own self inside in him. That filthy old slate-pencil (said Dowager when she heard the news) was as crooked as a dog's hind leg. It was high time (said Red Scissors with a devilish smirk) for another chapter to be written in the children's war against him and that was all the urge they needed.

These were summerlike days in early September, just before school began – days when the nuts were ripening and the rosehips were scarlet – days when the sun's red disc held mastery over everyone in Rookery Rally and over the children's own small bit of Paradise – days when the fairylike breezes each day came scurrying up to their bedside, telling them to rise up and go out and challenge the world.

Old Stroller with the help of Blue-eyed Jack and Fatty-Matty had safely secured his twenty trams-of-hay abroad in the meadow. As soon as the children saw this, they ran over the fields and attacked the trams the same way a band of reindeer from Bog Wood had done the previous year, sitting insolently on top of them and making hollow wells in them. For a pleasant hour or two they played *I'm the King of The Castle*, jumping up 'n' down (the impudent young puppies) on top of the old man's hay so as to ruin the trams.

And when they had grown tired of their play they made bird-nests in his trams – for themselves to lie down in and as though they were larks and they looked up at the blue of the sky. This was their way of chastising Old Stroller for drenching them in water. It was also a means of escaping from the daily job of bringing back buckets of water from the well.

In the comfort of their hiding-place they had plenty of time to do some serious contemplation. They were children that had never spent a day growing hungry. They had rabbits, fish, soda-bread-and-jam and lashings of milk each day. And now (ah, now) they had apples fine and plenty, hanging on the old fellow's trees in his orchard and looking across at them. They could see themselves sitting high in the dusky apple-trees with their sharp teeth crunching the juice out of his best rosy-red apples and rolling the taste of them round and round deliciously in their mouths. Ah, the temptations of Youth!

The Day Of Thievery Arose

The day for their thievery arose and the four lads (Warbling Will, Lofty, Stylish and Sammy-Joe) were up early. It was an excellent day and the apples all over Rookery Rally were about to blush red.

They ran out across the hazy mists that were still hanging over the Thistle Field, their bare feet drenching in dew-spray – feet that were well-hardened for climbing even the most awkward of Old Stroller's apple-trees.

The girls (like Little Nell and the now-chastened Darkie) were out early too, collecting field-flowers to make flower-chains for bracelets and necklaces, with which to adorn the younger ones (Deelyah, Tiny Jim and Little Dan).

The boys waved to these three little ones (the big girls were far too sophisticated for the entertainment of apple-robbing) and they beckoned them to come and join in the raid. Then the whole tribe went in through Sam's Gate, picking their feet through the hoof-wells left by the old man's cows and they headed for the trees.

Led on by Lofty and Warbling Will, they selected the better apples. The two-of-them scrambled up the trees like a pair of well-seasoned wildcats. The others looked on admiringly from down below as they started snapping off the apples and throwing them down as fast as they could pelt them. Oh, the heathens – the filthy little marauders!

Ever ready, the three little ones picked up the apples to add to their small collection of windfalls and they quickly stuffed the entire load inside their pockets and shirts. Warbling Will (the devil that he was) had brought with him three of Dowager's bigger saucepans (if only the others had thought of the idea) so as to fill them up with apples. Lofty, on the other hand, was wearing a raggy old ganzy belonging to Handsome Johnnie, which would do him well for holding more than enough apples to last him the rest of the week.

Once they had shared the apples out equally, their pockets and shirts, the saucepans and the ganzy would all be left half-empty before this band of raiders got home. Thanks to such an unimaginable feast-day, their bellies would be packed-to-death and in a woeful amount of pain with the gripe. It'd be a pure miracle if Doctor Glasses wasn't called upon to give them a dose of castor-oil or get Black Bess to carry the lot of them off to the Roaring Town hospital in her truck.

He Heard His Trees Rustling

In spite of the children's attempts at whispering while they were robbing his apples, Old Stroller was sure that he had heard his trees rustling a bit more than usual. Never a man to lie back dreamily in his bed, he rose from underneath his blankets and went to look out through his upstairs window.

There they were. He spent his next half-hour watching the merry young thieves. Patience – that was all he needed. He was like a heron that looks long and hard into the waters of River Laughter: waiting and watching: all the time waiting and watching. He counted seven of the young tramps in all, creeping round among the trees, as cheeky as rats round a turnip-pit. Look at them (he thought) – as brazen as hell, gathering in the best of his crop and (was his eyes deceiving him?) filling up Dowager's saucepans with them.

He spat out an oath to himself: 'It's gone on for far too long. It's time I put an end to the gallant adventures of mee dartin' young charmers.'

This was his moment – it had to be. He could feel it deep down inside him. He wasn't sure which was the better plan, whether to get the long washing-line pole and run down through the orchard and poke them in the arse so that they'd tumble down out of the trees and land in his arms where he could rope them up and take them off to the Guards – or whether (shudder the thought) to reach for his long double-barrel gun, the one that his father had hidden up the chimney when the Tans came calling on him.

He'd been anxious these past few days to get away from the house and go out into the faraway hills and smell the pine-trees and get himself a glimpse of Nature – also to get in a little bit of practice with his big gun. The children had seen him striding up the hill – himself and the gun. Gone to shoot a few rabbits – that's what they thought. But in truth he was hoping to use it to frighten the hell out of these young tearaways. With Handsome Johnnie lying sick in bed and not able to even get himself a smoke from his pipe, hadn't Lofty and Warbling Will enough to do besides gallivanting round in his orchard? Why weren't those young galoots helping Blue-eyed Jack bring home his hay?

The recent crude episode in which the children's hurleysticks had smothered him in dung and their artistry with the snow – not to mention the other rascally events like burning the arse, hay and hat off of Old Hayload – the disappearance of Glorious Glory-oh's turnips – the burning of Nance-the-Smith's oil tank – all these events gave him the final spur to use his gun and put an end to the misery of it all. It was as if a savage dog was snapping at his heels and he was unable to prevent it. His cold eyes were glimmering with poison and his face was as black as a missioner's venom during a sermon. His soul had delved down into a cave where joy could never enter in.

Time for Battle To Begin

It was time for the battle to begin. He blessed himself and said a silent prayer to the Virgin – to ask God to forgive him for what he was about to do. He took down his gun. He had primed it the previous evening with his oil-rags whilst sitting by the fire. Next to him was his box of red cartridges.

He loaded the gun. He had enough cartridges beside his foot to keep him firing for the next half hour.

'If it's war ye want, it's war ye'll get,' said he to himself.

He leaned out the top window and measured his aim. Then he let fly with both barrels – a shade or two above the tallest of the apple trees. It was a miracle he didn't frighten half the children in north Tipperary with the sheer volume of noise that his big gun made. No other gun could have made the racket that cannonaded off of his hayshed.

Like Frightened Hares

Such pace! Such speed! Like frightened hares trembling for their lives, seven pairs of heels somersaulted from among the trees. They ran this way and that, their hearts withering inside them – knocking into each other in an effort to reach the wire fence at the bottom of the orchard and escape from the bullets that would bring them their certain death. There wasn't a second to raise their heads or look back and see who was maimed or who was for the graveyard. They lept the two-foot fence, some of them tearing their britches to flinders on the wire. Even Darkie (with her hole-in-the-heart and her newly-acquired skills of an apple-thief) managed to run faster than the wind and leap out across the fence. They kept running, running, running like a pack of wild asses till they reached River Laughter and threw themselves into its waters. There'd be a neat pile of pissy britches when it came to next Monday's washing-day!

Their High Spirits Egged Them On

Surprising as it seemed, this fierce episode with the gun did nothing to cure them of their search for further bursts of roguery, their high spirits all the time egging them on in search of entertainment once they got the breath back in their lungs. It wasn't just Old Stroller's apples that they stole: they now stole his turf to make themselves a fire in Old Sam's Grove: stole his turnips to roast in the same fire and they sat around it, smoking their stolen fag-butts. Oh, Stroller – whatever next!

And so, a mere week after his attempt to kill them with his gun (or so they thought) they were on the march again to test out their gallantry in another bout of daring amongst his apple-trees.

Minnie-Ha-Ha

It was a Monday afternoon (always a sleepy-headed time) and Old Stroller would surely be in his dreamland, having his nap, himself and his ugly old gun. For their next bout of apple-stealing they left Galloping Gret's six-year-old daughter (*Minnie-ha-ha*) standing at the back corner of the old man's house, posted there as a look-out. Surely the old devil wouldn't try to kill so small a child as little Minnie with his gun. Alongside her they placed her cousin (*Noolah* – and she all of thirteen). She had the most beautiful flaxen hair and was already a spritely young madam, always paring her nails and polishing them with the dab of butter. By now this little charmer's lovely locks curled round into natural ringlets and she had developed a ring of yellow freckles round the bridge of her nose. Some of Dowager's older boys (even Stylish) were already feeling strangely and shyly uncomfortable in her presence. They knew what they would like to do with her – to roll her warm body round in their arms. But they didn't know how to go about it – not yet.

An Uncomfortable Day in Store

It was to prove an uncomfortable day for them. Old Stroller was far from dozing and it wasn't long before he was standing at his upper window and counting a pile of the same rascally children. It must be a dream (he thought). Some of them were sunning themselves on the ditch at the entrance to Sam's Gate. Others were sitting awkwardly on the stile. One or two of them were resting their bums cross-legged on the stone slabs bordering the well-hole in the dyke. All of them were deep in silence.

Ah-ha, the little featherheads were here again. He spotted Noolah and little Minnie-ha-ha underneath his window. Yes, just as he thought – on the look-out while the other crafty rascals were waiting for them to give a signal that all was clear for their next bout of apple-thievery.

It wasn't long before he saw the bigger boys huddled on their perches in the apple-trees, shading their eyes from the glare of the sun and nonchalantly chewing their juicy apples down as far as the core – with one eye on the window and the other on the river that would mark good their escape if needs be.

The scene was set.

His bedroom always had the smell of strong piss in it and the frustration inside him was now boiling over and telling him what to do next. Armed with his pisspot and without a moment's thought, he ran to the window (*I'll give them a bath they'll not forget in a hurry*) and let fly the contents, hitting poor Noolah full in the chest and damn near drowning her.

The other children heard the sudden roars out of her as she and little Minnie came flying out from the yard and up the Open Road like a pair of foxes with their tails on fire.

'Mee hair – mee feckin hair – mee lovely curls! The basthard has drowned us – look at the state of mee dress – he has drenched us with his piss!" She never stopped running till she fell into Dowager's apron. As for little Minnie-ha-ha, she was delirious from that day to this.

The rest of the children lept up on the ditch to see what had caused such an unholy volley of curses to find their way out of Noolah's mouth, a precious and immaculate young damsel up till then.

From his window Old Stroller (oh, the treachery of his black heart) was waving his empty pisspot triumphantly round in the air, showing them the snarl on his yellow teeth. The filthy blackguard hadn't cleaned out his pisspot for the last few days and by this time the piss in it had been almost pouring out over the rim. He had planned it all so well – had been waiting and waiting for just this glorious moment when he could tip the contents out the window so as to put an end to the young thieves ever again coming within a stepping-stone of his apple-trees.

Oh, Stroller, what on earth made you stoop so low?

Ah, me – you showed the children the worst sign of your nature – showed them your need for a terrible vengeance, the likes of which was never heard tell of before. The little robbers would have preferred your double-barrel gun.

Later that evening Warbling Will and Lofty crept discreetly back into Old Stroller's yard and they quietly took his horse-and-cart and fired it into the dyke. Then they took to kicking his two dogs (*Barker* and *Belch*) round and round until the poor creatures had almost collapsed before escaping out over the ditch – dogs that would normally tear the arse out of your britches if you ever crossed their path and hadn't brought a handy stick with you to leather into them if needs be.

Christians One And All

Being Christians, we are taught to forgive one another. Children and adults alike know when to restore peace – when to call a truce. It seems almost unnatural but after this last punishment at the hands of Old Stroller, there came a week or two of calm. Something strange was in the air. Maybe it was a visiting angel. For everyone in Rookery Rally finally saw a change coming about in the crotchety old fellow – a change that was like a bright new rainbow in the sky.

How did it happen? From far across the ocean in the Land of The Silver Dollar came Old Stroller's one and only sister (*Lizzie*) the left-handed fiddle-player. She came for the sickness of Old Stroller's young wife (*Polly*), who for some time had been silently wasting away in her own room with the dreaded disease of consumption stamping the dew-of-death on her face – the consumption that was so rife amongst our countryfolk and that would finally take her away.

Before the arrival of Lizzie, poor Polly (and she coughing raspingly) had been comforted on her journey to the Beyond by the daily visits of the nuns from Monks Abbey, who allowed Old Stroller to look in on her – but only from the safety of the doorway, lest he caught the contagion. Polly's breathing was very much laboured, having decreased to such an extent that it was only a matter of days before the good God-in-heaven would call her to come and join him beyond the clouds.

There she was, no bigger than a frail chick and the two pink spots showing on her yellow cheeks. She struggled and tried to sit up and then she gave Old Stroller a sad and final wave – her last mute stare. It smote him to the core and tore his heart asunder. He would never forget it and yet, until her dying breath, he could do nothing but stand there helplessly at the door, his awkward hat in his hands.

Polly (what must have been on her mind?) lay still – listening to the harsh winds and the rain ceaselessly battering against the walls and windows and gurgling in the tar-barrels at the hayshed. No more would she see or hear any of this. She closed her eyes for the last time and Old Stroller came in the door and threw himself on his knees beside the bed, Lizzie behind him, her hand on his shoulder. He prayed to God for the safe-keeping of his dear wife's soul and then (poor man) he threw his greatcoat over the bed-quilt to keep her feet warm and he sank his head down tearfully beside her on the musty pillow.

The next day the nuns, with himself and Lizzie, took Polly's remains into the Welcoming Room where she lay in her coffin for all the neighbours (children too) to come and see her and pray over her with their rosary-beads.

Two days later it was most unmerciful to see Old Stroller at the graveside in his black pool of mournfulness, his heart broken in two and he a mere shadow of his former doughty self. The sun had set on his life (he knew it) and would shine on him no more. It was hard for him to think that God was still a good friend to him. As he looked down into the grave he had time to think religious matters through for himself – time to think of the past – time to think of the present – think of the future.

The Needed Miracle

And then there followed a quiet hour or two – as though the spirit of Polly had returned and brought back the gift of *Calmness* with her. And the little birds outside the window – they too poured out their eloquence afresh, as though to celebrate the death of so fine a young woman.

This was the moment for Lizzie to prove her worth and bring on the needed turnabout to the poor man's life and drive away his sorrow. *She* would be the one that would work the miracle and ease the painful thorn from his chest. Lizzie – herself and her haunting notes on the fiddle – herself and her smile that could light up a town on a winter's day. She vowed there and then that she'd never leave her sad brother to cope on his own. The Land of The Silver Dollar could go to blazes for all she cared.

In the weeks that followed she proved to be a source of the utmost joy around the house. There was another thing that brought Old Stroller cheer: she was in her early forties and yet prettier than the rest of our women put together, what with her set of pearly white teeth and her round child-like face, plump and pink, and her thick black hair, though streaked with a little greyness, which she always swept back in a neat little school-ma'amish chignon.

She was practical too: making him batches of soda-bread (five at a time) and the finest of apple-turnovers: giving him fine feeds of spuds, bacon and cabbage, something he'd nor been used to since the days of Polly's cruel illness: giving him mugs of hare-soup from the burner and whaling all her meals good-naturedly into him and never losing that lovely smile of hers.

And abroad on the farm she was turning out (everyone could see it) to be a lion-of-a-worker: whipping the horse's hide in front of the speeding plough. Nothing could withstand her – not even Old Stroller's sad misery for the loss of his wife.

'Lizzie,' said he, 'ye're the angel that God has sent me down from heaven.'

It was true for him. Each night he got down on his bended knees and offered up a fervent prayer for the soul of his lost Polly. He said a second thankyou prayer for the timely arrival of Lizzie and the powers that were in her sweet nature. God listened to his prayers and he smiled down kindly on him and then he did the unthinkable: he threw Old Stroller's grumpiness away into Bog Wood.

It All Happened Suddenly

No-one in Rookery Rally – no-one except himself and Lizzie – knew why the change in Old Stroller came about. It had all happened quite suddenly. Ring out the bells! Ring them out loudly and clearly. He ran out from his front door and into the yard. He greeted the blessed sunshine of the new day, as if it were a new bride.

With what vigour did he pelt what seemed a ton of apples into the shoe-boxes that he'd brought out from the bottom of the press-cupboard – a gift for the children. Then he heaped a load of turnips into the two feeding-buckets – a gift for their future schoolday snacks. Then he strode humbly up the Open Road and into Handsome Johnnie and Dowager's Welcoming Room where he knelt down repentantly in front of the startled young Spallidaghs and their visiting two cousins, Noolah and Minnie-ha-ha:

'Forgive me! Forgive me!' said he, turning towards Noolah, 'for I have sinned a great sin against you and the little one standing next to you.' His eyes glistened with tears as he walked round and round the room, his hands clasped together as if he didn't know what to say next.

If you had hit Dowager between the eyes with a rock she couldn't have been more stunned. Had the old fellow (that *old slate pencil* that she'd recently called him) taken leave of his senses? The children as well – for a moment they had all lost their powers-of-speech. Was there to be no more joy, no more merriment for them from their ongoing bouts of devilment and warfare against him?

He gave each of them his hand-of-friendship. He gave each of them a juicy red apple and a turnip to go with it. He gave each of them his promise and his blessing.

'On-mee-oath,' said he, 'there'll be no more wars – no more gun – no more deluge from on high. Ye have mee solemn word.'

It was clearly a happy ending, as though he'd floated in through the door on wings to put an end to the roguery on both sides – his own and theirs. From now on as the children took their copybooks to the schoolhouse of Dang-the-skin-of-it, they found a welcoming greeting from the old fellow awaiting them on the ditch where he sat – an apple apiece for each of them as well as a turnip from his pit. He collected wild berries for them to trim their lunch-boxes off. He gave them a sod of turf apiece to warm the cold old arse (he said) of their mistress, Big Screech.

With these gifts from a reinvigorated old man the Spallidagh children were as cheerful as newborn lambs as they sped on their way towards the metal bridge. Old Stroller stood looking after them, chuckling with contentment as he listened to them reciting their singalong tables in order to shorten the three-mile journey.

He took his last glimpse of them as they glided away towards the Kill – off across Red Buckles' Meadow – out over the Difficult Stile and on towards Dang-the-skin-of-it and a wealth of new knowledge. Life and devilment would never be the same again – a marvel and a joy – and yet somehow… a thing of sadness too. Enough said.

FIVE

Cousin Daisy

Handsome Johnnie and Dowager slept in a cold and damp room which was called the Big Cave Room. The room had a broken clay and concrete floor and four potato-sacks spread strategically here and there around the room and there was an empty tea-chest beside the bed and one or two holy pictures on the wall. Their bed was tucked in close to the back wall, next to the henhouse where Handsome Johnnie was able to keep an ear out for the unexpected arrival of Mr Weasel or Reynard-the-Fox if they ever stole up from their home in Bog Wood for a raid on their fowl.

There was another bed in this damp room – the bed of the two older girls, Darkie and Little Nell (not little Deelyah) and it was placed next to the chimney that backed onto the Welcoming Room. The empty fireplace had never had a fire in it, although it would certainly have warmed the room greatly if from time to time a fire was lit there. It was covered instead with bunches of laurel leaves. Behind the leaves and throughout the summertime was hidden a mountain of frantically buzzing bees, fresh from their outings to the field-flowers. With all their excitement after returning from a day's work and not yet wanting to go to sleep, these wretched creatures were poor company indeed and were likely to keep the very devil awake.

In a little anteroom at the far end of the house slept the three younger children while their older brothers had to sleep on the floor in the settlebed in another anteroom at the back of the house. Both of these rooms were separated by a thin wooden-slatted partition.

The Grand Piano

In the middle of the parent's room was a totally out-of-place obstacle – the grand piano. For modesty and decency's sake it acted as a stop-gap between the parents' own bed and the bed of Darkie and Little Nell. For some unknown reason Lady Singleton on her deathbed had left it to Dowager as a reward for her ten years' service at the Big House. Still a child, she had gone down there on the day she left school, aged eleven, and she stayed there till the day she married Handsome Johnnie, ten years later. When news of the piano's whereabouts spread abroad, everyone was left scratching their heads for it was a very curious thing for a posh lady like Lady Singleton to have done since neither Dowager or her brothers and sisters had ever played a note of music and no music was ever heard played in the little Spallidagh house till years later when Handsome Johnnie played a few old polkas on his battered concertina. But even then, he did so only on a few special occasions like a child's baptismal day or (better still) the birth of a child.

You'd imagine that a showpiece such as Lady Singleton's grand piano would have been the envy of the open road – that it would have been displayed at every opportunity in front of the jealous neighbours. But no, not one of the Spallidaghs knew what to do with the wretched thing or even if it was a musical instrument at all and it was always covered in a thick film of dust, an act that some foreign grandees might have regarded as the next worse thing to blasphemy. Worst of all, inside its lid was kept some of Dowager's most precious items: the icing sugar, the nutmeg, the raisins. Family Law forbade the children to touch any of these items for their mother had eyes on her like a hawk and she assured them that they'd take the short road to hell if they ever stole from the grand piano.

From Their Hidey-hole They Listened

From their hidey-hole under their blankets Darkie and Little Nell were forever eavesdropping, listening to the talk of the cardplayers at the other side of the hob when these happy chaps came in out of the cold for the copper-counting and the serious games of card-playing. By this time Dowager had hurried all her children off to bed early. It was for the good of their souls (she said) since the cardplayers' language, depending on their excitement after winning a game, was somewhat coarser than usual – though it was rarely, if ever, over-polite on these good-humoured occasions.

There were other times (these were seldom) when the older children were allowed to stay up and sit on the cardplayers' knees in front of the cheerful fire. There were one or two lucky occasions when even the little ones were allowed to stay up a bit later than usual whilst the table and cards were being set out. This was by way of celebration; maybe Handsome Johnnie had sold a beast or two at the Fair. For the next half-hour they got themselves thoroughly spoilt before ending up kneeling down to say their prayers in front of the fire. After that, the girls shyly put on their chemises. The boys, like the men, did not have to undress as they always slept in the shirts that they wore during the day.

The general rule, however, was for Darkie and Little Nell to kneel on the damp potato-sacking in their bedroom and busy themselves with their long list of prayers – thanking God for his goodness and asking Him to bless their animals and crops – praying for the dead (even for their poor buried horse, Fandango) and for all the sick souls in Rookery Rally before ending up with the *God-bless-me* prayer. Heaven help the two of them if they made the mistake of creeping into bed before saying this almighty list of prayers for Dowager would have her hawk-eye ready and, as with any attempt to steal from the piano, would again threaten to beat them half-to-death with the broken leg-of-the-chair if they didn't offer up their nightly prayers to God before hopping in to bed.

After all the excitement of the card-games had finished and the cardplayers had stepped out the front door after taking the holy-water from the font, Dowager and Handsome Johnnie were at last able to get a bit of peace for themselves. This was a special time for them with no children or cardplayers left in the Welcoming Room to annoy them or interfere with their thoughts. That's when Darkie and Little Nell had their ears cocked close to the chimney-wall, listening to the lofty stream of conversation that always seemed to pour out of their parents' mouths. They'd stay glued there till their eyes grew heavy with sleep and even at that hour of the night it was the devil's own job to get a wink of sleep, for Dowager could talk the legs off of an ass and would stay talking across the firelight to Handsome Johnnie for half the blessed night.

The Subject Of Cousin Daisy

The subject of Cousin Daisy was often to the forefront in these nightly conversations. It was a time shortly after Old Stroller had converted himself to a new and better way of living and Darkie and Little Nell could hear their mother sighing over something that she called *Cousin Daisy's great sorrow* when herself and Handsome Johnnie could be heard offering up the odd little prayer for that young girl's well-being.

They soon learnt that Daisy was one of their nearest relations and lived three-quarters-of-a-mile from their own half-door – at a spot where the road dipped down at Red Scissors' Well and came to a sharp elbow-point leading up the lane to the Lofty Bald Plain. Running across the lane was a small stream, barely a trickle in summertime. If you turned the ass-and-car sharply left and followed the next winding lane still further uphill you'd come to a hidden nook among the pine-trees. In that sheltered spot lay the little thatched house of Dowager's older sister, Nancy. She had been married late in life to Dan-the-Cooper, a hill-farmer with oceans of black cattle to his name. Miracles do happen and in spite of their advanced years in life, God had been good to them and had given them the gift of four children: Jack, the twins (Ned and Nan) and Daisy. Daisy was the youngest of these.

Young Girls Off To The Convent

Many young girls – especially the daughters of rich farmers – were heading off in droves to the convents of the Sisters of Mercy. Poorer farmers were awfully anxious to be seen rubbing shoulders with those farmers who were higher up the social ladder and richer than themselves – farmers, who were out on Monkstown's grand golf-course or at the hare-coursing in Ballyhennery and on nodding terms with the clergy as they sat alongside them at the hurling-matches.

These soft-hearted men were as sad as a wet week when they found themselves driving their innocent young daughters into the Roaring Town Station. It was a terrible thing (they said) for a man's daughter to be seen leaving the nest and she a mere sixteen, no more than a child. Why, it was only the other day (they said) that these young girls were seen playing hopscotch and skipping their rope or rolling their bowlee-wheel up and down the road. At the time of their leaving it seemed as though they had gone from the earth in a puff of smoke – dead and gone forever.

Other Fair Damsels

Sad-to-say, there were one or two other fair damsels (ah, the little hussies!), who were forcibly dragged away from Rookery Rally for having brought everlasting shame on their family by giving birth to their babies at the wrong stage in their life. There was only one way for those families – indeed for the salvation of the entire community – to save these girls' eternal souls and that was to send them crashing in through the walls of a cold and distant nunnery. Tucked away out of sight, they were treated as a scapegoat-offering to God so as to avoid the punishment of hell that might otherwise await them as well as a dose of the drought or even starvation attending the rest of their family later on.

What on earth were some of the miserable Christian souls in Rookery Rally thinking of – to be downgrading these young girls in such a way as opposed to their tight-lipped respect for the girls who had gone off to enter the convent and become holy women? Whereas these newly-appointed nuns could be seen (to the surprise of their joyful parents) stepping down from the train on a return visit home, the other poor wretches were confined to the blistering heat of a convent's laundry where they washed and ironed the nuns' habits for them – never to be seen again till the day they dropped down dead from exhaustion or a broken heart – never to have seen the newborn baby that had been snatched from under their skirts the minute it made its way into the world.

All this, for a few moments of youthful pleasure, fleetingly discovered inside some ditch or other where no priest and his earnest lamp could spy on them after the Dance-in-the-Fields had ended. To what distant shores had the gift of charity flown? Where now was the pitying face of Jesus, who had stroked the sorrowful head of the Sinful Woman as she washed his feet with her tears?

The Forcing-away Of Young Girls

Apart from the convent and the laundry, there was yet another side to the life story of young girls. When a girl's father was unable to get her married off to a farmer who owned a profitable bit of land (it didn't matter how old the man was – unless he was the wrong side of sixty with a bald head and a mouthful of broken yellow teeth) the poor fellow was left scratching his head as to what to do with his daughter.

'Am I to keep this daughter of mine at home for the rest of her life – to spend her days in a state of sad spinsterhood?'

What he truly meant was 'Am I to be left feeding her hungry mouth three times a day out of mee own pocket from now until doomsday?'

Why, the mean old skinflint!

He saddled up the pony-and-trap and took the young lady into the Roaring Town. As soon as he got there, he gave her his handshake and his fatherly blessing – all the while dabbing at his eyeballs with the feigned handkerchief of sorrow. He was now rid of her and his wave-of-farewell was nothing short of a kick in the arse.

His daughter was now making the saddest of all journeys. But, though she hadn't heard the call to go spend her days close up to her Saviour on her knees in a convent, her future would be bright enough when she found that she was well-suited to a future life of nursing the sick in one of the big-city hospitals. Thereafter she never gave a moment's thought to the old skinflint who had hunted her away from home.

Like other girls, Daisy had also been given these simple choices: a chance to go off at sixteen and live the life of a holy nun inside a convent or a chance to go find herself nursing the sick in one of the big cities abroad. She was such a good clean-living soul that the shameful alternative (life in a nunnery's cursed laundry) would never have entered anyone's mind.

A Day's Labour

In her fifth year on earth – the year prior to attending Dang-the-skin-of-it's schoolhouse with her two big brothers and older sister – Daisy would spend the morning helping her mother keep the place ship-shape while Dan, her father, was abroad in the fields, working away like blazes at the hoeing and weeding of his early crops before going on to trim the briars on the ditches. He was a man, who never seemed to stop working – not even for a minute.

It was the same with Daisy's mother, Nancy. With a face as red as a turkey's gobble, she could be seen enveloped in the washtub's steam and soap-suds of a Monday morning, scouring and rinsing the bedsheets before laying them out the length of the haggart-bushes where they quickly dried in the ballooning wind. After that she had a hundred-and-one other jobs to do – far too many to mention and there was never a time for her to stand still gossiping.

Daisy was being brought up in the same vein. Her workload was a tall order for a child so young. She had to dodge the snapping jaws of the two fierce sows blocking her way to the haggart in her search for eggs hidden among the nettles. She had to tiptoe round the ducks who were drinking up the pissy swill at the Sinky Pool outside the pig-house door before she could collect the thorny bushes for her mother to light the fire. She even had to sweep the dung from the yard with the long-handled brush (*not too roughly lest you shift loose the cobbles*). She had to help her mother clean out the flies and the milk-scour from inside the two creamery-tanks.

A Day To Forget

From their nights spent listening at the chimney-wall Darkie and Little Nell were alarmed to hear that it was something of a miracle that Daisy was still alive, seeing the narrow escape she'd had from death in that very same year. What had happened to her was all-so-predictable – everybody said so at the time.

After completing her morning jobs, she wiped the sweat from her brow and went in the door to get herself a mug of water from the bucket. She was tired beyond belief and she sat down on her stool by the fire. Whereupon she slipped into a doze and fell with a crash into the hot ashes. The folds of her dress got caught on a burning log and the flames tore into her flesh. Her father was coming across the yard to get his billhook and to return to the field for the briar-cutting when he heard the roars out of Daisy. He rushed in the door and quickly wrapped his greatcoat around her. Her mother rushed in a second later and ripped the dress from off of her back to see for herself the damage to her child's body. The blisters were already forming round Daisy's waist.

A month previously a poor woman had scalded herself by tripping over her skillet-pot whilst straining the boiling water from her spuds. At that time Father Accessible had mentioned a widow-woman who lived at the back of Bog Boundless. He said that she had the cure for almost everything – especially the burnt limbs (even Doctor Glasses had said it) and that she had healed the burns and huge blisters on the poor woman's arms.

The same widow-woman now came down the hill. She was riding her piebald horse (*Black Jack*) and from her hip-pocket she produced her mother's own hand-me-down ointment that had been made from the heated paste of dried-out laurel-leaves, mixed up with a good dose of unsalted butter. A month later, after she'd ridden back home, there wasn't a single mark left on young Daisy's body – just like the woman who had been straining her spuds. It was nothing less than a miracle and it was talked about for months thereafter. Father Accessible and Doctor Glasses never stopped singing the healer's praises. Praise-be-to-God for the life-saving powers of the widow-woman from above in the mountains.

The Month Of May And Holy Mary

The next few years sped by all too quickly. And then came May – the first real month of the year when everybody had finally shoved to the back of their minds the harsh days of snow and winter. This was the loveliest month in the year with all those flowers and blooms to celebrate Our Blessed Lady and all those church processions and nasally hymn-chanting around the church grounds, carrying Our Lady's lofty statue on the shoulders of the red-and-white-robed altar-boys.

Father Accessible took a long look at Daisy. She was at an age when she was growing big and strong like the crops in over the ditches and he had no hesitation in picking her out to crown the statue since she reminded him of Our Lady's own good self, what with her clear angelic face and her fingers forever laced round her rosary-beads every Sunday during Mass.

A Rare Duck-egg Or Two

Her mother too was taking a long look at Daisy these days – days when her daughter would go off behind the cow-shed, searching for a surprise gift for her parents: maybe cutting a bunch of wild roses for the house-altar with her mother's scissors: maybe discovering a rare duck-egg or two. See Daisy with the ducks and the way they slowly rise up from their nests in the dock-leaves in front of her, almost tripping over her feet, the sunlight shining on their blue and green feathers – the way her nimble feet move towards the haggart-gap, dancing round a proud young hen as she parades her chirping chicks out the field-gate, guarding them with her motherly cluck-cluck-clucking.

May, the month of all months. Hear the whispering oak-trees on the ditch with their new leaves, shiny and clean as the holly. Behold the many hawthorn-trees trees too, showing off their snow-white flowers and the wild violets smouldering everywhere with vivid colour and spreading themselves round Daisy's bare feet. These mornings were a far cry from the day of her burnt body. They were Daisy's happiest time when the April showers and the dark clouds had finally drifted out across Galway and the sun had drunk up all the puddles. Like the flowers and the trees, Daisy could feel the fullness of life tingling around in her veins.

She was happy in other ways too, for it wasn't long since she had been freed from the imprisoning drudgery of her schooldays and the fierce temper of her mistress, Big Screech. It was a pleasure to have these precious mornings to herself whilst her two big brothers and her older sister were off in Bog Boundless, slaving away at saving the turf. Like the rest of the family, they too had been well-trained as willing work-horses.

An hour after her adventure behind the cow-shed and after handing her mother the two big surprises (the duck-eggs and the bunch of wild roses for her bedroom altar) the merry peals of Daisy's laughter could be heard ringing across the ditches as she went chasing the hysterical ass (*Jimmy*) round and around the field for no better reason than to see him dance his crazy jig-steps away from her. Nancy was taking in the bedsheets at the time and she stopped and leaned in over the field-gate. 'Why, this daughter of mine,' said she, 'is like a young calf that has recently been untethered and is about to go mad-capping round the universe.'

Yes, happiness was walking hand in hand with Cousin Daisy. It had first been noticed long before the day when Father Accessible had picked her out to crown Our Lady's statue – on the day of her First Holy Communion when she was nine-years-of-age. Her communion robes had an outstanding silky sheen to them that reminded the gathered congregation of how close to an angel-of-God this little girl had grown. Her face had taken on a new complexion like an innocent saint from the centre pages of her prayer-book. Up until that memorable day she had always been reluctant to kneel down in her bedroom during the long-drawn-out imposition of nightly prayers. But then – like an ugly duckling turning into a white swan – as soon as the blessed host passed her lips, she found she was a new child and had cast off her old self forever.

Ready To Be A Soldier Of Christ

It was now a year since Daisy left the schoolhouse of Dang-the-skin-of-it. It was the time set for her and girls of her own age to take the Blessed Sacrament of Confirmation. She was fifteen. Once more it was the month of May and Bishop High-Hat arrived in his posh motorcar from out of Clare. During the ceremony he was to give each child the traditional slap-on-the-jaw to remind them that they were now strong and perfect Christians – that they were nothing less than soldiers of Jesus Christ. Daisy was dreading this slap to the jaw as her mother had told her that one side of her face would be blood-red for the rest of the week. Shame on you, Nancy, for frightening a guileless child in this way. It wasn't only children that could lie like fair hell for the kindly old bishop merely gave Daisy's cheek a fond stroke with the palm of his hand.

Slap or no slap, after this new meeting with her Blessed Saviour, Daisy was seen to increase even more (if that were at all possible) in holiness and purity-of-nature. She knew what this holy sacrament had meant: she was going to show the world that she had become a soldier of Christ and would stand proudly beside him till the day she died. Wasn't that what Bishop High-Hat had meant when he bent down and whispered into her ear?

People Began To Worry

Before the summer ended people were starting to worry about her, seeing the extravagant differences between herself and other girls. Each day after dressing and washing her face in the freezing waters of the yard-stream and before she attacked the main tasks of the day with her brothers and older sister, she took her father's much-too-big twenty-six-inch-wheeler bike from the shed and cycled into town so as to attend Mass and receive the blessed host in holy communion. It was a miracle she didn't break her neck and kill herself on that ramshackle old thing as she hurried across the sloping hills in order to get there in time – five miles to town and five miles home again.

As she pedalled her solitary way home, no bird ever flew with such a light spirit as she did. Her cheeks were aglow with pinkness and her heart was full of a new burst of sanctity. In accepting the host so regularly on her tongue she had intensified her love of Jesus more than ever. She felt the tall trees were winking down at her, knowingly – almost whispering their softness into her soul. She hummed a juddery song to her bicycle, knowing that Jesus was all the time with her, deep inside in her soul and that he would never leave her.

Winter Came On

Winter came on. Father Adaptable (the kindly old priest inside in the Roaring Town) began to worry like everybody else had been doing. He could see that the farm at home was now taking second place to Daisy's desire to come to Mass each day. He had expressed his priestly anxieties to Daisy's own mother, seeing the way Daisy was becoming far too engrossed in her own saintliness.

Might this young girl be losing her mind (he asked himself)? Her mother had spoken to him about it the previous Sunday after Mass. For as soon as Daisy came home each day from church, her mother would take a peep out the half-door at her – only to see her on the upturned ass-and-car, dreaming her life away languorously, brought back to earth only by the anguished cry of an adventurous drake caught in the bushes round her mother's private garden. Listening to the worries of the poor woman, the old priest was left scratching his head. He'd have to do something – he surely would.

There was something else. By now Daisy was as slender as a blade of grass for she had begun fasting from food every other Friday in order to chastise her body. She had read about it in a book of the saints. This was a new one – starkly in contrast to the ways of her parents and to her big brother, Jack, as well as the twins, Ned and Nan.

One morning as she was leaving the church the old priest decided to act. He caught hold of her arm. It was a day that had started off bitterly cold when the snow was already a foot deep, capping the neighbouring fields and making the laneway behind Daisy's house far too treacherous on which to have been seen cycling her father's old bike. The holy man was bent on forbidding her from cycling all that way to Mass during the cruelty of this period of heavy snowfall and he advised her (he even begged her) to give the altar-rails a miss occasionally, at least on these fierce cold days.

'Even Jesus would not be expected to do what you are doing, Daisy. You're a pure saint – with one foot already inside the gates of Heaven.'

Daisy was quick to answer her priest. 'Yes, father,' said she (and he saw the worry-lines on her forehead), 'but if one foot is already in heaven, tell me this – where is the other foot?'

She already knew where the road to hell lay and the good priest was left scratching his head all over again.

This was a new one on him and he went off into his presbytery smiling reluctantly. He had lost his battle with Daisy.

The Father Of The Flock

Dan was the father of the flock and, though he'd always worked hard, he was now busier than a hive of bees, not stopping for a moment – not even for a cup of Nancy's strong tea. With the crops growing nice and strong he turned his eyes to other jobs. Even before the lark had finished her first morning song he had tackled up his ass *(Jimmy)*. He seemed to be permanently seated on the lace of his ass-and-car. It was as if his arse was glued to it (smiled the neighbours).

He couldn't stay idle. See him, his cap perched back-to-front on his head, driving off to get a load of ferns from Bog Wood for his cow-shed bedding. See him driving his ass-and-car back a second time for a load of logs and timber-lengths in readiness for next winter's firing.

He did not stop for a drink from the bucket but went off a third time – out to the hill to inspect his herd of black cattle. A miller couldn't keep up with the likes of him. People went on talking more than ever: did he ever stop to take a bite to eat? Did he ever stop to ease his bowels or wipe his arse?

It was no laughing matter. The pace of his work was making poor Dan grow old before his time. Nancy kept telling him to throw down the reins like any man of his age and let Time pass him by quietly from now on.

But he was like many men and never listened to his wife's advice. It was no surprise, therefore, when a sharp pain hit him in the chest one day and he realised he'd have to say goodbye to the work that he was planning: he'd even have to stop taking Jimmy and the ass-and-car down to Bog Wood for a load of logs and ferns – have to leave the work of farming to one of his sons from now on.

Jack

The eldest son, Jack, had already found a true vocation for serving God and was about to leave home. Being the son of a plain and ordinary farmer, he had his eyes set on going abroad. Not for him (said he) the fine old times of a priest in a parish at home in Ireland – though he had to agree that a priest being on call twenty-four hours a day in a parish at home and inescapably sharing in the sorrows and grief of a hundred souls at one and the same time was enough to send any young curate pure mad.

His younger brother, Ned-the-twin, was the winsome lad – always warning his older brother how much he was going to miss not being a stay-at-home priest – reminding him of all the adoring popularity amongst the women and all the summertime outings to hurling-matches and all the hunt-meetings with the men.

However, a month later and as soon as he had crossed over the seas, Jack realised more than ever that he preferred living among the black heathens in darkest Africa. That's what he said. Everybody crowded round to see the startling pictures that he sent home – pictures of himself in the middle of a village of smiling black faces and he dressed out in his long white missionary robes and the red fez hat of a White Father on top of his head.

Ned-the-Twin

Proud as they were of Jack, it turned out to be a lifesaver to have Ned-the-Twin still at home with Dan and Nancy and for him to take on the mantle of his father's ever-receding workrate round the little farm. However, if men thought that Dan-the-Cooper had never been able to stop working like a young horse, he was nothing at all when compared to his son. Ned turned out to be such a powerful worker that everybody wondered what sort of milk his mother had weaned him on or what sort of spuds and cabbages had he been reared on thereafter. And so prodigious was his output – so incessant was it – that he seldom darkened the door till the sun had gone to rest and the moon had risen high in the sky.

Thin As A Hayrake

The previous year had witnessed the international cyclists heading in a lightning volley of a hundred cyclists up around the bend at Sheep's Cross and speeding on towards the Hills-of-The-Past before anyone could get back their own eyeballs or their tonsils. Such excitement – such clapping of hands – such yahooing from throats – would it ever be forgotten? Powering away on their spindly set of legs, these cyclists were as thin as a hayrake but Ned was even thinner than them – thinner than a matchstick or a newspaper as a result of all the hard work he kept putting himself through. It was sure and certain (it was almost a prophecy) that one day soon he'd kill himself from such arduous work.

That's when Cousin Daisy found herself in a frustrating quandary. She could see how pale and shaken her brother was looking and she wanted him to take life a pace or two slower. She worried about him to such an extent that, whereas Father Adaptable had been unable to keep her back from the altar-rails and from receiving daily communion, she now felt a desperate need to support brother Ned. It was the least she could do. So, instead of cycling into town every day of the week, she gave it a miss now and then and took her pitchfork out to work alongside Ned and to ease the strain from his back.

Herself And Nan

By this time both herself and her sister, Nan, were fast approaching the first stages of womanhood. Nan was seventeen and she was sixteen. Their mother smiled and smiled. How proud she was of her two pink-cheeked beauties! 'As pretty as the sunshiny beauty of wildflowers in a field of thistles,' said she.

She felt she could almost write a song about them – their coral blue eyes sparkling like a sweet-gallon full of shiny water – like the dewdrops on a new flower in the early dawn – their teeth (unlike the rest of the young women) as white as a bone in the sun – their hair as wavy as the sea. These were her thoughts – if only she had the words to back them up.

But something was missing. Though they crossed the fields to get water from the well, they had never been known to mix with the rest of the growing boys and girls. They had never spent happy childhood days carousing along the riverbanks in the company of the Spallidagh children – *those young galoots* as their aunt Nancy disdainfully called them. They had never been seen at the top of the high trees, shouting and cursing like Dowager's wild children.

But, to give them their due, Daisy and Nan lived a good bit away from the rest of the children and were unable, therefore, to come traipsing down the road from their home beyond Sheep's Cross.

Maybe They Were Lonely

On mornings when Darkie and Little Nell were sitting on the logs in Old Sam's Grove, they'd think of Daisy and Nan and wonder whether they were a bit on the lonely side. From their home across the fields surely the two of them must have been tired of hearing the whole merry bunch of the Spallidagh children roaring and bawling from morning till night and thrashing the life out of the countryside.

Warbling Will and Lofty had other thoughts about Daisy and Nan – that, as lovely as their looks were, their two little noses were pointed a bit too high in the air.

'Let them go and bury themselves,' snapped Warbling Will.

'They are far too good for the likes of us with the smell of cow-dung on us – themselves and their skimpy dresses and they always shining like a pair of dolls,' said Lofty with an air of indifference.

There was no love lost between the two lads and their cousins, – or so thought Darkie and Little Nell. Yet, in spite of their strong denials, *the Temptation Fairies* (led on by the devil and his wicked band of fallen angels) had already come stamping in the doorway and were enthroning themselves blissfully in the hearts of these two doomed Spallidagh boys – especially Warbling Will. He was eighteen and had already been feeling those unmentionable hidden tremors in the blood of his lower body that had caused Dowager to drench him with a bucket of water the previous year. He was just a year older than Nan. Lofty was the same age as Daisy.

Had Dowager known the thoughts that were creeping into her two sons' heads, she'd have either put a hairclip in their hair ('Why, don't tell me it's turning into little girls that the two-of-ye are – with yeer sheep's eyes gawping at Nan and Daisy?') or have given them a wallop of her yardbrush in case their thoughts were brazenly given to lifting up the young girls' skirts to see the colour of their knickers.

The Spring-well

Do you know the spring-well below at Old Sam's Stile? It sometimes went dry during the summer months and Dowager's children had to take their buckets up to Red Scissors' Well at Sheep's Cross. It was at this well-hole that these two fair damsels – their shiny eyes and their smiling fat lips – came each day for their buckets of water.

Without looking up at the sun, the two lovestruck youths seemed to know to the minute the time when Nan and Daisy would be arriving with their buckets. You'd see the two fidgety simpletons – with a casual straw in their mouths and their faces for once washed clean as a new copper – dawdling in embarrassed shyness not far from the well-hole – as though they were in search of a new species of wild rosebush, so intently did they gaze at one bush or another. They were utterly unaware (it seemed) of the presence of the two fair damsels stepping down across the fields with their buckets.

Warbling Will began cutting off the heads of the nettles around the well hole, to protect the soft limbs of the girls when they arrived.

Lofty was expertly pulling up the roots of the thistles with the aid of his switch for a similar reason.

Our two young shining knights were making sure that the visiting girls would not get stung by the nettles or torn amongst the thistles and that their ladylike route to the well-hole would be unimpeded. They left no holds barred so that these fair creatures from Heaven's bounds could get into the side of the well-hole and fill their buckets.

The two stately girls arrived. They were dressed in their summery dresses. They brought to the well-hole their angelic smiles and their shiny eyes and teeth. They brought their polite laughter as well.

Warbling Will and Lofty had no words in their stuttery mouths to offer them. Why on earth were these boys so shy? What on earth was wrong with the pair of them? They were like fluttering birds inside a winter's cage at the sight of the girls' soft beauty. For as soon as Daisy and Nan got down to the task of filling their buckets, the two odd fellows could be seen running away towards the metal bridge and disappearing in over John's Gate and out across the Bluebutton Field.

That night as they lay in their settlebed next to Stylish and Sammy-Joe, Warbling Will swore that Nan's eyes were as blue as a robin's egg. Lofty swore that Daisy had hair as yellow as Lady Elegance's flax. Warbling Will vowed that he would give Nan the moon – if only he could get the price of it. Lofty swore that he would go one better and give Daisy the whole of the sun. Ah, such poets were they! And for the rest of the summer these two poor forlorn scholars sang like the very larks in the morning and the hearts in their chests went *tra-la-la* and *tra-la-la* time and time again.

An Uncertain Twist To Things

There was at times an uncertain twist to things – whether it was the sudden clouds speeding into Lisnagorna from the Kerry side of Ireland or the fierce new thunder and lightning abroad in Bog Boundless.

Out of nowhere arrived a homely nun in the shape of Sister Augusta from the Convent of Mercy in Limerick City. She was the one and only sister of Dan and the two young beauties' maiden aunt. She had come to celebrate the twentieth wedding anniversary of Nancy and Dan. What on earth was wrong with the good woman? Was she mad? Events such as this were never celebrated in Rookery Rally. Maybe the convent was teaching their nuns a new style of living these days: the only celebrations heard tell of in Rookery Rally up until then had been the Holy Mass or the birth of a calf or the fine bout of drinking after selling a few cows on a Fair Day.

On Across The Stiles

The holy nun (*call me Augusta*) walked alongside Nan and Daisy across the blooming meadows. The summertime sun was shining brightly and not a drop of rain had been seen for the last ten days. The yard streams could have done with a drop or two. The three of them proceeded over the stiles, Augusta all the time describing the charmed convent life that she was living – the fine high teas and cakes – the uplifting hymns that she was forever singing. She talked of the unfathomable happiness that was giving daily strength to her soul. She told them how God Himself had whispered in her ear one night long ago and how she had listened to his voice – how she had answered his call – how she had followed his footsteps every day since then in her dedication to Him as a Sister of Mercy.

That evening whilst Nan was sleeping beside her, Daisy's heart burst straight up into her throat. Her two eyes shone like a pair of saucers. She realised that she too was being whispered to by God.

She Set Off To See Her Confessor

Although Father Adaptable had finally put a stop to her getting herself to the rails of the church each day – although her brother, Ned, was glad of her help on the farm on those days that she wasn't cycling all the way to town, Daisy got up early one morning and decided to put on her best Sunday dress. This time she left her bike behind her and in her walking-boots started off on the much shorter journey to Copperstone Hollow to see Father Accessible rather than Father Adaptable.

After a heart-to-heart talk with the holy man she was once more seen on her daily journey to Mass and holy communion – not cycling her way into the Roaring Town this time but stepping out along the creamery road to Father Accessible's church in Copperstone Hollow. She could have straddled the old ramshackle bike if she wanted to but she needed this precious bit of time for a bit of quiet contemplation whilst she was preparing her soul for the reception of Jesus in her daily holy communion.

Life Moved On At A Merry Old Pace

Life was now moving on at a merry old pace and, if she had previously been seen as very different from the rest of the young girls, she now seemed to be floating like an angel through the skies. She passed the Blue Gates and sped her dreamy way towards the doors of the church. Though everyone had worried about her when she was a child, now no-one could handle the likes of her at all. 'Look at her – the most beautiful damsel in our midst,' whispered the Weeping Mollys. This time there wasn't a trace of scorn in their eyes – only praise and wistful admiration.

'God-love-her, she has never been known to see the image of her face in the eyes of a young man,' said they. 'She's forever casting her eyes up at the ten-foot crucifix above the altar.' Yes, Daisy was making her daily sacrificial commitment to Jesus all over again. She'd never find a bed for herself (they said) beside one of the hairy old farmers, all of whom would run faster than a hare to get her into their clutches and roll her round in the bed. That's what they said.

Black And Blue With The Cold

The year progressed and the weather turned harsh. Daisy's two feet grew black and blue with the cold when she was marching along the creamery road to the church-door.

Then the inevitable happened (there was no escaping it) and influenza caught a hold of her. A fit of coughing took hold of her lungs and yet she still weathered it all and went on making the daily trips to the altar-rails.

She was going on for seventeen and a few months short of taking her suitcase off to the gates of the convent where she was to become a postulant – a white-veiled novice – before finally taking her irretrievable vows of allegiance to God. She couldn't wait for that most happy day to come. Her heart was bursting with the joy of it.

A Very Bad Hand Of Cards

Then came another twist – one unworthy of her. Grief struck Dan and Nancy's house when the *Cruel Fairies* came a-calling. They handed Daisy a very bad hand of cards. It was getting on towards evening when the whole houseful started bawling. Daisy had gone down to Bog Wood to tell Ned to come home for his supper. He'd been cutting ferns like his father used to do and by now he should have been turning the ass towards home.

It didn't take Daisy long to find her brother. He was in the middle of his beloved Bog Wood. He had fallen down in a sudden fit from the lace of the ass-and car. As he fell he must have hit his head on the wheel. As the neighbours had long predicted, he was stone dead. Hadn't they all begged him not to work so hard? Hadn't they told him that this would happen to him one day – that he hadn't the mechanics of a clock?

The rest of the household ran down quickly. They carried him home between the four of them (Nan, Daisy, Nancy and Dan) and they laid him out on the bed. They placed the eight lighted candles for a happy death all around him and then their cries could be heard the length and breadth of Rookery Rally. 'What'll we do now? What'll we do now?'

Dan-the-Cooper Calls It A Day

Before the start of autumn Dan had reached the ripe old age of seventy – an age that many men would rarely be lucky enough to have reached. He was now too frail to fork the hay to his winter cattle in the shed or pick the last of the spuds. Nan, though older than Daisy, had always been a frail little chick and now her lungs had difficulty in getting a breath of air into her. Doctor Glasses had warned that this daughter's heart (like Dowager's daughter, Darkie) was far too weak for any sort of hard manual work.

As Good As A Punch In The Chest

Daisy, though the youngest, was struck a terrible blow. It was as good as a punch in the chest. From this day on, the household would be dependent on her own good self. What was she to do? Her sincere and deep devotion to the Blessed Sacrament – her promise to spend the rest of her life as a Christian soldier in the arms of her Saviour – was now challenged by an even greater need. She felt this higher calling – an even more noble calling than the walls of the convent – a sterner duty than joining the nuns: to protect the livelihood of her mother and father.

She would forego the Sisters of Mercy. She would become the lifelong servant of her mother and father instead.

Scrawnier And More Weatherworn

In the years that followed, growing older, scrawnier and more weatherworn by the day, Daisy continued to walk the three miles to the church in Copperstone Hollow and back home again. On her return she farmed the land every bit as good as Ned and her father used to do. Each new day, until the rosy sun disappeared from view and went down into the ocean – long after the harsh dews of twilight were gone and ever onwards into the lonely starry nights – Daisy worked like a steam-engine – as though punishing herself for not being able to accept the black veil of a nun.

Passersby no longer worried but pitied her as she dragged her wheelbarrow-load of dung along the fields to enrich the soil. Others marvelled at her when she led her mare (*Frisky*) out onto the headland and yoked her to the plough. The wonders of her workrate were the talk of Rookery Rally. Drudgery upon drudgery crept up along her bones. It reddened her alabaster cheeks and destroyed the porcelain beauty of this angel-upon-earth, whose looks had once outmatched the very stars. Had the neighbours the powers to look inside in her heart they'd have seen a broken-spirited woman, who never came to terms at not being able to fulfil her dreams of living her days in the convent and getting herself married to God with a nun's silver ring on her saintly finger.

Never A Cross Word

No-one ever heard a cross word out of Daisy as she pushed the ache back down inside her throat and kept her secrets locked forever in her heart. Not even Father Accessible or Father Adaptable were ever aware of the constant pain in her chest: only she knew the truth – that she had always been married to God – from the very first day when the sacred host first passed her young lips. But one thing the rest of Rookery Rally always knew (Dowager especially with her evening fire-side chats with Handsome Johnnie) – that there was a bed in heaven prepared and awaiting the arrival of Daisy.

Daisy! Daisy! Daisy!

If the Angel Gabriel were to slip down to Rookery Rally on a rainbow-glide – if he were to join in the company of the rest of us poor scholars – he'd surely have found out that you were one of the truest friends that the Son-of-God had ever laid claim to. Enough said.

SIX

Stylish and his merry soul

After the earlier antics of Darkie, it is time to take a step back and look closer into the life of one of her younger brothers. Somewhere in the middle of Dowager's brood of chicks there was placed this fat little nursling – later to be given the name of Stylish. Even as he crawled out onto the floor of the Big Cave Room behind the hob he seemed to be winking at the world.

His two big sisters, Darkie and Little Nell, hushed Handsome Johnnie and their three older brothers out of the room and coaxed their weary mother's aching limbs onto the settlebed that was spread out on the floor. They whispered encouragement to her in between cursing her to high hell for not hurrying on with the birth of this little fellow. Then with the lighted candles in under her skirts they helped drag him out of her belly and into the world in much the same way as they had once seen Warbling Will and Lofty helping Blue-eyed Jack drag a newborn lamb into the light-of-day from its teeth-chattering mother.

Their task was still not finished. They washed their mother's bloody clothes, the blankets and sheets in the yard stream and then they hung them on the bushes behind the henhouse dung-heap to dry. They threw the remaining blue-and-silver placenta-tube into the turf-fire and watched the fat sizzling up and dying away. They got busy (as their mother had shown them) and baked a fine big apple-batter in the burner so as to feed and fatten her limbs and bring back life and strength into her. The tears of joy rolled down Dowagers cheeks (theirs too) as they placed the wet lips of Stylish onto their mother's warm breast.

This Rosy-Red Child

By the time he was five this rosy-red child had a huge mop of hair on him, red as a goose's beak. He was soon seen as the wild one among the rest of the children and known for regularly doing what was unexpected of him. It often involved him in mischief.

He had what his big brother, Blue-eyed Jack, described as an air of *Plenty* about him, filling the open spaces round him with unfailing bouts of fun and energy and with an endless supply of cheerfulness and laughter.

See him chasing across the Bluebutton Field and trying to catch the flying clouds and stamp on them. See Dowager looking out over the haggart singletree and shaking her head in wonder at the sight of him for it seemed to her as though the sun shone out of him.

Handsome Johnnie too (when he managed to walk a few steps from his bed these days) could see such an air of playfulness in this little child – such an air of what he called *Carnival* in him – as though the world belonged to him.

Even at this early age the child was turning himself into a little roll-of-fat with a rounded paunch on him and forever loading his belly with whatever was at hand – especially the milk (lashings of it) and the eggs and spuds. But he was a fussy young eater and as soon as he hopped out of bed he'd ask his mother, 'Is mee egg ready yet – is it a fresh one this time?' And if there was the tiniest blotch of blood in the yolk, he would spend a good while scraping it off. Then he'd add a mountain of salt and butter to it and keep stirring the whole mess round and around, at the same time stuffing his mouth with slice after slice of soda-bread and yet having enough time to carry on talking nonsensically to the others, all of whom would like nothing better than to put their father's sock in his mouth and shut his gob for him.

Stepping forward a few years later you'd see him raiding like a hawk for a wider variety of food. As soon as he'd had his two (maybe three) eggs for breakfast he'd go digging into the burner for the latest cuts of apple-batter or rhubarb tart. You could set your watch by him. By one o'clock he'd be hungry again and with the complicity of Sammy-Joe he'd filch half-a-dozen steaming hot spuds from the skillet-pot and run out the half-door with them and squeeze them into powder in his fists before devouring them abroad on the ditch behind the cow-shed. By three o'clock he'd be collecting crab-apples and roasting them in the fire for yet another little feast.

When he was tired of all this eating – and with nothing else on his mind – he'd have an hour or two left to act the fool in front of the later arrivals, Deelyah, Tiny Jim and Little Dan, and go running after the ass, the Lightning Whoor, chasing him round and round the Bluebutton Field in an effort to get up on his back and ride him to kingdom come.

When He Was Six

Children have their ears as well as their eyes and are inclined to pick up and take to heart everything they hear. Even before he had turned six and was ready to follow Darkie and Little Nell off to school, he began to acquire the full flow of our lilting language – the polite words and (ahem) the bad and filthy swear-words in like measure.

Among the polite words there were so many tall tales and outright lies that he told – like the time he saw a ghost dancing round on the galavanize roof on top of the pig-house or the time he saw the purple cockerel (bigger than a sheep) dancing round and around in Galloping Gret's hayshed. As Dowager was fond of saying: 'The lies don't walk out of this little fellow's mouth – they come trotting out in a pure river.'

Before he had finished his first year at school (thanks to Dowager's fireside tuition) he was able to say a dozen prayers. He was better than a missioner (said Warbling Will). Dressed up like Father Laudable and wearing Handsome Johnnie's long white Sunday shirt, he would kneel in the yard and yell out the *Credo*, the *I Confess* and the *Hail, Holy Queen*– each prayer as long as a wet week. There wasn't a prayer that could beat the spouting mouth of this young whippersnapper. He could count passed a thousand and sing all six verses of *Moonlight in Mayo*. He was able to entertain the passersby on their ass-and-cars with:

> *'When I was young and able to hop,*
> *I soon found out mee father's shop.*
> *'Twas there I learnt to take a drop of Murphy's*
> *double-porther.'*

The cute little way in which he strolled round the yard astride his wobbly yardbrush, mimicking his father – the way he rolled out this last song as he swayed from side to side on the brush – made his brothers and sisters laugh till their sides hurt. They pictured him one day soon, sitting on a bar-stool in Curl 'n Stripes' drinking-shop with his father's cap tilted back on the edge of his poll and his little fist wrapped round a pint of the black-doctor stout. 'What rare gifts this son of mine has,' said Dowager proudly.

And shortly after his seventh birthday and when Christmas Day had come and he'd eaten nearly half the burner-of-rice, especially the crispy brown edges, and had devoured the best part of a goose as well, she paraded him down to the gates of Lady Elegance. You can imagine the surprise for the lady when Stylish gave her his latest acquisition – his rendering of the long poem he'd been learning from Darkie and Little Nell on the daily trek to and from school, namely *Dangerous Dan McGrew*. Yes, the clever brains and talents of his grandfather, Dandy, were alive and well in young Stylish. Ah yes, stylish indeed!

A Dark Cloud Lurking

So much for his choice of the politer words – a fine variety that would offend no-one and that would bring him nothing but praise, he being so very young and having mastered them all to perfection. But there was (alas) a dark cloud lurking on the horizon – a cloud that had always been there among his older brothers and sisters. Like the rest of their school-fellows they were quick to learn not only the holy prayers and the innocent hymns but a list of unacceptable swear-words in addition to the *feck* and *shite* words that children regularly used – a list that would never appear in any fairy-tale book. As with anything else that they did, they took their lead from the grown-ups living around them and the coarse language of the older farmers was sure to amuse them and bring tears of laughter to their eyes.

A Gap In Their Lives

Most days saw Darkie, Little Nell, Stylish – also his younger brother, Sammy-Joe – back home from school as early as mid-afternoon when they would join up with the three younger ones. For an hour or two they had a short gap in their lives with nothing left to do and a possibility of boredom settling in.

An hour later they'd be sitting down in front of Dowager and presenting her with their school copybooks and the homework exercises set by Dang-the-skin-of-it and giving her the news of the day – especially who had his little arse thrashed by Big Screech for nothing else other than stupidity.

For the next hour or so Dowager and Blue-eyed Jack (with Handsome Johnnie giving a hand now and then) were abroad in the cowshed, milking their seven cows. It was a blessed relief for the children to have this bit of time to themselves in between the drudgery of their school day and before their noisy pens started scribbling across their copybooks to the satisfaction of their mother.

They Raced Across the Flagstones

They threw their bag of books on the table and raced out over the flagstones in a rushing heap of arms and legs with Little Dan struggling along behind his bigger brothers and sisters. They went scampering up the Open Road and across the Easy Stile towards Red Scissors' Well.

Ahead of them in Free-and-Easy's field was a familiar sight – a little old man with bandy legs and a rolling stroll as though he were a sailor fresh home from the sea. When he saw them running towards him he stopped on the top of the slope. Behind his head lay Fort Dangerous and his shadow stood out like a halo against the backdrop of the blue sky. He was like Jesus in the children's Holy Book – standing there, as though he was about to start preaching his own particular sermon to his little flock. But the sermons of Jesus were far different from the sermon that this limb-of-the-devil was about to start preaching.

Jack Fart

The name of this rogue was Jack Fart. He was the son of Tom-the-Gosling and Roll-of-Steam and the children were full of joy as soon as they laid eyes on him. You'd think they were a pile of springtime lambs the way they went dancing round the field. They sat down and prepared themselves for the entertainment to begin and to hear the sound of his latest filthy farts and smell the perfume out of him.

They began chanting and clapping their hands: 'Coom on, Jack – fart for us! Fart, Jack, fart! Please, Jack! Let's hear yeer farts.'

He held up his hands and commanded their silence. This ritual between him and the children had gone on for the past few weeks – since the day he came home from the Roaring Town Hospital after the operation on his bowels. Those old gossips (the Weeping Mollys) had spread the rumour that Doctor Glasses had given him far too many tablets and lozenges for the recovery of his bowels. What on earth was the good doctor thinking of (they said)?

The Man-of-the-hour

The old schemester was now the man-of-the-hour and proved himself to be a born comedian, worthy of the Dublin stage. With his wild eyes bulging out of his head he began to look round him sheepishly as though he'd forgotten his pocket-watch and didn't know where it was. This (he knew) was a fine start and would keep the little devils enchanted and as frustrated as hell.

He threw his head sharply to the right. Then he threw it sharply to the left like a cockerel on the lookout for a spare hen. He leaned forward and stared straight into the three younger one's eyes and rattled his boots on the grass.

His work had begun. He raised his left leg slowly into the air. Then, putting his hand to his ear and cocking his head as though expecting the roar of a tractor from the far side of the hill, he cried out:

'Listen! Listen!'

'The cat's pissing!' the children roared back, rhyming their *pissen* with his *listen* and they all laughed heartily.

It was time for another breath-taking pause.

Then he whispered the same words again, but ever so quietly and ever so slowly – drawing them out as if to mesmerise them.

'Listen! Listen!'

'The cat's pissin'!' whispered the children again, mimicking his quietness and putting their own hands to their ears.

From His Rumbling Stomach

From his rumbling stomach Jack Fart then produced the finest variety of farts that Rookery Rally had ever heard tell of. He started off with a series of fluffy little ones coming out of his stinking arse like a purring kitten. This was followed up by the exultant children giggling and clapping till their hands were sore. It must have awakened the sleepy leprechauns inside in the nearby fort.

The man was in his element. He held the legs of his trousers with his forefingers and thumbs like a dainty housemaid. Then he gave his legs a good shake to let out the stinking air.

Once more he beckoned silence. The scene was set for his next bout of amusement – as amazing as any act performed by the man balancing the telegraph-pole on his chin at the Daffy-Duck Circus. It involved an even better series of squeaky farts, teased out sporadically, with unbelievable gaps of silence in between and sounding like little mice playing hide-and-seek in the chimney-breast. This part of the performance was greeted with tremendously loud applause all over again.

'Fair play to you, Jack! Fair play to you again and again!'

Him and his famous farts was the best bit of sport they'd had the privilege of enjoying since the day Zippity and Punch set Old Hayload's load of hay (his hat and arse) on fire above at Sheep's Cross.

The great entertainer finally turned sideways into what he called his *thunder pose*. He dragged the toe of his boot gently towards the back of his knee. See him there – frozen in time and space as though he was a Thinking Statue or an Ancient Athlete about to throw his discus. The children knew what to expect when they saw his elbow reach up to his forehead and his forehead reach down to his elbow and his leg reach up to the sky.

In recent months they were often seen kneeling at either end of Old Sam's disused drainpipe below in his haggart – blowing their tuba-like noises to one another through the length of the drainpipe and listening to their homemade echo. That was nothing compared to what was about to follow. Jack Fart let fly such a steaming volley of long-drawn-out windy thunder from the depths of his arse that the ditches nearly fell down.

'Cripes, byze! that was a good one!'

It shook the tears of laughter from the children's eyes and Darkie and Little Nell crossed their knees to prevent themselves wetting their knickers.

The children ran back down the hill, the wild man's ringing laughter ('Ah-ha, mee byze, but that was *indeed* a good one!') echoing after them all the way down to the Easy Stile. He had given them a sermon-and-a-half and they couldn't wait to run in the half-door and tell Dowager the merry news of their memorable escapade ('We have seen Jack Fart! We have heard his farts!') before the older ones got on with the serious business of completing their school-lessons.

The good humour created by the old rascal was followed by a bout of coarseness from Warbling Will and Lofty, each of whom, whilst they were all feasting on a hefty feed of spuds and onions, thought it high time to add a bit of their own impromptu amusement to all the fun and games and let rip a few of their own stinking farts whilst they were still sitting at the table.

'Put them out! Put them out!' said Dowager good-naturedly as she continued to peel a spud or two on her upturned fork for her three little ones. Then the whole household took a fit of laughing at the big lads' impolite interruption and went on munching their cabbage and spuds and drinking their mugs of milk as though nothing ungentlemanly had happened.

On The Upturned Ass-and-car

On the upturned ass-and-car you'd sometimes hear the ladylike chorus of Darkie and Little Nell singing to their little sister, Deelyah:

> *'Oh mee britches full of stitches,*
> *Oh mee britches buttoned on*
> *Oh mee britches full of stitches,*
> *Tell the ladies hurry on!'*

This had a few indicative words in it that bordered on the rude side but were nothing to get alarmed at. It was abroad in the fields that you'd hear the ruder songs when Blue-eyed Jack, Warbling Will and Lofty were hard at work on the land and singing their lungs out so as to make the day pass quickly. Maybe Warbling Will would entertain his brothers with his coarsely-spun song: *The butcher's wife pulled out her knife and cut off his taggledyowney.* Maybe Lofty would delight his brothers with his studied version of *If ye piss against the wind, ye'll surely wet yeer britches-oh.*

In the evening, when all the work was done and the door was barred for the night, the whole family (the girls included) might sit round the Welcoming Room's blazing fire and, before handing out the rosary-beads for the night-prayers, entertain the four walls with a few verses of an old hand-me-down song, which (after a long pause) ended each verse with the words *cold, cold arses*, at which they'd all raise a tremendous shout. That, however, was as far as coarse language ever went and it was part of the fun that made most days pass along merrily.

Stylish Had A Mind Of His Own

Unlike the rest of the children Stylish had a mind of his own and, young though he was, he could swear like a trooper, with a tongue on him as well-practised as any of the adults. His swearing skills started when he was seven, on the morning when Dowager's older brother (that wily old devil, Gooseberry-the-Pony) set the fierce sow loose across the yard in the hope that she might tear the britches off of the young fellow. Not only did Stylish wet his britches in sheer terror but, in his anger and to the amazement of Dowager, he also let rip a volley of unheard-of filthy language that lit up the yard. You should see the way old Gooseberry roared with laughter – something that made matters a good deal worse. For the child's filthy expletives continued to fill the yard, frightening the ducks and hens out of their lives so that they ran out passed the ass-and-car and flew out over the haggart singletree.

Worse was to follow when Stylish, realising the power of his cursing and how it had caused old Goosberry to laugh so much, went on swearing and cursing for all he was worth – especially where he felt the untold freedom of the open spaces in the Bluebutton Field and his filthy curses could be heard echoing as far away as Corcoran's Well. Dowager felt helpless and threw her hands up in the air. What would be her shame and embarrassment if the delicate ears of Lady Elegance or those of the devout Father Laudable ever got to hear such unimaginable swearing: they would die of heart-failure there and then.

Quite The Little Entertainer

From that day forth Stylish became quite the little entertainer, forever apt at embroidering and embellishing the more unedifying songs in Rookery Rally's repertoire. Now and then he'd walk the road with Hammer-the-Smith when that serpent-of-a-man was driving home his cows to be milked of an evening. At the drop-of-a-hat the little demon was soon singing the smith's most ribald verses to the merry passersby on their way to the forge or the creamery – to such an extent that they'd forget where they were going and even why they were doing it: they simply couldn't get enough of the little whippersnapper's attempts at acting the little man. Before the year was out he had become renowned for singing by far the filthiest of all Hammer-the-Smith's songs:

> *'a-down by the glenside I spied an old woman,*
> *a-pissing, a-shitting, she ne'er saw me coming,*
> *I listened a while to the song she was hummimg,*
> *Glory-o, Glory-o to the Bold Fenian Men.'*

It was an unbelievably crass derivation of a praiseworthy (almost sacred) Fenian song that was well-known and loved by everyone. Oh, the shame of it – it almost brought the world to its knees and left Dowager and Handsome Johnnie in the most dreadful state-of-mind for the well-being of their son's immortal soul.

Dowager Was Not Amused

When she found out the source of Stylish's appalling language, Dowager was forced to swear a mighty curse of her own: 'Hymph, that old ashy-arse, Hammer-the-Smith – even if he was shitting gold abroad in the field, you'd not catch me near him.' And she blessed herself and offered up three Hail Marys to the mother of God. For she was convinced that the wretched fellow was bent on delivering her son to the gates of hell with all his filthy talk. From that day forth she increased her fervour for the well-being of Stylish – to such an extent that she kept him praying on his raw knees for half the evening. But though she threatened to whip his hide with the yardbrush if he didn't control his gob (and he did indeed soften his swearing for a while) he was not yet entirely cured of his dirty talk and he kept back a few savage curses that he might need to use – that is until a sad day would come (and it did come, sooner than expected) when he'd have one or two more crucial things than bad language to occupy his mind.

Lord Elegance

It was a breezy morning in October when Lord Elegance had the breakfast eaten and, armed with his cane and gun and with his two dogs panting at his heels, came striding up the road. The children saw him hurrying their way from below at John's Gate. He was wearing his plus-fours just like his father, Lord Plus-Fours, and before that his grandfather, Lord Manners, used to do. He had the deerstalker hat sitting jauntily on his poll. You would think it was his own father was in it (thought Handsome Johnnie to himself).

He came to a halt at the flagstones over the yard stream.

'Good day to you, my good woman.'

'Good day to yeerself, yer honour.'

'May The devil shit in the ould madman's britches,' murmured Stylish. He still hadn't forgotten how to recall the mannerisms of his latest teacher, Hammer-the-Smith.

'Tell me, Mrs. Spallidagh, have you seen any birds flying this way today – maybe a few of my fine fat pheasants or a partridge or two for the pot?'

With her little finger cocked to her jaw, as though deep in thought, she pointed towards Stylish and indicated that her little son had come running in this very minute with the news that a dozen fine pheasants had been flying out over Old Stroller's haggart. May God forgive her, this was nothing but a damned lie. For, like the rest of her neighbours, she had no time whatever for this pompous old goat-of-a-man – though his wife, Lady Elegance, was loved by one and all.

The Ashy-arsed Ould Hangman

This was the chance for the verbal abuses to roll once more out of Stylish's mouth: 'Why, the ashy-arsed ould hangman,' he whispered – again imitating the words of Hammer-the-Smith as he stood behind Dowager's skirts and watched the lord and his dogs go back down the road in the false direction of Old Stroller's haggart. The old fool (thought Dowager) would be a long time shooting for his dinner in that hideaway.

Stylish made a dash out past the flagstones, shouting, 'Go and piss on yeer dogs, yuh ould fecker!' – but not until Lord Elegance was well out of earshot to hear such strong language.

When she heard her son cursing so profanely all over again, Dowager made a rapid sign-of-the-cross on her chest to avoid the presence of the devil. In spite of all her prayers and her weekly novenas for the soul of Stylish she began to wonder was it for hell or was it for heaven that she'd been raising him. She lept across the henhouse singletree and ran down the haggart where she prepared herself a sally-switch with which to redden her son's legs for him. Knowing when it was advisable to play the innocent repentant, the cunning little fox followed her round the back of the dung-heap – all the time dragging and clawing at her apron (what an actor!) and begging her not to kill him outright but to show him mercy. And such was the warm heart in his mother's chest that she took a fit of laughing before crossing the haggart-singletree hand-in-hand with the son she loved so well. She kept on shaking her head for, in spite of everything, she had to admire the bravery of the little upstart in putting his heart and soul into cursing the pompous old goat-of-a-man. And she thought to herself, 'What a cocky little shapester this child of mine is turning out to be!'

Then she had a second thought – a dreadful one. If this was the way he was learning to curse and swear, what must Dang-the-skin-of-it have been doing inside the school doors these past two years with a boy of such tender years as Stylish (he wasn't yet eight). What on earth could the schoolmaster do – what indeed, only whale the little arse off of him. And once more she took a fit of good-natured laughing when she pictured the prospective howls of Stylish holding onto his gable-end and the astonished look on his princely young face as the master gave him the medicine. Smiling to herself, she led him in across the yard – in passed the ducks and geese that were following her back from the haggart (you'd think they never got a bite to eat) and in through the half-door.

Airs-and-Graces

Airs-and-Graces was the son of Briary and Ruffles. He was a fine poacher and he lived inside in The Roaring Town. With his shy young son (*Boon*) he spent many a night catching rabbits above in the Valley-of-the-Black-Cattle. He was a hefty man with an imperious look about him – a bit like Lord Elegance (if you didn't know him). Apart from that he was always a jovial visitor, whom Dowager loved to see coming in the half-door for he liked nothing better than good company – especially the company of little children like Deelyah, Tiny Jim and Little Dan. And whenever he came calling, he would dig out handfuls of shiny coins from his pocket so that they could go to the shop and buy peggy's-leg sweets and (he said) rot their fine teeth for themselves.

When the October evenings were darkening a good bit earlier than before, Boon and himself were seen passing by and heading into the gathering mists. They both preferred the open spaces up around Saddle Wood and Lisnagorna where dwelt the finest of rabbits. No, not for Airs-and-Graces the cosy fireside chat at home or the big game-of-cards in the town's drinking-shops where he'd only lose all his hard-earned pennies. See him and Boon pressing their way out passed Sheep's Cross and into the Hills-of-the-Past, the lights from their guiding bike-lamps streaming on ahead of them.

The First Misty Shapes

It wasn't long before the two-of-them saw the first misty shapes of the rabbits and they busily nibbling on the moist grasses – waiting (shiver the thought) for Man to come and greet them with Sergeant Death, did they but know it.

Silently the poachers advanced on the rabbits.

Rabbits, rabbits everywhere – rabbits that Airs-and-Graces would sell next day by the pound-weight to the greedy shopkeepers in town. The price for them would keep his wife well-fed and trim and would buy her from Fanny Farthingale's Shop a posh fur-coat to put on her back when she was attending Sunday Mass. Nothing else would do him for she was the prettiest woman in the Roaring Town.

And now – thank God for the full moon that was lighting up his rabbits. He steadied his powerful flash-lamp in their direction, its brilliant light covering the breadth of the hill. The poor little innocents cowered in front of the fierce dazzle – frozen in fear, their spirits already dead inside them. There followed the quick chopping stroke-of-the-hand on the back of their necks – a death, however, that was far quicker than the one the fierce little weasel would have delivered for he'd have pierced their throats and drank the blood from them.

Dowager Ran Out to Meet Them

It was shortly after dawn when the two tired poachers came stamping down the hill, their billycans-of-tea empty and their doorstep sandwiches resting in their stomachs. Dowager thought she could hear them and she lept to her feet from where she'd been tending her fire. She looked out the window and saw the faint glimmer of their bike-lamps splashing on the road ahead of them.

She put on Handsome Johnnie's topcoat and ran out into the roadway. She gave a little yelp of delight when she saw that the bikes were fully laden with fine big rabbits and they dangling down dead and dismally from the poachers' handlebars. She knew there would now be the gift-of-a-rabbit for her, since her younger sister, Winnie-Anne, was the pretty woman married to Airs-and-Graces and had been for these last twenty years.

Brusque and brisk was the talk that followed ('Coom in and sit down by the fire.') and without another word Airs-and-Graces entered the Welcoming Room and hung three fine rabbits on the nails behind the door. Boon (like any quiet young man) was much too shy to impose himself on the house and he cycled on home into the arms of his doting mother. She'd be waiting for him and to hear his good news.

The children heard the sound of Airs-and-Grace's boots and they ran out from their beds and stood around him. They gazed up into his face, wondering from what far-off land-of-mystery he had been journeying this time. Before he sat down he handed them each their share of shiny money and gave Dowager the makings of a walking-stick so that she could chastise her cows when their shitty tails swished against her jaw while she was milking.

Everyone now sat round the fire – even the ailing Handsome Johnnie, still mindful of his previous quarrel with Darkie. With the corner of her skirts Dowager lifted the kettle off of the crane and she made Airs-and-Graces his mug-of-tea and handed it to him. He gulped it down – strong tea, the way he liked it.

She took out the bread from the burner and tapped it on the base to see if it was done. She took it up to the half-door to cool and then she cut huge skelps off of it and buttered it thickly – again, just the way he liked it. The poacher's eyes were soon sparkling with merriment as he dug into his little feast, swilling down the hot tea (better than soup, he said) and wolfing down gobfuls of the bread-and-butter. As if that wasn't enough the good woman gave him a slice of apple-batter an inch-and-a-half thick (the luxury of it – it had always been his fancy) and with the children's eyes steadfastly on him this little treat scarcely touched the inside of his jaws before he swallowed it down in a single gulp. Better than Christmas cake, said the merry old soul.

At last the table was almost bereft of food. The children had been standing quietly all that time. They knew their place and they knew their manners in front of such an important visitor. With a nod and a wink from

Handsome Johnnie they rushed up to the table, banging their knives and forks and pouncing on the carcass of the apple-batter. There followed five minutes of absolute silence before their father saw them licking their plates clean. He smiled to himself. As a child, he had been the very same as them. He could see that they were as healthy as dogs.

It was getting on for mid-morning and it was time for Airs-and-Graces to hurry home to bed. Before he left, there was the customary request from the children. He'd have to turn in to the fire and give them (especially the three little ones) the story they all liked best – the one about the *King of The Rabbits*, a great big ghostly creature that ran all round Ireland but was now dead.

'And did ye yeerself ever see him?' said Dowager with a wink.

There followed an unbearable pause as the wily old fellow puffed on his pipe in an effort to keep it alive. 'No,' said he, 'but mee father did when he was coming home drunk from the drinking-shop.'

This was followed by another knowing wink – this time from Handsome Johnnie.

And when the old poacher had finished his tale (the music in his voice, pausing now and then and every bit as good as Old Stroller) the children clapped and clapped. And then they ran off out to their secret hideout behind the ass-and-car. At which their old friend hopped up on his bike, his pockets now empty of shiny money, and he raced down the hillside to get home to his pretty wife, Winnie-Anne.

A Fine Sunday Morning

It was next Sunday morning – and a fine day indeed – when the Spallidaghs heard the rattling of a bike's mudguard and the jingling of a bell coming into the yard. The young ones ran out to see who was in it. It was none other than the mighty poacher himself – as if he'd never left them. The old charmer would be sure to leave them yet another handful of coins with which to buy their sugary sweets again and blacken their fine teeth.

Strapped on the back of his saddle he had brought a cumbersome-looking box and inside it there were three cages, each with a ferret the size of ten weasels. One was coloured a seaweed brown, another was yellow-and-cream and one was snow-white. He took them out of his box and held them to his chest. The children were captivated one and all. Oh, how lovely, how soft and furry the ferrets looked.

A few weeks previously Blue-eyed Jack had come home empty-handed from a rabbit hunt. He had lost Handsome Johnnie's one and only ferret (*Beauty*) as she lay entranced inside in a burrow whilst eating her way through the head of a young rabbit. She had been so engrossed in her feast that she'd forgotten her way out of the burrow. He could have kicked himself that he hadn't a second ferret on hand with him – one with a jingly bell round its throat – to go in and trace the whereabouts of Beauty. On his sad return home Dowager tried to comfort him and the other children, saying that *The*

King of The Fairies had found his way into the burrow and had killed the poor forlorn Beauty (to put her out of her misery) and had whisked her down the long tunnel that led to *Never-Never-Land*, from where she'd come back one day – born anew. And so, it was time for the Spallidaghs to get themselves a new ferret.

Forever Running Ferret Races

Airs-and-Graces was forever running ferret-races with his ferrets all over north Tipperary. Back home he had a dozen of the little charmers sitting coyly in their cages and as many painted drainpipes stored up for the races – drainpipes that he'd lay side-by-side in long lines when the time came for his ferret-races to take place. After collecting in the betting money at the start of each race he'd invite a dozen men to come out from the onlookers and open up the cages to start the race. Out would fly the eager ferrets, all racing like hell through the length of the drainpipes.

This Sunday there were no races to be run, the reason (he said) why he was standing at the half-door with his ferrets clutched to his coat. If Blue-eyed Jack had only known it, the old schemer was offering him the choice of one of these three ferrets only because of their unreliability at the end of every godforsaken ferret-race. These three devils were forever rambling off into the crowd amid the screams and shrieks of the young women. You'd think the damned ferrets were about to run up their legs and get into their knickers!

Dowager Chose the Yellow One

Dowager was entranced by the lovely ferrets. She chose *Honey,* the yellow-and-cream one.

'A good choice, she'll glow in the dark,' laughed Airs-and-Graces and he dropped the little creature into the cage in front of the dresser. Dowager gave the poacher a mug or two of her strong tea and the sweat was soon seen hopping off of his forehead from the heat of it.

His job was completed and he put on his cap and took the holy-water from the font at the door. He made a run at his bike and hopped up on it in his haste to get home to his dear wife and tell her the glad news.

The children hurried out after him to the flagstones and they waved him off, once more to the merry sound of the rattling mudguard and jingling old bell. They saw him tearing down towards Old Sam's Stile at a truly breakneck speed – in spite of the wobbledy old boxes and the two extremely frightened ferrets that he was carrying home with him, waiting for some other poor scholar to take them off of his hands.

Lofty

It was a week later. There was no school on Saturday but Dowager rose up early as usual and was out at the ash-pit emptying her pisspot even before the first blackbird had sung its song and while the lazy cockerel was still dozing in the hen-house. Together with the ever-ailing Handsome Johnnie, who was gamely trying to do a bit of work now and then, she placed herself on her green three-legged milking stool in the cow-shed. Soon she was whaling into the work of milking her seven cows. She was singing unmusically to herself (she knew all the words, but hadn't a stem of melody in her head) as she filled the bucket with the warm milk.

Her son, Lofty, had been dreaming of taking the new ferret out the hill to greet the rabbits and had asked Blue-eyed Jack for the loan of it. And this morning he trudged back home, weary but exhilarated, with a stickful of rabbits on his brush-handle. Beaming, he hung them on the back of the green door where the white enamel bucket of spring-well water sat on the soogan chair next to the axe. The blood from the rabbits ran down silently and made a ruby-red pool on the floor outside the room in which Dowager's sick daughter (*Deelyah*) would one day meet her death. The children gave the rabbits but scant appraisal, for (though young) they were well-accustomed to seeing animals meeting their death like these dead rabbits had done. They had seen their mother grasping a goose between her knees and sawing away at the little blood vessel at the back of its neck till it swooned away and died. In earlier days they had seen the death of the pig from the long black-handled knife skilfully wielded by their father abroad in the yard – himself and half-a-dozen other men holding down the serpent-of-a-pig who wouldn't die for them. The death of the hen and the drake too – all of these were as well-known to them as the bread on their table.

He Put the Ferret Back into The Cage

Dowager stood looking at the new rabbits. She glowed at the sight of them. Their pelts would make her a tidy sum of sixpences. She got busy with stuffed paper and the odd spud and her needle and thread to repair the damage that had been done here and there by their noble new ferret. Lofty put the ferret back into the cage in front of the dresser and he went out the door and headed for the pig-house gap to make his poolie on the ash-pit. He then set off up towards The Valley-of-the-Black-Cattle in search of the ash-tree that he'd seen an hour ago for the makings of a new hurleystick.

No-one Will Ever Forget That Year

No one will ever forget that year. It was the year that Stylish was ten. Nor will they forget that month or that very day. It was a Sunday morning and the family had all travelled to Mass in Copperstone Hollow – their mother firing four of them in behind her into the ass-and-car. Handsome Johnnie took another load of them in the horse-and-cart – in spite of the fact that he wasn't feeling too frisky. The liver disease, which was to shorten his life and carry him off to the Beyond, was already doing him more than enough mischief. Sad to say, he spent solitary hours these days in his shed in the grove, pining for the days of his lost youth and his six brothers and little Kate, who had all gone to seek riches at the far side of the map.

After Mass

After Mass Dowager and Handsome Johnnie drove the children back to the Welcoming Room and soon the fire was blazing away. The good woman was fanning it with her sweet-gallon lid and the kettle was singing on the crook. She cut up the soda-cake for the children and she gave them each a few black puddings and some eggs that Moll-the-Shuffler had exchanged with her. Then with Handsome Johnnie she went to the cowshed and took the chains from off of the seven cows that had been munching their hay contentedly there. The two of them strolled down to the Bull-Paddock with their cows, as happy as the day was long. They'd collect some mushrooms and a few cobnuts for themselves. They'd be back in half-an-hour.

Constant Mischief

Stylish (the devil-that-was-in-him) continued to be an arch source of mischief for he had far too much imagination, – be it in the praying, counting, swearing or telling his lying tales to the rest of them. For a child of ten years (said Handsome Johnnie) he was indeed a ripe young apple.

Some of the older children were at the front-table, patiently stacking up a house of cards while others were playing *Beggar-mee-neighbour* near the roaring fire. More of them were trying to wind up the gramophone to put on a record or two from the bacon-box in the absence of their mother and father.

Stylish hoisted himself up onto the back table where Handsome Johnnie kept his new and still-unused tobacco-pipe. He filled the bowl of the pipe with tobacco from the tin. He took a kindled twig from the fire and tried (*puff-puff-puff!*) to fire up the smoke and inhale the sweet juices of the tobacco by drawing in his cheeks the same way his father did in order to keep the flame going.

Honey, The New Ferret

The rest of the children were highly amused at the antics of Stylish as he began to parade up and down the floor, imitating the gimp of Handsome Johnnie, the father he so much admired. But from all the effort at puffing on the tobacco-pipe all he succeeded in doing was to sicken his stomach and for once in his life this put him in a fierce bad humour. Honey-the-ferret was similarly just as ill at ease in her new home and was restlessly marching up and down inside in her trapped cage. She could see the dead rabbits and their ruby blood on the back of the door and she was anxious to get out of the cage and get a taste of their blood.

Stylish put back the tobacco-pipe and leant down towards the cage. Maybe it was the suddenness of his movements that made the ferret feel alarm rather than the kinship, which she had felt towards Stylish and the others the previous week when she'd first arrived.

The Wild Eye Of Stylish

Stylish cast a wild eye at the ferret. He tried to daze it into a softer nature by the continuance of his stare. The ferret was having none of it. It looked back at him out through the bars. Stylish, still the mimic of his elders, reached back to the tobacco-tin. Soothing the ferret with the soft talk that he would often pour into his father's ass, he playfully lifted the ferret out of the cage, holding it by the back of its delicate neck, the way you would a cat. All that time he kept admiring its beautiful coat and stroking the warm smoothness of its back. Then, still staring into its eyes (ah, the little heathen!) he opened his eyes even wider and gave the ferret what all knew as the *come-hither* stare or *the evil eye*. Then he spat the spitty tobacco-juice into the poor ferret's eyes.

What Made You Do It?

Stylish! Stylish! What on earth made you do it? Had you lost all sense of reason? Such a commotion you never did see as what followed. Honey turned herself into an army of cats, filling the Welcoming Room with her own fear and the rest of the children with terror. She was like a cornered rat in a henhouse and ran up the side of the dresser where she smashed to bits the already-broken-lipped jug of sour milk that had been left there for the baking of Dowager's bread. Up the partition with her next where she succeeded in smashing the household guardian (the revered Sacred Heart picture) from off of the wall. It was a miracle that the house didn't fall down from such a sacrilege.

Round and around in circles the dizzy children ran in as much of a panic as the poor ferret herself. Like a chicken without a head they tumbled over one another in their fearful attempts to hide in Dowager's bedroom or under the bed in the Big Cave Room behind the hob. They knew that any ferret worth its keep would attack the throat of its enemy and they fingered their own throats anxiously. The three girls held their skirts tightly round their knees the way they'd seen the older girls doing when the big lads from The Valley-of-the-Pig came down to play snowballs and hide 'n' seek with them in the wintertime and tried to lift up their skirts and get a look at their knickers.

Their Screams

By now the children's screams had outshone the antics of the ferret. Hearing their roars Dowager came steaming in across the yard, Handsome Johnnie stumbling along a few feet behind her with an armful of little logs. She ran in through the half-door, almost knocking it off of its hinges. Like any distracted mother, she saw at once the cause of the ructions: the discarded tobacco-tin: Handsome Johnnie's tobacco-pipe: the untold destruction done to her Welcoming Room by the frantic ferret. Recognising the angry boots of Dowager stamping towards in her direction, the hissing ferret retreated to the corner of the room.

'I'll chastise ye,' screamed Dowager.

With the yardbrush she made a rush at the ferret who ran in under the table to find a hiding-place and nurse her sore red eyes, which were streaming from the tobacco-spit.

Scraping Away With Her Brush

Beside herself with worry Dowager started scraping away with the yardbrush ('Coom out, blasht you! Coom out to hell!') at the ferret that was seething at her. Alas, she made too hasty a grab for the ferret and found herself holding it by the middle of its back. Enraged and terrified and her piss running down along Dowager's wrist, the terrified creature twisted round fiercely and snapped her teeth round the outraged Dowager's finger, clinging on to it for dear life. Like the badger when caught in a fight with wild dogs, she wouldn't let go till she heard Dowager's finger crack and crack again, exposing it to the bone and breaking it in two. Immediately the poor woman's crimson blood spattered down onto the floor. The children were shocked out of their natural lives and they screamed and screamed, seeing that the ferret was about to destroy their mother's hand – the hand that was needed for baking her apple-batters – the hand that was needed for sewing socks and making their new suits out of old overcoats when it was time for their First Holy Communions and their Confirmation with Bishop High-Hat.

Handsome Johnnie's Saving Hands

Poor trembling Dowager had lost all her former serenity. She had turned yellow and withered in the face from the pain and anger at it all. Handsome Johnnie came staggering in the half-door with the logs. He saw the bloody state of his dear wife and the ferret still trying to suck the blood out of her. He hadn't a moment to think. He dropped the logs and rushed to the fire where he grabbed the wire tongs. As though he were at war, he placed a blazing sod-of-turf up into the ferret's arse. The creature gave one last roar out of it and dislodged itself from Dowager's disfigured finger and fell to the ground where it lay unconscious:

'Throw her into the fire! Throw her into the fire!' the children yelled.

They could see their mother crying unashamedly, her tears rolling down her cheeks – something they had never seen before. For all his anger, Handsome Johnnie couldn't do it. Instead he took the ferret outside with the tongs and he threw her behind the hen-house on the dung-heap to die. That evening the ferret had disappeared.

'Risen into life like a bleddy phoenix,' said Lofty.

However, when Blue-eyed Jack and Warbling Will were taking the buckets to Old Sam's well for the water, they thought they saw a wily fox crossing the haggart with the devastated body of the ferret stuck to his teeth – another tasty morsel for himself and his family.

The Witch's Finger

From that day forth Dowager's little finger looked the very same as a question mark – all hooked round and crooked as the witch's fingers in one of the children's storybooks. the Mountainy Men's older children, as they chased their younger brothers and sisters down to school, prodding them on with their sticks so as not to be late, would stop for a second or two at the Spallidagh flagstones and ask to see the famed crooked finger of *Missus Spallidagh*. The news of it had spread up the mountainside as far as Mureeny – how a brave woman had gone to war with a ferret. No one else in Rookery Rally had a finger like it. Satisfied with what they saw, these big mountain lads then passed the news back up the road ('We have seen the finger! We have seen the finger!'). Dowager's wound had become a badge of pride and honour and her star rose higher by the hour among Rookery Rally's little folk.

The Children Were Thinking Of The Ferret

The late evening sun was going down now and the day was in ruins. There was a peculiar silence around the little thatched house after the children had picked up all the broken bits and pieces destroyed by the ferret. Doctor Glasses would come in the morning to see the damage done to their mother. Meanwhile, the iodine and rags were wrapped firmly around the broken finger.

The brothers and sisters sat abroad in the yard beside the ass-and-car, the older ones on top of the horse-and-cart. They were thinking of the ferret. They were thinking of their mother and her tears and her blood-spattered finger. Dowager and Handsome Johnnie brought out all the chairs into the yard. They called for more chairs from Moll-the-Shuffler. The children knew what this would mean.

'We will have to go to law,' said Handsome Johnnie. 'Yes, by the power of the bellows, we will have to go to law.'

The Children Sat On The Chairs

The children sat on the chairs and turned in to make a circle round the yard. The hens and the geese looked on bemusedly. Each child would now get their turn to speak the law.

After they each had had their say and had spoken truthfully (as any Christian child should do), Dowager brought Stylish out and placed him in the middle of the circle. He now had the final word to speak in his defence. But not a word did he speak. He was as guilty as hell and he knew it. And another thing – at the sight of his mother's broken finger he wanted to take his punishment – he wanted to be punished severely.

The Sentence Was Passed

Handsome Johnnie passed the sentence on his ten-year-old son. He brought out the leather razor-strap, wincing at the thought of what was to come. He loved Stylish a great deal – almost as much as his favourite (Sammy-Joe) and his dear wife, Dowager.

And what of herself – the mother that had always adored Stylish? Wasn't it out of his backside that the sun had always shone? And now, though she had been driven out of her mind with the pain – though she had cursed him for letting the ferret out of the cage and bringing ruin to her finger – she would have wished to be anywhere else on earth other than sitting on her damned chair at the half-door, hiding her finger from the others and waiting for the child's punishment to begin.

'Who is going to administer Justice?' said Dowager.
'Who is going to deliver the medicine?'
'Who is going to give Stylish the skelping?'

Not Handsome Johnnie. He was too sick with his liver these days to raise a hand to anyone and the temper that had once been his in his treatment of his beloved Darkie had fizzled away to nothing.

Blue-eyed Jack (wasn't he the lucky fellow) – even though he anguished much over his mother and her broken finger – had his own share of trouble. The back of his hand was covered with Doctor Glasses' bandages since the day of the pig-killing in Red Buckles' shed. It was his first time using the long-handled knife and the enraged animal would not lie down and die peacefully before his knife. It had pinned poor Jack's hand between itself and the boards of the cart, rubbing it back and forth against the rough wood of the cripple-board that was crusted with cement. Poor Blue-eyed Jack! He was fortunate indeed not to have lost his hand altogether and he'd be lucky if he could use it even to light a candle let alone stick a pig for at least another month (said the good doctor).

Warbling Will

Whom could the father appoint? All eyes were cast down into the yard for it wasn't a job anyone would relish. It had to be one of the older children. That left only Lofty and Warbling Will, neither of whom said a word. But Dowager recalled the recent misdemeanours of Warbling Will and how he had brought shame on the family with his scandalous bouts of lovemaking with

Come-and-give-me-a-test. It was a chance for the guilty wretch to make amends and redeem himself in her eyes.

She pointed the razor-strap at him. Like all good sons, Warbling Will loved his mother dearly. The sight of her broken finger and his own desire to restore his good name and help bring back a sense of order to the household gave him little choice. Besides, if he had any doubt, his mother's steadfast glare at him was spur enough for him to do what was right and proper.

Handsome Johnnie Handed Him The Strap

Handsome Johnnie handed him the razor-strap and led Stylish out to the flagstones as though it were a place of execution. There wasn't a trace of the ducks or hens – not even the old sow and her enemy, the gander. They had all run for cover behind the dung-heap.

'Do it!' whispered Dowager and she turned her head away.

There was a hush before Warbling Will proceeded to cut the razor-strap across the seat of Stylish's britches and into his legs. The other children closed their eyes in awe, never having seen the law administered like this.

Half-a-dozen times did the older boy belt the razor-strap into his younger brother. A chill had crossed into the yard. No sound – only the fierce music of the strap. The sky seemed to have turned from blue to black.

There wasn't a whinge, wriggle or whimper out of Stylish. He took his punishment like a man – at least in the beginning he did.

But then, in spite of himself and he being just ten-years-old, he could hold out no longer. And as he felt his legs burn from the lash, he gasped and he shivered. He sobbed and he snivelled. Poor child – there wasn't a place on earth where he could hide. At the sight of the blood trickling down their brother's legs the rest of the children turned their heads away and wept.

Dowager was never inclined to keep up for long the anger that she'd previously shown with Darkie and she got up from her chair and barked out her orders:

'That'll do! That'll do! Enough is enough!'

She ran across the yard and snatched the razor-strap out of her son's hand before he could do any more damage. Though the law was the law and it had to be administered, Handsome Johnnie was now too sickened to remain in the yard. He turned into the bedroom, shut the door and closed his eyes.

She Bathed His Legs

Dowager took Stylish by the arm and stood him in the middle of the stream. Gently she tended his wounded legs, wiping them clean. She wiped the tears from his face and held him to her chest. The other children took back the chairs silently into the house and the hens, ducks and geese came back into the yard from their hiding-place. Though Justice had been done and dealt with, little did any of them know that this would be for the last time.

Stylish was weak from crying and his legs almost went out from under him. Unsure what to do, he let go of his mother's hand. It felt as though he were in a dream – a horrible dream as he staggered across the yard.

He stumbled passed the cow-shed and out into the field so he could hide from his brothers and sisters – hide from the wretched world and disappear forever.

The happy little bird that had always been in his soul – his childish devil-may-care – had scattered to the winds and vanished and he hadn't a single swear-word or curse to explain how he felt. All he knew was there'd be no more charming strolls with Sammy-Joe across the fields – no more rousing adventures in Old Stroller's apple-orchards. He was now disengaged and solitary like a monk in his cell – an irreparably lonely and distant child. And there he lay – with only the odd rusty bawl of the ass and the bemused cattle looking at him from the shelter of the ditch – his new and unearthly companions. He sank down in the middle of the field and was soon fast asleep.

The Sunlight Had Dimmed

By now the sunlight had faded into a dusty lilac behind Corcoran's Well and the glitter of the moon was starting to peep out at him through the bushes.

He was getting frightened. The silence was eerie. The pain in his body and soul felt much worse.

The crows had long since gone home, making little or no noise – in view of the punishment they had seen dished out. It was as if, like the children, they were sick from the sight of it all.

From now on it was farewell to the sun. Farewell to childhood.

Hello to Anger. Hello to a New Man.

The jay-like mimicry of his walking and talking, which had made him imagine himself a small man like his bigger brothers, was replaced now by a fierce feeling: *'I am a man – if only a little man – and a man in my own right.'*

From that day forth none of his brothers and sisters – not even his mother and father – would ever know what had now begun to grow in the heart of the former merry-hearted Stylish. For after his leathering with the razor-strap he had indeed become a new person and would walk hereafter in his own secret ways.

Dowager Sent for Him

It was well into the night – passed his bedtime. It was the first time that he'd not be kneeling at the fireside with the others, saying his prayers and preparing for bed. There'd be no peace for Dowager till she went out looking for him.

She was thinking to herself: what must he be feeling? How lonely the house was when he wasn't in the room.

She went quietly out into the haggart and out to the stick at the field-fence.

'Stylish! Stylish,' she croaked. 'Where are you?

'Coom in, child. 'Coom in and have yeer tea and soda-cake with the rest of us.'

It wasn't long before she found him frightened and asleep in the middle of the field. The dew had long fallen around him. He was cold and he was wet and the sympathy ran out from her. She rustled his hair coaxingly and gave him her sorrowful look. He blinked a bleary eye at her and gave both herself and her broken finger a brave look back. It was (she thought) as though his heart had been broken by the razor-strap.

He was reluctant to come in – the way he had hurt her – the way she had hurt him.

She sat down beside him on the wet grass and the two of them stayed there for a long while – the only two people, it seemed, in all the world, reflecting on the pain and the hate and the sadness.

She stood him up and wrapped herself around him to provide him with warmth. Humming softly to herself, she combed his hair with her fingers and patted him on the back so as to ease the pain in him.

Together they walked in across the haggart, passing the hawthorn-tree where the little family of wren-birds had their home and were now sleeping the sleep of peace – a peace that none of his brothers or sisters would share with Stylish for many a day to come.

SEVEN

How Stylish Redeemed Himself

Some grow up early. Some grow up late. Stylish was one of the former. Whenever he stood around the table with the rest of his brothers and sisters, drinking his mug of milk and his plateful of champ with doses of raw onions, butter and milk scattered amongst the floury spuds, he was consumed with a self-conscious guilt as he looked at his mother peeling spuds for the three little ones with her injured finger bent into a question-mark from the way Honey-the-ferret had snapped it in two and she rolling her tongue around on her lower lip as she always did when she was concentrating. The sight of it never left his mind.

Unmerciful Anger

Though he felt this guilt and an aching sadness for her and knew that her finger would never have gotten crooked if he hadn't let the ferret out of its cage and spat tobacco-juice into its eye, nevertheless he couldn't help feeling an unspeakable anger against Warbling Will and the rest of the onlookers for the way they'd let him be skelped.

He realised that the Family Law had had to dish out some sort of punishment but he felt that the savage beating with the razor-strap had been far too cruel for a boy of his age – the absolute indignity of it – the way he had been forced to swivel and twist his body away from the strap so as to lessen the full force of Warbling Will's lashes – the look on his brothers' and sisters' faces, sitting on their goddamn useless chairs in the yard and listening to the strange echo of the strap doing its work again and again on the seat of his britches and legs.

No-one else knew how he felt. How could they? He couldn't tell them. And even if he could, he wanted to keep these feelings well-guarded to himself. Unless they were pure magicians they would never guess the depths of what lay inside him – his broken heart – his anger – his distain – and, yes, even his hatred.

The Household Law Must Change

One thing he knew for certain: the law that insisted on such a harsh punishment for causing not only his mother's pain but the agonising death of Honey-the-ferret would have to be changed. For the moment he would feign and pretend – he would hoodwink the others into thinking everything was right with him. Actor that he'd always been, the bigger children, like

Darkie and Little Nell, saw him stepping out the day after his torment and returning (or so they thought) to his usual own old self.

The little ones were far too young to notice any changes whatsoever in him. They were too busy playing with their marbles and skittles.

With Handsome Johnnie it was different. Unlike Dowager, he had always kept his private feelings to himself (men in Rookery Rally usually did) and now he thought he could see something missing in his son: the lad's ever-ready smile: his ever-ready cheekiness: the way he'd always been able to make the rest of the house laugh till they were silly in the face. Would this gift-of-a-smile ever come back to Stylish? Would Dowager ever again hear him singing his filthy rotten songs? Shameful as much of his posturing had been, Handsome Johnnie felt that life in the Spallidagh household had lost its magic – lost its happiness. Would life ever be the same? He hoped and prayed that it would.

A Year Or So Later

A few years later at a time when Handsome Johnnie was growing sicker by the day and when Blue-eyed Jack and Warbling Will were doing most of the farm-work (except for the trapping of rabbits, a task which their father wouldn't let go) there came a Saturday morning when Dowager asked the two of them to go to town and bring back a bit of mutton for the Sunday dinner. It was the day after she had cashed in the monthly creamery cheque from selling their milk.

Before they cycled off, they went looking for Stylish in the haggart. He was mooching around by himself. That was usually his way of passing his Saturdays.

When he saw them he looked anxious, wondering what was on their minds. Was it good. Was it bad? These days he never knew what to expect from any of the family.

Blue-eyed Jack spoke up first.

'Stylish, mee ould friend, it's a fine morning – indeed it is.'

'Now that ye're twelve and will soon be getting into yeer long britches, I keep asking meeself: what sort of work can a youngster like you do for two men like meeself and Warbling Will whilst we're in town?'

Ever since his argument with the razor-strap they had grown tired of seeing him straggling around on his own as though he were lord-of-the-manor and not one single stroke of work out of him except running to the well for the odd bucket of water. It seemed as though the madamy days of Darkie were back all over again and that wouldn't do.

It was Warbling Will's turn now to step forward, shaking his head and with his usual crafty smile on his face:

'Stylish,' said he, 'for the last few weeks ye've been giving us a pain in the ear – telling us ye're as good a man as any man walking the road, if only ye were given the chance to prove it.'

'Coom on, blasht you,' said he, 'let's see this so-called manliness ye're always talking about – let's see whether ye're man enough to scythe down an acre of corn before we coom home this evening.'

The Lesson With The Scythe

Blue-eyed Jack led Stylish out the field-gap and across to the Deer Field where there was an acre of corn to be cut. He took the scythe down from its hiding-place in the bushes. He unclasped the emery-board from the scythe's handle and gave the blade a long and studied sharpening, testing it with his thumb before clipping the board back on the handle. He did all this with scarcely a word, giving Stylish time to think and observe what would be expected of him.

He then showed him how to cut his corn – the way that Handsome Johnnie had shown himself: spread the legs wide apart to keep yeerself balanced and place yeer body at the precise angle to the scythe – don't rush headlong at the work but spare yeer energy and take up the start of yeer scythe-sweep ever so slowly, bending yeer knees low before adding a swift follow-through. It was a tremendous amount for Stylish to take in all at once.

He handed Stylish the scythe and made him repeat the same scything action as himself, all the time prompting him with words of encouragement. It was the best he could do for his young brother after all the suffering he'd had to endure. He was hoping that in his attempt to cut corn Stylish would show everyone how contrite he was and how he would try anything to make amends for the ruination of his mother's finger. Only then (thought Blue-eyed Jack) would there be anything like peace inside the four walls of the house.

Then himself and Warbling Will headed out the gap and sailed off into town on their bikes. When the day's shopping was done they'd have time to regale themselves with one or two pints of the black doctor stout in the Widda-Widda-Woman's drinking-shop. Hopefully their mother would never get to hear of it for they were only too well aware that they were still not too big for her to leather their arse with the leg-of-the-chair.

'Dammit – the cocky little upstart will never finish cutting his acre,' jeered Warbling Will. 'Doesn't he know it's a man's bleddy work and not for a school-child to go play-acting at it. Hymph, imagining the likes of him thinking he's a man like the two of us. Has the little fool lost all sense of direction?'

Thanks to their unaccustomed feed of booze in town, this sort of merry chatter went on and on for the rest of the morning and they were still at it as they cycled back home – that is until they had rounded their bikes passed Galloping Gret's fierce geese and even fiercer sow and were almost back at the flagstones. At this stage they'd have to be a good bit quieter and more orderly (the rascals) and pretend that the day's shopping had been nothing but an onerous ordeal.

Cursing Their Disbelief

Meanwhile, silently cursing their disbelief in him and angered like he'd once been angered the time Gooseberry-the-Pony set the sow on him and forced him to wet his britches, Stylish bowed to the challenge of the scythe and swept along the rows of corn with an almost vicious energy. This was the chance he'd been waiting for. The welts on his legs might have healed. The welts in his heart had not healed. All this hard work would go a long way to easing the terrible pain in him – the hidden hatred in him.

'What's an acre of corn to a little man like meeself?' he kept telling himself as he strode his way through the first few rows of corn.

'Have the simpletons lost all their memory – have they forgotten how our grandfather, Dandy, had nothing in his fist but a small sickle to do work as tough as this – the same old rusty sickle that's lying dead above the hob?' With tears of bitterness and unseen by anyone other than the *Cornfield Fairies* he went on whaling into the work. He was ready for anything.

The sun was soon high in the sky, turning the neighbouring fields and the surrounding hills into honeyed gold, warming the ditches, the corn and his own backbone. By three o'clock his limbs were aflame with the joy and the richness of his feelings. He had scythed down the entire acre and had started binding up the sheaves of corn with the binding belts of straw – the way he'd seen his father do.

He was stooking up the last few sheaves into their tents when his brothers returned across the field.

Oh, to see their astonishment! Oh, to see their two sets of eyes bulging out of their heads! A mere boy – now a year-and-a-half older than the lad that Warbling Will had skelped with the razor-strap – had finished the work that a stout-armed man would take a day to finish. Blue-eyed Jack could see that his young brother's legs were as weak as water – too weak for him to walk a step. The softness in him rose to the fore and he hoisted him up on his shoulders and brought him home.

Unable To Move A Muscle

Stylish lay in bed for three long days, unable to move a muscle. Dowager was beside herself with sadness as she wiped the holy-water into his thighs. She said it was a miracle if he'd ever rise out of the bed. What on earth were the two eejits thinking of – letting a lad like him go try and best them with this sort of nonsensical bravado? It had been a man's work and the pair of them knew it – only too well.

But there was something that she herself had yet to learn (only Stylish knew it) – that the thing that had spurred him to cut so much corn – the thing that had proved to him that he was as good as any man – was nothing other than *Anger* – sheer unadulterated anger. What else could it have been that'd make him scorn his brothers' disbelief – the brothers, who (like the rest of them) had allowed him to be skelped by Warbling Will? Would he ever forgive any of them? No, never.

The New Ferret

After his triumph in cutting his acre of corn Stylish next showed his feelings for the family by doing the last thing any of them would ever have expected. For, in spite of the sorry state of Dowager's finger, he surprised even Handsome Johnnie by bringing home yet another ferret from Airs-and-Graces. He also brought home a new cage to go with the ferret. Then he took out the old one and he set fire to it abroad in the haggart – a sign (said he) that in the past it had brought him nothing but bad luck.

After his battle with the scythe he felt he had proved to everyone that he was a proper little man. So, to shake the house up still further, he would now take a run at the hills and alarm the peace and quiet of the rabbits. Yes, himself and his ferret would chastise the life out of those damned rabbits and bring back platefuls of meat for the table, knowing how much they all loved the rabbit's flaky meat. He intended to show the pack of eejits how wrong they'd all been to destroy the goodness in him with the act of a thrashing.

Brandy

He named the new ferret *Brandy*. Unlike the recently-disgraced Honey, she would now prove to be a noble asset. Before he went to school each day – and again in the evening – he spent time patiently training her to listen to his commands and his whistles. He kept her well fed and watered with milk and bran-mash so that she'd remain trim and healthy and be more than ready to go with him for their first kill.

In spite of the wound to his mother's finger he trusted the little creature's sharp teeth to do their dirty work on the rabbits and not on himself. Before the week was out it became clear to his brothers and sisters that he had charmed the life out of her and that she had eyes only for him. What wasn't clear (alas) was the fact that since her arrival she had entirely replaced in his heart the affection he once felt for the rest of them.

Another Little Miracle

When all the Spallidagh children were still asleep in their dreamland and even Dowager and Handsome Johnnie were wiping the sleep from their eyes, Stylish was already wolfing down a few cuts of bread-and-jam and a hurried mug of milk.

Then he tucked Brandy nice and warmly inside his shirt, her nose peeping out. With half-a-dozen rabbit-hole nets on his shoulder and his father's wide-brimmed hat on his head (it'd come in handy later) he crept softly across the yard. There was a determined purpose to his step.

It was daybreak – the time he loved best. He was glad to escape from his brothers and sisters and leave behind him his sadness and the memory of their cruelty to him. The hills and the hunt would give him the peace that he needed and take away from him all his cares and woes – at least for the moment. Every rabbit would be out and about, feeding and stretching their hind legs. He'd hunt them back into their burrows and with the help of his noble ferret he'd bring back as many rabbits as he could carry on his stick – more than enough to feed the entire family.

He strode on passed Shy Dennis's Shack, listening to the early birds playing their hide-and-seek games in the wiry hedgerows and beckoning him on. The clouds were already breaking up and letting in bits of the captive sunlight and he used his eyes and his ears the way he'd learnt from Handsome Johnnie – a father who had a deep affinity with Nature and had always yearned for the hills and the rippling sound of the river's song. He worked his way up towards the forge above Sheep's Cross and skirted the side of Bog Road, moving on in the direction of Lisnagorna and leaving behind him the grey-weathered farm-buildings for the churchlike quiet of the deserted hills. At last he penetrated the pine-forest and walked silently through its aisles before finally coming out at the Valley-of-the-Black-Cattle – the kingdom (his father once told him) of all the world's rabbits.

Tiptoe Tiptoe

This was the time for an anxious young hunter to be furtive and as quiet as the hills. It was tiptoe, tiptoe from now on with only the sound of Growl River nearby. He made a quick study of the slope of the ground and the nearby ditches. He kept himself downwind and studied the sun and the shadow – all of which might inform the rabbits that he was on his way to kill them. And then he saw the rabbits and his nerves tautened as all the zeal of an olden-day hunter arose in him. There was more than a dozen of them, sitting around motionless, wrapped up in their animal heaven and lifting their heads from time to time, sniffing at the scent on the breeze.

He remembered Handsome Johnnie telling him which burrows were linked to one another and as quietly as a hermit he crawled along the far side of the nearest ditch where he knew he would be shielded and hidden from the rabbits. Then he counted the rabbit-holes. There were six in all. He covered each of them with his nets to ensure there'd be no way for a rabbit to bolt and escape in that direction. It was time to go hunt and he coughed and clapped his hands loudly.

From all over the field the rabbits made a hysterical rush for the safety of their burrows, stumbling into each other in their haste to get home and the black crows screeched and flew far away. The field was now bare and not a rabbit to be heard or seen – nothing only the silence of the hillside.

A Bloodthirsty Venue

Stylish took Brandy from inside his shirt and whispered to her as he stroked her fur. Then he let her loose. She quickly found a burrow and worked her way into it – into what he hoped would be a bloodthirsty venue with a cowering rabbit. Seconds later he heard the excited rumble beneath the ground, the earth coming alive with the thumping feet of rabbits fiercely signalling to one another. He felt that same burst of energy rising up in him that he'd felt the day he cut his corn. He could picture a rabbit cornered by Brandy, its eyes glazed, its feet galvanised with fear at this sudden confrontation with Death. Where could the poor rabbit run to? Where else – only to the ditch-side opposite to where it had just been feeding – the side where he was now kneeling and ready to snatch each frightened rabbit into his father's outstretched hat. And then the first rabbit came crashing out into his net only to find itself inescapably trapped and imprisoned.

There followed the high-pitched squeals and the kicking feet as he disentangled one rabbit after another from the nets and with a swift chop of his fist dislocated their necks. There was not so much as a death-rattle out of them. He picked up each rabbit and with his father's knife he hamstrung their back legs, sticking one leg in through the hole in the other. He loaded his six rabbits onto his stick and threw the stick over his shoulder.

Ah-ha, mee byze, what fine bowls of soup we'll have tomorrow and for days and days to follow, said he to himself. It'll make the bleddy eejits at home sit up and think – make them feel as guilty as hell for the shameful way they allowed me to be trashed – as though I were nothing but a bleddy dog.

The Very Scourge Of Rabbits

He wound his way triumphantly down the hillside, tearing back to humdrum reality. He felt he had proved himself a man a second time – proved himself to be the very scourge of rabbits. He was almost home when he had a thought and called in on Moll-the-Shuffler to let her choose one of the rabbits for herself. She had always been a good friend to Dowager. The grateful look on the woman's face was hard to describe. Then he dashed the rest of the way home to show off his trophies.

Dowager stopped feeding her hens and ran across the yard to greet the happy hunter with his kill and his ferret. Bedraggled and leg-weary he stood there, looking at her.

Oh, what joy! Such fine rabbits!

My hero! My hero!' she laughed as she examined the rabbits – the joyful smiles pouring out of her. After they had eaten enough themselves, the rest of the rabbits would sell well down at the shop and make them a tidy sum of money for future days.

The Little Ones

The three little ones had been running races out in the Bluebutton Field but as soon as they heard all the fuss and excitement, they ran in across the haggart to see Stylish and their mother and the fine rabbits dangling down on their brother's stick. Awestruck, they stood there and looked up into the dead rabbits' eyes that glistened at them like jade buttons. Their joy, however, was somehow marred by the sadness they felt for the miserable death of these fear-filled rabbits – rabbits that'd no longer be running around in the hills now that Brandy and Stylish had killed them.

Stylish was tired and footsore and hadn't time to talk to them. He was parched with the thirst and went in the half-door to get himself a mug-of-water from the bucket. Ice cold, it tasted good – just what he needed. He drank it down fast and dipped his mug in for another mouthful. His mother stood there, all the time watching and studying him. He was replenished in heart and in soul and he lay his rabbits cross-legged across the middle of the table.

Handsome Johnnie came out from the bedroom where he'd been resting. Though sick and close to death, he was beside himself with joy at the sight of his son and his rabbits. As so often with him, he didn't know what to say or what to do. He had been a shy man all the days of his life – with the exception of the day he threw the bucket of water over his pet daughter, Darkie, to cool her of her temper.

He took a chair and went and sat outside the half-door where he could enjoy the sun shining in across the fuchsia-bushes. That's the way he always was – his ears cocked and listening to the songs of the little birds and drinking in the beauty of it all rather than come in and sit round the fire with the rest of them. But he continued to think of Stylish. When news of his son's rabbiting-success got around it would set the women's tongues ablaze all over Rookery Rally and they'd carry it round from house to house. He smiled to himself and was as happy as a thrush.

Dowager Skinned Her Rabbits

Dowager was bent on making money from the sale of the rabbit-skins. She forgot all the other jobs she was supposed to be doing and she put on her apron and took up her first rabbit. Skinning it would take her no time at all. She drew the hindlegs out through the skin, keeping the tail intact with the rump. She pulled the skin back as far as the forelegs, leaving the forelegs intact with the carcass, cutting round them with her good scissors. She got rid of the head. If she were she to leave it attached to the rest of the skin, she'd get only half the rabbit-skin price since the meat of the head was known to turn bad and rot the pelt. Last of all she pulled off the entire pelt.

Meanwhile, the house had remained quiet – the little ones spellbound at the sight of their mother skinning her rabbits. Blue-eyed Jack took this opportunity to beckon Stylish out behind the pig-house and help him saw a few whitethorn logs for the fire. It was merely an excuse and when they were out of sight he dug out a Woodbine fag from his pocket. He chopped it in half with his penknife. Then he handed one half of the fag to Stylish – his reward (they both knew) for his young brother having hunted so well. He lit both fags. It was Stylish's first smoke. The two of them puffed and puffed merrily in the quiet of the wood-stack, putting smoke to the heavens.

The Dusky Time Of Day

You'd think the rabbits had had enough excitement to last them a lifetime. Far from it. After his first success with Brandy there followed evenings when Stylish would attend to his work all over again. This was the dusky time of day when all the fields were gilded and gleaming and the dying sun was seen fighting with the night-clouds and trying to keep herself alive. The sight of the changing sky-colours and the glory of it all stole the young hunter's heart again and made him sigh.

At the same time, the pain inside him was driving him further and further from his brothers and sisters. They didn't seem to notice, so well-used were they to seeing him come home with his britches half torn off of him and his cheeks aglow and the occasional dab of rabbit-blood on the tip of his nose. All they ever wanted was to admire him for having scythed down a whole acre of corn and for bringing home rabbits in such great numbers on his stick.

Something That Only A Mother Could Feel

However, there was something almost sinister that only a mother could feel. She saw the way Stylish would throw his rabbits down on the table, almost disdainfully. She saw the way his previous vainglory and childish notoriety were replaced at times with a profoundly gloomy look on his face. She felt she knew the sadness that he was hiding from them. No, his recent outbursts of energy weren't able to fool the likes of her: himself and his corn – himself and his rabbits.

She could feel it in her bones. It was as if he was saying, 'I have paid ye all back – I have made up for my sin against ye all, haven't I? Yes, that's what he was telling her – telling all the others too, if only they could get a look inside his head and feel the wounds imprinted on his heart. Was there ever such a tortured soul as her young son (she thought) – her *half-child-half-man*, who had cut down his acre of corn in less than a day – who with Brandy-the-ferret had kept both herself and the rest of them in food for weeks to come? But even now, just as after his work with the scythe and the corn, there was something that Dowager wasn't smart enough to know: there was never a razor-strap invented that could pacify or destroy the bitterness and hatred her son now felt towards them all.

He Strapped His Rabbits To The Handlebars

When he'd eaten the evening meal Stylish strapped his rabbits to the handlebars of his father's bike and cycled down to Curl'n'Stripes' shop. In front of the astonished drinkers he laid his rabbits out in a row on the counter. The sight of it ('and tell me, Stylish, did ye yeerself catch all these rabbits?') left the lazy old time-wasters shaking their heads, their mouths gaping to such an extent that they forgot why they were there – to drink their couple of pints of the black doctor stout.

The news had already travelled the roads and all the drinkers could think of was Stylish and his skill with the corn – Stylish and his skill with Brandy-the-ferret – Stylish and all the money he was piling up from the sale of his rabbits. They'd be talking of it for days on end. Before the month was out his fame as a rabbiter was to make him a rival even to the great Airs-and-Graces himself.

Silver Coins And A Tortured Soul

Stylish returned home from the shop with fistfuls of coins from the rabbit-sale. Dowager could hear him crossing the flagstones, the sound of the coins jingling in his pocket. He slapped the money down on the table and once more she thought she saw the look of distain in him. Not a penny did he keep for himself but gave it all to her – to the mother who had ordered his punishment – the mother whom he had grown to hate as well as love at one and the same time.

'Here ye are, mother. Is that good enough for ye?'

Yes, he was paying her back with more than just rabbit-money. Merry little soul that he'd always been before his world had gone wrong for him, he was hoping that she would understand – that she would share with him the guilt and the misery inside in him for a crime which he'd unheedingly committed.

High-Jumping

A week later the pretence of Stylish at leading a normal happy life was seen to take a new direction. It was Saturday and, free from the imprisonment of school, he had oceans of time to plan his day. He took a few of his father's hazel thatching-rods and headed out to the Bluebutton Field. He cut the rods into different lengths and with his father's pocket knife made a cleft at the top of each one. Then he fixed the shorter ones firmly into the ground and placed the longest strip of hazel-wand across the sticks. He back-pedalled a few yards from the wand. He bounced on his toes like he'd seen the great jumpers doing at the Annual Show-Fair in town. He made a mad rush towards the wand (it was a mere foot high) and lept clean out over it. Easy does it (thought he to himself). By the end of the day we'll see how high a man as fine as meeself can jump.

The rest of the children came out to watch their big brother's latest achievement and see him jump over the wand. They had never seen such a spectacle before and they clapped and clapped. Once more he felt the unavoidable anger throbbing in him – this time against the outstretched wand, which (unlike his battles with the corn and the rabbits) might thwart him of success.

He raised the wand a bit higher and sat his young brothers and sisters down to watch his next attempt at jumping. His three older brothers were missing, busying themselves at turning and tossing the rows of hay in the Seventh Field. They'd never be seen wasting half the day in such childish games as jumping over hazel-wands.

It was time for Stylish to invite all the younger children to join in and take their jumps against each other. In less than an hour they had completed four or five rounds of fine jumping and by then there wasn't a crow or a sparrow left in the trees or hedges – they had all been frightened to death. The three little ones had long ago thrown up their hands in despair, having barely cocked a leg out over the first jump. At the two-foot mark both Darkie and Little Nell, though older, were forced to give up the ghost as well. That left only the gutsy Sammy-Joe, two years Stylish's junior, to make some sort of showing and try to keep pace with him.

He raised the wand up to the height of Sammy-Joe's chest and the little band of spectators sat down, transfixed and in silence. It was time for the two jumpers to play the hero and to put on a bit of a show for them. They spat on their fists and shook hands the way sportsmen were supposed to do. They'd seen all this at last year's Show-Fair.

They looked fiercely at the increased height of the wand.

The rest of the children rose to their feet, bouncing on their toes and impatiently urging on the two-of-them. They were as anxious as hell to know what would happen next: would Stylish and Sammy-Joe win their battle against the wand or would the wand turn out to be the real winner? They were scarcely able to catch their breath what with all the excitement.

The two lads made a mad rush at the wand and gave a great big shout. Then they ran back again. This was repeated a few more times – to show that they were the manly fellows, who were about to frighten the wand into submission. At last they took a run together (you'd have to close your eyes) and went sailing clean out over it – even Sammy-Joe. Was there ever such a beautiful sight! You'd thing they were about to fly off into space.

Alas, this marker was as high as the cleft-rods would allow them to jump and they were left scratching their heads: was there no other jumping-challenge left open to the two of them?

He Of The Harsh Razor-strap

For the last year or two Warbling Will (he of the harsh razor-strap) had been anxious to forget the day he'd ever brought pain to Stylish. He was now crossing the field with the sandwiches and gallon-of-tea to give his two brothers their dinner. He stopped a moment to look at the young ones idling around. It didn't take him long to see that the day's jumping had come to an end. This might be his one and only chance to put an end to his continued feelings of guilt.

It was that time of day when Old Stroller would be having his mid-morning nap and dreaming of the saved apple-trees in his orchard. Warbling Will left down the sandwiches and gallon-of-tea and ran down the road to the old man's yard.

He made two trips back, each time rolling one of Stroller's empty tar-barrels along the road. The children stood around him, puzzled and wondering what on earth he was going to do with these strange barrels.

Before they could blink he had disappeared again. He ran down the road and stole the old man's long plank from the stable behind his hayshed and came staggering back into the field with the plank balanced across his back. Suddenly they realised what he was up to. He placed the barrels three or four yards apart and got them to help him search for rocks to weigh them down. He ran the plank across the gap between the barrels. In spite of himself, Stylish was forced to smile, seeing how the heart of his former tormentor had softened so much towards him and the mad way in which he'd been running up and down the road, trying to prove it.

All was now ready for the serious jumping to begin. The news of the two great jumpers had quickly spread and a good crowd of children were seen thronging into the Bluebutton Field – those of Moll-the-Shuffler – of Smiling Babs – of Cackles – of Moll-the-Man. Such excitement was rare indeed, enough to scare even the devil in his corner in hell (said Dowager later).

Stylish took command and sat everyone down beside the barrels. Himself and Sammy-Joe stood aside awhile, whispering to each other and deciding the best way of tackling such a mighty jump. It must surely be four feet high. There was much to consider. Were they to take a fast run up or a slow and studied one? Were they simply to make a heedless rush and meet the wand head-on? Was it better to approach from the righthand side or the left?

'Coom on, blasht ye – what's keeping the pair of ye?' shouted Warbling Will.

They were all getting restless. The suspense was killing everyone.

For a second the world seemed to stop. Then Stylish and Sammy-Joe made a rush at the wand and at the very first attempt Stylish sailed clean out over it. It took his younger brother two more attempts before he too sailed out over it without scraping the plank. And as if that wasn't enough, they both went back and repeated it. Such celebrations you never did see as the little ones started spinning round and around in circles and the older ones started somersaulting and cartwheeling all over the field. The applause could be heard as far away as Corcoran's Well.

Suddenly they heard Dowager banging her tea-tray on the flagstones. It was time for the dinner and the crowd ran home. Dowager's little ones were first to burst in the half-door and tell her the good news and how the day's jumping had finished up and how Stylish and Sammy-Joe had jumped as high as the roof (the little liars).

She smiled as she passed the spuds and milk round the table. 'I was wondering what all the noise was for,' said she. 'It must surely have been heard above at Sheep's Cross,'

'Aye, faith,' laughed Handsome Johnnie, coming out from the bedroom, 'and even heard as far as The Valley-of-The-Pig – and that's almost a mile away.'

Dowager put down her knife and fork. 'It's a wonder that God-in-his-heaven didn't get to hear all the racket – surely it must have reached his ears up there in the clouds?' And she started laughing to herself. Ah-me, this was Dowager and her flowery talk all over again – herself and her tongue that was always running away with itself. Handsome Johnnie shook his head and smiled. It was nothing new to him.

Abbey Cross Sports

Such elation could only be beaten by taking a trip to the Abbey Cross Sports on Sunday week. Meanwhile there was much practising to be done. Sunday arrived with a smile and not a cloud in the sky. Red Scissors brought down one of his field-gates and set it out for the jumping. It had five loose bars to it that could be taken off or put back at the jumpers' request.

With the testing of the first and second bars a good number of young rascals succeeded in leaping out over them. Oh, what joy, to see their red-cheeked mothers clapping and clapping and (with many a tear) complimenting their sons and daughters for their fine bit of jumping. However, after the third bar was raised onto the gate and when many of the jumpers had tried in vain to jump over it, only four children were left standing before the next bar – the fourth one. All eyes were now on Sammy-Joe and Stylish and on Moll-the-Shuffler's sons, Zippity and Punch, the two previous slayers of Old Hayload's hat and hay. A few minutes later, however, both Sammy-Joe and Punch were forced to meet their fate and walk away, Only Stylish and Zippity had been able to clear this fierce obstacle,

The scene was now set for a grand finale.

It took all the energetic rage that was in Stylish's body – all the bitterness and hate – to see him leave Zippity behind him and vault clean out over the final fifth bar of the gate – a feat that had never been heard tell of before.

'Stylish! Stylish!' – roared the crowd.

'Stylish! Stylish!' – roared his brothers and sisters.

'Where in God's holy name did the lad get his spring from?' – cried the women.

'Is it feathery wings the young devil has on his heels?' – they said.

Spare a thought for poor Zippity who now came over to Stylish and shook him warmly by the hand.

Stylish with his final jump was the glory of the day. The crowd would never forget it. Once more it was the hidden anger inside him that had won out and had beaten the gate into submission – just as it had beaten down the acre of corn and the necks of several rabbits.

From that day forth Stylish would be recognised not only as *The Master of The Cornfield* – not only as the lad who had loaded Dowager's fists with handfuls of rabbiting-money from ferreting with Brandy, but as *The Jumping Master of the five-bar-gate*. He had won all the laurels handsomely.

The Hurling

By the next summer (his thirteenth year) Stylish was seen to excel elsewhere – this time at the hurling – not so much in the competitive use of the hurleystick but in the accuracy of his solo work. He took himself off to the Bluebutton Field where he stabbed two goose-feathers into the ground, a few feet apart from each other and some forty yards out from the ditch that bordered the

Hollow Field. His feathers were his markers, his guiding eyes, directly in line with two tall trees growing side-by-side on the ditch. They would tell him where the gap between the trees was so that even before he turned around to face the ditch he knew exactly the direction of the gap and where to strike his ball.

His young brothers and sisters gathered excitedly on the other side of the ditch and shouted, 'Ready, steady and strike the ball! Coom on, Stylish – strike the ball!'

Stylish glanced down at the feathers. He rolled the ball onto the boss of his hurleystick and wheeled around.

The children heard the zing of the ball as he sent it high in the sky towards the trees and the gap. See their eyes fixed steadfastly on its flight as it soared like a bird to its nest and hovered tantalisingly in the air. Hear their squeals of rapture ('Stylish! – oh, Stylish!') as it skimmed through the gap and curved down into the Hollow Field.

Oh, the excitement as they hurried down the field, vying like mad puppies to see who'd reach the ball first and bring it back to Stylish for yet another display of accuracy from him and his feathers.

Time after time he fired the ball in between the trees. Time after time his brothers and sisters ran after it till they were as tired as flies overcome with heat. They had seen the glory shining out of him yet again. Why (said Sammy-Joe), his brother was better than a cartload of circus animals.

The Bucket And The Rusty Milk-Churn

As if that wasn't enough, in the next few weeks there followed his venue with the bucket and rusty milk-churn turned up on their sides. Day in and day out he practised striking the ball at each of these obstacles – one to his right and one to his left in an effort to establish his prowess and make the ball lodge in the bottom of either one of them. As soon as he was expert enough to achieve some degree of accuracy he invited his brothers and sisters to see the cut of his hurleystick – the big lads too.

'Deaden it! – bury it!' they cried as they watched him slice the ball into the bucket or churn half-a-dozen times. Would they ever stop marvelling at him? Even the previous sneers of Lofty were missing and he had to shake his head in disbelief when he saw how Stylish was able to do what he liked with the ball. Not one of them could fathom what lay behind this most recent battle of his with the bucket and milk-churn.

And in the coming days the women at the well would speak of nothing else but Stylish: 'Where did our young enchanter come from – or was he born at all? Was he some sort of changeling-child brought back to earth by the *Good Fairy*?'

Stylish went from the field with a wave of his hand and a flourish of his hurleystick. He left behind him his afterglow. He took away with him his greatest asset: the hidden anger born in him the day of his cruel skelping

– the anger that would always be his inspiration and the centre of his many endeavours.

It Was Haymaking Season

It was now August and the haymaking season was thriving. Half-a-dozen men were helping to save one another's hay. As well as Blue-eyed Jack and his two brothers there was Gooseberry-The-Pony, Rambling Jack, Red Scissors, Fiddler Joe and even Tom Foolery (now chastened and back into harness again after his crude demolition of Yellow Patsy's flour). They were all working like blazes over in Handsome Johnnie's Seventh Field – some of them turning his hay for him as fast as they could – others raking it into huge heaps in preparation for the making of twenty or thirty haycock-trams, each eight-feet high. They would level down to five or six feet in a week's time.

From last year's reek in the haggart they made hay-rope soogans (two to each tram). They would criss-cross them tightly over each tram when the trams were made, fixing them firmly down at the butt of the tram to prevent the Kerry winds from rolling all the hay down into Bog Wood.

Meanwhile – and to keep them from getting in under their feet – the men shepherded all their own children into the Bluebutton Field for a day's racing.

Stylish and his good friend Zippity marshalled the merry little band down to the lower ditch and sat them underneath the Rotten Oak.

The races were to take place between the yellow ragwort bouhilauns – those damned weeds that had killed the unfortunate Fandango a few years back. Stylish and Zippity picked out a number of children for the short dash (Little Dan was one of these) and some for the double-field race up'n'down and round the ditches (Little Nell was expected to make a great show at this).

The two young race-masters had gone down to Curl'n'Stripes' shop the night before, looking for a crate of empty green and brown bottles. When they came home they smashed them into small pieces – the green ones as trophies for the winners – the brown ones for all the runner-ups. And that was every other child, all of whom were to be acknowledged as the very best of sportsmen. It was time for the racing to begin.

Stylish pointed out two clusters of the yellow weed, lying a considerable distance from each other. He and Zippity paced out the distance for the start and finish of the first race and for every other race (short or long) that was to follow. Zippity signalled the start of each race with a pompous lift of his hand. Stylish was at the finishing-line to judge the winners every time. They selected the girls for the first race and the boys for the second race. Sammy-Joe and Zippity's younger brother (*Punch*) were expected to make a great show just like Little Nell. As for himself and Zippity, they would be leaving school the following year and were far too big to be seen racing against the younger ones.

Hearing all the fuss and excitement, Dowager left off her work at the haggart-stick where she'd been feeding her lively calves with watered-down buckets of milk and chastising their bony heads with her ashplant when they attacked one another in an effort to steal each other's drink.

For the next hour she found herself spellbound, watching all the fine entertainment and all the rivers of energy flowing out of the children. She let out a sigh, thinking of the days of her own happy childhood. A heady laughter filled her soul to see the excitement in Stylish as he stamped up and down the field in the middle of all the amusement. He seemed to be back to his merry old self again. Ah, me, the poor woman still hadn't a notion (would she ever?) of the depths of his anger and bitterness and the welts he still felt in his heart – they'd never go away.

The Climbing

Stylish then pointed his finger towards the Rotten Oak. It would be the final race. Who would be first to the top? Who would win the big prize – the green bottle itself?

The children made a mad dash, giggling and squealing as they vied with one another to see who'd reach the tree first – who'd scale it to the top first. Up and up they climbed among the branches, the older ones leading the way. Higher and higher they twisted, their breath and excitement almost dislodging them. When Sammy-Joe found himself at the top, the others not very far behind him, why (bless my soul), who was standing there already but Stylish himself, having climbed up unseen from the opposite side of the ditch. He was like some ghostly apparition that had flown in on wings – his face sparkling with little sweaty diamonds on it. Poor Sammy-Joe had to make do with second place. He had to laugh.

Stylish pointed into the far distance, gently steering all the children's eyes in the direction of the town with its castle and blue church-spire.

'Can ye see the Roaring Town?' he asked them.

'Yes! Yes! We can.'

Then he gently steered them down onto the ditch.

Turning Their Trousers Inside-Out

It was time for all the boys to turn their trousers inside out so that the whites of them were shown as a hurling-togs the same as the ones Old Stroller had hated so much – the day of his dung-bespattered face.

Some of the girls sat with the little ones in the shelter of the ditch, away from the glare of the scorching sun. Others lay down at the top of the field and stretched out their legs behind them, warm among the thistles and dock-leaves.

With a mighty shout the battle of the hurleysticks commenced. The girls scrutinised the hurling and cheered the boys along. The boys whaled into the hurling till they were as exhausted as a cow that had just calved and the Bluebutton Field was almost reddened from their play. And all the while the sunlight overhead tilted itself down and swept the children along with it in their childish joy.

Stylish and Zippity led the children to the ditch and sat them down under the Rotten Oak. They handed out the prizes from all the competitions – the racing, the climbing, the hurling. These bits of coloured glass would be cherished for many a day.

'Fair play to you and to you and to you,' Stylish kept saying. 'Fair play to the lot of ye.'

It was the end of the day and the sunlight had waned. The merry little band left their laughter behind them and faded away from the energetic play that had left all of them as thin as storks. Stylish shepherded them out from the field – the hurling boys marching (*left-right! left-right!*) behind the girls and striking off the heads of those cruel ragwort-bouhilauns with their well-aimed hurleysticks. Would-to-god that Fandango had been here to witness it. Behind them a few sick crows, their bellies fully-laden, staggered home likewise from across the fields. The pale evening sky came in fast and a bat whispered its way out past the pig-house gap. Dowager's starving children stumbled into the Welcoming Room just as the last rays of sunlight ached through the bars of the upper goose-gate, shining red-and-gold over the deserted Bluebutton Field.

Ah, the races! Ah, the hurling!

Stylish had well and truly ambushed their hearts – yet again.

Hunting With Gooseberry-the-Pony

The following year Airs-and-Graces was stricken down with a severe dose of the cholic. There was no chance he'd be able to stagger into his clothes and head out the hills with his ferrets or his newly-acquired terrier-dogs (*Boxer* and *Slasher*) – at least not until his pretty wife had shoved a large bottle of Doctor Glasses' medicine down his throat. He had no choice but to ask Dowager's brother (*Gooseberry-the-Pony*) to look after his terriers for him till he was back on his feet. You should have seen the smile on the face of the old shapester, trotting the roads each day with his two new doggy-friends.

This was the chance for Stylish to strike out into new territory. He'd give his beloved little ferret, Brandy, a well-earned rest while himself and uncle Gooseberry spent their evenings rabbiting with the terriers in the old fellow's favourite haunts in the Valley-of-The-Black-Cattle.

It was to prove a good partnership that kept the rabbits pouring in the door of Curl'n'Stripes' shop. And so wondrous were Boxer and Slasher at tearing into every available rabbit-hole that within a few short days Stylish – in addition to their evening hunts – was forced to drag Gooseberry out of his sleepy bed to go on an early morning hunt with his terriers.

This was during September, the fourteenth year in Stylish's life when the school was about to start up again for himself and Sammy-Joe, Little Nell and Darkie (a well-reformed young lady these days). However, there was a quandary for him to fathom out each day: whereas his anger that had been a sufficient spur for him to succeed in all his past ventures, the question now was: would he be able to chase after his rabbits at such an early hour of the day and still be able to get himself to school in time for his first lesson? It was a tough test even for the likes of Stylish.

A Price To Pay

Sure enough, it wasn't long before he was seen racing like the devil across Red Buckles' Field so as to catch up with Sammy-Joe and his two older sisters. Damn-it-all, he was going to be late and there'd be a price to pay for his morning's rabbiting. He knew what the penalty for lateness was: he'd be asked by Dang-the-skin-of-it to take the school's knife down to the river and cut himself a sallyswitch, with which to receive a few strokes across the seat of his britches. However, after his first taste of this particular treatment, he found he didn't mind it a bit for, unlike the savage beating with Warbling Will's razor-strap, the soft taps his kindly schoolmaster gave him wouldn't hurt a fly and he was able to sit down thereafter with no soreness to his gable-end. Dang-the-skin-of-it was no fool and he knew only too well that Stylish might well have spent not only the previous hour or two but possibly half-the-night staring down into burrows with the rabbits staring back up at him so as to keep bread on the family table and money in his mother's purse.

It Was Mid-morning

After his gentle argument with the sallyswitch, Stylish (and he still breathless after his race to school) sat himself down at the Top Scholars' Table alongside the master's son, Satchel (a much-improved learner these days). Dang-the-skin-of-it stood in front of the blazing fire, restlessly bouncing up and down on his toes. As soon as the children's writings in their Daily Dictation books had been handed in to him, he wrapped his scarf and coat around him and got ready to lead his eager band of scholars out to his vegetable-garden for an energetic bout of marching and drilling.

Saturated with the dictated sentences that Dang had inflicted on them (today it had been about the ancient Danes), they quickly got themselves ready at the door. They were like a flock of goslings behind their goose for the morning's outing – down the lane – across the bridge – up to the gates of the master's garden where the tall breezy trees waved their branches in greeting around them and the leaves' shadows wove their patterns across the grass in front of them.

Once inside the gate the newer children gazed in wonder at the master's well-tilled garden and all its dazzling colours. For the next half-hour they busied themselves marching up and down the rows, chanting and pounding out the rhymes and rhythms of the many verses that the older ones had learnt in Recitation Class the previous year.

Wasn't Dang-the-skin-of-it the crafty old schemer, getting his children to march and drill and at the same time getting them to keep down his weeds, their boots stamping along the furrows between his cabbages and lettuces in time with each line-of-verse. The echoing hills and their troubled ghosts looked down on the charming antics of what looked like a gaggle of young fairy-folk.

With the weeds well-chastised by his scholars, Dang-the-skin-of-it marched them back down the lane and into the classroom. The monitors poured out the well-earned mugs-of-cocoa from the big jugs and handed each child a generous mugful. It went down well with the slices of soda-bread-and-jam that their mothers had prepared the night before.

The Little Breadwinner

Later in the day it was time for Story-Writing. The blaze from the merry fire shone round the four corners of the room, its flickering light helping the children to concentrate their minds in silence and to put a few words together successfully in their copybooks. From time to time Dang-the-skin-of-it stopped warming himself in front of the fire and tiptoed quietly up and down the rows of desks.

There was something unreal about these September afternoons when early autumnal changes were in the air and the last of the aching sunlight was forcing itself in through the windows. Dang-the-skin-of-it stopped his pacing and looked down admiringly at Stylish's lowered face and his studious copybook. The sun was shining directly on the young lad's head. He felt an incontrollable urge to reach down and stroke Stylish's hair for the traces of rabbit-blood were still smeared in it.

'Ah, the little breadwinner! said he to himself and he shook his head in disbelief.

'Why – dang-the-skin-of-it!' said he to himself, mouthing the phrase that had long since given him his name, and he went on twisting the waxed ends of his moustache. Then he tiptoed behind the blackboard so as not to be caught smiling and talking absentmindedly to himself as he continued to meditate on the young rabbiter, whose recent exploits with the ferret had caused him to take the boy to his heart.

There Was Much To Celebrate

September was the month when there was much for the farmers to celebrate. The harvest had come and gone. The fields of hay had all been safely secured into trams and the long reek in the haggart had been built up high and raked to perfection. The corn had been bagged and turned into flour at Liam-the-Miller's mill across from the shop. The turf had been brought home from Bog Boundless and the timber carted back from Bog Wood so that all would be snug and warm during the winter months. Both the turf and timber had been piled into two neat stacks, a job the Spallidagh children loved to do, abroad in the usual place behind the pig-house.

But, unlike the others, Stylish had paid little if any heed to all the harvesting. He continued to mix his days, staying with the others from time to time but keeping away from them whenever he could, telling himself that he didn't need (or want) their company in the first place and that his life would always be the same for the way they had let him suffer. Meanwhile he had come to terms with his twofold duties – that of a serious rabbiter and that of an earnest scholar. His ability to get to school on time had vastly improved.

Inspector Handyman.

Soon to be fourteen, this was to be Stylish's last few days at school. One fresh morning after dropping off his rabbits at Curl'n'Stripes' shop, he was belatedly hurrying after the other children and putting on such a great burst of speed, the steam rising up from his forehead, that he didn't hear the sound of a pony-and-trap's wheels coming up behind him until they were almost on top of him.

What a sight, to see such a beautiful object as this with its wheel-rims painted in a spanking new yellow and the black lacquer and sheen down the sides of the trap, similar to that on Father Laudable's motorcar.

'Hop up, sonny! Hop up!' said a strange man. Was it a dream?

Stylish had seen but few pony-and-traps in his lifetime and had never seen the gentleman who was now travelling the road with him, probably one of the posh gentry-folk (he thought) with his greased-back hair and his high starched collar and his tweed farting-jacket and gloves on him. Ever-anxious to forego a few strokes of Dang-the-skin-of-it's sallyswitch, Stylish was only too glad to oblige. He knew that the other children would still be ambling their way to school and filling their pockets with cobnuts to supplement their cuts of bread-and-jam. He couldn't help smiling when he thought of their open mouths – to see the dash of him as he sailed out passed them in a fit of royal splendour. It would make a rare introduction to the master's lesson (Is-There-Any-News?) as well as for all the disbelieving parents when the children got home in the evening to tell them of Stylish's posh new friend.

Stylish Did Most Of The Talking

There followed a pleasant few moments of polite conversation in the trap with the new visiting inspector (for it was he, Inspector Handyman, who was the driver of the pony and shining trap). It was as if they'd known each other all their lives – Stylish doing most of the talking and Inspector Handyman doing most of the listening – Stylish telling him about the numerous events that had of late taken place in and around Rookery Rally. For, among his other talents, he was gifted with his mother's rapid tongue. It took no more than five minutes before he had given Inspector Handyman the most recent news of all and sundry. It was a long list delivered at breakneck speed – like the names of those who got married the previous Saturday (*Nance-the-Sack* and *Paddy-Whack*) and the man who got waked and buried the week before that (The Gog's ancient father, *Silverlips-the-Fluteplayer*) – every noble deed and every misdeed, including his own crime of letting the damned ferret out of its cage to eat away half his mother's finger.

'Why (thought Inspector Handyman to himself), I should have been a saintly priest. It's almost as good as listening to the secret doings of all the locals inside in a Confession-box.'

He would have to say this again a minute later when Stylish, warming to his theme, began pouring out the more intimate details of the school itself : how the master was a kindly and charming chap – indeed a most excellent fellow – how he loved fine poetry and noble books – especially those that dealt with the patriotic forefathers and their renowned love of Ireland – how his wife, Big Screech, was a right old rip unlike the previous mistress, Gracious Mary, and how she never stopped beating the brains out of the children's heads and how all she was good for was rattling off hymns on her bleddy old piano and how she had caused most of the children to get their mothers to cut their hair down to the scut with the pudding-bowl, rimming it round about before the old stick's sharp claws pulled it all out by the roots.

Mercy-on-us, would the little windbag ever shut his gob? His detailed news and all its niceties were the finest information Inspector Handyman could have wished to hear – an inspection in itself and before they reached the school gate he had gotten himself everything he needed for the report that Bishop High-Hat had sent him to write – all summed up and neatly parcelled out for him by Stylish.

'Well, thank you, Stylish! Thankyou a-thousand-times over!'

He halted his pony-and-trap at the school gate and followed Stylish in through the door. You should have seen the self-important strut of the little turkeycock opposite the rest of his school-fellows.

Inspector Handyman spent no more than half-a-day inside in the school. He'd have plenty of time in the afternoon to use his fishing-rod at Growl River's fishing-hole abroad in the bog. But before making his hasty retreat in the pony-and-trap and giving them all his farewell wave with his ashplant there was one more job he had to do. Like the wise old prophet, Moses, he stood high up in the trap and after a cough and a calculated silence he looked down on the school and heaped his praises on Dang-the-skin-of-it for the excellence of his teaching and the fine turnout of his scholars.

After that he turned to face Big Screech and, raising his fist, he admonished her in front of the astonished children for her bouts of bad temper and incivilities (a word they'd never heard of till now). He promised that if she ever again grabbed any children by the hair-of-their-head and treated them so unmercifully, he'd have her carted back to the backside of Clare to spend her time picking spuds. His words were like a gift from heaven and the schoolyard almost burst asunder with the children's thunderous cheers at his words of warning. The next thing they heard was a flurry of skirts as they saw Big Screech fleeing from the yard in a flood of tears, almost tripping over Raggy, the wily thief-of-a-dog that had once stolen Little Nell's lunch on her very first day at school.

Fair play to you, Stylish! If you never again did the school and your fellow-mates a good turn, you surely did so on this memorable school-day.

'Why – dang-the-skin-of-it!' said Dang-the-skin-of-it to himself, 'I knew it would be none other than Stylish that would save the day.' For Inspector Handyman had informed him of the excellent report that Stylish had given him during their pony-and-trap ride to school. Only too well did the kindly master know his wife's little foibles and the badness that could be sweating inside in her at times. However, he felt that from now on things could only get better, thanks to what he referred to as 'the opportunistic intimations' of the young rabbiter. Words, words – mysterious words (thought Stylish). Weren't adults a peculiar lot – to be using such quare-sounding language as this.

Brandy Back In Harness

Stylish was never lucky enough thereafter to get a ride in such a beautiful pony-and-trap and he was soon back to his old ways, running like the wind after his brother and sisters so as not to be late. His haul of morning rabbits had never come easy on him and he was forced to wake up his beloved Brandy and take her out hunting again with uncle Gooseberry and the two terriers, Boxer and Slasher.

Sadly, the little ferret was now out of practice and what's more, she was frightened to death of the terriers. Once or twice she hid herself from them inside in a burrow, much too frightened to poke her nose out. Stylish and his exasperated uncle had to make use of the shovel and crowbar to dig her out or else she'd have stayed in the damned burrow the rest of the day. They dug and they dug (Stylish would certainly be late for school this time) until finally they found Brandy and she engaged in a morning's repast on the hind-quarters of a poor misfortunate rabbit. Weary and worn from his morning's work it was a very wonder if Stylish wasn't fast asleep before the end of the first school lesson – that's if he ever reached the school gates.

Thankfully, however, help was soon at hand when the news arrived that Airs-and-Graces had bounced back to health and was anxious to fetch home his two terriers. You could almost hear Brandy's squeals-of-delight when she saw the old poacher taking Boxer and Slasher away with him. Her life with Stylish now returned to the happy days of old – him and his nets – him and his father's big hat and she herself, snuggled up nice-and-warm inside his shirt and no wretched dogs anywhere in sight to worry the life out of her. Gooseberry-the-Pony, however, was saddened indeed to see his terriers go back to Airs-and-Graces and he never came back to join Stylish in his outings to the hills.

Dowager's Confession-box Horror

Brandy's anxieties hadn't been the only event to trouble the Spallidagh household at this time. During the last week of September Handsome Johnnie, in spite of his noble efforts to get up out of bed and do the odd tap of work like sweeping the yard and bringing in the logs, could be seen getting weaker and weaker by the day. Dowager was determined that from now on she would attend Mass and Communion on the first Friday of every month and ask God if he'd restore her sound man to good health.

She tackled The Lightning Whoor to the ass-and-car and took herself off to the church in Copperstone Hollow where she would offer up her Communion and spend the rest of her Mass-time praying – not only for Handsome Johnnie but for the soul of Dandy and all the Spallidagh ancestors – that they might escape too long a stay in the Purgatory's cleansing fires before taking up their place in the heavenly kingdom. When Mass was finished she'd go into Father Laudable's Confession-box and confess her recent sin (a big one) in the hope that the priest would treat her decently.

As she stepped up to the door of the Confession-box she felt very small and unsure of herself. It was worse than that: she was in dread of her life in case her sin was too great to be forgiven. What words would be suitable for Father Laudable's holy ears? The truth was that she had sinned most grievously when she deceitfully sold Curl'n'Stripes two patched-up rabbits that Brandy had half-eaten.

It was dark and gloomy in the Confession-box. It reminded her of the year she was seven and the week in May when she was getting ready to make her First Confession. Only too well did she recall how she had written out a long list of her harmless sins and how the door of the confession-box had been slammed behind her by her teacher (*Miss O'Hooligan*) – how she feverishly clutched the bit of paper with her sins written down on it. She remembered how she had shuddered when she breathed in the strange smells of polish and incense inside in the Confession-box and how confused and frightened she was to find herself in complete darkness and unable to read out to Father Simpleton the list of sins she had written on her bit of paper.

What could she do on that memorable day? What else, only to let a little stream of her warm poolie out the Confession-box-door and disgrace herself and her family opposite the rest of the smiling children.

But now – here she was again (a grown woman) – inside in the Confession-box. Once more she was in total darkness and thinking of her sin with the torn rabbits. Oh, the shame of it! Would she have the barefaced nerve to speak the name of this sin to a holy-man-of-the-cloth? As yet no-one but herself knew how she had stayed up half-the-night, doctoring and making whole the two shabby rabbits with her needle-and-thread and a few wads of brown paper and soft-boiled spuds tucked inside them.

There was, however, one little bit of comfort that she had brought into the Confession-box along with her. She had always been a good woman – almost a holy woman with few if any recognisable sins to confess other than her wrath when belting the backbone of her cow too severely with the corner of her stool after the misfortunate beast had whipped its shitty tail across her face. No, it was the rabbits – nothing but the damned rabbits, which were the cause of her present fall-from-grace and might lead her to the gates of hell if she didn't confess them and say sorry.

It was going to be a difficult few minutes – she knew it. For the way she had disguised and sold Curl'n'Stripes her half-eaten rabbits was as bad as stealing money out of his money-box. Oh, dear – oh, dear!

She gave a little cough to let the priest know she was there. She hung her head and sank low on her knees as if to hide herself from him. Then she blessed herself and began to confess her sin.

There followed a lengthy pause and she began wondering if the good priest had fallen asleep on her.

Suddenly the slide-door of the Confession-box was swung open, almost violently. Father Laudable was wide awake and listening after all. To see the slide-door open was a new one on her, for the secrecy of the Confession-box insisted that no priest was allowed to know the identity of the confessing soul and here she was (she could hardly believe her eyes) looking up into the priest's angry red face confronting her.

'Dowager, tell me this – am I hearing you correctly? You sold two diseased rabbits to Curl'n'Stripes – is that what you're telling me?'

'I did, Father, I did.' And she lowered her shameful head even further so that he wouldn't see her guilty face and the tears welling up in her eyes. 'And believe-you-me, Father, I am heartily sorry for mee sin. Will you please ask God to forgive me – if only this once?'

'Faith 'n you'll be twice as sorry when you hear the lengthy Penance I'm about to give you, the rogue-of-a-woman that you are.'

'For your Penance you'll have no more soft *Hail Marys* or *Our Fathers*.'

'No, you'll have to walk to the well barefooted for the next three mornings.'

'You'll have to be on your knees for the rest of the week, praying for God's forgiveness and for the neighbours to see the shame of it when they see the heathen you've become and the Penance I've been forced to set you.' He closed his eyes and wiped the sweat from his forehead.

'Ah, Father, aren't you the very cruel man!'

'A cruel man is it? You have the devil's own cheek to tell me this – after you sold diseased rabbits to Curl'n'Stripes and made an ass out of him.'

'I'm a thousand times sorry, Father – indeed and I am.'

'And to whom do you think Curl'n'Stripes sold one of those diseased rabbits?

He paused for a confounded second so as to give Dowager time to think.

'It was to *me,* Dowager!' Goddammit – it was to *me!'*

A Bout Of Unbearable Laughter

The silence was unbearable. It was followed, however, by a bout of uproarious laughter on both sides of the Confession-box. Oh, how the rascally Father Laudable had led poor Dowager on and on inside in the box! But to hear such unbridled laughter coming out of the holy place – how shocked were the poor women in the pews as they waited to pour out their womanly emotions and anxieties to him, never having been able to do so to their dull and unfeeling husbands.

Surely Father Laudable wasn't drunk (they whispered) at this unearthly hour of the morning – or was he?

'Get along home with you, Dowager, and sin no more,' said he.

'I absolve you from your sin with the rabbits. Your best road from now on is to sell better rabbits and not have them landing on a poor scholar the likes of me.'

After that he gave her the usual three paltry Hail Marys to say for her Penance and in her relief from anguish she almost ran out the church-door. She couldn't wait to get home and unburden herself to Handsome Johnnie. She'd remember the shame of her big sin (she hadn't any others worth mentioning) till her dying day.

The Cattle-drove

Now that the two pits of spuds and turnips were covered with straw in the haggart where no rat could get at them, it was time for farmers to sell some of their cattle. They couldn't keep foddering all of them during the winter months. Some of the hillsmen had up to a dozen two-and-a-half year-old bullocks (and maybe an old Kerry-Blue cow to be sold for calf-meal) to take into the Roaring Town's market-place.

Handsome Johnnie, still sweating from his ill-health, was making a great effort these days to show he could still hold his own. After helping Blue-eyed Jack and Lofty dig the hard-soiled haggart pit, he had plenty of time to spare and his thoughts turned to Stylish. The lad would be fifteen the following month. From among the school-leavers he had been selected to assist in the six-mile cattle-drove to town – himself and half-a-dozen Mountainy Men and their black cattle.

The field behind Curl'n'Stripes' house was the half-way stage in which to lodge their beasts before reaching the Roaring Town. They'd be glad of the usual overnight sleep in his back-kitchen. Besides, they'd have time to get a few frothy pints of the black doctor stout poured down their bellies – not to mention the ham sandwiches and eggs, the charge for which would eventually be taken out of the sale of their cattle.

On the day before the cattle-drove Stylish and his bedsheets and blankets arrived late in the evening at Curl'n'Stripes' back door. He was taken into the back-kitchen (a rare treat) and directed to his bed-space in the corner along with the other drovers. It was going to be an early start next day and soon he was fast asleep, his young head full of golden pictures of the journey he'd be making with the cattle to town and all the strange faces he'd be seeing.

His peaceful sleep didn't last long for it was scarcely four in the morning with the dew-whitened dawn still a longways off when the shouts of Curl 'n' Stripes and the banging of his tea-tray roused all the drovers from their dreams. The cattle were already bawling at the lower gate, anxious be out on the road and off to town and unaware (poor things) of their imminent death at the hands of the butcher's knife in Limerick City.

A Scene Fit For The Last Supper

The scene that followed was fit for the Last Supper. Stylish and the drovers came out from the back-kitchen and sat cross-legged in a circle on the bar-room floor. They were handed out a dozen hardboiled eggs, each one tapped with the spoon, and three cuts of soda-bread with salty ham rolled up inside them. After much munching and crunching, the well-fed assembly got down to the more important nourishment – that of their immortal souls. Curl'n'Stripes ceremoniously showered them with holy-water and handed each of them one of the rosary-beads he'd borrowed from Father Laudable

The drovers sank to their knees and with much fervour – much striking of the chest – they began to recite the five decades of the rosary so that next day's cattle-sale would be a success. The wondrous spirit in their uplifted eyes – the sing-song sincerity of their loud praying at this unearthly hour of the morning – was a sight to behold.

It Was Stylish's Turn

It came to the turn of Stylish (a new one on him) to introduce the prayer-book's second part of the litany, *the Litany-of-The-Saints*. After each mention of a saint's name the gathering would lower their heads and devoutly give the traditional response *Pray for us! Pray for us!*

As ill-luck would have it he found he was next in line after the best praying-man among them – Curl 'n' Stripes himself. This ancient seer had just finished reciting the first part, the part echoing *the Praises-of-Our-Blessed-Lady*. The drovers had greatly admired the nasally way he had delivered it. After all, wasn't it his own family that were renowned for their ability to breed clergy? Wasn't it *he* that could throw out his chest and boast how his forebears, the Hartigans of Toom, had produced four nuns, two priests and even a holy bishop? It was going to be a devil-of-a-job for Stylish to follow the excellent praying of this holy specimen.

With a prim little smirk-of-the-lip Curl'n'Stripes passed the prayer-book to Stylish, pointing to the page with the *Litany-of-The-Saints* and to the sacred phrases and names with which they were to be honoured.

The Devil Was Wide Awake

But the devil was already awake and at work at this early hour of the day. Himself and his minions were lying down beside the knees of Stylish and whispering sweet words of roguery into his ear. Suddenly Stylish began to get nervous and in his fit of the fidgets he let the holy book drop from his hands.

He hastily picked it up – too hastily, for he was now on the wrong page. He started pouring out the noble phrases in honour of Holy Mary instead of those honouring The Blessed Saints. There was no time for him to change course and stop.

'*Morning Star*,' he shouted, hitting his breast fervently and giving Our Blessed Lady one of her many titles.

In spite of the phrase being from the wrong page, this was a good start and Curl'n'Stripes was seen to smile warmly.

'Pray for us! Pray for us!' roared the circle in response.
'*Ark-of-The-Covenant.*'

Pray for us! Pray for us!' they roared again. Things were going well.

'*House-of-David,*' shouted Stylish. He was becoming almost as good as Curl'n'Stripes as his devout words gathered speed.

Once more the bar-room echoed with the shouts of 'Pray for us! Pray for us!'

On and on went Stylish.

At this unearthly hour of the morning the drovers were beginning to get tired of praying for the success of their cattle and one or two of them were already yawning and nodding their heads. Then, when no-one was expecting it, the devil flew into the room and got to work. He gave Stylish a wicked pinch in the side.

'*The Hartigans-from-Toom,*' piped up the young rascal – as though this was some newly-named saint to be honoured.

Before the drovers could check themselves (or maybe the old sleepy-heads weren't paying too much attention to the prayers) they again shouted out their hearty response – 'Pray for us! Pray for us!

'Put him out! Put him out!' roared Curl'n'Stripes, suddenly springing up off of his knees. 'Put that limb-of-Satan out!' His face had turned into a motley of red and purple and he was fit to burst with rage. It was bad enough to make a mockery of Our Blessed Lady as well as the Blessed Saints. But worse still was it to have shamed the name of his own noble race (the Hartigans of Toom) on this most solemn occasion. And another thing – after this bit of outrageous impudence from Stylish how was the cattle-sale ever going to succeed?

It was the end of the Litany and the bemused men got up off their knees. Curl'n'Stripes led Stylish out of the bar-room by the scruff of his neck and forced him to face the back of the door inside in the chicken-shed till the drovers were assembled for the long haul into town.

Fair play to you Stylish! Fair play to you again and again! The hypocritical praying of Curl 'n' Stripes, who was always boasting of his holy lineage and yet ready to grasp the last shilling out of the poor hill-farmers, had been soundly trumped by a mere boy. The Mountainy Men spent the next week spreading the news – how Stylish had added one or two little niceties to the established Litany-of-Our-Blessed-Lady!

There was further good news later in the day when Stylish was handed his six bits of silver for his six-mile walk to town and was praised for the way he had conducted himself. Like a proper cattle-man (said the drovers) – as good as any man around. In the course-of-the-day Stylish managed to visit a number of drinking-shops and by mid-afternoon he had forced twenty-two bottles of lemonade down his throat. Later that evening he was seen bursting in through his mother's half-door with the manly walk of a newly-established cattle-drover: Cripes, byze, I'm sweating from all the fine lemonade I've been drinking after mee work as a cattle-drover!'

For once in his tortured life he had been treated as a grown man and could afford to let out a little smile. He said not a word, however, about his scandalous early-morning attempts at re-directing the traditional prayers. Who knew when the lash of the razor-strap might strike again!

A Time For Vengeance

Not since the previous year had Handsome Johnnie been able to go out to the hill and shoot a few rabbits for the Sunday pot. All he was able to do these days was go down to the Bull-Paddock and lay one or two snares and rabbit-traps.

For some days he had noticed that his snares and traps were not in the places where he'd left them overnight. Everything else was as it had been: the rabbits' little black droppings among the broken-down ferns: the main trails leading out from the ditch at the side of Bog Wood where he had meticulously laid his snares and traps. After years of rabbiting he was no fool and it was as clear as the day that there was roguery afoot. He was fit to spit vengeance.

Stylish was preparing himself for bed and saying his prayers silently on his knees alongside his brothers and sisters in front of the dying fire. For the thousandth time he had asked God to drive away the unholy anger and hatred against the rest of the household that still lay smouldering in his chest. But there was no shaking it.

His father tapped him on the shoulders and beckoned him to join him outside the half-door.

'A vagrant has been tampering with our traps and snares and has had the nerve to coom stealing the rabbits out of them' said he. 'I need your help tonight.'

'The two of us and our hurleysticks must catch the basthard and give his ribs a right good skelping. Tell me, Stylish, after your gallant day's cattle-droving are you man enough for the job of pulverising the villain?

Stylish jumped at the chance to redeem himself in his father's eyes and nodded.

'Get dressed, then, and coom with mee so that we can catch the filthy whoor.'

Stylish had never used a hurleystick on a man's ribs before. But, as with the scything down of the corn, he felt he was every bit as good a man as his father and now was the chance to prove it.

So, when the rest of the children had left the fireside and were safely wrapped up in their nests of sleep he put on his best Sunday boots, the dripping grasses being too cold for his bare feet. By this time of the night the coppery moon was high in the middle of the sky, breaking up the clouds and there was no haze. Wrapping their coats firmly about them, father and son set out into the velvety dark. The stars shone above them in their gleaming millions, quivering like shiny flies hanging above a dung-heap.

Handsome Johnnie pinched the ruddy cheeks of Stylish good-naturedly as, armed with their two hurleysticks, they headed out across the Bluebutton Field. They took a roundabout route that would finally lead them to the Bull-Paddock and the edge of Bog

Wood. The winds whipped down from the crests of the Lisnagorna pine-forest and cut into their limbs like a knife as it clasped itself round them.

Soon they found themselves at the lower end of the Deer Field, this side of Corcoran's Well. They tiptoed on to where Handsome Johnnie had laid his recent traps and snares and found a trap not yet taken and a buck rabbit squealing for its life and trying to bite its own leg off. Handsome Johnnie opened the trap and Stylish gave the poor creature a playful tap-of-the-fist on the back of its neck and carried its warm body further across the field with him.

It was now past midnight. Handsome Johnnie had scarcely time to look at his pocket-watch when he saw in the far distance the form of a man coming out from Bog Wood.

'Ah-ha, the poacher of mee rabbits, I do believe. We have him at last, Stylish. Patience! Patience! What a fine skelping he's going to get from our hurleysticks!'

It Was Poesy

Nearer and nearer came the vision of the man. But there was something wrong. Handsome Johnnie began to shiver. Were his eyes deceiving him? He knew who it was. It was Poesy, Dowager's dead brother – dead these past twenty years – Poesy, the best friend a man could ever have. Handsome Johnnie remembered well the day of his death. After beating a field of the lord's flax with the other men (it was Lord Manners at the time) Poesy had gone back for a dip in the lord's lake where he sadly sank to the depths – never again to emerge and walk dry land. Cramps, it was said, had taken hold of his legs, weary after their day's labour. Older heads, however, said that the *Water Fairies* had snatched him away since he had always been too delicate a blossom for this world.

Yes, it was Poesy alright, his own drinking-companion. He'd know him anywhere – the cock of his cap, as clear as daylight – the tobacco-pipe firmly clamped in the lower corner of his mouth so as not to let it fall.

The ghostly shade was less than a hundred yards away and steadily heading towards them. There was no mistaking him – and he awkwardly picking his dainty steps as of old so as not to wet his socks with the long grass.

Stylish, wishing to appease his father for the ruin of Dowager's finger, was twisting the hurleystick in his fists and getting himself awfully excited. He had never skelped a poacher before and hoped they wouldn't kill him outright. Little did he know that the miscreant was Poesy's ghost, freshly back from the other world.

Handsome Johnnie took him aside from the track and whispered in his ear:

'Stylish, avic, let's go home. There'll be no need of our hurleysticks tonight.'

He gave such a violent shudder (Stylish couldn't help noticing it) – to think that they were about to have used their hurleysticks not on the ribs of a poacher but on a man, who'd already been dead and drowned many years back. He took Stylish by the arm and led him away towards the Deer Field.

'What is it, father? Can't ye see our poacher heading for our traps and snares? It's time we chastised him and gave him his thrashing.'

There was a bit more to it than this: he didn't think it right that he should be the only one ever to have received a good thrashing.

The ghostly spectre was now within fifty yards of them and seemed to be staring at the two of them – staring right through them. Suddenly it passed them by and faded away out of view as though it had never been there in the first place – as though it had all been a mysterious fairy dream.

The Fear Inside Stylish

Though Stylish was well-used to hearing tales of the ghostly spirits that wandered round Rookery Rally, he now realised that for the first time in his young life he had witnessed the apparition of a ghost. And whereas others would spend the rest of their lives sitting round the fire, spouting manly yarns about it, the effect on him was more than startling. As they hastened their feet from the field his fear was exacerbated even more when his father explained that it was the ghostly spirit of Poesy, the friend of his youth, and that no harm whatever would befall them.

They crossed the Bluebutton Field, repeatedly making the sign-of-the-cross and saying prayers for the repose of Poesy's soul. Handsome Johnnie led the bewildered Stylish into the Welcoming Room. He was as yellow as a lemon and he fell on the floor in a pure faint, sweating in every pore of his body.

Limply he lay in his bed for the next fortnight – alone and all the time thinking of the ghost and the reason for his appearance – until the young Clare curate and the sweet melodies of his melojun eventually hoisted him back to life and gently walked him out of the bedroom, persuading him to leave his fears behind. Stylish tried valiantly to block from his mind the terrible thought – how himself and his father went hunting the thief of their snares and rabbit-traps and found themselves about to belt the ribs of the ghost of Poesy. Like Dowager and her Rabbit-Confession it was something he was never likely to forget.

Stylish Gets Back To His Roguery

Yet (damn the bit) it was impossible to control the energy that had always been there – driving Stylish on and on. A few weeks later he was seen leaping out over the ditch near Dowager's ashpit and storming into Simple Simon's haggart. The old farmer was always a fortnight behind everyone else when it came to thrashing his corn. Once more the rogue that was inside Stylish got the better of him and he was up to all sorts of devilment – especially amongst a family of rats that had come to attack Simple Simon's haggart whilst he and the neighbours were busy at the thrashing.

The young rascal came out from the back of the reek and tied two dead rats' tails together inside the sleeves of Simple Simon's discarded coat. When the old man went for his first mug-of-tea and sat on the rats' heads, he would dance a few of the liveliest jig-steps ever seen around the haggart.

An hour later Stylish was back a second time. The tar-barrel at the end of the haggart was half-full of water from Red Scissors' Well. He rested a plank of wood halfways across the barrel and he spread out a handful of haw-berries on cuts of bread and placed them on the plank. He enticed two playful young rats to walk up along the plank towards the haw-berries. Ah, yes, bitterness and sourness were still alive in him. He stood back and he watched. It wasn't long before he saw the startled creatures falling down into the inescapable waters of the tar-barrel – into their grave. Sadly, the way he laughed was as good as Tom Foolery all over again.

Before the day was finished he gingerly approached two screaming rats, caught in two of Simple Simon's earlier morning traps. He turned the two traps in to face one another. He pushed the rats and the traps… slowly… tantalisingly… closer and closer together – the demented creatures growing fiercer and fiercer by the second until they were as close together as possible and he could watch them tearing each other to pieces in the battle for their lives – in much the same way (he felt) that he himself had once been torn apart by the cruel savagery of the lash. Was there ever such a wicked devil inside anyone as the devil lying in the heart of Stylish? Ah, Stylish!

The Call Of The Bar-trade

He had reached the age of sixteen and had long left the schoolhouse of Dang-the-skin-of-it, taking with him the master's compliments and with him his best marks in the subjects of Euclid and mental arithmetic. How proud Dowager was of him! It didn't take her long to make up her mind as to the road that lay ahead of him. She recalled the way Handsome Johnnie's young sister, Kate, had been forced to leave home of old and head for foreign shores. Like the child's mother (Sadie-from-The-Well) she herself would now have to let Stylish go. With his alertness and quickness at mental figures, together with his innate gift-of-the-gab, he'd be more than suited for the bar-trade. It was time to say goodbye.

She had a connection above in the Big City– in one of the several drinking-shops. Many years previously her older brother, Pat (later to be renamed *Busy-Bee*) had left the quietness of Rookery Rally and headed for the maelstrom of city-life a hundred miles away on Ireland's eastern seaboard. It had come as a great shock to her to see her brother leave. For up until then he had been an easy-going sort of lad – with his feet in the ashes and his head stuck in an old book. But a year after he stepped off the train at King's Terminus he found he had a newly-awakened energy given to him from out of nowhere. It was referred to as one of the holy miracles when news of his sudden achievements came back home to Rookery Rally.

From the minute he set foot in the city he applied himself as never before, taking up jobs in the building-trade – especially in the construction of new homes to replace slum-dwellings along the banks of the docks and the Regal Canal.

Busy busy busy! That's the way it was with him from now on. And a few years later he came to own the Busy-Bee Firm with his name plastered in black lettering on signboards throughout the city.

Sad to say, such a strenuous outpouring of labour from a man like Busy-Bee (how well he had earned his new name) couldn't be kept up forever for he hadn't the mechanics of a thrashing-machine and he ended up dead at the ridiculously early age of fifty-three – worn out like an old plough-horse. It was a sad and sorry state of affairs (thought Dowager) – to see how the tremendous pace of his house-building had killed Busy-Bee and for days on end she wept over him. Why did he have to work himself to death like a damned racehorse? Why indeed! It was to show the simpletons back home that he was no longer an idle louch, too lazy to wash his own face – that he was a changed man with the makings of an even better man always inside in him. Many country lads before his time had done the very same thing – changed gear the minute they left home and reached the city – took with eager fists the chance to make themselves a rich and successful life. Fair play to them all! Fair play again!

But Busy-Bee hadn't died in vain. He was a good straight man and, knowing that he was soon to meet his Maker, he set his two sons, Matty and Pat, up in their own walk of life as owners of two spanking new drinking-shops in the centre of Riverstown.

And now, with this in mind, Dowager got out her copybook and in her best handwriting wrote a lengthy epistle to her two nephews, outlining the superlative charms and talents of their young cousin, Stylish. Wasn't she the mighty woman with words – the way she could write. For in less than a week she received a letter back, beckoning Stylish to catch the next train and direct his footsteps to Matty's drinking-shop to take up his next step in life – learning the bar-trade.

The Dilemma

As the previous years of his adolescence had rolled by, Stylish had grown more and more restless, almost nervous. Yet now, when he was about to leave home and all its memories, it was not the easiest of tasks for him to undergo. Half of him wanted to stay where he was – walking through the hills and the pine-forests – gazing at the springtime calves and lambs, the new wild-flowers, new birds – savouring it all – wandering with Brandy-the-ferret after those little rabbits that were begging to be turned into soup. All that and much more was deep down in his soul. The other half of him wanted to put his past life aside and run for the train as fast as he could gallop (he'd never even seen a train before) – wanted to skedaddle to the Big City where gold lay in heaps everywhere only for him to put it into his pockets.

Outside The Half-door

The evening before his departure he took a chair and sat with his father outside the half-door. Dowager stopped her darning and she peeped out the window at their two silhouettes. What was in the mind of her lovely son – the son she loved best – the son she'd soon be bereft of? She yearned to get inside his head. In her heart-of-hearts she knew one thing – that on this, their last evening together, Handsome Johnnie and Stylish would be sharing the peace and strange luminosity of the yard and the stream, their ears attuned to the last songs of the little birds in the hedges – attuned to the crows calling each other back to Old Sam's Rookery and the cows bawling to one another on their way to the river to drink. Down in the valley the Roaring Town's street lamps were already glowing a smoky orange.

As soon as Dowager lit the oil-lamp, father and son brought their chairs back into the house. They sat in silence in front of the fire, watching the faint yellow light of the oil-lamp start to glow into a cheerful orange, illuminating all four corners of the Welcoming Room and casting massive shadows up towards the rafters as it burnished the walls.

Midnight

An hour or two later, when midnight came and all was quiet and the Spallidaghs were asleep in their dreamland, Stylish walked out the door and stood at the flagstones. Stars in their thousands spattered the sky's blackness above him. He strayed over to the singletree in Old Sam's Grove and stayed sitting there a long while – thinking of the past – thinking of the present – thinking what might lie ahead of him in the future. He knew that the dawn would be coming in soon. And then he heard the first shy songs piping from the little birds' throats to awaken the insolent cockerel and give the hens a nudge. Somewhere behind Old Stroller's hayshed a dog barked as if in tune with them.

An hour or two later he washed and dressed himself in his one good suit (his Confirmation suit, now a little too small on him). It was a difficult moment – not knowing whether to run or stand still – with an awkward silence between himself and his brothers and sisters. None of them knew what to say – whether to smile or to cry – knowing that Stylish was leaving them all behind.

But childhood is a fickle time and as soon as he was gone, the rest of them would be off out the fields, running their races and climbing the Rotten Tree.

With Stylish it was different. He would remember this morning. If he'd been able to put it into words, it had an almost pentecostal feel to it – as though his life was about to begin afresh – with all the excitement and all the wonders that lay ahead of him in his bright new world, a far-off place where he could forget the memory of his thrashing.

And now, in sympathy with the all-too-familiar scene of a son leaving home, the rain began lashing against the windowpane and the wind from furthest Kerry began rattling the horse-chains and tackling on the back of the door. Abroad in the yard the ducks and hens had danced their way to cover and, heedless of all the fuss around the would-be traveller, were already nestling themselves under the shawl of the fuchsia-bushes at the pig-house wall,

Dowager came to the half-door. She showered the holy-water over him to keep him safe and guide him in his future footsteps.

Like Dandy, His Grandfather

Handsome Johnnie drove him to the station. Stylish had with him his little bundle of treasured school-books and his rosary-beads and the Sacred Heart badge and medals that Dowager had pinned onto his vest. The scene would remind you of the Galway farewell taken by his grandfather, Dandy, after his defeat by Foxylocks in the schoolyard debate. As with Dandy and his satchel of school-books, Stylish was now well-armed for the life ahead – not only with his school-books, but carried in his hip-pocket a fine character reference from his priest and an even better one from Dang-the-skin-of-it, the schoolmaster who was his lifelong inspiration.

Later that evening his brothers and sisters moped listlessly around in the yard, realising that Stylish was gone from them – that the life-and-soul of the house was gone for good and they began to cry. They ran out across the flagstones and looked down the lonesome road and they went on bawling like a pack of sick donkeys after him. They were lost. They were bewildered. There'd be no more jumping of the five-barred gate – no more tying of rats inside the sleeves of men at thrashing time – no more interrupting the saintly prayers of Curl'n'Stripes. There was a lengthy list of *no more and no mores* and the long and the short of it was that the laughter and fun had been knocked clean out of them and that life was never going to be the same again – that Stylish had fled like a ghost in the night.

Dowager And Her Tears

Handsome Johnnie would be back from the station in an hour or two. Meanwhile Dowager lay in her bed, her two eyes red from weeping. Her mind was full of Stylish – especially those images of his earliest efforts to say the long prayers and his memorising of the long poems. What a marvel he had been! She had once held high hopes that he'd be sent by Father Laudable to Mount Monastery and become a holy priest of God. Others from Rookery Rally, like Curl'n'Stripes' cousins, had done so before. Why not him? She had spoken of it to Handsome Johnnie. She had spoken of it to Stylish himself. But the rage inside the lad was enough to have ruled him out for such a priestly office for he was in no fit state ever to forgive his tormentors. Besides, remembering his filthy swearing and the rascal and rogue that he was during the recent praying of the Holy Litany, no-one in their right mind would ever have believed him worthy of a holy priest's white collar

Dowager, therefore, had been forced to put aside her ambitions for Stylish. But that didn't stop her. She knew what a mother's duty should be. All she had ever wanted for him (as with all her children) was to see to his happiness. She made sure that he had his two references safely tucked away in his coat-pocket and his rosary and religious medals with him. Then she gave herself a comforting little thought: priest or no priest – sending him off to the Big City wasn't such a bad thing, was it? Didn't any fool know that the bar-trade was the next best thing to becoming a man-of-the-cloth? It was an established fact.

She stopped her crying and gave herself a good shake. What on earth was she thinking of? The chores of the day were screaming at her. She couldn't hide under the bedsheets, moping for the rest of the day and she made a step or two out the bedroom door and took a drink of water from the bucket. Then she went to the half-door and stood there, breathing in the fresh air. Life would go on. It had always gone on. She felt sure that Stylish would find fame and fortune in his new role as a bar-tender.

His Training

When Stylish arrived, he was met at the train-station by cousin Matty, who almost shook the hand off of him. He led him promptly to his expansive mansion in Riverstown for a right royal greeting before finding him a suitable lodging-house nearby. Stylish found the mansion a strange place to be in – the finery, the wealth of it all – not a bit like his little thatched home back in Rookery Rally. Above the fireplace was a photo of the famed hurlers of Riverstown Club, the team that had won more than one championship towards the end of the previous century. He couldn't help smiling. All the hurlers looked like peas-in-a-pod with their peaked caps and their droopy black moustaches. And among them was Matty's father, Busy-Bee, who had hurled for five years with this famous club.

After a fine feed of spuds, ham and cabbage and a hearty good sleep Stylish was up early next morning, dressed and ready to start his training that very day – learning the many skills that the bar-trade would require of him: the requisite temperatures for various beers and wines: the intricacies of gravity flow: the cleaning of the several pumps: the counting of coins and notes and the speed at giving back change (accurate to the penny): the pouring out of the creamy Guinness with the little shamrock to be etched on top of it.

To Matty's astonishment his young cousin made fast progress in all of these skills and before his eighteenth birthday he could be seen leaping out over the bar-counter with two jugs of brimming booze in each fist – adding up the cost of the four drinks in his clever little head whilst sliding the pints of beer the length of the bar without spilling a drop. And another thing – at just eighteen he had already begun to fill out across the broad of his back and shoulders and the muscles in his upper arms had a bulge in them – to such an extent that he was able to eject the rowdiest of drinkers onto the street – doubtless a rare occurrence, as his natural charm usually got the better of even the most sour-headed boozers.

He Was The Devil's Own Shy One

It's often the way with growing lads like Stylish: he was unaware of his charm and good looks. When the urges of springtime came upon young women, a number of these rosy-cheeked damsels could be seen flocking towards him, entranced by his energy and his polished wit. They loved to listen to his lying tales of Olde Tipp'rairie and see the twinkle in his roguish blue eyes. Meanwhile the men frowned and envied him his natural graces – so much so that they'd like nothing better than to buy him a train-ticket to high hell or to whatever damned corner of the earth he'd come from.

Ah, springtime, the season of Youth – the time when the raging blood of adolescence might have caused Stylish to spend his spare time tumbling the bedsheets and thrashing the heated limbs of one or two damsels that he'd coaxed into his arms. But the jealous men needn't have bothered their heads about him for, thanks to the anger twisting round inside in him, poor Stylish was unable to acquaint himself with the mysterious intimacies of *Love* and *Romance*. There was also a further side to him: as with many a youth from the far-off slopes of Rookery Rally he was the devil's own shy one. Shyness, it must be said, had been bred in him. Whereas he was brave with the hurleystick and was manly with the scythe, he was cowardly when lying in the arms of a damsel and he'd leave her screaming for this baby-of-a-man to do or say something romantic – like inviting his lips to meet with her lips or (in the case of one or two bolder hussies) to test the inside of her skirts. Yes, this soppy fellow from the back-lands of Tipperary was the breaking of a good many young damsels' hearts.

And yet, he wasn't unhappy – far from it. What with his extra tips and his long-hour bonuses, he was making heaps of money so that like his grandfather, Dandy, he took to wearing clothes of a very fine style. He bought himself a blue silk shirt, the best that money could buy. It complimented the blueness of his eyes. He bought himself a couple of hard white collars to go with it. He bought himself an exquisite brown suit of Jewish gabardine and a pair of brown shoes also. He bought himself half-a-dozen striped ties – to match the suit and the shirt. You'd have to stop and stare at him, so fine and dandy a fellow was he.

The Call To Come Home

Little did he know that Rookery Rally and his childhood home would be calling him back before the year was out. Handsome Johnnie continued to ail and he seemed to pass most of his time closer and closer to the house – apart from a small bit of rabbitt-trapping. No-one knew how long he was going to live.

One Monday morning whilst Stylish was shaving in front of the mirror he received a knock on his bedroom door and was handed a letter by the woman-of-the-house. It was from his mother. He recognised the writing. In it she suggested he might like to come home and spend a few days with them and be near to his sick father. In truth, it was she herself who more than anyone wanted to see Stylish come back – however briefly. So much did she miss him. And though he was now settled in his new life and felt more and more estranged from the Spallidagh household, he decided to return home for a few days – to see and chat with Handsome Johnnie as of old and to go trap the odd few rabbits with him. He took pen to paper and wrote back, telling Dowager he would catch the Limerick-bound train the following week.

If You Listen...

And now, if you listen, you can hear the excitement in the air of the house: in the yard: in the haggart. 'Stylish is coming! Stylish is coming!' With his bucket of white distemper Blue-eyed Jack is already halfways round the gable-end of the house. And when he's finished the walls, he will paint the house-door a deep and richer coat of green and even the henhouse door will get some of the paint. The frames of the soogan-chairs will get a new coat of purple paint and the willow-pattern plates on top of the china-press – some of them big enough to hold a pig – will be brought down and scrubbed clean of cobwebs. The yard will be swept spotless and freed from chicken-and-goose shite and the cow-shed will get a few more sheets of galavanize on top and will put a smile on the cows' sad faces.

In truth, the big fellow was anxious to see Stylish again – more than he himself realised. The need to re-affirm his friendship with his young brother was always at the back of his mind, for there lurked in him (he couldn't escape from it) a guiltiness for the time he'd stood back helplessly and watched the blood running down the back of his young brother's legs from the savage strokes of the strap.

His Visit

Quicker than a blink Stylish arrived at the Roaring Town Station. He hadn't given his mother the time or date of his arrival and none of his brothers would be there to meet him with the horse-and-cart. That's the way he had planned it and he caught a lift in Danny-be-Quick's posh motorcar. He had to smile when he thought of the day he had ridden in the splendour of Inspector Handyman's pony-and-trap and the grand entrance he'd now be making when he stepped down onto the home flagstones.

During the drive from town he kept on telling himself how glad he was to be back in Rookery Rally with all its favourite haunts. But was that the truth? For the nearer he got to home, the more he found that there was still no peace inside him. There never would be and that was the saddest part of all. However, for the few days he was going to be home he would go on like he always had done and keep his anger locked away inside him. Not a soul would ever suspect that after all this time the heart of an entertainer like him was as hard as a pebble and that anger was still alive and burning a hole in his soul.

He Came In Across The Flagstones

After closing the henhouse-door and counting her hens up onto their roost for the evening, Dowager walked back across the yard. The children had been busy helping too. Sammy-Joe had been counting the hens, ducks and geese with her. Darkie and Little Nell had been washing the dinner-plates and leaving them to drain. Deelyah was putting the knives and forks back in the drawer of the press.

It was at that precise moment that Stylish stepped down from Danny-be-Quick's posh motorcar and came across the flagstones to meet his mother.

Was she dreaming? Could this be her Stylish and he now a gentleman? So proud was she at the sight of him for he was like a flash of sunlight coming back into her life and her heart missed a beat. She ran across the yard and shook him warmly by the hand. She was itching to throw her arms around him but custom forbad it.

Then she stood back to take a good long look at him – what with his copper-shining hair and it greased back smoothly on his poll and the glint in his teeth and eyes and the pink in his jaw and the musical notes of his voice. Yes, he was taller now. He was more solid-limbed than earlier and he still had those hale blue eyes of his, deep and as luminous as the bluebells – though (as Handsome Johnnie was later to remind her) he was a good bit plumper now around the belly, the result of all the fine living he'd been used to above in the city.

And then, the older brothers and sisters came running out into the yard to meet and greet their long-lost brother and they too couldn't help staring at him and his rich clothes – feeling the texture of the cloth and admiring his newfound style for he was wearing a remarkably expensive suit that contrasted strongly with their own almost raggity shirts and britches. They loved the sight of him and they wondered when (if ever) it might it be their own turn to leave the nest and fly off like the wild geese of old to city-life for all its excitement and wonder.

And then – Deelyah and her two little brothers peered out over the half-door at their big brother, frightened to death at the sheer brilliance of him. That didn't last long, for Handsome Johnnie kept shoving them forwards and he himself came out behind them to take a look at Stylish and welcome him home. 'Ye're a rale punch-of-a-man,' said he proudly, prodding Stylish in the side and there was nothing but genuine love in his eyes.

Stylish sensed all their happiness and he passed out cigarettes to Handsome Johnnie and his three older brothers. They were used to tapping their Woodbine fags on their box to firm them up before smoking but Stylish produced from his pocket a fine silver cigarette-case with a little yellow band across the inside to steady the line of his fags. And as soon as he had handed out the fags he snapped the case closed again with a firm and delicate little clasp – something everyone greatly admired. Yes (like Dandy before him) he was indeed the swanky fellow.

It Was A Special Occasion

The excitement was mounting and they all trouped into the Welcoming Room. This was a special occasion and Dowager covered the table with the oil-cloth which she usually reserved for Christmas Day. She got busy with the banging of cutlery and saucepan-lids and the swish of her skirts seemed to be everywhere. She filled the kettle with water for Stylish's tea and she hung it on the crane, keeping her eye on the lid till the water was bubbling and hissing. And all the while she kept up the immensity of her chatter – bending her son's ear with details of Rookery Rally's latest news.

There was some hare-soup left over in the burner. She poured him out a delicious mugful, showering it with pepper, and Stylish gulped it down greedily. There were plenty of spuds left over from the family meal and Dowager gave a plateful to him and mixed up the spuds with lashings of milk, butter and scallions and some thick cuts of cold ham added on. This was followed by a healthy helping of her special apple-batter cake. After that, Stylish thumped his belly a couple of times and smiled happily round the room. With such a fine feed after his long journey he felt fully replenished and he rose from the chair and spun around the room, laughing. Then his brothers and sisters, awkwardly silent up till then, relaxed a good bit and they all laughed with him.

Good To Be Back

And when the table was cleared and the fire heaped high with logs – when the little ones had said their prayers and toddled off to bed – they tucked their chairs in round the fire and sat under the hearty light of the oil-lamp. It was a moment of magical intimacy – here in this little thatched house and they all knew it.

They talked and talked for hours on end, the memories flocking back: memories of the good times of olde: the pitch'n'toss and the horseshoe-pelting: the hide-and-go-seek and the mountainy-men chasing after the screaming children and the stamp of their big boots running down the pig-house gap and the older and bolder girls running up from Saddle Bridge and joining in the games and romping with the men behind the hayreek before running back down the road (pretending to be shy) and lifting high their skirts and giving the old schemers more than a glimpse of their knickers to take back home with them. Weren't those the best of all days? Ah, yes, indeed they were! And as the Spallidaghs warmed their shins round the fire, they shook their heads and laughed all over again.

The clock on the wall kept ticking away and from time to time Dowager poked the fire to keep the blaze high and inviting. The laughter took hold of them again and one or two of them remembered Stylish's last and final villainy the year before last – the time the infamous rogue stole Ducks-and-Drakes' brand-new bicycle and went speeding like the wind up'n'down High Straits, challenging the surrounding hills for a morning of rare pleasure. Dammit, the sheer impudence of the young rascal!

His Feverish Tongue

When they got up next morning, it was the same track all over again. The laughter of Stylish was infectious – as though he had forgotten the hurt and bitterness that was inside him. His feverish tongue (like Dowager's) kept running away on him as once it did in the pony-and-trap of Inspector Handyman – so much so that before they had finished eating their eggs and drinking their milk he had them all (the little ones too) splitting their sides with laughter – telling those huge lies of his and how he stole the duck-eggs from Maggie-the-Shine's bowl and brought them to the priest as a humble and holy Lenten Gift – how he informed the hillsmen that Old Noah was dead and how those simpletons went up to say the rosary over the poor man's corpse ('He's upstairs adin in the bed,' said Noah's wife) and how they reverently crept upstairs on their tippy-toes only to find Noah sipping his tea and sitting up in the bed.

At this last outrageous lie of his, Dowager almost fell off of the chair from the fit of laughing she took and she smacked her son's knee good-humouredly, her eyes filling up with happy tears at the sheer size of his wicked yarns. For it was to him out of all her children that the *gift-of-lying* had been given on the day he was born. But there was one crucial thing (apart from the unreported absence of Brandy-the-ferret) missing from all their merriment: not one single word was said about the love and the hate that was mixed up inside the heart of Stylish nor the reason why it was ever there.

Putting On A Brave Face

Then it was the next day and a Saturday. In these few short hours of his homecoming Stylish couldn't sit idly by and stay looking into the fire each morning. Life's springtime was rising up inside him, now as ever, urging on all his spellbinding energy. His very essence (albeit disguised) was crying out to him to get himself off out to the fields and put on a bit of a show for the younger ones. What better way of entertaining them than to express his hurling prowess. It had never left him and he'd make this a day for them to remember.

He got up from the chair and he walked over to his suitcase at the half-door. Whatever else, he was determined to put on a brave face and hide his sadness – just as he had done in days gone by when he carelessly jumped the five-barred gate and practised all sorts of devilment in front of the rest of the family. He unstrapped his new white hurleystick from the belt round the suitcase and passed it round among his brothers and sisters. They marvelled at the newness of it, for all that they'd ever owned were the broken bits of hurleysticks thrown away by the senior hurlers of Abbey Cross.

'Follow me,' said he to his brothers.

They didn't need asking twice and they ran out the door after him and into the Bluebutton Field. It was getting on for mid-morning with the hot sun already glaring down on them and not a single cloud in the sky

Stylish hurried towards the middle of the field, sweeping his hurleystick this way and that way and jumping over-and-back-and-over-and-back across it, his knees bent high up almost to his chin. Ah-ha, the athlete that was in him!

He pelted his coat into the ditch and threw out his chest, breathing in the air of an almost-forgotten Rookery Rally – air that was pure and heavenly compared to the dingy smells and fumes of the dung-laden streets of the Big City. It was doing him a power of good.

The little ones had also left the fireside and, climbing over the haggart-stick, they quickly reached the field. They stood at the ditch, staring at their big brother's thick-set body and the wrinkles on the back and belly of his lovely blue shirt. They saw him take a shammy ball from his pocket. They saw him stare at his hurleystick, twisting it round and round in his big fist. He had wrists like butter and his fingers rippled on the hurleystick.

Then all was quiet and hushed as he threw the shammy ball into the air and raised his hurleystick. He curled one trouserleg round the other and, writhing like a hammer-thrower, he made a mighty roundabout swing and sent the shammy ball soaring high in the sky where it hovered for a moment as if it were on wings. They all got a dizziness in their head from looking up at its flight and then looking back down at Stylish. Oh, how nimble were his pudgy legs as he flittered back and forth across the field – his eyes all the time following the shammy ball's journey. Before it could come back down to the ground he met it fair-and-square with his hurleystick and sent it flying back up on another long career high in the sky.

That's when the surrounding hills re-echoed to the roars of the children ('Sky-high, Stylish! Sky-high!') as they stretched out their necks from their perch at the edge of the field.

Dowager and Handsome Johnnie had left off what they were doing and had come out and were standing behind the children at the haggart-stick. They saw it all – saw the wonder in the eyes of the three little ones and the rapture in them at the blaze of their big brother and his shammy ball: the hollow ping of it: the rubbery hum of it off of his hurleystick.

'Do it again for us, do it again!' pleaded Tiny Jim, as time and time again Stylish sent the shammy ball up into the clouds.

And oh, how his big brothers and sisters also loved the sight of it – loved the sight of Stylish the new man.

Neither could Handsome Johnnie stop from smiling at the glory of his son – at the sunlight shining out of him, a sweat-stained youth as of yore when once he scythed down his acre of corn.

Ah-ha, (thought he, nudging Dowager) isn't our Stylish the mighty-mighty man!

Why (said she), he could do what he liked with the shammy ball. Aye, he could make it talk.

The Upended Bucket And Churn Again

In the late afternoon the neighbouring children – Zippity and Punch among them and even the oafish Tom Foolery – joined in with the Spallidagh children. They all returned to the Bluebutton Field to watch the mastery of Stylish enervating them all over again. See the way they held their breath while he made one of his juggling solo-runs with the ball stuck like glue to the tip of his hurleystick – down the length of the field to the Rotten Tree – back up again – all the time bouncing the ball and turning the boss of his hurleystick up'n'down, up'n'down without letting the ball drop to his feet as he sped towards the little ones and frightened Little Dan and Deelyah out of their wits with his sheer speed.

The older ones clapped and clapped and sighed and sighed with a rare pleasure at this particular piece of trickery. And Tiny Jim cried out, 'Stylish! Stylish! Do it again for us! Do it again – gwan, do!'

And then, to see Stylish whaling the shammy ball at the upended bucket and the rusty churn – just as he did in days of olde – and they all counting the number of times he was able to fire his pucks into the depths of the bucket or churn.

And then to see the smart way he rolled the shammy ball out of the bucket and up between his shoe and the boss of his hurleystick before taking a mighty swing at it and sending it high over Old Stroller's hayshed where it landed in a little scrape of stones outside the old man's back door.

And now, the flaming sun began to fade away, its rays travelling off stealthily into the purple and lavender afterglow. It had been a day of all days when the world of childhood seemed to hold lingeringly onto the last few white clouds of the late afternoon.

And then, the silence of twilight came along and put an end to the hurleystick amusements of Stylish. A few inky clouds were already appearing from beyond Corcoran's Well and invading the sky over the Bluebutton Field. The children in a great big heap came scattering in across the haggart to tell the news to Dowager and Handsome Johnnie (who had both long left the haggart) – how Stylish and his hurleystick had teased the very life out of the white clouds and out of the sun herself (the little liars all over again) with the magic of his shammy-ball hurling.

Quicker Than An Eye-blink

That evening, that night and all of the next day seemed to pass by quicker than an eye-blink and it was time for Stylish to leave his home for a second time. Dowager and Handsome Johnnie came out to the flagstones where they lashed the holy-water onto his forehead and blessed him with their tears and best wishes. His brothers and sister – the neighbouring children too (led by Zippity) – came down the road to watch him placing his polished shoe a step inside Danny-be-Quick's posh motorcar. There wasn't a single smile out of him ('See the sad look on his face and how sorry he is to be leaving us,') and one and all they made great use of their pocket-handkerchiefs and their melodious tears.

'Coom back soon, Stylish! Coom back soon!' But they never saw him again.

Famed Riverside Park

Ever the showman, Stylish returned to the big city where he quickly bounced back into his citified life. A few weeks later, though still a youth, he was given the privilege of hurling for *the Commonside Wanderers*. It was to be his first and only hurling-match in the famed Riverside Park.

Listen to the noisy din of the streets. See the young men and women speeding their way to the match and jostling at the gates to get in – some on foot, their feet stamping the pavement in time with one another – others on bikes, their bike-bells and mudguards rattling and the laughing children getting a safe carrying on the crossbar of their father's bike.

The Twisting, The Tangling

How happy was Stylish on this the most memorable day of his life. He had his boots and his hurleystick well-oiled and ready for him to show his mettle. It was his chance to shine and make his mark in the Big City like his uncle, Busy-Bee, had done before him. The world was at his feet (he was sure of it) and from the very start of the match he gave it all his skill and energy, enjoying every moment of the twisting and the tangling: the fray and the tussle: the mass of the clouting hurleysticks: the cries and the roars of the crowd.

But alas, soon there was to be heard a far different cry. Woe and woe a thousand times over: if only the hands of Time could have been stopped on the clocktower.

The Lugubrious Fairies

Lo and behold, the *Lugubrious Fairies* were out and about on that breezy afternoon and they now came hurtling down from the nearby mountains. They flew into the Big City – a-hunting and a-searching for Stylish and eager to catch a hold of his soul.

May the good-God-in-heaven spare the young hurler (*Diamond Jack*) whose hurleystick struck the savage blow down on top of poor Stylish's skull in a misplaced attempt to clear the ball upfield before Stylish himself could bury it passed the goalie and into the net for the opening score.

Ah, Stylish, Stylish! Why had it to end this way?

In A Haze Of Unconsciousness

He fell to the ground where he lay in a haze of unconsciousness. The spectators were hushed into silence, horrified at the sight of the blood they saw puddling out of Stylish's sad wound and spattering onto his hurling-jersey.

In a fierce hurry the ambulance-men carried him away, his head in a mummified bandage, as far as Riverside Hospital where the surgeons and nurses (some of whom knew Stylish well) worked a near-miracle in an attempt to cure and save him from dying.

In the end they put a small steel plate inside in his head, hoping that he would recover and then they placed a hurleystick on the wall above his hospital bed. It would be good for nothing but a showcase offering for they knew his head was never going to get right again.

The steel plate grew heavier by the day and still heavier by the month and before the year had ended the weight of it had shattered almost all of the brains left inside him. Poor Stylish! He, who had given so much of himself to the entertainment of others, now got the severest of headaches. He realised that he hadn't much longer left on earth – that he'd have to be quick. There was still a little time for him to make his peace with God and Man.

He Couldn't Hide From God

He knew that he couldn't hide from God and that the unforgiving nature of his sour anger was still alive inside in his heart, even after all these long years.

God came close and he looked into the depths of his secret soul.

He excused him for his anger.

He did not excuse him for his hatred.

Before Stylish faded away altogether, he was spared a little more time – just a week or two – in which to examine the thoughts that had dogged him ever since the day the ferret had destroyed his mother's finger.

'I cannot die a bitter man. I'd be in Purgatory's flames, forever burning, if I hadn't the heart to forgive mee mother and father – forgive Warbling Will, whose hands delivered the savage blows with the razor-strap – forgive mee other brothers and sisters, who watched it all and said not a damned word to save mee hide.'

God came to his rescue and told him what to do. He gave him just enough brainpower to sit down and write to his mother. Stylish took out the pen and paper – something he had never thought he'd end up doing – and he wrote Dowager a letter that was most heart-breaking. In it he spoke of his forgiveness for the savagery of the belting and the raw bleeding of his legs the day the blood ran down from him and into the stream. His words were simple but their meaning was clear. He forgave them not only for the savage hurt to his arse and legs but for a much deeper hurt – the hurt to the very spirit that was the core of his child's soul, leaving it bruised and torn right up until these last few hours before his death.

At the end of the letter he hastily scribbled his last few sad words to Dowager: 'Dear God-in-heaven, don't let me die a bitter man. Forgive me for my coldness to ye all!' He hoped and prayed they'd understand.

He Had Forgiven Them All

His letter arrived home a day after his death. It took time for them to understand it. He had forgiven them for having sat like cowards in the Law-circle of chairs abroad in the yard, condemning him to the harshest of punishments. Likewise, he had asked them to forgive him for the hate and anger that he'd nourished in his heart against them these many years.

The letter was a great shock to them and with many a tear around the house they forgave him wholeheartedly. It seemed a moment of Redemption for both himself and themselves. If only they had had the chance to write back to him before his death and to whisper their words of forgiveness into his ear so that he could have known the truth at the end of his days and died in peace.

A Dark Shadow

He was in his chair at the evening fireside and gazing into its embers when a dark shadow passed over his eyes. He was sitting there alone in that solitary space – just himself and his little dog (*Savage*). He had nothing else to do but think about his life and a fierce yearning came over him – for the past and for his home and his kith and kin.

He was far away from Dowager – far away from Handsome Johnnie – far away from his brothers and sisters and his olden-day school-friends, all of whom would live and die one day back home in Rookery Rally. An unbelievable sadness took hold of his heart as he cast his thoughts back to those earlier times – times when the shrieks of his boyish laughter could be heard all over the fields – all over the rivers and woods – to the days before the Family Law had delivered him his skelping.

What Were They All Doing Now?

What were the Spallidaghs and the rest of the old folk doing back there in Rookery Rally?

Sitting on the singletree at dusk in Old Sam's Grove and smoking their Woodbine fags.

His younger brothers and sisters, playing their skittles on the flagstones.

Sammy-Joe and his friends, Zippity and Punch, taking the ambling horse up to Hammer-the-Smith's forge for a new set of shoes.

Dowager, feeding her morning-time hens and ducks and listening to the terrible racket they made beneath her feet.

Handsome Johnnie, fixing his rabbit-traps and snares and thinking of his dead friend, Poesy.

Blue-eyed Jack, going off to Bog Boundless for a cartload of turf and searching out a hurleystick-makings from an ash-tree.

Warbling Will and Lofty, going off into the Roaring Town for a fine day's outing and boozing at the Show-Fair.

Darkie and Little Nell, making their daisy-chains for the three little ones' necks in the Bluebutton Field.

And the three little ones, trying to build a house of cards for themselves on the front-table.

No More...

His mind could picture it all. No more would he fetch the water from the well. No more would he cut an acre of corn. No more would he leap the five-barred gate or climb the Rotten Tree.

A day later when the door was broken in by his cousins, Matty and Pat, they found him sitting on his chair in front of the dead fire-grate. The woman-of-the-house hadn't seen him since the week before and by now his legs were as stiff as a board. When this fact – the saddest of all news – reached Rookery Rally, those cruel old gossips (the Weeping Mollys) had the nerve to say that in the meantime his little dog, Savage, had grown so hungry that he had chewed not only the ends of Stylish's trousers but had eaten half of his right leg and was casting an eye on the left leg as well. Oh, the hard-hearted harridans – to be saying such things about a youth as noble as Stylish! Would God ever forgive them? Would hell itself be good enough for the likes of them?

He Arrived Home In Style

Stylish arrived home in style and was buried in Abbey Acres. The full attendance of Rookery Rally's people was there in the little wooden church in Copperstone Hollow. It was a grand and ceremonious occasion, full of blue and yellow sunlight at the windows and not a cloud dotting the sky. It seemed as though a hundred flickering candles were lighting up the church. The scene was heightened all the more when Dowager and Handsome Johnnie stepped up to the coffin and placed a brand new hurleystick on top of Stylish's coffin. It was wrapped in a blue-and-gold Tipperary jersey.

That evening, long after Curl'n'Stripes had thrown a last wreath, (delivered from the Hartigans of Toom) down into the grave, Warbling Will took the razor-strap from its place beside the broken bit of looking-glass in the Big Cave Room. The rest of the Spallidaghs surrounded him at the front-table. He layered it with goose-grease from the bowl next to the sour milk jug on the press. Reverently he laid it in the blazing fire. They watched it shrivel up and disappear out of sight. There'd be no more beatings and humiliating of a child's legs with a razor-strap. Then Handsome Johnnie said a prayer that the burning of the razor-strap (but he wasn't sure how) would now free the family from its guilt and give their souls a fighting chance of heaven in the hereafter – that it would cancel out forever the anger caused to Stylish and set his own soul at peace – that it would free him to soar towards his Maker in The Beyond.

They All Began To Look Back On Themselves

Stylish's letter had made them all take a few steps back and cast a long look inside themselves. They began to ask themselves: had they been so blinkered all these years as to forget the rules of Nature – the stories of asses and horses that had been harshly beaten and how these hurt creatures, when given half-a-chance, made unexpected raids on their cruel masters and chewed the arm off of them or had nailed them to the ground with a fierce kick from their hind legs? Had they not realised that a child, like any trashed ass or horse, was never likely to fill the world with dimpled smiles or genuine laughter?

Suddenly it dawned on them: what a great actor Stylish had been all this time – the way he'd entertained them with his athletic and hurling skills and all his roguery – the way he'd let not a single frown or scowl ever run across his face. They felt like a pack of thundering eejits. Never could they have imagined the bitter anger and hatred that must have been engendered in his cheery nature as soon as the first stroke of the lash had hit him – the aching pain and sadness thereafter in his heart – all of which had grown and festered undisturbed in him throughout these years.

A Moment Of Enlightenment

This was the moment of Enlightenment for the Spallidaghs. They read his letter over and over again. They talked about it for days and days thereafter. They couldn't get Stylish out of their heads – couldn't forget the comical and energetic boy, who had spouted prayers and curses in equal measure and had made their sides burst with laughter throughout his childhood.

It was the end of one chapter and the start of a new one. The letter of Stylish had achieved its purpose. There'd be no such humiliation ever again. There'd be other ways of carrying out the Family Law from their circle of chairs in the yard. And they – in the act of burning the razor-strap – and with a commitment to change forever the penalties of Family Law – had each sought forgiveness from the ghost of Stylish.

From now on the lives of the Spallidaghs would be different.

From now on they would find peace within themselves.

From now on they would realise the dignity that lies in the hearts of everyone.

God (they hoped) would find it in His heart to smile favourably on their little thatched house so that at the end of their own days on earth He might see fit to welcome them into the realms of heaven – to join with that wonder-of-a-man in his new home beyond the skies – the inimitable and once-in-a-lifetime Stylish.

EIGHT

Sammy-Joe's sorrow

Some fifteen years before the tragic death of Stylish, Dowager and Handsome Johnnie were again overjoyed when they realised that another little blessing from God was about to come into the Spallidagh household.

It was a Friday morning late in March when Sammy-Joe was born. It was during the last knockings of the Great Storm that had enveloped Rookery Rally throughout the winter. The weather had been even more foul the previous week, carrying old and young alike off to their death by the severity of its gales – either drowning them in bog-holes or causing them to shiver to death despite being placed in front of their blazing fire.

And now, as Dowager lay in her bed, awaiting the birth and wonder of this new child, she feared the storm anew. From her bed in the little birthing room opposite the Welcoming Room fireplace she could hear the wind whistling as if it were a banshee and the crows calling to one another as they came flying frantically back to the safety of the trees in Old Sam's Grove – a sign (said she to herself) that another blast of the storm was brewing nearby. And then – as though Nature had been reading her mind – the wind turned into a roar similar to the roaring of Growl River abroad in Bog Boundless and it rattled its way straight across the haggart in an effort to get in through her bedroom window.

At first the older children, led by the eight-year-old Blue-eyed Jack (though his eyes at that time were not yet that lovely cornflower blue that would one day set the maidens' hearts a-fluttering) paid little or no heed to all the fuss-and-bother around their mother as she lay struggling to give birth.

It was nearing the holy weekend of Easter and they had the run of the yard and the fields to themselves. They were free from school for a week or two and they felt able to terrorise the geese and the sow and frighten them off into the haggart. Even Darkie and her hole-in-the-heart was able to run after the hens and the ducks and make a grab for their tail-feathers so as to dowse them with a dab of salt.

Meanwhile, their mother clung to her rosary-beads and blessed herself and said her favourite prayer to Saint Jude. After that she heard another roar – a different kind of roar – a better kind of roar. Handsome Johnnie had brought in an armful of logs and had heaped them up onto the fire. The flames were now roaring up the chimney, as if bravely fighting to protect the house from the threatening storm outside. In spite of her backache in attempting to give birth to this latest child, she felt safe and comforted.

Bless-my-soul, a minute later there came a third roar – a roar in the shape of her newborn baby boy (Sammy-Joe) as he made his struggle into life and started roaring like a lion for the next half-hour before finally wearing himself out and falling into a peaceful sleep on his mother's breast.

And then the children rushed in the half-door when they heard the crying squawks of their newborn brother and they stood on their tippy-tiptoes and looked in over the handles of the crib so as to get a proper peep at Sammy-Joe. It was as good as a Christmas Day. They soon found that the little infant was no company for them. He slept throughout the hours of daylight but he kept them all awake, roaring like a bleddy lion the whole night long.

Handsome Johnnie and Dowager had to change their sleeping habits. Instead of the customary welcome for the cardplayers as they came in to while away the dark evenings with their tales and their bouts of roguery, the two of them were so tired and weary that they found themselves staggering round the house in a daze and ready to fall down.

Dowager laid her baby gently under the warm blankets in his crib next to her bed – just in case she should fall asleep after all her tiresome labours and roll over on top of him. Then she opened wide the bedroom door so as to let in the warmth from the blazing fire. After that she spent a precious moment looking down into the baby's crib, all the time wiping the happy tears from her eyes and smiling down at the little fellow. She felt well-and-truly satisfied. She had done her duty: another living soul for Holy Mother Church. And from the rafters overhead the ghosts of her ancestors looked down on herself and her baby. She felt their presence now as always – felt that they were her guardians and would always be near her to protect herself and the Spallidagh household – just as she would protect Sammy-Joe from all harm so that he'd never hereafter have to know the meaning of fear.

Little did she know what lay in store.

The Following Months

In the following months she couldn't take her eyes off of him. The other children had to laugh, seeing the way she bounced and dandled Sammy-Joe on her knees after dressing him and the way she whispered in his ear her own childhood nursery rhymes – especially the one she loved best:

> *Johnnie when you die will you leave me the fiddle-o?*
> *Johnnie when you die will you leave me the bow?'*

Sammy-Joe was beginning to thrive and already had the start of a fine head of hair on him. It was pure ginger, unlike the hair of the children that came before him – indeed unlike any of his previous ancestors. It was the colour (said Dowager) of the highly-strung mule belonging to her brother, Gooseberry-the-Pony.

And in those early months whilst he was lying in his crib in his mother's room and when he wasn't deep in sleep's dreamland, what else had he to do but drink in gallons of his mother's milk and open one eye after the other and gaze up at the hazy picture of The Virgin hanging down on a bit of string and the picture of the bespectacled pope on the wall opposite her and listen to the birds singing outside his window and hear the frantic bees in the hedge outside the back window, humming their latest news to one another after their outing to the field-flowers.

Cradle In Front Of The Fire

During the daytime Sammy-Joe's cradle was taken out from the bedroom and placed in front of the fire where the child could look into the flames or across the room at the yellow rays of sunlight coming in the half-door or watch his mother washing the delf in the enamel pan or cleaning out a chicken at the front table. If nothing else, he could listen to the tick-tock noise of the clock on the dresser. That's when the neighbours started to come in and gaze fondly down at the little dear. They were always sure to put a bit of silver ('for luck, you know') in Dowager's fist and say a prayer or two over her latest arrival before going off on their merry way.

Each night Handsome Johnnie conscientiously prepared his own sleeping quarters in the Big Cave Room so that Dowager could be left alone in her little room and have the space she required for tending to the basic needs of her newborn son. Before he headed off for his own nest, however, he made sure that his wife had all she wanted. He brought her a hot jar to wrap round her toes and he gave her a few slices of bread and blackcurrant jam and a mug of milk to wash it all down. With loving gaze (he couldn't stop his tears of joy) he gave her forehead a few drops of holy-water and added a few drops to the baby's forehead. Then, well-satisfied with all the arrangements, he left his good wife in peace for the night – or rather left her alone to have a great big fight against the devilish noise that Sammy-Joe was bound to make the whole of the night. No, Handsome Johnnie was no fool: he knew he'd got the best part of the bargain – a narrow, if sly, escape from hard work and a peaceful night's sleep for himself instead.

The Next Year Or Two

And in the next year or two Sammy-Joe would come to the fire and kneel beside Dowager as she taught him how to join his hands in prayer and how to say his first sincere *God-Bless-Me* prayers. And again, the smiles and the laughter of the six older children when they recalled how they too must have been infants once – just like him – and must have felt (could they have put it into words) the close beating of Dowager's loving heart before falling asleep on her lap.

However, his slowness of speech during these first few years of his life was something that Dowager couldn't stop fretting over and the way the little fellow always kept looking round him as though he was expecting the world to pounce on him. Nevertheless, by the time he'd reached the age of four he had the freedom of a young calf and was able to edge his way round the back of the house and into the haggart. But his joy was constantly marred with fear – a fear that he had already developed of the Sinky Pool outside the cowshed, the result of listening to the visiting cardplayers' tale of a drowned man's ghost and his squelching wellingtons that were sometimes heard rising up from that slimy spot (or so they said). His mother knew that these newborn fears were nothing but the result of those cursed *nerves* that the child had inherited from his ancestors and which had plagued the lives of a number of earlier Spallidagh children.

Sammy-Joe's Bad Luck

In this fourth year he had the bad luck to contract the measles, a singularly sickly disease that was rarely, if ever, experienced by the children in Rookery Rally. It had unusual red spots, as if Sammy-Joe had been a naughty child and playing with the red sheep-rodden and dabbing it all over his body. It caused everyone in the house to stand and stare and wonder at the sight of him. As soon as its ugly head was raised, Dowager knew exactly what she must do: she took Sammy-Joe into her bed, away from Blue-eyed Jack and the other children in case they caught its contagion.

Lady Elegance (always a bountiful woman where there was a need) brought up a huge bowl of red jelly with fruit in it. To cap it off she added a little handful of cornflour, which (unlike the local stirabout) was well known amongst the better-offs in Rookery Rally.

There followed what was nothing short of an open rebellion as the other children refused to get themselves hunted from the bedroom door. After all, they weren't a bunch of intruding hens (they said). Dowager surprisingly relented. They peered in the bedroom doorway, puzzled and bewitched at the sight of Sammy-Joe and the bowl of jelly upturned on his mouth and rapidly finding its way down into his throat. This was a sight worse than death and one-and-all they had an ache in their guts – to see their young brother attacking the sweet medicine with such a gusto. It must have been doing him a power of good (they could tell).

'Ah, this lovely new food! Ah, if only we could get our hands on some of it!'

As soon as Dowager got out of bed and put on her boots to go out and feed her hens, they made a headlong dive in the direction of Sammy-Joe's bed and leaped in on top of the poor sick child:

'We too want to catch the measles.'

'We too want to catch the jelly and the cornflour.'

'We too want to catch the lovely fruit in it.'

It was not every day that they had a chance to get themselves both the measles and half a pudding-bowl of jelly, fruit and cornflour to whale into their bellies and they almost suffocated the poor child as each of them piled in on top of his head, squeezing him to death.

The Special Bond

It was in these formative years that the special bond between Sammy-Joe and Handsome Johnnie first became noticed – as if the father was the son's shadow and the son was the father's shadow, forever following each other round about in the morning sunlight.

An attachment such as this wasn't easy to explain. After all, there were four older sons, Blue-eyed Jack, Lofty, Warbling Will and the departed Stylish (God rest him) as well as Darkie and Little Nell. But just as a man can stand before a dozen damsels parading themselves round the floor of the Platform Dance-in-The-Fields and only one of them is able to catch his eye, so too was it with Sammy-Joe and Handsome Johnnie for the child had the unnatural gift of catching his father's eye in such a way that the poor man was like a moth bedazzled by a candleflame – all the time fussing round the little fellow in a way he'd never been able to do with the other children.

The Joy Of Sammy-Joe

As these early years rolled on, the joy in each other's company became clearer and clearer. It was especially true when Handsome Johnnie required Sammy-Joe to stay at home from school and help him plant the latest trees at the bottom of the haggart, a task that would keep back the fierce force of the Kerry winds. On these occasions the father was the finest of teachers, having been good with plants throughout his life – skills he had learnt from his own father, Dandy, who in his turn had been drilled by his father in the posh gardens of Lord Allsworthy back in Galway. And so, he took the greatest of pride in teaching his young son how to place the stronger roots on the south-west side of the trench – how to hold them firmly and vertically in place whilst he himself pelted in the clay and firmed it roundabout with his wellington-boot. What need was there of school (he would ask himself) when he could see for himself that Sammy-Joe was learning so much at home?

Some Saturdays the two of them would head off to town and to the market-cross to make a study of the corms from which to grow the seeds for more new plants. Handsome Johnnie would cast his eye at the tree-saplings on display. With his finger on his lip he would stand back and gauge their future heights ('I think this one'll make thirty feet – that one next to it'll make forty feet.') and he'd pat Sammy-Joe on the back to make sure that the latest lesson of Nature was going into his head and up into his brain.

On other Saturdays it was Sammy-Joe and not the others that went with his father to the creamery, the two of them lining themselves up with the other farmers' horse-and-carts out passed the graveyard and the gates of Lord Elegance. On these mornings the child had nothing to do but listen to the trundling sound of the cartwheels from his unsteady perch between the roped tanks of milk on a sop-of-hay with last year's harvest-scent on it – listen to the jingling rhythm of the mare's harness and her rhythmical farts, accompanied by his father nasally singing one of his old favourite melodies, *A lamp shining bright in the window*.

When they reached the creamery gates ('*whoa! whoa!*') there was always something new for Sammy-Joe to occupy himself with ; the grating carts circling round in the white yard ; the rumbling sound of the great big milk-vats as the strong arms of his father helped the creamery-manager lift the tanks up onto the milk-stand : the sight of the men leaping down from their cart, searching for their pipes of tobacco before lighting them up (puff! puff!) and putting smoke to the heavens and then the sheer delight on the faces of this vast congress of men (there wasn't a woman in sight) as they all strived to talk at one-and-the-same time, each one louder than the next, before taking their turn to exchange their milk for butter and semi-skimmed milk.

The Most Intimate Of Friends

In ways such as this the father and son continued to work daily side-by-side till they became the most intimate of friends – Handsome Johnnie teaching his son a list of new and practical skills: how to shoe Moll-the mare: what was the best way to tame an ass: how to recognise wild birds' eggs by their shape, colour and speckles: how to get milk out of a sheep. And on each occasion Sammy-Joe showed himself to be the most willing of scholars, taking his father's words seriously to heart – taking them deep down into his soul, a joy that would last him all the days of his life and make him a most willing slave to Nature – make him what Handsome Johnnie would refer to hereafter as 'mee one and only *True Man.*'

A Record Man

And now, a year after the tragic death of poor Stylish, some men seemed to have forgotten the towering strengths of *that* young man and they began to sing the praises of Sammy-Joe instead.

'An arch man – that's what he is,' they'd say whilst supping their pints of the black doctor stout. This was high praise indeed. They then went a step further and invented a new credential for him: 'Sammy-Joe is nothing short of a *Record Man.*' It was a title, which meant that in their eyes Sammy-Joe, though still a fifteen-year-old lad, deserved to have his name recorded in the annals of Rookery Rally.

Unique praise such as theirs might well have been given to him a few years earlier by these same seasoned drinkers if only they'd been sitting beside him at their old school desks. For on the days when he attended Dang-the-skin-of-it's schoolhouse, Sammy-Joe proved (like Stylish before him) to be the brightest of stars when it came to the use of the book, pencil and slate.

On those days when Inspector Handyman was due to pay the school a visit and when Sammy-Joe was likely to be at home working with his father, a message would be rushed across the fields to Dowager, informing her 'be sure and send that lad to school tomorrow.' For there was none but he who knew how to pin the donkey's tail blindfolded on the requisite part of that animal during the lesson of the Blind Coordinates – none but he who could sail through the advanced books of Euclid and memorise the several verses of poetry in the two languages, English and Irish.

Surprisingly, however, such a repertoire as Sammy-Joe's was not enough to win him the accolade of a Record Man. There had to be something even more telling than his brainpower at school: it was his expert use of his well-hooped hurleystick which was to mark him out as a youth worthy of even higher acclaim.

A Wiry Lad

He was a wiry lad, so thin, said Dowager with an exaggerated smile on her face, that you could put him in a lemonade-bottle. And at first sight he had all the appearance of being on the weak side. His looks, however, were deceiving. For the minute he stepped out on the hurling-field he was seen to be made of sterner stuff. No-one could understand how the quietness in him could change so quickly into a raging vitality or the reason why this strange new power came storming through his body. After all, he was shyer by far than his older brothers – even a mouse could frighten him – and his nervous lips never expressed a single word of anger to anyone during the rest of the week. When asked to explain his shyness, Sammy-Joe would shrug his shoulders. 'There's enough tongues (he'd say) to be making noise without me putting meeself forward and adding to the list.' Those few words might be the only bit of speech his brothers would get out of him the livelong day.

Dowager was well aware of her son's gentle nature. To some extent she even admired it and, when chatting with Handsome Johnnie at the milking, she would often echo the lad's words with her own bit of motherly wisdom (though nobody understood a word of it): 'There's more badness comes out of the mouth than ever goes into it.'

The Abbey Rovers Juveniles

On the days when Handsome Johnnie took Sammy-Joe down to Abbey Cross to hurl with the Abbey Rovers Juveniles – and after he had given him his fatherly blessing, accompanied by a good-natured smack on his arse – the lad's whole frame would shudder inexplicably. But, as soon as he put on his hurling-togs and entering the hurling-match frenzy, his demeanour would change as if struck by a magician. And when he turned his eyes towards the sideline, all he could see was the smile and happy laughter spreading ear-to-ear across his father's face and he shaking his fist encouragingly and urging him on.

'Be a man, mee son.'

'Be a proud man.'

'Be yeer father's son.'

His words were not in vain. For as soon as the priest put the whistle to his lips to let play commence, Sammy-Joe with a belt of his hurleystick made a painful dent in the arse of the lad he was marking and put the fear-of-god in the poor fellow. From then on it was as if the sun had come out from behind a smudgy cloud – as if the soft chalk in Sammy-Joe had turned to bell-metal, so fiercely did he wield his hurleystick round the middle of the battling field.

'Keep back from me! Keep back, I say! Be-the-holy-crypes, I'll make ye keep back from me!' Wasn't he the miller-of-a-man!

Fair play to him (thought Handsome Johnnie) and his face reddened with merriment ('that's mee son out there!') at the dash of Sammy-Joe.

That was all the encouragement the lad needed to dazzle and shine even more. He took a tremendous cut of his hurleystick across the startled lad's shinbones and followed this up by almost ruining the fellow's ribcage – digging the heel of his hurleystick in through the poor lad's stomach so that he was scarcely able to cough for the rest of the match and was seen running like blazes away from Sammy-Joe.

With the field to himself he had space now to pull on the rising ball. Zing-zing it went, cutting the air like a scythe as it sped towards the opposing goalmouth.

As the match went on his father nudged the man next to him, pointing out the way Sammy-Joe had placed himself beneath the arc of the dropping ball after the opposing goalie had taken his puck-out – the way the sly young devil, who a minute before had been seen strolling around with an air of aimless disinterest, was now running forward and eyed the ball's downward journey, not bothering to catch it in his fist but meeting it fair-and-square and sending it back to where it came from. You'd give anything to see the gaping eyes of the goalie as the ball sailed high above the crossbar and out into the next field.

It was then that the drinking-guzzlers thought of their new title for him (a *Record Man*) and Handsome Johnnie was more than glad to agree with them, so proud was he of his young son.

The Children's Greetings

In addition to the hurling there was something else – seemingly trivial at first glance – which would mark Sammy-Joe out from his brothers and sisters. In their babbling infancy each Spallidagh child was heard to utter the pleading word *mammy* when they needed their mother's milk. They shouted the word *da-dah* when they saw Handsome Johnnie coming in through the half-door and firing his cap onto the nail under The Sacred Heart picture guarding the Welcoming Room.

In the following few years, however, they became somewhat coy and self-conscious and forgot the sentimental word *mammy*, replacing it with *ma'am* – a posh throwback expression from the days when their grandfather, Dandy, had worked for Lord Allsworthy over in Galway.

As for their father, the other children, once they reached school-age, also changed tack and gave up the childish expression of *da-dah* and greeted him with the much more formal greeting of *father*. For, in spite of his warm and almost childish nature – in spite of his rousing singing and the way he played his battered old concertina – there was in him (something they couldn't put into words at the time) an inexplicable sense of nobility and a serious grandeur that made him the omnipotent lord and master of his household. In their books at school they had learnt how Jesus used to look up to his own heavenly father and pray to him. They took it for granted, therefore, that there was no more important man on God's earth than their beloved father.

The exception to the rule of using *father* when greeting Handsome Johnnie was Sammy-Joe, who continued to refer to his father as *da-dah* – himself and his revered father being as close as ivy to the ash-tree – and *da-dah* would be the name forever on his lips.

The Wretched Pains In The Liver

A month before Fandango arrived from Galway and made his ill-fated appearance amongst the Spallidaghs – that was when Handsome Johnnie's health had first started fading with one or two pains in his liver. Dowager was beside herself with worry and she told him he was a silly old fool to be working so hard and that his health was what mattered and not to be spending all his time mollycoddling Sammy-Joe.

As soon as her daily chores were done she insisted on spending an hour each morning trying to comfort the poor man in case he'd start fretting about his health. Oh, how he relished these precious moments when all the children were out of the way. She too loved this closeness. His ears would prick up like an ass as he listened to the embroidery of her words whilst she was tracing the pedigree of one family after another. For she knew to her little fingernail the ancestry and burial mounds of most souls in Rookery Rally – knew their strengths and their weaknesses – and her broad knowledge of events included her own past family-members, some of whom had been no angels from time to time.

The Three Wise Men

It was during the following year (just after Stylish passed away) – a day when Blue-eyed Jack had taken Handsome Johnnie over to get Doctor Glasses to take a good look at him – that a group of strangers came into the lives of the Spallidaghs. Dowager was later to refer to this group as the Three Wise Men and she would remember their arrival as the month that Handsome Johnnie started to grow much worse with the liver-pains.

The day they arrived was a cold and frosty morning. Stepping out from their silver motorcar, they stood in a row on the Spallidagh flagstones. For once in her life Dowager was struck dumb and with finger on lip she quietened her excited children, who were already tugging at her apron and demanding answers to their whispered questions.

She could see by the rich cut of their clothes that these smart-looking men had come from the Land of The Silver Dollar, the place that was fondly referred to as Ireland's thirty-third county, our country having but thirty-two to call her own. What a long journey (she thought) the three of them must have made across the stormy waves of the ocean: they must be famished with the hunger.

The three strangers walked over to her little garden, which was edged with her sweet-william flowers and they gazed in over the privet hedge. In the centre was the American grass and behind it was an ancient pile of yellow stones that were the twelve-foot-square remains of an old blacksmith's forge. No-one in living memory had ever paid the slightest attention to these stones or had even bothered to ask why they were there or who put them there in the first place.

Dowager came out from the half-door, wiping her floury hands on her bib for she had been making the weekly preparation of her batches of soda-bread.

The Three Wise Men tiptoed across the yard. The children stood silently behind their mother's skirts and their eyes were quick to make a study of these remarkable visitors – how they were wearing new and double-breasted gaberdine suits, green as the blades of grass on the ditch – how their brown shoes were as shiny as the Christmas berries in Old Sam's Grove – how fair their hair was (their own head-of-hair was as black as tar) and how their faces seemed to reflect the light from the sky.

We Are The Carmidys

The men held their hats respectfully in front of them and they made a bow towards Dowager and the little thatched house.

'We are the Carmidy brothers,' they said.

After this introduction they informed her that they had come from far-off Baltimore all the way over the ocean.

At once Dowager recognised the name. For in her long list of tracing she had taught her children how, many years before the Spallidaghs ever came to live in their own little thatched nest, a dozen of the Carmidy family had lived on the very same spot as the Spallidaghs – along with their father (*Hop*) and their mother (*Lily*). She had told them how The Great Famine had once threatened to destroy the entire nation and how the whole crowd of the Carmidys – with whatever bits of money and few possessions they owned – had piled into three horse-and-carts and headed south for Cork County and Cove Harbour. That was all she could tell them and no-one had ever heard a word about the Carmidys since the day they departed, leaving a tearful gathering of neighbours and their wet handkerchiefs behind them down at the Kill before vanishing into the early morning mists.

She Made Them Her Best Bow

Dowager made the three gentlemen her best bow. She led them into her humble abode and offered them the holy-water from the font. She quickly put the kettle on for the mugs of strong tea and the soda-bread with blackcurrant jam.

Somewhat ceremoniously they sat themselves down beneath the Sacred Heart picture. They looked around the Welcoming Room where their ancestors had eaten and slept those many years before. They seemed bewildered by all that they saw. It was as though they were trying to memorise everything in front of their eyes: the dresser: the hob: the Saint Brigid's Cross: the horse's collar and haymes: the goose wings at the side of the hob: the hooks on the hob for the fletches of bacon: the tapestry that covered the length of the open fireplace: the oil lamp: the blazing fire: the blackened burners and skillets and crane: the Thomas Hood picture under the font with the words on it: *the little house says stay and the little road says go*.

After all their glorified living back across the ocean (thought Dowager) this must seem a very strange place for them to come visiting.

The strangers weren't the only ones bewildered. The older children were somewhat timid and stood close to the half-door in case they might have to escape and make a bolt across the yard.

With the younger ones it was different. Tiny Jim and Little Dan were unsure of themselves at first for they didn't know how best to approach the new men in their midst. Little by little, however, they started to get a bit brave. They slowly started to edge their way forward towards the fine-looking men, who were busily preoccupied, talking to their mother. They knelt down on the floor beside the strangers and with their grubby little hands began to feel and examine the threads in their creased trousers. They put spit on their fingers and tried to trace the intricate pattern and the sheen in the men's shoes. It was as though their new visitors (unlike the poacher, Airs-and-Graces) were a set of angels that had arrived from somewhere close to heaven in their posh silver motorcar.

Growing Thinner And Thinner

The distraction of these dazzling strangers couldn't have been more welcome, seeing how Handsome Johnnie had been growing thinner and thinner during the previous week. It was clear to Dowager that there was nothing but miserable death facing his handsome face.

The coming days would prove the saddest time in the children's lives with the younger ones playing on the floor round his sick-bed in an effort to bring him back his old cheerfulness – the older ones praying for his well-being outside in the Welcoming Room. When they were all safely tucked in bed and sound asleep Dowager would still be wide awake, watching Handsome Johnnie as he coughed up bits of his liver in the quietness of the night.

Supping Their Tea

As the Three Wise Men went on supping their tea they told Dowager how their family had set out from the coast and after much turmoil and seasickness had at last reached the Ohio River – how three of them had died of starvation on their way across the sea – how, in spite of all the hardships that they'd endured in their new land, they, the Carmidys, had kept to their ancestral task as blacksmiths and had grown steadily richer as the years rolled on.

As their tale continued, Dowager's ears were glued to every word. Never in all her born days had she heard such an enormous amount of adventurous news. She had to smile at some of their story – especially when she heard of the Ohio bank-manager handing them tea in his silver teapot and huge lumps of chocolate cake and rubbing his greedy little hands together (she could picture it) when he saw the piles of Carmidy money coming in across his counter.

Where did the money come from?

The Carmidys were the first migrants to set out each day from their forge in Ohio and take their tools and skills out onto the ranches to mend the farmers' broken ploughshares. Other blacksmiths hadn't the same foresight and they waited for the distressed farmers to bring their ploughshares into town, thereby wasting their valuable farming time.

Weren't these Carmidys the wisest of men? For in this canny way they soon outstripped the rest of the blacksmiths, who were headstrong enough to go on mending the farmers' ploughshares at their forge inside in the town.

They Finished Their Tea

The visitors finished their tea. For a moment they seemed not to know what to say. The school was closed for the long holidays and Dang-the-skin-of-it and Big Screech had taken themselves off on their annual pilgrimage to some holy shrine in the far west.

That was a great pity for the Three Wise Men were unable to visit the school and show their appreciation for the lessons the teachers had once taught their forebears.

They fumbled in their pockets and to everyone's astonishment they each took out a fifty-pound note and gave it to Dowager, asking her to pass the money on to the master and mistress for books and equipment and the school's overall improvement as soon as they came back from the holy shrine. It had been their father's dying wish (they said) that they do him this small favour and return one day to Rookery Rally to show his personal respect and gratitude for the master who had taught him and Lily so well. Fair play to old Hop Carmidy!

Dowager had never seen so much money and she swore an oath on the Sacred Heart picture that old Hop's wishes would be her wishes too. In the space of a few months Rookery Rally was to see plans for a new schoolhouse taking shape, thanks to the visitation of the Three Wise Men.

It Was Turning Into A Fairy-tale

The early afternoon was turning into a fairy-tale. First there was the arrival of the Three Wise Men in the silver motorcar. Now there was this story of their wealth and the three fat fifty-pound notes lying in Dowager's fist for a new school.

The day wasn't done yet and they asked Dowager to show them the little garden once more and asked if she'd allow them to step in over the privet hedge and take a walk round the seven-foot high American grass and would she lead them behind it to have a look at the pile of yellow stones. For these (Hop had told them) were the remains of where their father had put shoes on his last horses – the three horses that the Carmidys had driven in the carts so as to catch the boat from Cork and cross the ocean.

This spot was one of the children's favourite places where they hid from one another when they were playing hide-and-go-seek – just an old heap of broken stones at the back of Dowager's garden and never imagined as the remains of the Carmidy forge.

Dowager led the three gentlemen into the forge the easier way around – from the back of Simple Simon's lane. The three strangers stood in the middle of the yellow stones for what seemed an eternity. This is where it had all begun for the old Carmidy blacksmiths. All that was left of their forge were a few large stones and the two bigger cornerstones, most of the rest of the walls having been carried away long ago by one farmer or another with a better use for them. There were also three rusted galavanized sheets that had once been the roof of the forge.

The strangers tiptoed gently round through the ruins. They carefully (almost reverently) dislodged three handy-sized stones, frightening the little hen (*Speckles*), who had been secretly laying her eggs there and almost tripping over the fat rat, who had been regularly breakfasting on poor Speckles' daily eggs.

There was a further moment of silence in the middle of the lopsided ruins – as though they were praying. The three-of-them sighed and they wiped the tears from their eyes. The children stood in front of them at the hedge and gazed in wonder at their soft tears. Were they sad? Were they happy? They thought it a very strange thing for their visitors to be doing – standing there in the middle of a heap of old stones and ready to burst into tears as though they had caught their foot on a sharp thorn. But they were still young and had no way of knowing the rich feelings in the hearts of returning emigrants. It would take them many years to fully understand the depths of the Carmidys' joy. If the three strangers had a pencil handy, they would have written a small tale (even a poem) about Hob and Lily Carmidy and the little band of their twelve children – a tale about the long journey across the windswept seas – about the strange and bustling new land in which they found themselves.

The Day Was Moving Along Speedily

The day was moving along speedily and there was an increased urgency among the three men. They asked Dowager if they could carry away three stones as a heritage. Then they asked her for a few straws from the thatch above her half-door. The children thought they must have lost their wits entirely as a result of the very long distance they'd been travelling across the ocean waves. For what the devil were they going to do with the straws and the stones? Were they going to use the stones to build a little house for a family of leprechauns? Were they going to play gob-music on the straws?

Dowager gave her guests a mug of spring well-water. Then she shook each of them solemnly by the hand and blessed them again with the holy-water from the font. The children lined up in a row and they too shook the strangers' hands. It was all very grand and very unreal for them to see their mother kindly thanking the strangers for coming this very long journey to see and honour her Welcoming Room with all their finery.

Then she pointed her finger towards the Valley-of-the-Pig.

'Take that road – up by Sheep's Cross. It'll lead ye to the burial plot of yeer ancestors in the graveyard in Camel Hill – just behind the old church ruins. Ye can't miss it. That's where ye'll find the final resting-place of yeer ancestors. Yeer great-grandfather and a number of his brothers and sisters are buried there beneath the wheel-band belonging to their old horse-and-cart – the last bit of Carmidy workmanship some years before yeer people left this land for good.'

It was a long-winded bit of talk to have made – even for Dowager with her gift for tracing family roots – almost a sermon – for the ancestral Carmidys, being the finest of blacksmiths, had fashioned the wheel-band into a most artistic Celtic cross-and-circle and if a shower of silver had dropped from heaven, the visitors could not have been happier. They snatched up their hats and almost knocked each other over, disappearing out the half-door like a bolt from the blue. Then their silvery motorcar put dust out over the ditches as they stormed away towards Camel Hill and the graveyard to see the unique monument to their forebears – the blacksmith's cross-and-circle.

The Sad Morning Came

A day or two later – and after all the excitement of the Three Wise Men and their gift was over and done away with – there came a very sad morning when Handsome Johnnie started coughing up more and more of his liver. Dowager knew that the worst had finally arrived and she was forced to hurry Blue-eyed Jack off for a second time to fetch back Doctor Glasses quickly.

As soon as he arrived he could see the houseful of children sitting on the floor round the bed. He didn't want them to see their father dying in front of their eyes and he got the nurse (*Black Bess*) to bring up her truck and rush the poor man into the Roaring Town Hospital.

Dowager's uplifted spirit was now replaced by a river of the older children's sombre tears at the thought of their father lying in some godforsaken lonely bed in the town – the thought (worse still) that they might never be let go to town to see him or to say a little prayer over him. The three little ones were too young to know that they were about to lose forever their beloved father, never having lost him before, and they were soon abroad in the Bluebutton Field playing leap-frog when Black Bess and her black truck took Handsome Johnnie away with her and roared away down the slope.

Ah, the poignancy of it all.

The neighbours (forever mindful) came down to add their own bit of support and to comfort Dowager. When they saw the unbearable grief of the Spallidagh household and how empty the place was of all its previous joy (a pity the charm of Stylish wasn't here) they turned on their heel and respectfully left the yard at a quiet pace.

No Longer The Brave Hero

By this time Sammy-Joe had turned into a miserable waif – no longer the brave young hero of the juvenile hurling-field. His brothers and sisters had always understood his quietness and had accepted it. Nevertheless, it was very sad to see the way he retreated behind the ass-and-car and ran in beneath the hollybush to disappear from the world. It was as if he were trying to bury himself in the clay amid the furry caterpillars and the red ants that lived there.

It was worse for their mother – so much had she loved her sound man all the days of her life. The look on her face was heart-breaking as the misty memories of her country lad came flooding back to her: memories of his doughty days as a ploughboy below at Lady Singleton's: days he had spent winking his gladsome eye at her with his nose squashed up against that good lady's kitchen window while young Dowager was peeling her spuds: days sitting with her (*'mee precious jewel'*) on the sheltering singletree, heedless of the rain's noisy racket hopping off of the roadway and singing her his homespun songs whilst fingering his battered old concertina: summertime days when he held her boater-hat in his hand and carried her out through the muddy pig-house gap so as not to spoil her lovely flowing dress and walked with her over the flowery fields – especially the day he proposed to her and with his penknife cut her a beautiful bunch of wild roses from the ditch at Corcoran's Well.

Ah, yes, those were the happiest of days when he chased after her long enough till he'd won her heart: days without a sunset as once were those far-off days when Dandy-the-Galwayman walked his beloved Sadie down to the well and back: days that would surely vanish forever from Dowager.

To think of it, her beloved Johnnie and he not yet fifty-years-of-age and as handsome as ever – as if he was still in his youth and prime. What on earth would she do (shudder the thought) when he was no longer hidden under the warm blankets with her in the night but was about to leave her all on her own and with all these young mouths to feed and no-one ever to replace him or support her in the years to come? Worst of all, she knew that his death was going to be most painful (Doctor Glasses had told her so) with Handsome Johnnie spitting up more and more of his liver in front of the nurses and doctors.

Those Tarnished Old Gossips

These were sad days elsewhere in Rookery Rally. For it wasn't just Handsome Johnnie that was a source of grief. Each new day saw someone or other moving towards an untimely death – either from tuberculosis or the double-pneumonia or the cancerous inward pain-in-the-stomach. And on days like the present one in the Spallidagh household – that's when those tarnished old harridans (the Weeping Mollys) were ready once more to come into full force with their gossipy tongues; they couldn't keep their mouths shut for they loved nothing better than lofty description when it came to spreading misery round about Rookery Rally. It was like some sort of disease inside them. Before the evening was finished, their miserable lips had turned rumour into a fine art with a set of newly fabricated misrepresentations: 'We hear that the doctors have cut poor Johnnie's stomach wide open and that he's absolutely rotting away with the inward pains inside in it – that the poor man's belly is riddled with it – that the pains have spread down along his legs – down to his very toenails, turning them purple.'

But this time round their twisted old tongues had been a little bit too quick to roam out of their mouths, not knowing that it was not the stomach but the liver that had finally begun to disintegrate inside the poor man.

He'd Escaped From His Savage Illness

It was a Thursday evening – just as Dowager and Blue-eyed Jack were whaling the last few drops of milk into the buckets from their seven cows – that they heard the news from Herald-the-Post as he came cycling into the yard: Handsome Johnnie had finally escaped from the savagery that had turned his liver into mush. Herald told her how it had happened just after he'd given his last farewell to the assembled patients, who had risen up ghost-like from their hospital beds and staggered across the floor to hear him sing his favourite old song (*the Bird in the Gilded Cage*) and that he had then fallen back on his pillow and died with a smile on his face.

Dowager said nothing but made the sign-of-the-cross and came in and joined her children in the Welcoming Room. Without a prompt from her they knelt beside their mother and, with only the sound of the blazing logs crackling in the fireplace, they said their fervent rosary for the repose of their father's soul. It was an unreal moment in their lives – a sorrow unlike any previous sorrow. But in one sense it was a great relief to Dowager to think that her sound man was no longer in pain.

Nick-the-Devil's Son

Nick-the-Devil's son (*Timmy*), a mere lad of eighteen, brought Handsome Johnnie's corpse back to Rookery Rally. With his father's famed black mare (*Big Betsy*) he came in the pitch black of night when all was quiet except for the raging howls of Growl River in the far distance. It was a small blessing amidst all Dowager's new troubles for there'd be no fussing or bothering from the well-meaning neighbours, who'd be sound asleep in their beds at such an ungodly hour of the night. She'd be glad to miss out on the sincere handshakes and the *sorry-for-yeer-troubles* speeches that the kindly folk would have wanted to bestow on her if the poor man's body were to be brought home next morning rather than now at night. The hearse-man was a thoughtful young man and he had known that such a number of handshakes would be enough to break poor Dowager's arm and prevent her from milking her cows for the rest of the week.

He Stepped Down Reverently

Timmy stepped down reverently from his black carriage. He wasn't a bit like his devil-of-a-father. His sympathetic words were like a beam of light – the gentle way he greeted Dowager ('we all know yeer poor man is now with his heavenly Father').

Nick-the-Devil had been a notorious villain and his name was rarely mentioned by any of the older people – himself and his black hearse-carriage (and colourful language to match it) and an old hag-of-a-tinker-woman sitting on the high seat beside him and he driving around the countryside as drunk as a bleddy mule – stopping in one drinking-shop after another on his way back with a misfortunate corpse to throw it down carelessly on some poor snivelling widow's doorstep at three o'clock in the morning.

The old madman hadn't a drop of consideration in his withered body and he galloped his mare fierce-and-recklessly through wind, rain and storm with the speed of the devil (hence his name). This was especially true when he, thanks to all the fine drinking he'd been doing, knew he'd be late in getting a corpse home for its wake or getting a child that was shivering to death with the scarlet fever or a ruptured spleen into a poorhouse bed before the sorry lad decided to die entirely on him.

For once in their lives the Weeping Mollys had been right ('a fine guardian, that fellow is!') in belittling the antics of the old rogue. It was a veritable wonder how more than one corpse hadn't been flung out over the side of his carriage – to find itself in a far different burial-site than the Abbey Acres Graveyard, namely scattered in the depths of some black, boggy ditch!

They Solemnly Led Big Betsy

Blue-eyed Jack was now the man-of-the-house. Himself and his mother solemnly led Big Betsy across the yard where the well-trained mare stopped at the half-door. With the help of the young hearseman they gently lowered Handsome Johnnie's corpse down from the carriage and laid him carefully onto the settlebed.

Lady Elegance had discreetly sent up her best white sheets and an embroidered bolster so as to make Handsome Johnnie decent for his wake and for his last journey to the graveyard next day. Fair play to the nurses in the hospital – they had done a grand job too, adding the finishing touches to him by dressing him up in his best dark suit – the one that the Two Little Tailoresses from beyond the Pool Field had made for his wedding – the suit with the narrow red lines running in squares across it.

Blue-eyed Jack Comforted His Mother

And now the moonlight's ghostly gleam came streaking in across the Welcoming Room and lit up the settlebed. It made the dead man look as though he was indeed ready for his own wedding-day. His face was free of wrinkles and he appeared (thought Dowager) the very same as the boy she had danced with at the Harvest Barn-Dance in the Year-of-the-Big-Wind.

Blue-eyed Jack comforted his mother throughout the long night. They placed themselves at either side of the settlebed, guarding Handsome Johnnie till the cockerels began to crow again. The only sound puncturing the eerie solemnity was the tick-tock of the grandfather clock. Before the dawn Dowager must have said a hundred prayers for the salvation of his soul.

As soon as the golden sun sang its way in through the windows she summoned her children to her side. Though bleary-eyed with sleepiness, they soon were wide awake. A dead person was nothing new for them to look at (not even their father's corpse) for they had been to half-a-dozen wakes before now and one by one she led them round the settlebed so as to take a last fond look at his handsome face and say their Act of Contrition over him.

Dowager (fine teacher as always) told them that it wasn't their father – merely the remains of his life – that was lying there on the settlebed. Though the three little ones weren't old enough to make sense of her words, the rest of the children knew from their school-lessons with Dang-the-skin-of-it that this was a solid fact – that their father's soul had flown off into what the schoolmaster called *the stillness of Eternity* – that he was right now in front of Almighty God and that Almighty God was sifting through all the good deeds that he'd done whilst on earth and that He was separating these good deeds from the bad deeds.

Even Darkie, who once had his bucket of water lashed down on top of her head for her bout of impudence to Dowager, had to admit that her father had always been a saint-of-a-man. The other children too recalled him as the kindest of fathers and could never remember him doing a bad deed. Like their mother, they knew he was now in heaven and that fact in itself should have been enough to bring them a bit of good cheer. However – in spite of their mother's comforting words, each of them felt a sharp pain in their heart, striking them in underneath the chest-bone. No more would they hear his courtly songs under the oil-lamp – no more would he bounce the three little ones on his knees – no more would his nimble fingers trace out *the Stack of Barley* or *the Cat's Ramble to the Saucepan* on his battered old concertina.

The Crowds Came Into The Yard

The Welcoming Room had turned into a corpse-house and the crowds came from all sides to pay their final tribute – so many that they couldn't get in the half-door but knelt down respectfully on the hard cobbles of the yard – back as far as the haggart stick – and prayed there throughout the morning. Some of the women had taken their handkerchiefs from their limp wrists and were dabbing at their eyes.

Dowager's older brother, Gooseberry-the-Pony, was the last one to attend. He was somewhat drunk in his sorrow and he fell down in a heap on the flagstones. Grief or no grief, it was a terrible thing for Dowager to see her brother in such a state of drink and behaving like this – a disgrace that would surely be talked about (not least by the Weeping Mollys).

The rest of them now recalled (as no poet could have done) the long list of Handsome Johnnie's doughty deeds: his love of his children: his horse-riding them round the floor: his nimble fingers playing the polkas on his battered old concertina. It was a never-ending reflection, delivered in the loftiest of language.

Curl'n'Stripes bent the rules and from his shop he sent up three bottles of his cheapest rawgut whiskey and a dozen bags of good tea for the women. Dowager could pay for these later from the tick-book – that *book of shame*, which children all over Rookery Rally dreaded, finding themselves shouted at in front of the other customers whenever their mothers sent them down to humbly beg for an extended bit of credit.

After all the prayers had been said, the women came in and stood round the walls of the Welcoming Room, anxious to get a last fond peep at the handsome man ('I never saw him looking better').

For the men it was different. They didn't mind if they never saw his corpse for they knew that the poor man was finally gone to heaven after all his wretched pains and that nothing was left of him. See them there – like awkward geese – standing on one leg against the pig-house wall. It was a moment of joy amid their sorrow – a moment for their own words of praise as they quietly ran through the list of Handsome Johnnie's earlier mightiness and gusto in whatever he did: his strength and bravado in his famed fist-fights and the use of his cudgel whenever he needed to defend the honour of his family – not to mention his ploughing, his singing of old airs and his double-whistle like Dandy, his nightingale-of-a-father and they smoked their fag-butts one after the other till the yard seemed to be full of smoky clouds.

The spectral dusk was collecting itself from the yard stream and aching in along the yard when some older keening women, hired for the few hours, arrived in the door. They had come from way back yonder and they hurried over towards the flickering firelight to warm their hands before sitting themselves down by the settlebed, quietly moaning and puffing fiercely on their clay-pipes so as to ward off with their tobacco-smoke any putrifying spirits that might make their evil way into the corners of the Spallidaghs' little thatched house.

The Sudden Change In Sammy-Joe

Dowager suddenly noticed the strangeness in Sammy-Joe's appearance. He was now what was called a half-man and half-child, like his big brother, Stylish (the time when he was scything his acre of corn) and it was the half-child that now broke down. He strayed over near the fire and gazed silently at the thick fur on the hob. His mother could see him shrinking into himself as he cocked an ear and listened – listened for what? For the ghostly shrieks of the ancient ghoul of his earlier childhood (the Boodeeman from the Black Place)? Expecting it to bring its clodhopper boots whistling down the chimney and pounce on him and put him in his Devil-Bag? She could see him trembling and knew that his heart was beating fast and his feelings (those old Spallidagh *nerves*) getting the better of him. She knew it – she could see it. He was frightened and he wanted to take flight.

He went and stood at the half-door. He looked out at what might be eternity, listening to the chirping birds in the pink honeysuckle and the tears rolled silently down his jaw. With shoulders shrunken, head bowed, arms dangling, he walked for a few laborious steps across the yard – breathing in the rich smell of the dung that was wafting itself playfully towards his nostrils from outside the pig-house door.

He came back in to join the keening woman and stood there, shivering and staring down at the remains of his father on the settlebed. It seemed as though a black cloud had come to rest on his shoulders – as if a demon from hell had fixed a metal bolt into his soul. Dowager saw that his face had turned into a river of sweat like the prayer-book-picture of Jesus in the Garden of Gethsemane the night before his sad death – and she shuddered.

He Was Thinking Very Hard

Sammy-Joe was thinking. He was thinking very hard. Though his father had ached over Stylish the day after his thrashing – so much so that he had felt forced to distract him and take him night-hunting so as to belt the hide off of the thief robbing his rabbit-traps – at all other times it had been *he, Sammy-Joe*, to whom his father's undivided attention had always been given.

But now, no more would he sit by his father's sickbed and roll the plug of tobacco in his fists for him or light the pipe and offer it to him: no more would he top his egg for him with the knife: no more would he traipse in the footsteps of the man he loved best in the world so as to lay out the rows of young spring cabbage-plants: no more would he help him clean the backs of their few sheep under the bridge in River Laughter: no more would he help him wash the tired hocks of the Lightning Whoor: no more would he help him plant the young conifer-trees in the long trench at the lower end of the haggart: no more would he twist the ropy hay-soogans with the twister (*'walk easy, lad!'*) so as to firm and guard the hay against the prevailing Kerry winds that yearly threatened to topple the reek and the thirty trams: no more would he match his father step-for-step at the digging of the sloping pit for the spuds and turnips and the strawing-up and the top-soiling against the army of haggart rats. It was a long list that had always welded father and son together and showed the eternal love they'd had for one another – as if they'd been joined together at the hip-bone. It had always made Sammy-Joe's brothers and sisters laugh nervously.

The Children Ran Out The Half-door

With the exception of Sammy-Joe, Dowager turned her children out the half-door and told them go play in the Bluebutton Field. Grief was a fine thing for herself and Blue-eyed Jack but she felt that the rest of them had mourned enough and needed a distraction – that there'd be time next morning for them all to pour their renewed tears down onto their father's coffin when they went to the graveyard and stood round him.

For them, poor dears – what was sorrow (she thought)? The only sorrow that they'd ever known up till now was when the evening dusk came on and put an end to their play – when night's shadows drew a curtain over the day and the pink coppery clouds sailed off to Galway after a last smouldering.

They Stumbled Out From The Haggart

They stumbled out from the haggart and into the Bluebutton Field and didn't say a word to each other. They would always remember this day. They couldn't get their heads round it. From the field they could hear the long psalming of the neighbouring adults praying in the yard. They felt the need to share the moment with them and had no heart for running races among the wildflowers: no heart for climbing the Rotten Tree at the lower gap and indeed no heart for anything only their own undisguised sorrow. This was the one time in their young lives for serious and adult reflection – a time not for laughter and fun or for anything that might show disrespect towards their dead father and they passed the next hour silently making chains from the daisies and buttercups. They bound them round their wrists and got one another to join their two wrists together with the binding of the colourful chains before solemnly marching back in home.

The Shrivelled Sammy-Joe

Dowager and Blue-eyed Jack stood at either side of the shrivelled Sammy-Joe. They were awed at the sight of him as he tried to say a few words to them. However, like Zachary in The Good Book the day he was struck dumb when he was purifying the sanctuary with his incense, the poor lad couldn't get a single word out of his mouth and, after a first few fretful stammers, they realised he had lost the power of speech.

Dowager (oh, the poor woman) was beside herself with anguish – to see her tormented young son fading away to nothing and she promised she would take him into her own warm bed and comfort him till the day he was able to speak again.

When his brothers and sisters returned from the Bluebutton Field the sight of their brother was like a second death to each of them and their hearts went out to him. They stood there helplessly. They knew how close he had been to his father but not one of them could fathom the depth of his pain – not even Dowager. She took her apron and wiped the few bits of spittle from his chin and she dried the silent tears that continued to trickle from his eyes and down along his jaws.

Had he been able to utter a word, they would never have believed him. He'd have told them how his father's ghost was standing next to him – almost touching him – telling him that the-two-of-them were still united and to remain steadfast in his love.

But there was no-one now to turn to – no-one, to whom he could convey the immensity of his unspeakable grief. He turned his eyes towards the vision at his side and prayed that his father's ghostly self might understand and even welcome this terrible speechless sign of his love, a grief that was too sacred even for his mother to assuage.

That Old Depressive Streak

There was no mistaking the look on Dowager's face. No longer could she control her worry and sadness. More than anyone she knew the depressive streak that was always lurking behind the gaiety of the Spallidaghs. At the tender age of nineteen, Handsome Johnnie's own cousin

(*Donie*) had lost his sweetheart – drowned (said some) abroad in Bog Boundless – carried away (said others) by the *Wilderness Fairies*, who lived at the solitary rowan tree in the centre of Bog Boundless. Dowager trembled when she thought how the poor lad had been every bit as sorry and heartbroken as Sammy-Joe now was and how he had taken to his bed and hidden his face in the bolster – how he had then turned his face to the wall and stayed there till he died of a broken heart a month later.

Grief was a terrible thing. Surely (she thought) this couldn't be let happen all over again?

The Funeral Niceties

The next day the raindrops were hanging on the morning leaves like silver berries. A few minutes later a legion of new and sombre clouds would appear over the hills. Dowager planted a soft kiss on Handsome Johnnie's cheek and then the coffin was nailed down by Lofty and Blue-eyed Jack.

Soon afterwards the Spallidagh children trudged down to Abbey Acres to respect the funeral niceties of burying their father. Their mother hid her face low down so that no-one would notice her tears.

Led by the hired keeners and Father Laudable in his vestments, the rest of Rookery Rally traipsed along behind the coffin – their hobnails ringing on the graveyard lane and their chins buried into their coats – until they reached the graveside. The women quietly sobbed, lamenting the departure of such a fine man. The men took off their hats and stood bareheaded at a respectful distance away from the graveside.

Then the older children came forward and laid their father's coffin in the cold clay, each of them holding the handles on the sides.

Dowager had not forgotten her duty.

Forever mindful of the days when Handsome Johnnie had courted her at Lady Singleton's and proposed marriage to her with a bunch of wild roses, she now threw a similar bunch of wild roses, picked freshly from Corcoran's Well, down on top of his coffin – so much had he loved Nature and the wild and it had always called to him.

The parish priest, Father Laudable, gave a eulogy that was fit for an orator.

Blue-eyed Jack, Lofty and Warbling Will took their shovels and covered the coffin with sods of turf.

Of all the people Sammy-Joe was the only one too sick to attend the service. Himself and the newly-ordained curate fresh in from Clare (*Father Grieveless* was his name) had stayed behind in the deserted Welcoming Room, the young man holding the sad lad's hands in his own and trying to comfort him.

Father Grieveless

The day after the funeral saw Father Grieveless coming up the slope and bringing his buttoned melojun with him. Dowager had asked for his music in the hope that it might soften and soothe away some of the ache in Sammy-Joe's heart. For as when Saul once found himself in a drawn-out bout of gloom – a gloom that was soothed only by the harp-playing of David – it was now the curate's turn – him and his music-box (she felt) to bring Sammy-Joe relief and help him regain his speech.

The priest was a shy and sensitive young soul and felt Sammy-Joe's heartache deeply. But he was unsure of himself and his music. For a day or two he hadn't the courage to step inside Dowager's half-door but sat down on the flagstones and began to play the haunting airs that his own father had taught him as a child.

He played them quietly.

He played them gently.

The music echoed out across the stream and on over Old Stroller's hayshed.

A Day Or Two Later

A day or two later he came a few steps further in and sat on the upturned ass-and-car in the yard where he played a new set of heartfelt airs – lofty airs that the harpists of olde had played in the court of the High Kings of Tara.

He played with more confidence this time.

The rest of the Spallidagh children stood around their sad brother's bed. They said not a word but held their breath and listened to the charm of the music as it rolled across the yard and in at them through the half-door. The music had a magic in it that was sweet enough to captivate the devil himself and none of them – not even Dowager's own good self – did a stroke of work for the next blessed hour. It was as if they'd all been mesmerised by the music-box and while it lasted the mother clasped her son's hand in her own and kept on praying in silence.

Dowager Blessed Him

At last Father Grieveless took courage. He entered the half-door and sat cross-legged at the foot of Sammy-Joe's bed. Dowager gave him a liberal dose of holy-water and blessed him and his music-box with the sign-of-the-cross in the hope that his fingers might draw more and more elaborate music out of the buttoned keys on his melojun.

He played his latest set of airs slowly.

He played them delicately.

And then… a strange thing happened.

It was as though Sammy-Joe was beginning to recover from a blow to his skull for he opened wide his eyes and looked down at the cross-legged priest at the foot of his bed.

Then he sat up and cocked up his ears like a young fox listening.

Then he gave a loud sigh and opened wide his mouth as if he wished to say something.

There wasn't a murmur from anyone else in the house.

They could see the tremor on his lips.

Might not the music of Father Grieveless be at last entering not only Sammy-Joe's ears but entering his heart – entering his very soul?

The Holy Man Took Him By The Hand

The following Sunday morning, whilst all were out at Mass in Copperstone Hollow, the young priest took Sammy-Joe by the hand and he led him out of the house and down passed the haggart as though this half-man were a small child.

He walked him down across the Deer Field as far as the river.

He took off his own black socks and shoes and he walked the barefooted lad into the murmuring waters of River Laughter, the black flies dancing around them in under the echoing bridge.

They stood facing one another in the centre of the freezing current. By this time the two-of-them were far away from the rest of the world.

Father Grieveless took a palmful of the clear water and he poured it over the head of Sammy-Joe. In his inspired eyes it was the same as a second baptism – a renewal of birth unlike the finality of Handsome Johnnie's death and funeral. And then rifts of wind suddenly stirred up from their hiding-place and a light breeze came down on them from out of the sky. It poured its strength into Sammy-Joe's youthful soul and he knew for certain that inside this breeze was the spirit of his father.

He let out a little whisper.

He then let out another one – and then an almost silent whistling noise came out of him – like Handsome Johnnie used to make when intent on sawing his logs. And then, with his eyes lifted up towards the clouds, the half-child let drop a solitary tear and at last broke his silence, calling aloud to his beloved father (*da-dah! da-dah!*) the words of greeting that he had always used since his earliest cradle-days. It was as if a putrifying gas had escaped from a cow lying dead in a drain – like the air let loose from a dead pig's bladder – as his load of sadness scurried away beneath the bridge, frightening the *River Fairies* in its effort to join up with some poor forlorn waif, who loved his own departed father with a love just as beautiful and intense as Sammy-Joe's.

The youth would remember this singular moment for the rest of his life – the water of River Laughter shivering over him from Father Grieveless's palmed hands and pouring down over the bridge of his nose – the breeze coming down on him from out of the clouds – the presence of his father oozing into him as though Handsome Johnnie's ghostly spirit had refused to depart from his side – from the child he loved best (mee one *True Man*). It was miraculous for both Sammy-Joe and the priest to behold when he found himself at last freed from the mightiness of his miserable grief, his father having taken it all away from him. He realised that henceforth the ghost of his father would always be there to temper away his natural shyness and encourage him as of old to bouts of vitality whenever he had need of them. There'd be times in the years to come when he would lift his eyes to the sky and call on his father – times when Handsome Johnnie's ghost would come dashing down and pour itself in through his mouth, down into his throat, filling his heart with the powers that once had been part of his own life.

Then Sammy-Joe would hear the voice of his father whispering in his ear:

'You know I am here with you, mee son.'

'You know I will never leave you – I will never let you down.'

He Could Never Tell Them

Throughout his life he could never tell his brothers and sisters any of this – how his father's ghost would come back from the after-world and infuse itself into him. They would think he had turned into a complete and utter madman. But his father's presence was no mystery to him. Hadn't Handsome Johnnie himself seen the strangest of things – a ball of fire rolling down the hill towards him at Free'n'Easy's Stile so that he'd flung himself in over the ditch? No, what other explanation could there have been for the change that had now happened to him and that would continue henceforth to turn a quiet lad like himself – a lad that had walked the roads with his head hung low – into an inspired lion-of-a-hurler as in his juvenile days of yore? It was so outrageous that he shuddered at the thought of it – almost like witchcraft for which there was no church-pardon and he daren't tell his mother or (more importantly) confess it to Father Grieveless inside in the Confession-box.

Gently He Led Him Away

Father Grieveless led him gently away from the river. A few more illuminating drops of rain had fallen on the leaves and bushes as the young priest held his hand in his own and walked him back along the edge of the Bull-Paddock and up though the Deer Field where together they climbed out over John's Gate.

They were a strange pair – the young priest and his battered melojun strapped onto his shoulder and the two-of-them soaked to the skin.

They passed Old Sam's Grove and strode purposefully in over the flagstones, greeted by the last hoarse song of the rookery crows and the hens bunched up beneath the house-eaves in preparation for the rattling storm that would dump itself soon on Rookery Rally.

There was a light shining in Sammy-Joe's eyes. His mother had been looking out over the geraniums in search of him. She saw him and she recognised the change in this lost son-of-hers. Her heart almost burst with joy at the sight of him and she ran out the half-door and across the few feet of yard to meet him. She wrapped him in the folds of her black apron and the tears of her joy were imprinted on her heart forever.

NINE

Deelyah, the little saint

It was now four months since Handsome Johnnie met his death. Folks still talked about the day that followed his funeral – the coldest day ever known to man when a great flood tore down the Open Road and smashed into matchsticks the old wooden bridge across River Laughter. But now there was something else for them to talk about. From the same little house there was to be another death for the frail form of Deelyah was soon to give up the ghost and die on them. Like her poor brother (Stylish), the little girl was to be remembered for years to come: the whole of Rookery Rally would agree. May her name last as long as there are fishes in River Laughter and blood-red apples in the Spallidagh children's secret haunt in Old Stroller's orchard.

Dowager, As Silent As A Monk

Since the death of her sound man Dowager had been as silent as a monk. You only had to look at her to see that she was forever daydreaming her life away. She kept on bringing back that earlier day when the poor man found himself at the very doors of death. The children, even the older ones, hadn't been able to understand the depths of her sadness. From time to time some of the passing women would put their head in the half-door to keep an eye on her – dumbfounded to see the little ones, Little Dan and Tiny Jim, patiently building a house of cards on the front deal table or Darkie and Little Nell quietly arguing with each other as to which priest gave the best sermon or spent the shortest time on the altar at Sunday Mass. Already they seemed to have forgotten their father – as though they were almost indifferent to their mother's grief. The truth was they were too young to realise the serious consequences of life without their father. After all they had never seen the poor man die before.

The older brothers were out in the Bluebutton Field, hurling unripe mangolds until they and their hurleysticks were nearly senseless, wearing themselves to a thread with their playfulness. Darkie and Little Nell sat on the upturned ass-and-car, quietly playing their card games of *Old Maid* and *Beggar-mee-neighbour* and humming to themselves like happily buzzing bees in a lilac-bush.

'Ah, the poor children,' sighed Moll-the-Man. 'Bless them, they don't know a thing!'

'And their father not long gone from them,' nodded the sympathetic Cackles, as she rushed passed Dowager's yard-stream flagstones and hurried off to Old Sam's spring-well for the buckets of water.

The farmers and their ass-and-cars and their two creamery tanks were busily wending their way down the Open Road on their way to Copperstone Hollow. They stopped from time to time to look in across the flagstones at the children playing their games around the yard and the fields.

'Will ye look at the crathurs!' shouted Bill-the-Bear as he gave his ass the ashplant across his scabby old back to hurry him away from so sad a scene. Like the other farmers he couldn't understand that life amongst Handsome Johnnie's children simply had to go on and put itself right again.

Most of the neighbours had the good grace, however, to keep well back from Dowager's half-door, knowing that she was full to the gills with her tears. They didn't want to cause her the added pain by coming in and crying their hearts out alongside her during these sad times. And yet, they could see that from the day she'd laid her lovely man in the clay life had all been too much for her in her black widowhood. There was no-one for her to turn to and she tried to hide herself out by the ash-pit where she cried bucketfuls.

A Cold Determination Creeping Into Her

But seasons come and then they go away again and at last the children woke up to the reality of life. In their alarm they could see a change creeping steadily over their mother – a change from her sorrow into something resembling a cold determination. For she was expecting Handsome Johnnie's final gift to her – another child to be born in a few months' time and was constantly on her knees, praying to his ghost to return and stand alongside her and to give her the strength she so badly needed in these days of her weakness with so many children to bring up on her own and educate in the Christian way of life.

Among her fears and worries there was yet another one – little Deelyah. She was a puny bundle, no bigger than a turkey and she now lay sleeping long hours within the black pool of shadow that was her crib. Dowager prayed another decade on her rosary – that from his new home in the Beyond Handsome Johnnie's ghost-spirit would come back and bring comfort not only to herself but also to this little girl and that he'd warm and enliven her small heart.

In answer to her prayers Handsome Johnnie came back each night, strolling in across the fields, the potato-sack on his back as of yore. He stood over Dowager for a minute or two before merging back again into the darkness of the Bluebutton Field.

'Biddy! Biddy! Biddy!' he would say, 'please forgive my poor sad soul for all my sins against you and the children?' Biddy was his intimate name for Dowager, she having been christened Bedelia.

'What sins, I ask you?' sighed Dowager back to his ghost. For in truth the few debts that he'd left behind him had already been paid off by Dowager at the three drinking-shops in Abbey Cross, Copperstone Hollow and the Roaring Town – thanks to the silver shillings she was receiving weekly from her older sons and daughters in their services at Lord Elegance's Big House. Praise be to the lords and their ladies. But, to be fair to him, Handsome Johnnie had had little to regret. The only over-indulgences of his pockets throughout his lifetime had been on Fair Days in the Roaring Town when he'd sell his best two-and-a-half-year-old bullocks and treat his townie sisters to a few rounds of whiskey and brandy and sing them his famed unheard-of songs till the rafters shook all round him and the cocks were damn near crowing.

How Did It Begin?

How did it all begin? A few months after her father's death and the hay being harvested everywhere, the new stallion (*Blackie*) which Blue-eyed Jack had brought back from Tipperary town to replace Fandango was working in the Seventh Field. If you were standing below at the Kill (a half-mile away) you'd hear the laughter of little Deelyah re-echoing across Corcoran's Well. The last of the summer days seemed to be a carefree part of a heaven-on-earth as the final tram-of-hay was being winched up along the hay-cart. Higher and higher the screeching chains winched the hay – nearer and nearer to the horse's back. Deelyah was lying back against the front of the tram, humming merrily and a straw stuck between her lips and waiting for the tram to bounce down onto the cart's shafts and force her to laugh and giggle in girlish excitement as she'd done with each of the previous trams.

The Changing Clouds, The Merry Sun

The dreamy little girl's thoughts – the changing clouds and the merry sun – were pure poetry and she was not holding onto the tram as tightly as she had been taught to do. The cart slammed down with a sudden heavy bang onto the cart-shafts, rattling the chains on Blackie's back. Unexpectedly losing her footing, Deelyah found herself embroiled with the horse's tackling as together the two-of-them – the hind legs of the alarmed horse (he was young and still untrained) and the spindly knees of Deelyah – struggled in a twisting mass beneath the haycart of hay. No-one knew (though it was often discussed) if the cracking of her skull against the horse's hooves was the cause of the innocent child's impending death.

Dowager Had Begged For A Girl-child

Alone among her brothers and sisters the firstborn girl (*Cathleen*) had died just three days after she was born. The sorrow of it had left Dowager crying in the arms of Handsome Johnnie and begging him to give her yet another little girl-child in addition to Darkie and Little

Nell. Her wishes were granted and another girl-child was born – as though to bring back the spirit of her lost Cathleen. The baby was given the name *Deelyah* after her mother's baptismal name, Bedelia.

Like all the children in Rookery Rally Deelyah had been as free as the birds in the sky. She had a reasonably charmed and happy life – but uneventful up until her sad accident with the haycart and Blackie. And now, after rescuing her from underneath the horse's feet, Blue-eyed Jack and his demented mother carried her gently back into the Welcoming Room. With the other children's help they opened out the settlebed onto the floor, all the time whispering words of kindness and warmth into the unconscious child's ear.

Doctor Glasses

It was a sad Thursday afternoon when the neat and tidy Doctor Glasses and his green tweed suit came running in the half-door. He laid his leather bag on the front deal table near the St Brigid's corn-cross. He was all alertness and action. An hour later he was standing at the half-door step, tucking away his spectacles and gazing down awkwardly at some imaginary drake that seemed to be occupying his sad mind in the corner of the yard.

At last he faced Dowager and spoke to her with a doctor's grave finality. 'Dowager, you will never need to unbutton your purse or give me another silver shilling for I never met such an unhappy case as this before in all my day's travelling.'

Then he paused, seemingly stuck for words.

'The truth of the matter, Dowager, is this: Deelyah has been stricken down with the dreaded bone disease. I cannot mince my words: God is going to take this little girl away from you – back to the angels from where she came.' And with that, himself and his watery eyes slumped out through the midst of the hens and ducks and vanished across the flagstones by the yard-stream

Within A Few Weeks

Within a few weeks the wasting bone disease began to set into Deelyah. A few days later this piece of misfortunate news spread itself across the length and the breadth of Rookery Rally. Men on their creamery carts spread it along the creamery road. Herald-the-Post on his letter rounds cycled the news of it into a dozen more thatched houses, scarcely giving himself time to take off his bicycle-clips. The holy man himself, Father Accessible, was met at the foot of the stairs before he had time to fasten on his starched priest-collar or eat his bread soldiers and the two boiled duck-eggs.

She Was Dying

Deelyah, an eight-year-old little girl, was dying. There was a gloom in every Welcoming Room in Rookery Rally as the soreness and the aching took a hold of men, women and children. In this small community the news of Deelyah blotted the sun out of the farmyard. It quelled the laughter from the rest of Dowager's children and they called a halt to their games of skittles on the flagstones by the stream.

Poor Dowager – after only recently losing her own sound man!

Daily she lifted Deelyah's wasting limbs from the crib and she whispered her own childhood prayers into the little girl's ears. She took her out to the blazing turf-fire where the flames growled in the fireplace under the hob. She sat her on her knees and she dressed her, all the while crooning those musical rhymes and rhythms into her soul. She could feel Deelyah's small heart throbbing breathlessly against her own heart. And then she sat her on the little stool that Handsome Johnnie had made for the three little ones (herself, Tiny Jim and Little Dan). With her weak strokes Deelyah marked out pictures on the furry soot of the hob with the metal tongs. Dowager looked on, the fresh rosy cheeks of the little girl's brothers and sisters contrasting with her own paleness.

Outside In The Yard

On brighter days the sun was blazing down merrily outside in the yard. The windows of the Welcoming Room were bright and the red geraniums were shining in through them from their home in the green window-boxes. A few fat flies shot in and out of the dust-laden bars of light.

Dowager took Deelyah outside the half-door and she sat her on the stone steps. The sun shone even more brightly on the cobbled yard and the stream's flagstones. The farmyard fowl were scattered about colourfully. Deelyah was glad to be here in the pleasant air after the hot turf-fire inside in the Welcoming Room. She could smell the summertime flowers, especially the rambling wild roses and the sweet-williams in her mother's little privet-hedged garden. She could listen to the cheerful tinkling of the yard-stream, fragile as a hen's egg and as scintillating as a feather, as its brown and golden waters swelled and flowed over the smooth stones.

The whole yard seemed to sparkle with flies. The bellflowers on Simple Simon's ditch were all a living flame of reds and yellows and blues, pressed all around by summertime's warm air. Their peculiar fragrance, scented with lavender, was a joy to her. Cackles' dog (*Rosey-Nose*) had come down into the yard and was sitting by the whitewashed walls, warmed by the glorious rays of the sun. She stretched herself and she rolled and re-rolled her back in the dust, flapping her ropy tail.

Smiling Bab's wild cat (*Henchaser*) slept blissfully on the bit of straw on top of the empty ass-and-car.

Across the stream the ducks tossed and curtsied and seemed to be gliding as they sped away downstream beneath the pink hazel catkins hanging down like caterpillars. The springtime ducklings followed their mothers awkwardly into the stream and were soon cocksure of themselves as if they'd been in the water all their lives. The gander stretched out his long neck whenever he saw the sow coming near him from her home in the pig-house. He turned about and flapped his wings, frightening the daylights out of the bold cockerel. Out underneath the haggart singletree went the goslings, a good bit older now and no longer fluffy and green-yellow. They waddled unsteadily as they paraded off down the haggart through the wheel-ruts and the dock-leaves.

Under the horse-and-cart stood the hens, waiting for Dowager's skillet of bran-mash and spuds. Black and white and red and yellow, they turned their heads with sudden jerks, this way and that. The cockerel came out from under the ass-and-car and strutted self-importantly and once again winkingly defied the gander. Once more the hens and their rusty feathers, on seeing the cockerel, glistened like gold. They ruffled them so as to attract his eye and they shook and pecked underneath each wing. All this Deelyah could see and hear with a greater intensity than her brothers and sisters. It was as though she knew that her life was going to be cut short and that she wouldn't have long to enjoy this beautiful world.

Warbling Will

Next in age to Blue-eyed Jack was Warbling Will – a year older than Lofty and born a year after The Year of The Big Wind. He was the most enthusiastic fellow imaginable when it came to the natural order of the world around him and to oblige his little sister he went off looking for wild bird's nests and eggs. In the evening, just after milking time, he brought home an abandoned nest. Eagerly he pointed out the style of its making to Deelyah – to show her how clever these little birds were.

One evening he became even more cavalier and brought home a baby rabbit, not long born. He intended to make a pet of it for Deelyah and to build it a wooden hatch and a netted lane to run around in. How frantically did Deelyah scream at the sight of the newborn rabbit – so much so that she nearly fell in the fire from the rocking she made on her stool. With a wisdom well beyond her years she had become increasingly aware that the day was soon coming when she wouldn't be left to look after this tiny rabbit. Also, at the back of her mind she feared that when it turned into a fully-fledged rabbit her big brothers would kill it and eat it or maybe throw it out in the field for the wild foxes.

Another evening came and went and Warbling Will returned with a crane that had recently died in Bog Wood. The other children gathered round him, their curiosity mingled with excitement and they begged him to cut it open and satisfy their beliefs in the number of little fishes that a crane could hold in its belly.

Snip-snip-snip went the scissors of Warbling Will. Deelyah again took up the harmony and her eyes shook with water as she beheld the sad relic of such a noble bird – to see it here on the front table when once it flew (if only she could put it into words) so majestically above the hills and valleys and to see the many small fishes that were inside in its belly. It was all too much for her.

Not Many Months Left

There were not many months left in Deelyah's fast-spinning life. Things were different now and she no longer had the strength to sit outside the half-door and view her world. But from her threepenny-stool by the fire she listened to *Windy* as he did his huff-and-puff dance against the rattling windowpane. Dowager was at the half-door, looking out at the daffodils blowing on the side of the ditch. Deelyah would see them no more. Only last springtime she was seen with her saucepan of rainwater, filled from the big black skillet-pot that lay on the corner of the pig-house wall and she carefully washing the daffodils one by one. After that she took three carrots from the vegetable-pile in the shed and broke them up and put them into the saucepan. Then she took them in the half-door and gave her mother and father a fine dinner of carrots.

Though she could no longer visit the yard, she could sit near the window and hear not only Windy but the raucous crows and chirpy robins – the gabbling ducks and the geese – the grunting sow – the cackling hens celebrating the fact that they had laid yet another egg abroad in the nettles in the haggart. Through the open window she could breathe into her the brightness of the sunshine on another glorious summer's days as the creamery-tanks and the carts' wheels came clattering along the Open Road. Voices from beyond the flagstones were muffled in the distance. Barking dogs were being called in for their bran-mash and the ass in Moll-the-Man's Thistle Field (*Lazylegs*), was being cursed-to-death yet again. Cows and horses were coming into their sheds, mooing and braying in subdued tones. Cackles was leaning out her half-door, calling on her children to take the buckets to the well for the water for the skillet of spuds and the washing.

In contrast Deelyah's brothers and sisters (it being Saturday and no school) sat silently at the half-door where once she used to sit and they gazed dreamily at the farmyard scene in front of their eyes. Unlike her, they still had the good fortune to be able to watch the ducks tumbling with a splash into the stream – to watch the old sow attacking the gander unsuccessfully yet again. They laughed to themselves. Then Deelyah found herself laughing too. Dowager was watching all this and she was wondering what it must be like to be inside the head and the heart of her little daughter, who must now surely know that she was soon to die.

'Until we're able to milk bullocks (she would say to the rest of her children) we'll never see another child like Deelyah.' It was true for her.

Her Reflections

In spite of her spindly little legs and arms, which could do little or nothing, the little girl's soul shone through her earthly flesh more and more clearly as the days loomed onwards towards her inevitable end. Her skin was even more satiny white now – almost yellow – and her eyes were a doll-like china-blue in their fairy-like delicacy. She had all the time in the world to reflect. Her brothers and sisters, from the first day they could walk a step, had yearned to be out in the summer airs and breezes. She too wished for this previous happiness but in vain. For inside in her head, in her heart, there had now grown a weariness over her sad fate: no more to go to the spring well: no more to go to the cow-house and get her eyes squirted with cow's milk by her rascally big brother, Blue-eyed Jack.

Desperate For Her Happiness

Her brothers and sisters had become desperate for her happiness. What could they do? They hit upon a plan. In the early evening they ran out past the yard-stream and onto the Open Road. From there they reported back their latest bits of news, shouting at the top of their voices to Deelyah as she sat on her three-penny stool inside by the fire:

'Cheerful Nan's bull has escaped again and he is running across the heights towards Old Stroller's hayshed to get himself a feed of oats.'

'Uncle Bohorlody is doing his famous trick and is hanging down by his two heels from the branch over the stream. He is like an old bat.'

'Jack Gallantry has just gone by. Will ye look at the antics of him, tearing down the bumpy road, his two knees balancing on the saddle of his bike. His hair is plastered back on his poll with the soapy water from the pan.'

Such an amount of news did they give her, bringing a lift to her ailing heart. Once more Dowager sighed and her thoughts strayed from the spuds and cabbages that she was boiling in the skillet-pot. How good it was to see and hear the laughter of her other rosy-cheeked brood. Alas, how it contrasted with the frailty and the pain of Deelyah and her rickety spine.

And when it was time for bed, her brothers and sisters vied with each other to sit with their little sister under the oil-lamp beneath the hob tapestry. They brought down the bacon-box that housed their schoolbooks and prizes. They showed Deelyah their copybooks and taught her the simpler words. They taught her to shape her own name with her weak fingers.

When she had the slightest thirst on her they ran to the bucket to get her the mug of spring well-water behind the door where the axe was kept.

'It's better for you than stout-porther,' laughed Dowager.

Some of them went one better: they ran to the jug of foaming milk and they watched Deelyah drink it fast, making a white moustache over her lips. And then they all laughed until their sides hurt them.

At the end of the day they knelt and said their prayers and each evening they took it in turn to help Dowager make up Deelyah's tiny crib. They carried her weightless body into the crib and tucked her in. With Deelyah soundly asleep Dowager returned to the fire. Her heart lay heavily in her boots. She felt like a dark cloud crossing Growl River abroad in Bog Boundless and was forced – just like after the death of her sound man – to run behind the pig-house and bury her tears in the ashpit.

The Last Few Weeks

It was the last few weeks of Deelyah's life. Once more she said her morning prayers with Dowager. She prayed that the blessed saints would come one day and take everyone in Rookery Rally away – to live happily together with Jesus in his heaven. She prayed that whilst here on earth they would all have lots of rich living – lots more cabbages, spuds, eggs and milk to get their teeth into each day, now that their father was no longer here with them to work the land and help them with the crops.

Each day saw another change coming over her as she patiently sat underneath the oil-lamp hanging down from the tapestry across the fireplace. By now the black metal tongs was too heavy for her but with the wire tongs she continued to draw on the velvet soot of the hob. She drew her mother and she drew her dead father. She drew her brothers and her sisters. She drew the Holy Family – Mary, Jesus and Joseph. Humming cheerfully to herself, she was the image of good cheer and managed to keep the light of Dowager's heart aglow, in spite of her sadness.

Tiny Jim

Each morning her big brothers and sisters set out for Dang-the-skin-of-it's schoolhouse. Even Little Dan was going by now. When they were gone Deelyah felt a deep loneliness coming over her. She missed their merry laughter. She missed their tears. But close beside her she had her brother, Tiny Jim, who, like Darkie, had been judged too delicate to enter the schoolhouse for yet another year. He was a year younger than Deelyah and was the skinniest little fellow you ever laid eyes on. Everyone thought he had worms in his belly. But, though he was frail, he was as neat as a new pin and in later life he went by the name of *Jimmy-the-Cardplayer*.

When the three older lads were at work in Travellers' Rest – handling the plough or looking after the horses for Lord Elegance – it was left to this little fellow to entertain his dying sister during these last few weeks of her life. When Dowager was out in the yard, feeding her hens and her ducks, or scuttling up the Open Road with half-a-dozen eggs for Cheerful Nan, he sat at the front table and took down his mother's tin of buttons, all assorted sizes and colours. He laid them out carefully across the soogan chair, making a large patient square of them followed by an increasingly smaller set of squares inside the outer pattern. The colours made beautiful and imaginative shapes. Himself and Deelyah spent many playful hours rearranging the colours of these buttons from the tin.

Then he took the silver gramophone needles and put on *My Old Home Town*. He marched across the floor from the dresser to the half-door with Blue-eyed Jack's hurleystick strapped to his shoulder. *Quick march! Attention! About turn!* After that he strutted across to the hob at the fireplace – then off into the Big Cave Room where he gave as long as half-a-minute shouting orders – then marching round the dusty grand-piano, inside the lid of which was Dowager's icing sugar and flour.

Not satisfied, he took the pack of playing-cards from the side of the bacon-box. He knelt on the chair beside the Thomas Hood framed poem of *the little house says stay* and forgot everything else and gave his entire concentration to building a card-house for Deelyah. He was soon able to go past a double storey of cards. Then (and not entirely by accident) his elbow hit the edge of the new card-house. He jumped up-and-down in feigned desperation, theatrically bemoaning its sudden destruction. He built the card-house again and again, each time showing his mock frustration by shaking his fist and threatening the cards with dire mischief if they dared fall down on him again. And as they fell down once more, Dowager, who was still feeding her hens or pretending that this task wasn't yet finished so that the two children could be left to themselves, heard the shrieks of Deelyah's delighted laughter echoing down to her by the hen's galavanize sheeting near the ass-and-car.

The Old Pair

Dowager and Deelyah's big brother, Blue-eyed Jack (and he almost a man) were forever known as the *Old Pair* – now that Handsome Johnnie was lying in his grave. Some of the young children nearby, not knowing the entire story, even believed that they were man-and-wife, there being but twenty-three years between them and just as many years between Blue-eyed Jack and the unnamed baby about to be born in October. At cock-crow the two of them would be abroad in the cow-house at the morning milking before Blue-eyed Jack set off to rise up a brood of pheasants for Lord Elegance.

On these occasions it was left to Tiny Jim to take his mother's place and lift Deelyah gently from her crib. Already she was feeling pains in her shins and spine from the spreading disease. Young and frail as he himself was, he had learnt how to dress her with care. After that, he sat her down on her penny-stool and gave her Dowager's rosary-beads to hang round her neck. Then she started praying – the way she saw her mother praying – with her eyes lifted up to where she imagined her father was sitting in heaven and smiling down on them.

When Tiny Jim saw her growing tired from saying so many prayers he sprang out on the floor and made half-a-dozen cartwheels for her. Then he stood on top of his head and sang her a few verses of his favourite song, the *Green Bushes*. He was almost as good as Stylish when it came to entertaining. He climbed onto the front-table (the devil that was in him) and tried to jump up as far as he could towards the black thatch and catch a bit of straw for her. Then he lept out as far as he could from the top of the table – to see how far from the dresser was his jump and again Deelyah squealed with pleasure and pride in him.

If she fell from her stool Tiny Jim grew frantic and gave the floor and the stool a mighty sound thrashing for trying to harm his dear sister. And then Deelyah started laughing all over again. And when he fell over the self-same stool and was sent hopping off of the hob he roared with the pain of it. 'And now (thought Deelyah) I can never take my bold stool to heaven with me'.

When he had to leave her and go fetch the buckets of water from the well the little waif turned back to her mother's rosary-beads, asking God to help her get into heaven. She knew it was going to be soon. On her lap she fidgeted with Dowager's Saint Brigid's corn-cross and thought of poor Jesus and his bleeding feet and hands that were nailed into the wood and the spear that drew the water and blood out of his side. She thought of the floggings he had suffered and the purple cloak drawn away from his back, bringing his skin cruelly away with it. She thought of the crown of thorns. Thorns? Unlike Rookery Rally's children, what would a silly little thorn in the foot be to the likes of Jesus? 'Faith 'n' if I was Jesus, I wouldn't let them soldiers do them bad things to me,' she said, shaking her angry little head.

Death Was Near

She felt she was very near death, its door beckoning, almost creaking. She wanted to be in heaven beside Jesus – and soon. She gazed into the turf-fire – into its blazing redness. What must hell be like? She thought she saw agonising souls in the flames. She heard the kippens sizzling and hissing as though screeching with their pain. She retreated to her prayer-book, the one with the shiny pictures of the saints and the angels in it – as smooth as a pig's bladder.

She began her long litany of prayers. And this is what she prayed:

> *the Our Father, The Hail Mary, The Glory be*
> *to the Father,*
> *Oh, angel of God, my guardian dear,*
> *Oh, Sacred Heart of Jesus,*
> *Jesus, Mary and Joseph, I give you my heart*
> *and my soul,*
> *the Hail Holy Queen,*
> *the Act of Contrition.*

And then she was finished and fell asleep contentedly.

Father Sanctity

A month to the day since the momentous predictions of Doctor Glasses a new face came into view. It was Father Sanctity, the newly-ordained curate from Clare. Men and women tripped over one another as they lept over stiles and ditches so as to kneel at his feet and get his first-ever blessing. They knew (everyone did) that a blessing from a newly-ordained priest had special powers in it and would bring each of them a significant deal of good fortune.

The young curate was informed of the holiness that shone out daily from Deelyah's innermost soul and he hurried up the Open Road where he stood on the flagstones in whispering conversation with Dowager. 'Make sure to call me,' he said, 'when the time of her death comes – any time of day or night – it doesn't matter. A saint like little Deelyah is a rare sight for the world to behold. We must all gather together and bear witness when her soul takes its final departure and gets carried up to heaven.'

A Bad Friday

The next Friday was not a good day. Blue-eyed Jack returned home, tired and weary from his day's ploughing for Lord Elegance. He took his small wages from his trouser-pocket and handed it to Dowager. Like all newly-established men, he never kept money for himself. All that his jacket owned was his penknife for a squid of tobacco, the tobacco square itself, his dead father's pipe and the box of matches to light it. Dowager insisted, however, that he kept back a shiny sixpence for himself. He gave these sixpences to Deelyah to store in her bib, a little present for her to keep and to treasure. A sixpence was worth a small fortune but it gradually gaining dust in her tiny fists. Soon she had a pile of the shiny coins – coins for which she had neither want nor need. For what did silver mean to Deelyah?

Believing that she was nodding off with the blazing heat of the fire her big brother tiptoed into his mother's room. In the drawer amongst Dowager's mothballs she kept a bag of her favourite boiled sweets. When he thought that no one was watching he took a sweet from the bag. But (ah the rascal, to do such a theft!) Deelyah saw his hand in the act of stealing the sweet. She had always felt that just one bad deed was enough to make her unworthy of heaven – that it would deprive her of everlasting happiness. No one had ever recalled her committing a single wrongful act against man, woman, child or beast. Constantly she reminded her brothers and sisters what God would do to bad people and how the angels would soon be coming for her – to carry her off to an even better crib somewhere in the Beyond. This caused them (you can imagine) to rush out the door and burst into a fit of unstoppable tears in the yard.

Seeing Blue-eyed Jack's theft of the boiled sweet she let a plaintive little screech for she knew that by his sin of theft her lovely Blue-eyed Jack (whom she adored even more than Tiny Jim – if not quite as much as Jesus) would now have to go down into hell for all eternity. She was inconsolable and in her unbearable sorrow she offered a score of prayers up to Jesus, asking him to pardon Blue-eyed Jack's soul on her behalf and not to disown him altogether.

Her Meaningless Confession

The last few days of July arrived. She couldn't get up off of her stool. All she could do was imagine the sunshine outside and her brothers and sisters playing in the yard and fields and she unable to share in their childish happiness. Another day and another hour came. Would the priest ever get here (thought Dowager to herself)?

Father Sanctity stepped in across our flagstones. 'God save all here,' he said and he bowed. He had brought with him his mother's book of prayers and a gallon of holy-water with which to bless the house and ward off the devil from Deelyah. Silently he raised the wooden latch of the Big Cave Room door. His tall shoulders stooped in over Deelyah's crib. No longer could he see that bright-as-noonday-sunshine in the young girl. Everybody left the room and the holy man took out his missal. He kissed his stoll and he put it round his neck. He had come to bring Deelyah the sanctifying grace of the Last Sacramental Rites and to hear her small confession. Dowager stood outside the door, her eyes red with weeping.

Confession (he thought)? What had this little girl to confess to? Everybody knew that she was as innocent as a newborn lamb and had been since the day she was born.

'It's a mockery,' he said, knowing that Deelyah had no sin on her soul. 'Surely it's this little girl that should be hearing my confession rather than me listening to her?

A Tender Moment

Father Sanctity was about to turn this into a happy and tender moment for Deelyah. He had been told in some detail of her agonies concerning Blue-eyed Jack – of the stolen sweet and the gates of hell. Raising himself to his full height he made Blue-eyed Jack kneel in front of the Sacred Heart picture and solemnly confess his sin of stealing the boiled sweet – confess it not whisperingly as in the church Confession-box but out loud for all his brothers and sisters to hear. Blue-eyed Jack dutifully confessed his sin and promised never again (by the living Lord – *never!*) to steal a sweet from his mother's drawer. Father Sanctity was satisfied and he gave Blue-eyed Jack his Absolution and blessed him with the sign-of-the-cross. 'I absolve you from your sin, my child. God has forgiven you.'

Once more the heavens opened and the sun shone down on the recently depressed face of Deelyah. From the depths of her blankets she smiled faintly at Blue-eyed Jack. Wistfully she started making her humming noises. She was happy once more.

The Last Week

As the very last week of her life drew near, she seemed rapidly to lose the last bit of flesh left on her and to grow more and more mystical in the face of the pains affronting her. Her prayers took on a new meaning. She wanted ('please, dear heavenly Father!') to be removed from this earth tomorrow if not today and to be carried up to the blessed saints in heaven.

The young curate often came now. Like Father Grieveless before him, he'd bring with him his father's melojun and gently play for her those haunting airs, which seemed to raise her spirits in those morning hours when most of her brothers and sisters were off at the school-house of Dang-the-skin-of-it.

The Last One Or Two Days

The last one or two days were here. Dowager and Blue-eyed Jack carried the meagre little girl and her crib into the small room at the far end of the house where Dowager herself slept. This was for privacy's sake and for Deelyah to be near her mother during the long remaining nights. They cleared out the laurel leaves from the inside of the chimney and the hive of honeybees had to depart from the empty fire grate while the turf-fire was lit. The holy picture of the Sacred Heart and the big blue picture of Our Blessed Lady on the far wall were cleaned and dusted. The dozen candles for a happy death were still not lit but were ready with the matches in the drawer. When lit, they'd light up all the dark corners of Deelyah's fading world and would banish those haunting spirits that came in the night in the shape of Boodeemen to bring evil to the dying child. Hour after hour Dowager and Blue-eyed Jack spent beside the crib, their long shadows stretching out across the back wall. Spiderweb stillness filled them and the room.

Her Brothers And Sisters

Returning from school the rest of the children sat silently on the floor around Deelyah's crib. Tiny Jim was heartbroken in his grief over Deelyah, who, for the next day two, was on the borders of life and death. Dowager could feel the child struggling and she tried to share in her pains. Deelyah smiled back brightly but her thoughts were now far away outside their world. Something extraordinarily good was going to happen to her – in another place – the Beyond. This she knew full well as the holiness fermented more and more into her soul.

The Day Of Her Death

The day came for her to die and the death-dew was on her forehead. In her tiny fists she clasped the ginger-glass rosary of her mother – to be buried with her and for company on the long journey to the Beyond. She said she could hear unusually sweet music, unlike any other music she had ever heard before. It was coming from far away. She could hear the laughing voices of bygone children. All that her brothers and sisters heard was the loud sound of the grandfather clock ticking away her last few breaths. They were all kneeling on the Welcoming Room floor outside the bedroom door.

There followed a last plaintive look in Deelyah's eyes. Dowager was fussing like mad, trying to avoid letting out the tears that were blinding her eyes. She lit the dozen happy-death candles so that the bedroom was a blaze of church-like glory. In the yard outside the half-door a crowd had already gathered, their rosary-beads in their fists. Even the hens and the geese were quiet. The yard-stream itself seemed to be hushed into silence in honour of Deelyah.

Wasting away to nothing (thought Dowager to herself). Mere skin and bones in the middle of the quilts and the little blue veins on her extended fingers. She could count them one by one. The child's frail little neck shaking giddily.

Deelyah tried to speak: 'Mother! Mother!' she began to whisper. 'Come and take me! Come and take me! Oh, mother, will you come and take me?' she kept crying.

'I am here! I am here, my child,' said Dowager softly. 'You know I'll take you,' she added.

Blue-eyed Jack, his heart bursting inside his chest, was slouching tearfully behind his mother. He glanced back over his shoulder at the picture on the wall – at the portrait of the Blessed Virgin in her blue-jay robes – at the heavenly mother who seemed to be smiling calmly and gently down into the crib – the mother with the child, Jesus, in her arms. It was clear to him that his young sister was being blessed with a happy vision at this untimely moment of her death:

'Mother! Mother!' again the child cried. Her eyes were full of starry joy and a pure bliss unknown to anyone in Rookery Rally. It was like a dart from the skies.

'I am here! I am here, child,' said Dowager.

'Mother,' said Blue-eyed Jack, almost reproachfully and gently tapping his mother on her shoulder, 'Deelyah is not talking to you – she is calling upon her heavenly mother, Mary, behind us in the picture – she is talking to the mother of Jesus.'

As if she understood Blue-eyed Jack's intervention, Deelyah extended her two matchstick arms towards the picture, her eyes steadily transfixed on the eyes and face of her mother, Mary. And then, in spite of her weakness, she sat up fiercely in her crib and shouted in a huge rapturous voice full of all the hope and tenderness she possessed:

'Mother! Mother! Mother! I am coming. Please take me. I am coming now. I am coming home.' And with that the black cowl of Death reached out and took her away

Below In Abbey Acres

Deelyah was buried below in Abbey Acres Graveyard, next to her father, Handsome Johnnie. On holy days her brothers and sisters would traipse down to the graveyard to tidy up her grave, picking wildflowers such as honeysuckle and foxgloves on the way. Once more Dowager took down a big bunch of wild roses to lay reverently on the grave alongside the children's bunches, all in a colourful pattern as once amused Deelyah when Tiny Jim set out his mother's tin of coloured buttons. For an unreal moment they prayed to Deelyah above in heaven – prayed to the little saint from Rookery Rally. God be good to you, Deelyah.

Before July Was Over

Before July was over a cry filled the slopes of Rookery Rally as Dowager struggled to give birth to her final child. Only the day before, she had been carrying home the bag of spuds on her stooped back. Cheerful Nan and Cackles hurried down to help with the birth. The room still smelt of mothballs and happy-death candles. They took off their scarves that were tucked under their chins and they unwrapped the potato-sacking from off their backs that they'd brought with them to keep off the rain. It was going to be a long night. They had brought with them some grains of tea, some soda-bread and some jam. They had a few candles and a candlestick holder to light up the belabouring skirts of Dowager. They filled the kettle with hot water, to clean down Dowager and her newborn child when it arrived. Cheerful Nan nodded to Cackles.

'There'll be another soul in Dowager's family tonight.'

'Yes,' thought Cackles. 'Deelyah is lying low in the graveyard. A new baby is taking her place here tonight.'

An hour later Dowager lay back on the bed, exhausted, her new baby beside her. It was as if the sunlight of Handsome Johnnie had come streaming back into her life and she was content.

And long after the birth, when they found themselves returning home before the pink dawn had arisen, the two women looked up hopefully at the faintly lighted moon that was like an old lemon about to depart. Cackles took her leave of Cheerful Nan and went off towards the Valley-of-the-Pig. Cheerful Nan lifted up her skirts to ease herself in the ashpit at the back of her carway.

'Yes (said she to herself) Deelyah is dead and Dowager's heart is broken for the loss of her little saint. But little Biddy has been born (thank God) and Dowager will be glad once more.' She tidied up her skirts. The smell of spearmint filled her nostrils from her little haggart. Her yard-stream chuckled over the stones. She was full of rich feelings.

Next Evening Closed In Achingly

Next evening closed in achingly. The last ribbons of sunlight were leaving the sky behind Fort Dangerous and the Danes' Hill. The yard-stream gurgled with a greater intensity than usual down near the rusty blue kettle at the little waterfall. Blue-eyed Jack and his dead father's ashplant led his little flock of ewes out the haggart gap. Along the winding path through the ash trees at the side of the Bluebutton Field he drove the sheep towards River Laughter to slake their thirst. There on the dewy bank the big man hid his face among the ferns and rushes. In the semi-darkness where no one could see him he began to howl like a lost dog for Deelyah. The very fairies that dwelt on that riverbank stopped their evening dances to look upon him as he mourned in secret for his little sister.

Back in the Welcoming Room, Dowager put away the happy-death candles in her drawer. They'd not be flickering on the mantle-shelf for many a year to come (she hoped). In spite of the tiny baby girl lying alongside her there was a darkness in her soul – to think that Deelyah was no longer with her.

'I must be busy,' she said with a tearful shake of her head. Her clickety-clackety boots echoed away from the room as she left behind her the scenes of her daughter's recent death-crib.

The next few weeks passed quickly. Each night it was the same. The hens had been fed and watered and had been counted and shushed back into the henhouse. Then came the quiet time when the nights seemed strangely deserted. Out of respect, the rabbiters and the pitch 'n' toss boys stopped their storytelling on the singletree in Old Sam's Grove and the road-menders put away their shovels and quenched their Woodbine fags.

A Little Dusty Breeze

In the silence of the night a little dusky breeze blew up, pretending to be a whirlwind. Dowager was lying in her bed. She turned and twisted nervously, trying to find a comfortable position. The air was breathless. She felt the ache of Deelyah's loss in a pain just underneath her heart. From far below Rookery Rally she heard a goose in Ducks 'n' Drakes' farmyard. It was caught in a fox's snapping jaws. She finally fell asleep. She continued to dream away her sadness. The lemony moon peeped in the window of her room. Beside her lay Biddy, her newborn baby. The drowsing infant snuggled up closely to her sleeping mother's breast. The two of them lay there warmly in the big straw 'n' lat bed with the fat blankets round them.

What was that? The half-sleeping Dowager turned in the bed. Was it a flickering of the moonlight trying to climb in through the back window? Was it the ass (the Lightning Whoor) trying to draw her attention as he had often done by bawling her awake with his *eey-yaws* in the dawn of morning?

No, it was something else – here in her simple little thatched house. It was something beyond the poor woman's understanding. She felt a tranquillity as never before – a feeling that was once in the heart of her daughter at the time of her death.

A Noble Radiance

Rapid clouds had sailed silently off towards Galway and the moon had risen high over the slopes of Rookery Rally, looking down on the little thatched house. The ghost of Deelyah, in robes that sparkled in silver, her features as white as a lily, crossed over the haggart and came as far as the bedroom window. Her noble radiance shimmered in through the glass and surrounded Dowager's bed. In spite of her semi-conscious protests the coverlets were pulled back gently from the mother's shivering grasp.

Instinctively she pressed her baby closer to her heart. Surely it was not the *Cloud Fairies* come to take this child from her in order to keep Deelyah company in the skies beyond?

The smiling face of the ghostly shade of Deelyah leant in across the bed. Her angel-face gazed down at her baby sister – the child that had not yet been born when she herself had been carried away to her own life in the Beyond – allowed back into her previous world just this once so as to get a glimpse of her newborn sister. The ghost of Deelyah smiled a smile that no-one could paint. Not once did she look at her mother. She put the coverlets back tidily, almost fussily, around Dowager and the newborn Biddy. Then, armed with a secret not to be shared, she vanished away, out past the cow-shed.

Dowager turned in her half-sleep. She pulled the coverlets in around her ears. She pressed the baby's warm lips to her milky breast. It was almost dawn. The dying moon, still round and yellowy, was giving up its ghost to the skies.

TEN

Fingers-Jack

Let me introduce you to the Spallidaghs' close neighbour, Fingers-Jack. With his slappy wellingtons, cut down to half-size and also his black-banded yellow-stained hat forever glued to his head – the one people swore he slept in.

His grandfather was the Drummer Boy, the son of the Cow Doctor, and still a mere boy when he was playing his drum at the battle of Sebastapol beyond in the Crimea. In his later life he was married to Quack-Quack, supporting her by turning himself into a blacksmith – starting off with only an old claw-hammer and an anvil and rasp.

Before the first year or two was out he had fixed the drum-rod in Rosy-Lee's mowing-machine better than any foundry inside in the town. From where on earth did he get his knowledge? He heated the metal expertly – not too hot and not too cold lest it would brittle and break on him and so fine was his work that no-one could see where he had joined it.

Fingers Jack's father was Old Banyan, renowned for catching oceans of trout above in Growl River – big five-pounders as long as your elbow – and selling them to the high and mighty inside in town. He was married to Twinkle, known as the Invisible Woman. She was so shy that she was never seen or heard by a single mortal soul and it was more than a miracle how Fingers Jack ever got to be born for it must have been a great shock to the poor lady when the old fellow got up to his antics in the middle of their wedding-night.

Old Banyan was the first heard-tell-of bonesetter in these parts. If a man's knee was sprained he brought him a shovelful of fresh cow-dung and made a mixture of it with cream before plastering it on the fellow's leg. It cured the damage within weeks but if that didn't work, he always had the milky juice of the redshank to get the fellow back on his feet. And in his bag-of-tricks he also had a poultice of flour to put on a man's leg – to get rid of his blood-poisoning.

The Man Himself

And now for Fingers Jack himself. He was a man whimsical in some ways for he loved nothing better than a bit of Christmas cake from Lady Elegance and more than anyone else loved to decorate his Welcoming Room with new holly-sprigs throughout the twelve Christmas days and with layers of white wool stuck round the Sacred Heart picture to set it off – all that, as well as a merry crisp fire to burn his shins from where he sat, almost on top of the flames.

Looking at his fingers, one would think that, given the intricate skills that were in them, they'd be long and spidery like a holy bishop's or a house-dance fiddle-player's. But no, they were small, pale and neat and the palms of them were as soft as his own dead mother's (God be good to her). Of course, like all the rest of us, he had only these ten fingers and yet, from far and near, he was known for the unique use he made of them when it came to repairing a broken arm, a rib or a leg. Hadn't he heeled Old Gentility's broken thighbone so perfectly that Doctor Glasses himself said he would have been proud to be the owner of such a marvellous pair of hands?

Like any craft – be it in the making of fiddles or the ability to make the double-whistle with the lips – Finger-Jack's craft had been handed down to him from his father and from his father's father before that and his gift as a bonesetter was as natural as a blackbird's sweet throat. Being the only bonesetter for miles around, he was as busy as a bee from morning till night.

You'd spot him a mile away with his peculiar yellow hat stuck on his head. He'd remind you of Yellow Patsy with his cart of flour for most men dressed in their peaked caps rather than in those old-fashioned hats. That was a bit of snobbery on their part – to make them look like the well-dressed townies or the clean-cut cattle-dealers that came in from Limerick with their cute little canes and their leather gloves. No, Fingers-Jack kept his father's yellow hat all the days of his life. Holding it respectfully in his hand, he even had a song (*the Hat mee father wore*) that he proudly sang on Fair-Days whilst the money was still fresh in the heel of his fist for a few drinks.

For a small man, he walked with a very long stride – the same as the Mountainy Men living further up the hills. This was coupled with an air of solid determination whenever he entered a yard or house to do his work on broken bones. See him in his long black coat – reminiscent of Red Scissors's long gingery coat. It must have been six feet in length and reached down to his toes. He always left it unbuttoned with the coat flaps forever sailing away behind him, flailing in the sunlit breezes that rushed down on him from the Mighty Mountain behind his house.

A Picture Of Liveliness

He was a picture of liveliness – him and his wet lips and yellow teeth – and was never known to have missed a hurling-match, be it a scrap between two local juvenile hurling-teams or a full-blown county hurling final in the Roaring Town. With his long coat hopping off of his wellington-boots he could be seen running onto the pitch from the touchline, holding at least a dozen newly-made hurleysticks in his arms, the product of Tasty Handler's workshop below at River Laughter's mill.

'Will ye look at the get-up of Wyatt Earp,' said Dowager, seeing the way he strode through life as though he were a cowboy from the wild west.

'A hurl! A hurl!' shouted the full-forward from his own Abbey Rovers team, twirling his broken hurleystick in the air and waving it towards Fingers-Jack, showing him how he had used his hurleystick to deadly effect on the shinbones of the opposing centre-half-back.

Fingers-Jack sailed in like a bird from the sideline, brandishing a new hurleystick. See the speed of the little fellow, desperate to keep the movement of play going at its present fierce pace. Look again at the speed of him (twice as fast) as he made a dash back to the sideline, quick as a bolt of lightning so as to escape getting his head broken in two from the renewed hurly-burly.

His little legs, as Dowager's brother, Gooseberry-the-Pony, remarked, were a good deal shorter than Bishop High-Hat's and would never leap the five-barred gate like Stylish once did. The holy man had recently thrown the ball in amongst the hurlers' legs to start the senior county match inside in the town and to the amusement of all had rushed back unceremoniously to the sideline (like the goodly bonesetter) to escape a similar belt on his holy poll from the manly hurleysticks. But, smart though the Bishop High-Hat was, if you were to put Fingers Jack in a race against him – even a short dash across the haggart (picture the thought) – his own little legs would beat the holy man's legs into a cocked hat. That's what Gooseberry-the-Pony said. So much for the wisdom of Dowager's older brother and his prodding tobacco-pipe as we leave Fingers-Jack jostling his way back up onto the bank among the crowd with the two bits of broken hurleysticks wrapped in his long coat.

Apart from supplying urgently-needed replacement hurkeysticks on the hurling pitch, he also acted as the chief steward to the Abbey Rovers Hurlers and had the sharpest of eyes when looking for homegrown talent in the developing schoolchildren. Ever quick to spot the hurling skills manifested in their solo runs and their striking and pulling on the hurling-ball, there was no better man for instructing the youth and praising their awakening talents (unless it was Dang-the-skin-of-it in the schoolhouse itself) and it was said that he was better than many a schoolmaster in the judgements he made. Would you believe that?

The Fixed Chain Of Command

Life was always the same in Rookery Rally since there was a fixed chain of command. Near the top of the list was Bishop High-Hat and over and above him sat the bespectacled Pope. Below him was the beloved Father Laudable, a fine man who could deliver his Latin Mass in a little over twenty minutes. 'Where on earth did he get such a head on him – where did he get his schooling?' said his congregation admiringly – especially the men, who were anxious to break out from the church gate and wrap their fidgety fingers round a Woodbine fag and have a smoke at the side of the Conifer Wall.

Next in line of command came Doctor Glasses and his leather bag and smart motorcar. Only the Bearded Vet had a newer car than him – red like one of Old Stroller's apples. But Doctor Glasses was the only man in Rookery Rally (apart from the priest and Lord Elegance) to have a radio-set to his name. Like many men in high places he was known as the Invisible Man and people seldom saw him since no one had a brass copper to give him. Nonetheless, he was a good man, trusted and respected the length and breadth of Rookery Rally. He'd be here in a flash if he were called upon. With his green tweed suit and his curt moustache and reading-glasses you'd know he was a man of distinction – the saver of lives whereas Father Laudable was the saver of souls.

Doctor Glasses had an understudy whose name was Black Bess. She was the nurse and had a famed rattle-truck-of-a-van whose roaring engine could be heard a mile away. Like the doctor she was a rare one to be seen and a woman would have to be almost dead with the pains during an unusually fierce childbirth before herself and her bag-of-tricks darkened the door. 'Is that the ambulance-driver gone up?' sneered Red Scissors, laughing at the van's lack of speed.

When necessity struck members of a family, men could always call on other men of distinction as well as the priest or the doctor or nurse. If the ass-and-car or the horse-and-cart was damaged in the wheel or the frame and shafts were cracked open, it was Tim-the-Wheelwright who had the fixing of it with his wood-plane and his red paint and his carpentry tools. If there was damage to your plough (especially the ploughshare) or to the axle of your cart, you'd see Hammer-the-Smith and his sinewy muscles getting ready to cure the ache in plough or cart – or in as little a thing as knitting together a man's cart-chains or the rim of his creamery-tank. And another thing – your mare could be tripping over her feet and her knees skinning the road in lumps but such good care did Hammer take of her shoes that she'd be dancing a hornpipe off of the road the very next day.

As for Fingers Jack, whereas the man-in-black talked a goodly sermon on Sundays, he himself was seen to talk an even better sermon when a break or sprain had ruined a man's limbs and, unlike Doctor Glasses, he was a good bit cheaper in the pocket (a gift of a sack-of-spuds would do him). With the subtle and mysterious workings of his gentle fingers and the accompaniment of his kindly words he had the surest of ways to soothe the depression out of a man's mind as well as carry away the mischief to his broken bones for he used the very same words as those he used when caressing the ears of the young hurlers. As he himself said: he'd have damaged men as playful as lambs on the green before the month ended. Fair play to you, Fingers-Jack!

Black Bess

Everyone remembered the harvest day when they saw Black Bess and her van – the van that was infamously labelled *the truck,* she not having a properly-shaped motorcar to call her own like the priest or the vet or the doctor. The Spallidaghs saw her clattering up the brow of the hill at the Kill, next door to Galloping Gret's red roses. The smoke from the engine was rising to the heavens like a battered old tractor and herself and her cheeks were as red as the rosebushes in Fatty-Matty's garden.

Her chief claim to fame was the black soot-drop that she painted onto her cheek each morning. It was pasted just below her left eye. The Spallidagh children had never seen her before and they were awfully anxious to get a proper look at her soot-drop. Alas, from where they were helping Blue-eyed Jack and Lofty to turn over the hay in the Seventh Field, there was little chance of that.

In her truck she was carrying all the *medicinaries* (her word) that she'd require: the iodine: the smelling salts: the temperature gauges: the bandages and safety pins and so on. Had the children been able to join up with her, she'd be seen entering Sissy Hopalong's half-door. The misfortunate Sissy was expecting her first child, the product of several brazen bouts of summertime tussling and tumbling when she'd initiated a brace of inexperienced adolescent boys into the sporting realms of pleasure above in her hayshed.

Black Bess was in an awful hurry to get to her as this was going to be a difficult birth and maybe Sissy would be dead before she arrived. The haymakers in all the fields were looking out over the ditch and left scratching their heads. This was a new one on them – to see a nurse and her truck steaming up towards Sheep's Cross where no one in living memory had ever seen or heard tell of a nurse hurrying up the Open Road.

The children stood on tippy-toe and watched the trail of smoke from her receding van. Blue-eyed Jack and Lofty left off tramming the hay and Warbling Will and Sammy-Joe (his own normal self again) left off gathering in the dried-out hay-rows towards the trams. Why on earth would a nurse and her van be coming up their quiet hillslope?

A day later the Weeping Mollys brought back the reason for summoning Black Bess: Sissy was forty-five (although she always said she wasn't a day over forty) and she had never given birth before. A first birth at such an advanced stage of life was a thing unheard of and was thought to be impossible for any woman to achieve.

How grateful everyone felt that evening when they learnt of the wonderful skills of Black Bess and how, after a labour of only four hours, she had safely delivered the new baby (*Tom-Tom*) into the tearful arms of Sissy. They blessed and crossed themselves for the skilful work the nurse had done. Maybe the Guards would leave Sissy alone and stop pestering her over her love of young lads. Maybe Father Laudable would let her keep Little Tom-Tom and not carry the child away to the Orphanage in Thurles or snatch the poor woman off to the Nunnery in Kilkenny. Maybe next year Sissy would forego the tussling and tumbling with her lively young lads.

The Screams Of Little Dan

The workers turned back, each to their own meadow, and they began applying themselves vigorously to the next bout of haymaking. Suddenly they heard a child's horrendous roar and they looked for its source. It was coming from Dowager's youngest son, Little Dan. His screams could be heard echoing from John's Gate beside the Bull-Paddock. A short way below the gate they saw Fingers-Jack – or rather his yellow hat streaking along at a tidy pace a foot above the ditch.

They dropped the forks and they listened. A short while later they heard the little boy's previous wild howls being replaced by tiny whimpering noises – like a puppy-dog pining after its dead mother. These whines then stopped altogether and they nodded and smiled at each other for they guessed what had happened: Fingers Jack had meandered his soft hands gently across Little Dan's shinbones and had found the source of the child's pain.

In an hour or two they'd all know the reason for the child's screams. A few minutes earlier Dowager's grumpy old ass, the Lightning Whoor, had been carrying the child and his mother back from Abbey Cross. The lad was sitting contentedly on the lace of the ass-and-car and Dowager was seated above him on the latboard's straw-bag. The old ass seemed very anxious to get back to his hiding-place under the oak-tree in the Bull-Paddock for he took a sudden mad fit-of-the-gallops. He was usually a lazy sort of creature and this abnormal burst of speed didn't become clear till later on – the fact that he had just been stung by a swarm of horse-bees introducing themselves in under his tail. You know the way these devilish little insects love the smell of the ammonia around an ass's shitty arse.

Up until then Little Dan had been bouncing up and down merrily on Dowager's best tartan rug. Everyone knew how she mollycoddled that little whippersnapper and always took him with her wherever she went, he being her youngest son.

Bumpity-bumpity-bumpity!

Unknownst to the poor child, his little bum had been bumping further and further out along the lace – nearer and nearer to the edge of the ass-and-car. Dowager had been in dreamland, thinking of Sammy-Joe and his recent ups-and-downs – thinking of poor dead Handsome Johnnie and Deelyah lying in their graves and how much she was missing them. She hadn't noticed the dangerous possibility that Little Dan might possibly bump clean off of the lace and out onto the road.

It was at that moment that the horse-bees started their sudden stinging raid on the sweet arse-smells of the ass. Startled as never before, the Lightning Whoor took off with the speed of a Limerick train – with the result that a most unceremonious tragedy followed when Little Dan, unable to catch himself in time, stumbled and fell down off of the ass-and-car. Horror-of-horrors, to see his little body rolling along the road and the iron wheels of the ass-and-car racing unstoppably towards his legs. There was no way he could escape disaster. The demented Dowager could only look on from her high perch on the latboard and watch the wheels slowly and cruelly cross over Little Dan's shinbones. They'd surely make mush out of them.

Where Was Good Fortune?

Dowager began cursing like blazes, all the time bemoaning her miserable lot in life – Handsome Johnnie dead – little Deelyah dead – and now this. 'The blessed saints in heaven, where has Good Fortune gone to?' she cried. 'Where are the *Kind-hearted Fairies* on a morning like this when I need them the most?'

And then (bless my soul) there came out of nowhere a vision from heaven – none other than the great man himself – Fingers-Jack. He had been over at the priest's house, tending to the broken ankle of Sally-the-Housekeeper.

Dowager looked back in utter disbelief when she saw him just a stonethrow away and racing at a devilish speed up the slope. He lept down from his mare and reached out his hands towards Little Dan, who was now lying in a heap behind the ass-and-car. The old ass was contentedly nibbling on the ditch-side thorny grasses and the horse-bees had departed in fright at the startling roars out of the child. If ever a guardian angel was needed to tend to her endangered son, it was at this moment and Dowager promised that she'd make a devout novena to Our Blessed Lady at the first possible opportunity.

Fingers Jack was moved with pity when he saw her weeping by the bucket-load over the state of Little Dan for she didn't know whether he was alive or dead. She had got down from the ass-and-car but didn't seem to know where she was or which way to turn or what was going to happen next.

She stood looking over her son. She'd do anything to distract herself from the sight of the child's pain and as the bonesetter came up to her he saw her stroking the head of the Lightning Whoor. She must have been out of her mind with grief (he thought) at a time when anyone else would have been whaling into the shitty-arsed ass with the heel of their ashplant for causing the child to fall down from the ass-and-car when he had made his sudden bolt away from the stinging horse-bees.

From Behind The Black Clouds

And now, as the sun comes out from behind the black clouds, the scene suddenly changed. 'Ha-ha, mee byze,' smiled Fingers-Jack to himself and he shook his head in disbelief and amazement. 'Not a single break this time, Dowager – just a badly-bruised sprain, that's all. Would anyone ever again disbelieve the powers of The Good Lord and what He can do underneath the wheels of a cart? Aren't miracles the most wonderful things on this earth?'

He smiled up into Dowager's eyes and her own eyes lit up with a love for this saint-of-a-man, who had appeared on the road like a gift from heaven.

'What holy saint are ye Spallidaghs praying to these days, Dowager?' went on the soothing voice of the bonesetter, doing his best to distract her out of her shocked state of mind. 'Whoever she is, please give me the prayers that ye're saying to her holy name so that I can start praying to her meeself.' And with that he took off his long coat and ladled Little Dan up tenderly into its folds to keep the warmth fresh in his body. With Dowager at his heels, he slowly marched him up the hillside and in through her half-door, all the time humming into the frightened little boy's ears those loving words of endearment, the way he would do to a ruined horse.

In what seemed less than a minute he made the hop back up to his own house, returning to Dowager with his hot poultice of laurel-paste and plenty of wadding and paris-plaster to wrap round the shins of his small patient.

'In a week or two this little rascal will be as lively as a goose running away from a fox,' said he, leaving the poor Dowager copiously weeping – tears of joy this time round. Then he lept up onto his horse and without so much as a sip from the proffered mug-of-tea, gave Dowager a regal bow and went galloping up the slope in a fog of dust towards the Valley-of-the-Black-Cattle. Wasn't he the marvellous bleddy man (said Blue-eyed Jack)? 'Deed-and-indeed he was.

The Silence Of Winter

Time flew by and the silence of winter was soon upon Rookery Rally. It was the time of the heavy snow and layers of it could be seen, crisp and crystalline, around the Spallidagh yard, covering the pig-house gap and the hen-house stick.

The children looked out the half-door at it. It was like the icing sugar hidden inside the lid of Dowager's grand-piano. It's strange what joy a good fall of snow can bring to a child. They suddenly forgot the recent death of their father and their sister, Deelyah – forgot their serious appraisal of the yard and the sad ducks and chickens and the antics of the mischievous sow in her war against the gander, all of which in days of yore had brought to the surface the melancholy poetry that lay in their young souls. For the snow's arrival had turned all of them (even Darkie with her hole-in-the-heart) into wild and raging creatures – running out the half-door as if they had never before been alive and sniffing at the new snow's crystals, plastering their laughing faces with it.

From the safety of their hidey-hole under the ass-and-car the ducks and hens thought it very strange indeed to see the way Dowager's children had turned themselves into snow-clad dancers. In disbelief they watched the children racing across the flagstones and out onto the roadway where they stood listening for the muffled wheels of any cart that might pass by and for some poor misfortunate eejit who might have the temerity to be out as early as this in the morning – waiting to see his shocked face and feel the ambuscade of the many snowballs they were busily preparing for him.

'Will ye look at them young galoots,' laughed Dowager to Blue-eyed Jack, taking up the derisory name given to her scholarly children by Cousin Daisy's mother (*Nancy*). Her children were business itself and it wasn't long before they had a wheelbarrow full of fresh snowballs, each one hardened and moulded as their deadly weapons for a hopeful bout of warfare against the next traveller to show his head above Old Sam's Stile. They waited in silence as in their playful games of *hide-and-go-seek* in their secret hidey-hole behind the bushes. In their mind's eye they could see what would happen in a few minutes time when they'd paste the head off of the next passerby as soon as his horse-and-cart reached the flagstones and their yard-stream.

The Rattle Of The Wheels

They heard the faint muffled sound of cartwheels rattling up the slope. It was Finger-Jack's cart, his blue turf-cart with the high boards added onto the sides and the tailgate. As usual he was standing high in the cart and delicately twisting the loose reins. He was in the merriest of moods having accomplished a pair of new shins for Little Dan a few months back and having recently restored the broken wrist of Madge-Roundabout, that well-known trainer of any stubborn ass with her hot beetroot administered in a stocking up into you-know-where. They could hear him whistling – like a man returning from town after making a small fortune selling a flock of sheep at the Market Fair. His big black mare (*Nelly*) was breathing hard and was wearily drawing her iron shoes through the snow.

On seeing his cart edging its way up by Old Sam's Stile, the children (like the bonesetter) were full of their own merriment. By now they were well-prepared and had stored a countless army of snowballs at various vantage-points inside the ditch: up beside the pig-house: underneath the fuchsia bushes: inside Dowager's privet-hedged garden. Fingers-Jack was in for a memorable drubbing and by the time he got home he'd remember this winter's morning with a sore jaw on him. By the holy Moses, he would.

The First Volley Of Snowballs

From his safe perch Fingers-Jack had least expected the first volley of snowballs, which came from behind the American grass inside the ditch. The next volley came from down near the stream's little waterfall. But the children were inexperienced and their aims were far from good. Every one of their snowballs missed Finger-Jack's saintly face by the width of a barn-door.

He stopped his cart and the weather suddenly changed when his normally smiley face turned into a black look of anger. He was never a man to let others take centre-stage and he threw down the reins and cocked his finger to his nose in an aspect of utter disrespect. And then, in a vile litany, he read the children his sermon for the day and in a voice that could win next year's election he rained down curses on their heads – telling them in no uncertain manner the dregs of their family pedigree and cursing poor Dowager, the mother who had reared them.

It was great fun – the best bit of sport they'd had since the Daffy-Duck Circus – and the children split their sides laughing at the sight of his angry face. This seemed to make Fingers-Jack angrier than ever and he had an even fiercer look in his eyes.

'Will ye look at John-the-Baptist,' laughed Dowager, seeing the get-up of him and (with recent memories of the scene with Jack Fart) the way he was performing for her children. The bonesetter was getting himself worked up into fine fettle and he began embroidering his cursing – cursing Dowager's own mother and her mother's mother before that – all of whom (it seemed) had allowed the likes of these young galoots ('ye little feckers!') to live on this earth. Even the younger children were almost wetting themselves with glee.

The Wily Old Devil

Fingers-Jack had always had that little bit of fierceness about him but he was a wily old devil and you never knew what he'd do next. However, the children were no fools and even they could see that all his anger – all his savage cursing – was a pure sham. He wasn't angry at all.

He proved this to be true as he leaned out from the horse-and-cart, making several ape-like faces at them and encouraging them to throw more and more snowballs at him. Soon the old rascal would have enough of their precious snow in his cart to firm up and make a few snowballs of his own and fire them back at the little devils with greater marksmanship than any of them had shown.

'Look at the appearance of that bad-mouthed article and his wicked curses,' laughed Dowager, looking out from the half-door, as Fingers-Jack danced and dodged around like a strange gesticulating lunatic inside in his cart. You'd have paid good money to see the dance-steps of him. They were good enough to be included in the Daffy-Duck Circus.

His Black Tongue

As though he was out of breath, he stopped his ranting and sermonising. Instead, he showed the children his black tongue that was stained from chewing tobacco. Then he waggled it round in his mouth at them and made his eyeballs bulge and disappear up into his head, leaving only the whites of them visible. It was enough to frighten the devil's own self and you'd hear the screams of their laughter down as far as Old Stroller's yard. The sport was getting better by the minute.

Then, oh the heathen, he took off his long black coat and he threw it down in the cart to show his further contempt for the children. He rolled up his sleeves and he took off his galluses. Then he dropped his trousers to give them a full inspection of his properties – his bare arse. The older boys hid the eyes of Darkie and Little Nell underneath their armpits. Oh, the absolute shame of it! By this time Blue-eyed Jack and Dowager had a pain in their sides from their fits of laughter at the humorous scene going on outside their flagstones.

This was now an open act of warfare but the day wasn't yet lost to the children. For, unknown to Fingers-Jack, other children – including their friends Lippity and his younger brother, Punch, as well as the chastened Tom Foolery – had come to join in the fun. They were hiding in Simple Simon's lane some sixty feet further up along the ditch. These little dragoons were well-armed with at least a dozen snowballs apiece, stored in the depths of the dyke for just such an unexpected operation as this.

Fingers-Jack felt safe, having escaped the raging snowballs that were being hurled at him from the flagstones. He was in the best possible humour as he continued to belittle the breed of the Spallidaghs for he had succeeded in cursing their family back as far as Brian Boru – as far as the borders of hell itself. He had shown them his black tongue and his white arse.

The Spallidagh children let Fingers Jack know that they were well beaten and that the fight had gone out of them – that their mood had changed, having listened to his curses long enough, and that they had nothing left but their frustrated rage. He was winning the sport by a mile and he almost felt sorry for the helpless state they were in. He almost felt like crying for the way he had treated them. He could see that there was nothing left for the poor dears to do but watch the likes of him dancing around unchallenged above in his cart. Not a single one of their snowballs had hit him in the gob to silence him.

'Hee! Hee! Hee! The shitty-arsed Spallidaghs can all *see* me!' he roared as he bobbed up and down defiantly in his cart.

'Hee! Hee! Hee! The shitty-arsed Spallidaghs can never *hit* me!' said the old devil and the spits flying out of him. Oh, the scoundrel. He was beginning to make his own snowballs from the pile of snow in the cart – to fire back at his attackers when he had enough of them made. 'Ah the poor little Spallidaghs and they looking so crestfallen,' he shouted and not a mark or a dent on his fiendish face from their mis-hit snowballs.

By this time his mare was ambling of her own volition up towards the gap at Simple Simon's laneway. He shook his fist and he and the charm of his mouthful of broken teeth looked back triumphantly at the children.

How little the old fool knew.

The children were every bit as good as himself when it came to pretence and jack-acting and the sadness that he saw in the way they'd lowered their downcast heads was every bit as big a sham as his own mockery had been – as good as the actors in a Lenten play. If only the big man could see inside their far-from-innocent heads and the merry ache in their chests that was bursting to get out. They had cast their own smart web and they were ready. They could hardly keep the laughter locked down their throats, knowing what a dreadful fate was in store for him and his filthy antics when he reached the gap at Simple Simon's lane and before an angel from heaven could come down and rescue him.

At Simple-Simon's Lane

He reached the lane. From their ambush out stormed the rest of the noisy children, led by Lippity and Tom Foolery, who this time, unlike his upturning of Yellow Patsy's flour, was about to prove his worth. The first volley of exploding snowballs hit Fingers Jack in the right ear and almost bowled him over. The second volley rebounded off of his neck and the third one trimmed the stubble of his beardy face and powdered him all over. Oh, the chill and the burn of it! Was this the way to treat an honourable man – this the way to paint a crimson picture of his face? 'Twas a miracle that Nelly-the-mare didn't take flight. Why, the very ditches seemed to be laughing at the joyless state of him.

Listen to the uproarious shouts of them as they whaled snowball after snowball into his astonished head, leaving him a spectral ghost of himself and kicking his heels in the air inside in his cart. Worse still, his famed yellow hat had fallen off into a straggly hollybush and for the first time in their life the children could see that his head was as bald as his arse and that himself and his long black coat were a pure wreck. Fair play to ye, byze! They had given him and his long coat a good soaking and had shut his unruly gob for him.

A Joy Short-lived

Their joy at winning the war against Fingers-Jack was to be short-lived for at that precise moment the sledgers and gliders were a stone-throw away, up at Fort Dangerous, preparing for the downhill slippery slide. It was the only field steep enough and long enough for the fine winter sports.

The day was marked out as a bad one for the tallest lad imaginable (*Mick-the-Walking-Hayshed*). He should have been celebrating this week more than anyone else, having left the imprisonment of the schoolhouse of Dang-the-skin-of-it for once and for all. He was not, however, full of the joys of the other boys and girls but as good as heartbroken not only over the recent death of his sheepdog (*Rose*) but (far worse) over his beloved father's untimely death from long days feasting on rawgut whiskey.

His mother had forced him to take out his thick-latted belly-board to enjoy himself and give himself a bit of distraction on the snowy slopes. But his recent sorrow was nothing to what was now awaiting him for in a minute's time he was to be introduced to the real meaning of childhood sorrow.

He was the last to come sailing down the slope.

'Here comes Mick-the-Walking-Hayshed!' roared the sporting hordes of sledgers as they encouraged him on his downhill slide. All eyes were glued on him.

'Keep the way clear, lads!'

With an increasing rush he stormed on and on. See the sway of him – a sight for sore eyes.

'Here he comes!' – a-skidding and a-flying and a-leaping – his ruddy face ablaze with unspeakable joy. He was like a chased hare.

His face suddenly registered absolute terror when he realised that himself and his belly-board couldn't stop. He hit the ditch with a terrible rap and like a shot from a gun went sailing out over Free'n' Easy's crab-tree and landed in the road at the side of Fingers-Jack's blue cart. The poor lad – you should have seen him. His face had the whiteness of death stamped on it and he looked like an ancient leprechaun.

No Longer The Playful Buffoon

'Stand back! Stand back!' cried the suddenly-authoritative voice of Fingers-Jack. He was no longer the playful buffoon, the jack-actor with his lowered trousers in the blue cart. He was Fingers-Jack, the bonesetter.

Down onto his knees he lept from the cart. He beckoned the children to his side and in a gentle whisper he ordered them to run into Dowager and quickly bring out the blankets and bolsters.

Meanwhile, he kept speaking in a strange and musical voice into the ears of the injured youth. With his skilful fingers he kept testing the limbs of the lad, like a fiddler tuning his strings or rosining the horsehair of his bow.

The children's eyes were all peeled on him – those of the victorious snowballers and those of the sporting sledgers alike. The road ached with a moment's unbearable silence and not a single bird's song could be heard. Was Mick-the-Walking-Hayshed alive or was he dead? The crowd of children stood there wondering and one or two of the girls said a silent prayer that Fingers-Jack and his magic would somehow turn the trick and revive the hapless lad.

These last few months had been an eventful time for their bonesetter – what with Madge Roundabout's wrists and Little Dan's two shins – but nothing like this. He turned his eyes up to the sky as though (like Sammy-Joe) he was asking the help of his father and grandfather. Then he gave a smile that lit up the road like a blast of orange sunlight. He knew that the breaks to Mick-the-Walking-Hayshed's two wrists were thankfully as clean as a snap of wood. However, the lad seemed most unlikely to be stepping out behind his father for the sowing of the spuds in the coming springtime and he'd be fortunate indeed if he could use these wrists to twist the same spuds from their stalks when harvest-time came on next year.

The older boys who were standing close by – particularly the two nature-lovers, Warbling Will and Sammy-Joe, who had closely watched the serious skills of Fingers-Jack at his work — knew that if anyone could now change the fate of this lad, it was Fingers-Jack, a man of the purest tenderness whenever he was at his work.

The rest of Dowager's children, all of whom had just pasted the snow-sodden features of the bonesetter and had beaten him into humiliating submission in his cart, now found themselves looking into the enlightened soul of a far different Fingers-Jack – namely Rookery Rally's one-and-only gifted healer of bones. It was better than a school education and it suddenly struck them (they knew it — even before Fingers-Jack said so himself) that before the next year's Saint Patrick's Day was seen and gone, Mick-the-Walking-Hayshed would have new wrists on him – that Fingers-Jack would have made them as sound as bell-metal and as strong as the cartwheels of a pony-and-trap or the handles of a plough.

Without a note of ceremony and heedless of the children's applause the great man hopped back onto his cart. By now the sky's wine-colouring was rolling its final farewell down the late afternoon and Fingers Jack was as contented as any man could be. A few minutes later he entered his house and lit a candle. He was tired and weary and he headed for the settlebed in the small room next to the hen-house. He was soon asleep and now as ever the hills around him were silent and the first winter stars were soon high in the sky. Neither wind or rain or children's snowballs would bother him for the time being. And yet… tomorrow would be another new day and no-one could know what it might bring him.

ELEVEN

Little Nell's journey

Dowager's children were mostly born in the Big Cave Room behind the chimney, one every second year, as with most households in Rookery Rally. The children of Red Scissors were a mere two in number and people politely coughed up their sleeves and wondered what was wrong with his private manly regalia. From time to time the women were caught short and couldn't cross their legs any longer. They'd be out in the springtime fields, alongside the men, weeding and hoeing, laughing and carolling as they worked. They'd be exchanging bits of their story-land tales, taking swipes at the clergy, who never seemed to visit the poor. The men alongside these women had different thoughts – hoping and praying that their country would one day be free from the bleddy foreigners and be master of its own fate.

Dowager Was Thinning Turnips

It was late one springtime and a long time before Handsome Johnnie had been called away by his Maker. Along with half-a-dozen other men and women, Dowager was thinning the turnips with the potato-sacks around her knees. And that was the day when it all started – abroad there in the Turnip Field. It was the day when Little Nell decided to make her way out of her mother's body.

Dowager had been walking, drill by drill, a stone's throw away from Handsome Johnnie when she suddenly felt a pain in the lower part of her spine. A little while later she felt another pain – this one a good deal sharper. It was ripping her inside in her belly. Her guardian angel came down and she roared at Dowager to hurry on. She herself knew what was happening to her for it was but natural – as with the cows and the mares. It had happened often enough to the women who came before her and she now had to think fast. There was no time to make her preparations and, like any wildcat, she struggled and crawled in over the ditch for privacy's sake. In the peace and quiet of the hollows where only the birds and the cattle could see her, she knelt herself down and she prayed to her God-in-heaven as she looked down at her sweaty face in the waters of Corcoran's spring well.

An hour later Dowager eased her baby daughter onto the grass. There was not too much blood. It was her fifth child – Little Nell. The spring waters in Corcoran's

Well seemed to stop their murmuring for a while in honour of the birth. Dowager's own guardian angel gave a little smile. Handsome Johnnie, at the lower end of the Turnip Field, was all the while whistling and singing to himself and hadn't even missed his good wife going away from the work.

Dowager took a fond look at the baby girl – so small that she looked like a long pink rat. A sudden bit of fear now grew inside in Dowager's chest. She gave the baby's forehead a fistful of the spring well-water and she reverently blessed her, baptizing her with the sign-of-the-cross. Then she took off her potato-sack from round her knees and untied the bows of her navy apron. She wrapped her baby in its warm, sweaty folds and went back into the Turnip Field where she showed the infant to Handsome Johnnie. He took one look at the frail little girl. He couldn't help himself as he began to bawl like a sick calf. He was the happiest man on God's earth.

Frail And Small

Weak at birth and still frail as she began to grow, Little Nell was by far the smallest of the family up until that time. She had been born a month earlier than expected and Dowager was wise to have had the good sense and the speed to give her the spring well baptism for she did not want any child of hers to die without the blessings of Holy Mother Church. She did not want her child to end up in *Limbo* outside of heaven.

Less than a generation before, when there might already have been a dozen children elsewhere around some mother's table, a newborn baby (as frail and as delicate as her own little heroine) might well have been left abroad in an open-air pram in all sorts of weathers. No-one seemed to know if this was done absentmindedly or with wilful neglect. Only God-in-heaven knew the answer to this query. A baby, left sleeping the night away below the hay-reek or at the back of the hen-house, had little or no chance of crying its lungs out when next morning arrived. The month before the birth of Little Nell Dowager had heard tell of a pair of baby twins (and not many twins were born those days) down near Gortnameena, who'd been left abroad during the night. The little mites did not cough another breath next morning.

Apart from being a burden to rear, delicate children in their future years would bring in no money from work as servants in the Big House of men like Lord Elegance or even in the houses of lesser-known rich farmers like Sallyswitch. They were unemployable and on the morning after the death of any newborn child, you'd see the sad mother bawling at the haggart singletree while the men were taking their milk to the creamery. You'd see the theatrical downcast look in her eyes. You'd see the shrug of her shoulders. You'd see the dreary look she gave upon the godforsaken earth, which had robbed her of her new child, as if to say, 'God's will be done!' But if you were to get inside the heart of women like herself, the prayer they were silently praying was, 'Thanks be to

God!' For as matters stood they hadn't enough stirabout in the cauldron over the fire to feed the rest of the huge family and nobody was bewildered or shocked by the news of an infant's sickness and untimely death. They were simply relieved.

God Sent The Best Of His Angels

And now we see the *Smiling Fairies* pursuing Dowager's household and God standing watch over Little Nell. He sent down the best of his angels to keep an eye on her as she grew. There was now hope and there was sunlight for her as in stops and starts her frail body increased in strength each day. People began to notice things about her. She was seen to have a wiry knot of lively black hair – as shiny as a jackdaw's wing. She had the lovely sloe eyes of her mother and as with the flowers in Dowager's garden, there grew in her a beauty that manifested itself in both her movements and her form – a beauty which sent a loving ache into all the souls who passed by the yard-stream and into the hearts of her three big brothers – if not entirely into her older sister, Darkie.

Sadly, it was a loving ache that lasted only too briefly.

She Loved Her Schoolbooks

This was the time when her sister Darkie had left school and was still sitting at home with her feet in the ashes, waiting to find work. Little Nell was the oldest child of the Spallidaghs still left at school. She was always the first of Dowager's children to rush out the door each morning – so much did she love her schoolwork – so much did she yearn for the knowledge and the learning in her schoolbooks. She didn't mind whether it be the mental quickness with the sums or the long-winded poems like *the Lady of Shallot* or the songs of pure beauty like *Barbara Allen*. She also loved making the cambric shirt and her imagination ran riot when it came to Dang-the-skin-of-it's special love – the subject 'Point to the Map'.

She well remembered her first day at school when she waved back at her mother across the half-door as she gleefully trotted over the yard-stream flagstones and followed along behind her older brothers and her sister, Darkie. Thanks to her mother, before she reached the schoolhouse she was already well and truly versed in the two times table and the repetition of the first page of the catechism – especially the bit which said 'God made me to know Him, love Him and serve Him in this world and to be happy with Him forever in the next world.'

February

It was February, a few days after her thirteenth birthday (of course there were no birthdays to celebrate in Rookery Rally since no one knew the meaning of the word *birthday*) and Little Nell was stricken low with a strange fever. The snow was constantly pouring down and the window-ledges and the house thatch and fuchsia bushes round the yard were a mass of linen white. Doctor Glasses himself came out to cast an eye on her. He threw his leather bag and stethoscope on the front table and pronounced his sentence: 'The child has the yellow jaundice.'

News travelled quickly that day. No one had ever heard tell of this illness or how serious it might be. Lady Elegance (kind soul) brought up a big bowl of ice cream. Such items as these were rarely heard tell of in Rookery Rally.

What do you think happened next? Why, Little Nell's three older brothers – and even the lonely Darkie – fought gallantly with each other in their attempts to throw themselves into the bed beside her. The four of them were fever-mad, all wanting to catch a hold of the yellow jaundice so as to get their claws on some of Lady Elegance's ice cream.

On Monday morning when Dowager was busy with the Rickett's blue for the week's washing and hanging her sheets and shirts on the haggart bushes she saw a little army of the Mountainy Men's children arriving on her flagstones.

'What do ye want at this hour of the day when ye should be beyond in the schoolhouse?' said Dowager, her sharp eyes noticing their cowdungy legs.

'Do they ever wash?' said Blue-eyed Jack to himself as he threw his leg over the crossbar of his twenty-eight-inch wheeler and went off to plough for Lord Elegance.

'We have come to see the yallah child,' said the biggest mountainy child stubbornly.

'We want to see the yallah face of her,' pleaded the smallest urchin from behind his brother's legs.

Dowager softened a little. They had come a very long way.

'Ye can see her this once and this once only. Then be off with ye to school before yeer master takes the sally-switch to yeer arses,' she said with a laugh.

Such excitement, to see the children dancing up and down on the flagstones. Their waiting was unbearable but at last her mother brought Little Nell out. She was like a holy church statue as Dowager paraded her around by the pig-house and down passed the hen-house. She didn't bring her too close to the mountainy children for fear they'd all catch the yellow jaundice themselves. After all, she loved their parents wholeheartedly and they loved her back in turn. They had always been ready to throw into her lap a freshly-caught salmon from Growl River or a snared rabbit from the Valley-of-the-Pig whenever they came down with the horse-and-cart for the monthly supplies of flour and meal at Curl 'n Stripes' Shop.

The Week Of Confirmation

Springtime seemingly was over before it had begun and the summertime and the flowers were here. The month of Our Blessed Lady came on – the glorious month of

May with its masses of white hawthorn blossom and wild honeysuckle and bellflowers. Little Nell was now thirteen years old and, though still somewhat on the small side, she was as healthy as a dog and could drink a gallon of morning milk if you let her.

It was the time for her to meet with Bishop High-Hat from his palace in Ennis. He was to visit the parish church at the Two Goats Hill and to administer the Sacrament of Confirmation, which would make Little Nell and her schoolfriends *soldiers of the risen Christ*. The holy man would give them the customary slap on the jaw to show them what fighting little soldiers of Christ they had become and Dowager coached Little Nell in all the catechism answers. Bright girl that she was, she had already memorized three-quarters of the long catechism answers, which might be needed in front of the bishop before he departed back home to Clare.

Confirmation week arrived and Bishop High-Hat stood in front of the children. None were more spotless than he – in his long purple dress with the big sleeves. He carried a shepherd's stick in front of him, handy in case he'd slip in the mud or the horse-dung as he came across from the master's house. In his spare hand he was carrying a black book with all the questions and answers in it for him to test the children's knowledge and understanding. The clergy from far and near followed along behind him like a line of goslings. Then came the children with their best side out. It was as exciting as a hurling-match and they were all dressed in their best finery – even the poorer children in their most suitable hand-me-downs where a sleeve had to be shortened or the trousers to be repaired at the knees that had been worn away from contact with the flinty stones when sowing spuds or thinning turnips. In earlier days Dowager had been up all night and had cut asunder three greatcoats belonging to Handsome Johnnie and his own father, Dandy. With these she had made a reasonable attempt at four new trousers and jackets for her previous children when they were to be confirmed. Fair play to you, Dowager. Little Nell looked a pure picture on the day and felt as holy as a walking nun. She asked the good God-in-heaven to take away any hatred that might still lie in her heart and prayed that He would help her come to love her older sister, Darkie. It seemed that He turned his ear away for this young lady continued to lord it over her and to set herself up as the veritable queen of her mother's Welcoming Room for much of their childhood.

Jack-the-Herd's Son

The Sacrament of Confirmation had gone smoothly enough – except for Jack-the-Herd's son (*Tommy*), who had disgraced the gathering entirely when he was asked for his new Conformation name.

'*Brian Boru*,' said he, proudly throwing out his chest. He had been put up to say this just as he was about to enter the church door by some of the wily men on their way home from the creamery. How was he to know that

Brian Boru was the most famous of the warriors of yore and not one of the blessed saints? Such a commotion followed this little outburst and the poor lad was swept away off of his feet and into the sacristy. There he was given the new name of Finbar by the startled parish priest, who wished that the floor would open up beneath his own feet. He'd be having the most unpleasant of tea and sandwiches alongside Bishop High-Hat when the crowd had gone home after the ceremony.

A Week Or Two Passed By

A week or two passed by and, with Handsome Johnnie dead, Dowager found herself very short of coppers in her purse. This shortage of money wouldn't do and would have to come to an end sooner or later. She cast her eyes about her in the direction of her eldest daughter, Darkie – the girl with the hole-in-the-heart. Then she turned her eyes towards Little Nell. She could see that her second daughter was growing stronger and stronger each day as a result of flexing her growing muscles as the household's little workhorse. For it was Little Nell that used the goose's wing liberally in all four corners of the Welcoming Room – that climbed up by the side of the tapestry and the oil lamp and took down the collar and haymes from the ledge beside the hob so as to put a shine on them. It was she that took out the shoe-last from the press-cupboard and polished all the boots and shoes for Sunday Mass till they shone like glass – arranging them in a row for Dowager's inspection. If there was time, she cleaned the blue delf and made sure that the jug with the broken lip, which held the sour milk for baking, was always replenished. There were a hundred and one jobs that this little girl was able to tackle – all of them without a murmur. Wasn't she the mighty child!

Dowager Made Up Her Mind

Dowager made up her mind there and then: she was going to have to tear Little Nell out from the nest and get her suitable employment. She would sort out this mess this very week. She knew that there were several big landowners like Sallyswitch who were only too willing to employ a stout-hearted girl for the customary ten shillings a month. The child would be trained to spend a year or two at the farm-labouring. And then, if lucky, she would spend another year or so at the cleaning out of the ashes and learning the household niceties, such as polishing the apostle-spoons, laying out the cutlery and folding the napkins. In the end she'd have the honour of waiting on the high and mighty at their top table and topping their eggs for them. Yes, there would be increasing loads of work for a girl like Little Nell as she grew in strength. But what Dowager didn't know was that if Little Nell was fortunate enough to gain such employment, she would not be allowed to give up the first job and replace it with the second job and later with the third job. No, she would find herself increasingly doing all *three* laborious jobs rolled into one: in the farmyard: in the kitchen: in the dining room.

Like A Thief In The Night

Little Nell was by now the top scholar in her age group. In a day or two, like a thief coming in the night, it was all to be torn away from her. She was to be dragged from the doors of the school, never to return amongst her friends and she cried herself to sleep each night in the dreaded preparations for this new life of hers.

It was the month of June and the sunlight danced in through the window on a dust-laden beam of light. Young farmyard fowl came out from their hidey-holes and were everywhere. The music of the ducklings echoed around the rocky edges of every yard-stream. The unsteadiness of new chicks, still unsure what to do, caused them to be blown sideways down the yard in the wake of their mother. The wobbly goslings caused the children to laugh heartily as the little creatures struggled their way across the haggart and frantically followed behind their mother on the long journey through the wheel-ruts to the Bluebutton Field. Little Nell was also about to make an unknown journey as her mother roused her from her bed and scrubbed her till she shone like a new sweet-gallon. She could do nothing with the child's wiry hair but put a few clips in it here and there.

She got ready the ass-and-car and they went on their speedy way, avoiding the gossipy questioning of

Galloping Gret and her prized turkeys below at the Kill. From Abbey Cross they went on through Travellers' Rest and its famed orchards. The wind whipped the clouds along in front of them in whisking gusts as they turned left and went down by Ranters' Cross before entering the huge red gates that stood some thirty feet in the air.

Dread

The dread was already setting into the soul of Little Nell as down the steps from The Big House came Sallyswitch himself to greet them. He was a great portentous fellow and had put on his best cap and not his working cap. He helped Dowager down graciously from her poised toe on the wheel of the ass-and-car. She didn't miss much. He was a dandy-of-man with a reddish face and the odd wart here and there and a mouthful of rotten yellow teeth. Well accustomed to inspecting his previous maidservants, he now eyed Little Nell up and down. She kept her eyes held low as he slowly walked around her. Was he about to kill her? She felt like a cow in the marketplace inside in the Roaring Town.

A little bit on the frail side (thought he to himself).

This is the way it is with the Limerick pig-buyers inside in the Roaring Town when they bargain for the fine fat pigs taken in with the horse and blue-boarded cart (thought Dowager to herself).

She herself was wearing her best gloves and her blue-basket hat. She was dressed in her best grey coat –

the one with the ribbons wrapped inside in it. She was at her proudest so as not to be a shame to her ancestors or the spot where she came from. She had been dreading this moment. She felt awkward.

Slowly she raised her eyes to Sallyswitch. Would he trust her as she started to assure him of the excellences of Little Nell?

A Slave – Or Not To Be?

A slave to be or not to be? That was the question now for Little Nell. Sallyswitch put his fingers round the child's biceps. He tested the muscles in her arms and the calves at the back of her legs. He almost took to looking inside her mouth to see her teeth – as if she were a horse.

'Damn his hide!' thought Dowager, nervously twiddling with her ashplant.

Sallyswitch ran his hands across the broad of Little Nell's back. His wife (*La-Dee-Dah*) came out running to join him and she too walked several times around the silent and motionless child. Little Nell knew that this was a moment of trial. She didn't want to let her mother down.

The two upturned noses were undecided about taking on so small a child and they went off down the yard for a private chit-chat.

With baited breath Dowager waited, fingering her rosary-beads and praying as hard as she ever did that Sallyswitch would buy the services of her daughter and make her his little servant-girl. At the same time she knew the tremendous load of work that was in store for Little Nell.

'Ah, the poor child!' she sighed. 'What have I done?'

At the lower end of the yard Sallyswitch started speaking earnestly to La-Dee-Dah: 'Will this child be able to rise with the cockerel at five in the morning? Will she be able to fill the fifty-gallon cauldron with the several buckets from the icy well? Will she be able to pulp the mangolds in the ringer in the turf-shed? Will she be able to feed the fierce sow with her thirteen little piggies at the crack of dawn? Will she be able to take our inexperienced young bull (*Brownie*) to the cowshed by the reins and bull-ring and help him to rise to the occasion and inject the young heifers with joy?'

Coming back down the yard, he stared deep into Dowager's eyes and put these questions to her. And to each fresh anxiety Dowager gave a quick but firm nod of the head. She knew her place as a suppliant and in desperation she crossed herself and swore a vociferous oath in Little Nell's favour. At last the good man struck the deal with her. He had bought his little slave-girl for ten shillings each month, the money to be sent home in a matchbox with the lads coming home from the creamery.

The Following Sunday

The following Sunday the final preparations were made for Little Nell's transfer. They were indeed sparse.

Dowager summoned the bewildered child and told her of the fine prospects that lay ahead of her.

Little Nell took a dazed look all round her. She gazed at the Welcoming Room where she now found little if any welcome – where all that she had received in welcome hitherto were the bruises inflicted on her by her older sister, Darkie. And what of Darkie? As usual she was jay-acting along with the younger children abroad in the Bluebutton Field and firing sods of turf at them, trying to blind them. Little Nell turned back her gaze and saw the guilt and the downcast eyes of Dowager. Prospects indeed – you'd think that she was being asked merely to go out and bring in the hens for the evening roost!

Her mother had made ready the child's working clothes and her Sunday dress for Holy Mass days when she'd arrive at the Big House. From the press cupboard she brought out her tattered shoes and polished them – the ones handed down to her from Darkie so as to avoid being barefooted for the rest of her life. Up until then she hadn't had much use for such items since all children until they were sixteen went in nothing but the bare feet between May and the end of September

The Penny-go-cart And Rosary-Beads

Still a child at heart, Little Nell took the penny go-cart that Big Paddy had once made for her in sympathy the day Darkie fired the stone into her head. She had hidden this toy cart in the henhouse, free from Darkie's jealous gaze. She also took the wax doll that Lady Singleton had brought up the previous evening and kept thinking: if only there had been a place for her to do some sort of servant-work with that good woman, but Lady Singleton couldn't afford to hire her at the present time.

Dowager solemnly handed Little Nell the white rosary-beads to bring her good luck – her own ones that had been handed down to her from her own mother, Nan. She pinned the Sacred Heart card to Little Nell's vest – the card which Bishop High-Hat had given her when he gave her the Sacrament of Confirmation and the second name of Magdalene. Little Nell's own sufferings were to be a mirror of the biblical Magdalene though she knew it not.

Ten O'clock

It was ten o'clock in the morning and the daylight was threateningly eerie. The cattle were bawling on Cheerful Nan's Heights as though rain was expected and the hens and the ducks were already asleep after their mid-morning feed of mash from the galavanize sheeting behind the ass-and-car. Dowager took the holy-water jar and placed it in Little Nell's fist and she blessed her solemnly. Then the tears silently rolled down her cheeks.

She whispered into the ears and nose of Moll-the-mare and then stealthily threw the reins and blinkers across her neck and the cart was got ready in the yard.

Suddenly her tune changed and that was unusual in a mother as kind and gentle as herself. 'Sight! Blasht you, sight!' she roared, now supplanting her betrayal of Little Nell with her vexation at the guiltless Moll. The bewildered mare was then showered with the holy-water and the cart and tackling were blessed too. Little Nell and Dowager hoisted themselves up onto the horse-and-cart – the ass-and-car being too menial for such a prodigious farewell journey as this. Mother and daughter looked around fretfully from their high seat on the straw bag and latboard and Dowager fumbled with her handkerchief. There was an unreasonable confusion in the air – a confusion that no child could comprehend. To which was added a huge hurt inside in Little Nell. She looked at her mother. Her mother looked at her. There was a little forlorn wave-of-the-hand from the other children, who all went inside, as if to hide themselves. They sat by the fireside and wept bucketfuls for the departure of their sister.

A Flick Of The Whip

Dowager and Little Nell wrapped the tartan rug around their legs. A flick of the whip and away the cart sped across the yard-stream flagstones. The rocky road under the mare's sparkling hooves seemed to make the child's vision glaze over. Already dazed and weary, she tried to concentrate on the new dizziness inside in her head. She looked down at the dung-stained cartwheels and the flies in the horse-dung on the Open Road. She tried to forget the fact that, upon leaving the only home she had ever known, her heart was about to break into a thousand pieces.

They at last reached the high gates of Sallyswitch. The dread from the previous visit set itself again into Little Nell's soul when the cart stumbled across the yard. Then the gates were slammed behind them. Little Nell was now a prisoner as her mother handed her down from the horse-and-cart. There were never any slobbery kisses in Rookery Rally. She looked her daughter in the eye and shook her by the hand. Then she turned on her heel and fled. Were he alive, Handsome Johnnie would be drinking more than the one pint of the black doctor stout on this sad evening if he were to wash the stain of family guilt away. Little Nell was still but a child.

The Silenced Priest

She was marched across the yard where she saw the stables and the eight tan-coloured racehorses looking out disinterestedly at her from their steamy-breath stalls. La-Dee-dah took her to meet the older workers and servants, the grooms and the maids. She introduced her to the silenced priest (*Tom*) in his small room above the stables. Tom had gambled away his soul at the races of horses, dogs and hares and was now an outcast from the family – treated like something that the cat brought in.

He was craving for some kind company and he saw his chance with the arrival of this little girl in the farmyard.

There was a story behind Tom. It was usually the sons of poor hill-farmers, who found their way across the ocean as priestly fodder on the Far Eastern and African mission-fields for converting the native flock. But, being the son of a rich farmer, Tom had been destined for a more prestigious mission at home here in Ireland. With men of Sallyswitch's high stature, to have a priest or two – even a nun or two – in the family was always a badge of honour as a result of which he could hold his head up high at every drinking-shop in the county. Sallyswitch had known that as soon as Tom was ordained, he would have the pick of several parishes in Clare and Tipperary and that all types of sorrow thereafter would be unknown to him. For he could have anywhere he chose on both sides of the Mighty Shannon River where the money from rich spinsters was good and where the football and hurling matches and the hare-coursing were regular amusements. Ah yes, thought Sallyswitch to himself, my son will have the hunts, the balls and the golf course and a lovely dwelling for himself. He will have the odd servant girl for him to lay his hands on – one who will warm his bed for him if he chooses. It would mean the introduction into high society at card-tables and gala-balls. It would mean even a stroll round the Ascot Racehorse Ring beyond at the English Racing Derby.

From his earliest schooldays, however, Tom had wished for the saintly work of an overseas missioner. A natural scholar and the reader of large books, he had set his heart on going far over the ocean and helping his poor African brothers, who had no knowledge of God.

'What's this I hear?' snapped Sallyswitch when he heard this news. He was in a froth of anger. No self-respecting son would do such a thing. Tom, the son of a rich farmer like Sallyswitch. What on earth would the neighbours think of a rich man's son used as fodder in the mission-fields abroad in Africa?

Poor misfortunate Tom found himself forced away from the high aspirations of his youth. He'd have to forget his dreams of working with his African brothers in the building of villages and the sinking of wells and the sowing of springtime grass-seeds. He'd be forced to work on the home mission instead. As a sop to Sallyswitch, who had paid the bishop a bob or two, he was soon made the inspector of religious finances and the guardian of the rich purses of the diocese. But, clever as he was in other ways, the poor lad had no head for figures. He couldn't handle it all – the money and the book-keeping of large sums of silver.

Then along came the gambling – whether at horseracing, greyhounds or cards – and it proved to be his downfall. He fell into the temptations that only money could bring and it brought him to the sorry pass in which Little Nell now found him. The destitute purse which was found in his pocket (for he had gambled away church monies) ensured that he had to be punished and forever more known as the *Silenced Priest*. What he couldn't bear (and it broke his spirit entirely) was the fact that he was forbidden by the bishop ever again to say Mass. On Sundays, the nervous Sallyswitch placed Tom on a chair inside in the sacristy a minute or two before Mass started. He hid him there, behind a curtain, for fear the congregation might find out that Tom was guilty of wrongdoing and had been *silenced*. Such shame could never be let abroad. The good name of Sallyswitch and La-Dee-Dah would have been tarnished irreparably forever. It was as though Tom was some outcast leper. His long-lasting grief matched the present heartbreak of Little Nell.

An Everlasting Bond

From the moment their two sets of eyes met, there was to be an everlasting bond between Tom and Little Nell. Each morning Sallyswitch and La-Dee-Dah would sit at the high table. Rolling their hypocritical eyes upto the rafters, they'd start the day by giving thanks to Almighty God for the fine food on their table. To her horror Little Nell could see that Tom was treated like a stray dog that had come in through the doorway – always summoned to his so-called meals like a naughty child – forbidden to dine with the lordly twosome – forced to sit in silence at a separate bare-board table along with herself and the other servants in the lower adjoining room. When he had finished his own meal, Sallyswitch with a snigger passed Tom the leftovers from his plate. When no one was looking, Little Nell gave half of her food to Tom to keep him from starving.

Her First Day

On her first day she was taken across the puddledy yard (in places almost a lake) and introduced to each of the animals – especially to the dreaded sow and the eager young bull (*Brownie*). In the far corner of the yard there was an outhouse. It had once been a pig-house but was now the laundry-room where all the linen was kept. In the middle of it a ladder rose up. If you climbed it, you would eventually reach the icy loft. This was now to be Little Nell's new home, far away from all her brothers and sisters.

The Bit Of Money

How breathlessly did she wait for the money to get into her fist at the end of her first month! Herself and her bulging eyes gazed at the new brown ten-shilling note – a sum of money such as she had never seen before. She stuffed it quickly inside in a matchbox. An hour later (she could hardly wait) she handed the matchbox to Hammer-the-Smith as he was wending his way home in his rattle-cart with his skimmed milk from the creamery.

It was such an exciting day for Little Nell and as the morning wore nearer to dinnertime she kept looking into the sky and studying the movements of the passing clouds. As the clouds crossed the sky they sent dreamy shadows across Polly's Hill above the schoolhouse where a month before she had been reciting her poetry into the welcoming ears of Dang-the-skin-of-it. The progress of these clouds would now be her guide and she knew to the minute when the money would at last reach the fists of her mother.

'Hammer-the-Smith's cart is now at Ranter's Cross,' she said to herself. 'He's now at the Abbey Cross turn. He's now at the Kill.' Each cloud-shadow told her a different story of the journey her ten-shilling note was making.

'And now mee mother has the money in her fists,' she cried triumphantly after all her hard work. She laughed to herself almost conspiratorially and heaved a sigh of pleasure. In the silence of her head she spoke to her mother from all the way across the open fields:

'And will you now be rich, mother?'

Of course, the answer, if it could have come back to her across the rushy fields, would have been *No*. Nevertheless, the money would go a long way to keeping the wolf from the door and it would keep her younger brothers and sisters in clothing fit for school and Holy Mass.

Sobbing Her Tears

More than once during the early days of her slavery Little Nell could be found sobbing silently in her cold icy attic. Her hands were blistered and her back was sore from the lifting of the heavy buckets and sacks. The morning sun shone fiercely in through her open window – even at this early hour of the day. An hour or two later the school children – her own younger brothers and sisters amongst them – were out on the Open Road and taking the long trek to the schoolhouse. You'd think her heart would burst when she thought of the difference between her new situation – out among the real world of drudgery – and the other children's playful activities on that sunny morning. The very sunshine seemed to be laughing at her.

The other children, some of them her own age, trotted jovially along on the other side of the hedge. Unlike our little heroine, they were counting the weary schooldays till the time would come for them to leave school. It simply couldn't come quickly enough for them. They were unaware of the blinding tears of Little Nell as she listened in desperation to the tinkling laughter of Matt-the-Hare and Bill-the-Bears's son, Micky. With Sallyswitch's pisspot she ran down to the bottom of the haggart to empty it in the ashpit where she herself discreetly made her poolie. There was a hole in the hedge and with tears blinding her eyes she tore her way out through the little gap. Picture the look of astonishment in her school friends' eyes as she begged them to tell her mother how unhappy she was and pleaded with them to take her with them to her desk in Dang-the-skin-of-it's schoolhouse.

Not A Moment To Spare

She hadn't a moment to spare. She asked them for all the news – especially concerning her best friend (*Leggy Peg*). She begged them for news from the previous week's schooling. 'What are ye learning now? Is poor Muddlesome Tom still left sitting on the plank along with Pinfeather and the little six-year olds? Is he still the helpless and hopeless scholar with his writing and reading and are the sums all the time baffling him?' She had several hurried questions and not enough seconds left before Sallyswitch would come after her with the yardbrush. 'I'll be here again tomorrow. Be sure to bring me yeer news and don't forget to tell mee mother that ye saw me and the terrible soreness in mee hands and the tears in mee eyes.' A second later the children were gone and Little Nell was left kneeling on the road and sobbing bitter tears.

The Wiry Yardbrush

'Is it tears ye want?' roared the salivating La-Dee-Dah as she clambered out over the ditch with the wiry yardbrush. She had a face as angry as a mad devil in hell.

'I'll give ye reason to cry.' She drove Little Nell back into the farmyard, whaling and walloping into her wherever she could get a good swing at her with the yardbrush and reddening her legs till they bled. She hauled her back through the hedge and shouted after her. 'Get on with you, ye heathen! Get back to the two pigs that we are fattening for market and go and give them their mash.'

Determined To Fight Her Corner

A day or two later and unable to stop shivering and sobbing, Little Nell could bear it no longer. Her prayers to her guardian angel were suddenly answered and, just as in the days when Darkie had driven her demented with her bullying antics, she found that she had a heart and a determination to fight her corner. It came rising up from deep down inside her so that in the middle of the night she packed her few belongings and tiptoed out the gate that led towards Ranters' Cross – to Dowager and the home that she had recently left behind. The silver moon ran along behind the entangled trees on the ditches. It shone radiantly through the clouds and glittered them above her in the black sky. The stars spattered all round her and luminated the milky road ahead of her. All this lifted her spirits so that she feared none of the nightly ghosts. But after half-an-hour when the misty rain came on she was forced to silently hum *Barbara Allen* to herself so as to keep her company and ward the wicked Boodeemen away from her. She was suddenly frightened of the dark roads, having never travelled at so late an hour before.

Daybreak

Daybreak came and with it the stormy conversations of the young birds flying about. It found Little Nell, her hair soaking wet, lying outside her own half-door. She was exhausted after her long journey and was lying there in a deep sleep. Could you but see the shock when Dowager beheld the state of her child. She was joyful. She was angry too – to think of all the ten shilling notes she'd be missing if she was to keep Little Nell at home and not to send her back, She gave her a few playful little cuffs of chastisement across the head and sent her to bed for the rest of the day. Now she'd have to collect her thoughts and get the apologetic ass-and-car and take Little Nell back. But she'd warn La-dee-Dah not to beat her too severely as she had already given her the thrashing of her life.

Back Behind The Big Red Gates

Next morning Little Nell beheld the thirty-feet high gates all over again. She was dragged back into her slavery and the gates were slammed behind her. As she drove her ass home Dowager's heart was torn apart – glad of the money – tormented at the treatment meted out to such a frail child as her daughter and she recalled the child's dramatic birth at the side of the Turnip Field ditch. The doubts now came crowding in on top of her: would Little Nell be able to bear it all?

The fun now began in earnest and Little Nell was made to work harder than ever. They half-starved her of food. And yet, they couldn't completely starve her or she'd be unable to work the harsh hours they had in mind for her.

Tom was her one true friend. He had kept back a few silver coins in a chest under his bed and late that night he threw on his top coat and whisperingly climbed up the ladder to her attic room. He told her of his silver coins, which were of no use to him anymore. He placed them tenderly in her hands. One day, when she was older (he told her) she was to run away. He had a cousin in the far-off Great City they called Pandemonium, across the Herring Pond. He gave her a piece of paper with the address on it.

'At sixteen you'll be let loose to the Roaring Town to shop for La-dee-dah's finery and cosmetics. At seventeen you'll drive Sallyswitch and the two fattened pigs to the market and you'll steer the mare home with Sallyswitch blind drunk behind you in the cart. At eighteen your time will have come. Trusting you, they'll let you take the two fattened pigs to market all by yourself. That's the day your slavery will be done for that's when you'll strike out for your freedom. You'll take the money from the sale of the two pigs – don't for a minute think of it as stealing – you've earned it ten times over and you'll get yourself on board the mail-train. They'll send me out to search for you. I'll find the horse-and-cart in the Widda-Woman's yard and I'll bring it home. I'll show them the note that you're to leave behind – a note that will misguide their search for you, telling them that you have gone to join a nunnery in county Kilkenny. Have no fear, Little Nell. I tell you, the money from the sale of the two pigs is rightfully yours – it's worth half a year of your wages and that is the very least they owe you.'

In such a way spoke Tom, the saviour of Little Nell.

Her Eyes Lit Up

For once in her life the eyes of Little Nell lit up as she warmed to the advice of Tom. He had come to her attic as a truly good friend and had left it again, his fingers on his lips and a wink in his eyes – as though he were the unbelievable fairy godmother in the story of Cinderella. For the first time since her arrival she felt a warmth in her bed as she slept that night – and for several nights thereafter. Tom was the answer to all her prayers and had shown her a vision of her happy future. She now knew that she would have to serve out her slavery for just a few years more and not the entirety of her life and she laughed her way all the way to sleep.

The Rats In The Rafters

Days followed nights and nights followed days with Little Nell listening to the rats in the rafters. She cautiously tiptoed to the door. She placed a chair underneath the door handle. She turned up the sides of the bedclothes and looked underneath her bed. No rats in here. No rats able to enter the doorway or the window. But the loneliness of her room continued to fill her with dread and the bedclothes were almost wet with iciness. She used both sets of fingers to fold down the small inner flaps of her ears. Then she covered the flaps with the floppy outer flap so as to block out the rats and the caterwauling howls of the nightly foxes and the nightly creaks and cracks that the Boodeeman was renowned for making, when he came peering in over sleeping children.

It was difficult to sleep in this strange house – in this strange room – in this strange bed. She was a small solitary bird trapped in a cage, even after all these weeks. She walked across the dark room towards the window. She opened the shutters half-ways and looked out at the black and silver tunnel of the poplar-trees fringing the carriageway and up at the high moon and banks of clouds like rags blown along in the night's gale. She gazed up at the innumerable clusters of riotous stars in the Milky Way, necklace upon milk-spattering necklace of night lights hanging down from the sky and twinkling and winking at her.

'How many stars are there in the heavens (she asked herself)? 'Is each one of them a saint? Will I return to the stars one day? Is that what heaven is like, a place of bottomless Joy – a collection of stars?'

Returning to her bed, she pillowed her head into the bolster and melted down under the blankets. She said a very short prayer-of-hope and tried to sleep once more. But it would be dawn in an hour for she heard the first shy songs of the little birds awakening. She heard Sallyswitch's insolent cockerel answering them and then a dog barking in tune with them. She missed Darkie, the sister that had caused her so much grief at home. How good it would be to put her two feet between her big sister's ankles during the night and to snuggle up beside her warm body. Instead of counting sheep, she counted the stars and imagined them falling from the black velvety sky and landing splashing into the yard stream back home. Thousands and thousands and thousands. And at last she fell into a bottomless sleep.

Above the farm of Sallyswitch the stars continued to twinkle merrily – far happier than Little Nell. Next morning came too quickly upon her and her nightly fear of the dark was replaced by the knowing urgency of her everyday workload. It seemed that no sooner was she asleep than daylight threw her out of her bed again.

Dawn followed dawn followed dawn. With her head splitting, she was awakened each day by the first light of the sun coming in the window in a silver ribbon across her attic bedclothes. A new morning. A new backache.

The Rusty Pulper

Five o'clock in the morning and she hurriedly threw on her dress over her chemise and put on her wellingtons. She descended the ladder and hoisted herself off to the barn where the rusty green pulper was awaiting her. From the corner next to the piles of turf, she got herself an armful of the sweet-smelling turnips and mangolds. *Pulp-pulp-pulp!* She fired them into the pulper until a huge heap of them lay in shreds at her feet. The two pigs and the nearby sow in her sty were in for a royal treat this day and the unweaned piglets too for after her feed of mangolds the milk from the sow would be all the better for them and their daily growth.

The Fifty-gallon Cauldron

She returned to the scullery where she found the huge fifty-gallon cauldron – the one she could not carry to the well. She found the brown papers and the paraffin. She found the candle pieces in the jar and she found the kindling and the matches. From last night's still-glowing embers she soon embroiled all these into a roaring blaze and with the turf heaped on, the fire was soon as hot as hell.

She lugged the cauldron over to the fireplace so that it'd be ready for the first buckets of water when she came back from the well. Back and forth she dragged her weary wellingtons to the icy well. She cleaned the top of the well and swirled her bucket around and around to throw away the top-water and the flies and insects. She scooped up dozens of buckets of water – filling them to the brim to save time and legs and energy. Before you could blink she had filled up the huge cauldron over the fire. And yet, this was the most exquisite hour of the day with not a soul to bother her – not a sound even from the mad old cockerel or the blathering crows. In spite of her labours she was for a moment or two as content and happy as a peaceful soul above in heaven.

Fear Of The Sows

Now it was time to rouse the sow for, before any thought of her own meagre breakfast, she must ensure that this sow and the two pigs were well fed. Her mother had long warned her there was nothing as dangerous as a sow with her family of new piglets.

Little Nell had but few fears but one of these had always been the sow. She could not forget her regular early encounters with Galloping Gret's fierce sow when she was trying to pass by with her mother's note to Curl 'n Stripes shop for a few needed supplies on his *tick-book*. It wasn't just her war with the sow: stamped on her memory was the snappish humiliation poured down on her head in front of the other customers and the pipe-puffing drinkers and the smirks of them. It had always infuriated her and each time she told her mother that it would be the last time she'd be running the gauntlet of Galloping Gret's sow and the agonies of asking for the *tick*. 'Let Darkie go down to the shop and ask for the *tick*. She's big and ugly enough and she's braver than meeself. Her hole-in-the-heart isn't that weak, is it?'

La-dee-dah's Sow

And now (warily, warily) she threaded her feet inside the sow's sty with its pissy straw. She could see that La-Dee-Dah's sow was an even more dangerous rogue than Galloping Gret's fierce sow for she had thirteen piglets to guard and protect.

In a storybook she might have read the mind of a grunting sow: 'Who is this entering my stall? Who is this unrequested stranger opening my creaky door?'

She smiled at the sow. She almost bowed down before her. She waved her first buckets of mashed turnips in the sow's direction. The sow stumbled to her feet. She had managed not to kill any of her piglets by sleeping on them during the course of the night.

The signs were good. Little Nell carefully filled the trough, spreading the mashed turnips out gingerly. The piglets made up a fine morning chorus around their mother as she gently kicked them aside. She now had better things on her mind than playing with her offspring. Grunting happily, she lay into her feed with vigour. Little Nell looked on silently. What if this huge creature's hunger was not abated? Would she turn around and try to tear the leg off of a child like herself? With palpitating heart she threw the last of the mash in from the doorway and then she showed a fine pair of legs as she retreated to the safety of the farmyard.

Escape From Her Duties With Brownie

A stroke of luck came her way. Brownie the young bull was fattening up by the minute, so spoilt was he. You'd swear that Sallyswitch had adopted him as a child for he kept him in the farmyard and gave him the best stable he had. He brought the heifers to Brownie and ensured that the love-making procedures were carried off handsomely. For once in her life Little Nell was spared her blushes.

The Nerves Were Getting To Her

But a new and frantic time now put its head forward. She couldn't stop crying and was getting regular headaches. She was all the time gasping and couldn't catch her breath and the night breezes were like unearthly voices outside her window. She knew it was her aching nerves getting the better of her and she felt she was sickening. She threw wide the window and leaned out. She took great gulps of air from the cold night.

'Ah, the nerves! Them blashted Spallidagh nerves!' she moaned.

She was now a victim to the same *nerves* that, ever since the death of Handsome Johnnie, covered Dowager in red rashes at times – the *nerves* that had caused her father's young cousin to die of a broken heart.

Little Nell felt that she too might die of a broken heart. However, it wasn't her nerves that were causing her trouble. No-one had told her what was happening to her body: the backaches: the headaches: the stomach cramps. It was the time for her first menstruation and it came as a great shock to her to see so much blood. The poor ignorant girl thought she was about to die. Surely only the pig and the goose had ever been seen to lose so much blood. There was no one to comfort her. No one had ever warned her that such things could happen. And what could she say even to her one and only friend, Tom? Nothing. So, when no one was looking, she stole Sallyswitch's socks from the clothes-line and she stuffed them up inside her and in this way soaked up the blood.

Next day we find her dreamily looking in the direction of home and her mother. By now she was anything but fond of her mother – the mother, who had sent her back to this house of drudgery and all for the sake of the brown ten-shilling notes.

'Another five years of this blashted slavery!'

And yet a mother is still a mother. Dowager was the only one she could now turn to and like a sick lost calf she bawled her wild call in the direction of Rookery Rally: 'Oh mother, mother, come and take me home!'

She Fell Into A Doze

Lacking sleep and finding no compassion, she put the big cauldron onto the fire. She threw on the turf and the dry logs and the fire blazed up. She fell into a doze by the fireside. She fell off of the stool and fell into the fire. She was badly burnt and ran for the bucket of water. To this day her screams echo around the house and the yard of Sallyswitch and hop back off of the red gates.

After a hurried visit with her to see the doctor inside in the Roaring Town, Tom was allowed to drive her home to her mother. Sallyswitch threw three ten-shilling notes hastily into the cart as it sailed away down the avenue. He then went back to the stables to take a studied look at his racehorses. He took a good swig from his whiskey-flask and wiped the memory of a burnt child from his lips.

Tom had learnt a great deal in his former priestly life when he was travelling the roads of the diocese. He rode his horse to Dowager's door and gave her a lotion that he had made up in his room. It was Fingers Jack's mixture of laurel-paste and other hidden ingredients, mashed together with the pestle and mortar. Dowager followed his instructions to the letter and made a bandage with the boiling hot paste which she stuck into the screaming body of Little Nell. By some miracle (surely sent from heaven) her daughter recovered from her wounds before a month was out. There wasn't a mark left on her body.

She'd No Longer Wait

She thanked God for her cure and then promised herself she would not wait another five years to make the escape that Tom had planned for her. She vowed that the first time Sallyswitch let her go to town by herself and sell the two pigs, she would be off and away, never to set foot inside those godforsaken red gates again and ridding herself forever of the brutality of Sallyswitch. She was now fifteen-and-a-half. She got down on her knees and listened to the voice of God inside in her head: 'You're strong enough now to fend for yourself.' That's what God seemed to say to her.

The Lovely Racehorses

In the following months the one and only pleasure she found was looking at the lovely racehorses which Sallyswitch kept and nurtured. Rich farmers took their horses to the Annual Show-Fair in the Roaring Town but her master was too high and mighty for this local event and took his better racehorse to the Big City and from there to the Land of John Bull and to Newmarket itself where he would sell them and bring home others.

Her Master Cast His Eye

By now she was allowed to make up the beds and lay the tables. On these occasions she saw Sallyswitch dressing in front of the mirror. These days he was hitting the whiskey-flask fairly hard. She saw him dabbing a bit of white powder on his ruddy nose. He put on his buff trousers in front of her and he put on the canary waistcoat, squeezing himself into both. He had a red tie with a pin in it and he had a starched shirt and collar and a few red pimples on his neck from the starch. He had ruddy brown leggings or gaiters, which reached the thigh and he had the boots to go along with them so that it all looked like one long wellington that reached almost up to his fly-buttons. He looked slyly at his little servant. 'Not yet, my girl,' thought he, 'but any day soon you and myself will be taking the high jump in the bed.'

He marched out the door, carrying his whip nobly and headed away to the Big City and the boat that would take him and his racehorses across the sea, five hundred miles away. Little Nell could see it all – how he loved these over-pampered horses with a civility unknown to herself – them and Brownie the bull. Why couldn't he see that she was worthy of far more kindness? There was one relief: she was now learning the delicacies of her new womanhood and La-Dee-Dah at last forced herself to give her the few bits of rags and linen that she'd require to hide her shame in future months and prevent her insides from falling out. She was beginning to come to grips with it all.

Saturday Night, Getting Ready For Mass

On Saturday nights she got ready for Sunday's Holy Mass and busied herself washing her wiry hair, polishing her boots and grooming herself for the receiving of the blessed host next day. See her standing in the laundry and cleaning the farmyard dirt off of herself. She placed two chairs turned in to each other and she put the big tub on top of the chairs. Then she stripped to the waist and washed herself vigorously all over – as though the splashing water could wash away slavery itself.

At these times, whilst she was washing her body, Sallyswitch took to entering the laundry room. Looking at her growing young breasts, he would pick a row with her for the smallest mishap – be it the feeding of the sow or the cleaning of the dishes. Oh, the heathen! He would catch her by her bare body and beat her with his fists across her back and chest. Little Nell bore his merciless cruelties with a patience that the Magdalene herself would have been proud of.

Her Time Would Come

Her time would come. The beatings were bad enough. But the de-womanising of her – for Sallyswitch to be beating her exposed body – was an act of degradation which drove her almost demented and sullied her soul for many a blushing month with memories of those Saturday nights and the lustful man's merciless dealings with her in that ill-fated laundry room.

For three more wearisome years she served Sallyswitch, waiting for the time to come ripe. The day finally arrived. She went to the Roaring Town with the two fattened pigs and the blue-boarded horse and cart. She stood before the Limerick pig-buyers, who lept up onto her cart and prodded her fat pigs here and there.

'How much do you want for these little pigs?' they said in their strange singalong voices. Little pigs, be damned! They were both as big as a cow.

She Ran To Fanny Farthingale's Shop

With the sales money in the heel of her fist – and the silver coins from her heroic Tom – she ran into Fanny Farthingale's Dress-Shop. She bought herself two sets of underwear and two dresses and shoes to match. She bought a suitcase in Sadie O'Keefe's. Then she made a discreet retreat as far as the Station Yard. Her head was spinning and she was confused and in great fear lest she was seen and caught. She stood at the entrance, afraid to go in and feeling guilty as hell for having taken the money. Her eyes were blinded with tears until she saw a tinker woman inside the gates dressed in nothing but rags.

'Gimmee a copper, gwan do!' said the tinker woman.

It was just the same as many years before – the time when her grandfather, Dandy, had passed the tinker woman at the Portmantle Bridge and was promised the world for his kindness. She gave her a handful of her silver coins. She gave her the old clothes. The tinker woman loomed up before her as though she were an angel and she called down a blessing from heaven:

'May your children and your children's children reach the stars and get to see Glory!'

The Limerick Train

The train from Limerick came lumbering in, bound for the Big City and carrying the mail. It filled the station with its raging roars and its clouds of steam. Little Nell stepped on board and away she flew – into the flood of the future – into the world of the unknown. Faster and faster went the wheels and her racing heart.

Dusk stole into the crevices of the Dublin Mountains and filled them with black mist as the sun began to knife behind the hills and fade away. The evening church-bells tolled in the Big City's harbour as she entered the cattle-ship. She stood at the railings of the ship. She saw a shadow and looked up into the sky and saw a black cloud slowly spreading out and drifting like some huge stalking cat towards the sun. It was the shape of the lion in her school storybook that told the tale of Androcles. It twisted into a serpent as in Eden and stood there still and blocked out the sun – as though blocking out the sunlight in her own heart and soul.

Meanwhile, with the stolen money from the pig-sale she felt more and more like the biblical Judas and felt that hell was opening beneath her feet. She looked down at the bewildered cattle in the ship's cavernous hold – cattle that were bound for John Bull's island and the slaughterer's knife. She felt the sorrow of these poor misfortunate beasts as they filled the boat with their loud and prophetic roars. She cried with them and, like any stray lamb, she cried for her mother and cried to the ghost of her father.

'Why didn't I run home once more? But what would have been the use? Mee mother would only send me back again – and all for the money she so desperately needs.'

The journey was long and arduous. However, the next day when the train reached the railway station in the heart of the City of Pandemonium a little dance of sunlight shone in the window. The good women from Mary's Holy Legion met her and before the night came in they had settled her into suitable accommodation with the promise of work as a hospital ancillary. Life could only get better from now on. She would return all the money to Sallyswitch without so much as an apology. He could go to blazes and drink it away to his heart's content – in over the counter at the Widda-Widda-Woman's drinking-shop – and she herself would thereby ensure that she wasn't damned forever in the furnaces of hell.

And what of the horse-and-cart? What of the empty palms of Sallyswitch when no little slave-girl – no handfuls of cattle-money – no horse-and-cart returned through his red gates? He had his suspicions of Tom (the blackguard) but his son feigned ignorance – only to innocently hint that Little Nell had mentioned running away to Kilkenny (or was it to Cork?) to join a nunnery. In this way he stopped the search for Little Nell even before a search could begin.

A Time For Penance

The time for Penance had come and Sallyswitch now had a harsh retribution to pay back to his Heavenly Maker. He had to look out for another little slave-girl – one, whose legs La-Dee-dah could whallop with the yardbrush and one whose youthful body he could in time molest. But by now the ruffian had other things on his mind. The good God-in-heaven decided to send down on him a few of the Egyptian plagues for all his sins. His own two daughters in the convent-school in Tipperary got taken up with a child apiece and seemed surprised by the outcome of their own lusts. It was an unbearable shame in the family.

The eyesight of La-Dee-Dah was getting worse by the day – what with the cataracts in both her eyes. With her lighted bedtime candles she took to inspecting the sheets in the laundry room. Alas, she left a candle smouldering one night and the laundry went up in a blaze. Her alarmed shrieks saved the day and the house itself was not completely gutted but the laundry where Sallyswitch had brazenly treated Little Nell was gone forever.

Sallyswitch's favourite racehorse (*Dazzler*) was in foal. He came every day to inspect her progress, rubbing his delightful hands across her belly.

'My beauty!' he said, kissing her ears and kissing her nose.

It was a windy October evening and the time of the milling rains that spattered and bounced off of the roads

– the time of storm-scattered trees and bushes and of lanes high-packed with clay. Sallyswitch's sheep (tellers of weather) had moved quickly to the lee of the hill. Dazzler stopped grazing and took shelter in underneath a tree. The branch above her head broke in two and fell onto her back. She panicked and away she fled – in no particular direction. She attempted to leap the wire fence at the lower ditch. The wire and the spiky wooden fence pierced right into her side. It was sure and certain now – what with the laundry fire and now with the mare – that God had marked out a severe punishment for Sallyswitch. The lightning bolts of storybook Zeus could not have done a better job for the stake had pierced not only the belly of the lively mare but also the unborn foal inside in her.

Sallyswitch took the wide haycart down along the field – the haycart which they used for winching up the trams of hay each harvest like the misfortunate one that had brought on Deelyah's fatal injuries of old. He brought home the miserable twosome, the dead bloodstained mare and the stake still in her side and the unborn foal. The scene in the yard was like another cross on Calvary. He took to the whiskey-bottle in real earnest after burying his beloved mare and her foal in the Callow Field down by the river. He came home nightly from the Roaring Town's drinking-shops footlessly drunk – one foot in the stirrup and his head trailing the roadway – the clever horse delicately and oh-so-patiently carrying her master home and in through the high red gates.

And Finally...

And now... it is but right and fitting that we end this tale with a wish. May the blessings of heaven be heaped on you, Little Nell – little slave girl – in that new land across the sea – a land where you settled, rarely to return to those green fields and purple hills in Tipperary and the mother that brought you into the world in that quiet ditch beside the Turnip Field at Corcoran's Well – never again to hear the whistling and concertina-playing of your father, Handsome Johnnie.

Like Job, you survived the early days of your drudgery back home in Ireland. As the tinker-woman prophesied you indeed came to Glory long years later when heaven (one must surely hope) took you into its arms as a just reward for all your endeavours and where you wait (methinks) for your childhood companions back there on the slopes of Rookery Rally to follow in your footsteps towards the eternal joys that lie in that great borne beyond the skies, beckoning us all to come home. Enough said.

Author's Afterthought

Today – some seventy years after the end of the Second World War – I find myself returning hotfoot to the scenes of my early childhood in north Tipperary, racing across the fields and tiptoeing into the graveyard where I stand before the graves of my old guardians. Instinctively I close my eyes and lose myself for a moment, thinking I hear their voices humming their way into my bemused head as of old. It's just a dream. I imagine them smiling at me from across the grave's void – aware now that, through my few small bits of writing, I have paid my humble respects to them for looking after me in the first five years of my life – have paid my respects also to the folk who lived and died on the purple hill-slopes above Dolla – a place similar to Rookery Rally – folk who gave the green fields of north Tipperary their vibrant colouring and life-force.

I am but a messenger. It is the many tales of my guardians and those of the card-players and poachers – those of the men on horseback and abroad in the bog and the meadow – that have become the seeds of my writing and have compelled me to lay my hands to the plough and till in prose the rich life of rural Tipperary with my own particular crop of corn – a crop similar *to their own. I have watched it rise up, ripening in colours that have varied (it must be said) from an almost sickly lemon to a somewhat improving gold.*

And now, in peace and tranquillity I can return to my home in the Kent countryside and sit back and burn my toes in front of a blazing fire. I can tie on my boots and in the noon-day breezes take my stroll through the nearby fields and woodlands. Together with my close friend, my wife, I can sip my beer in a quiet olden-world hostelry. Isn't it time for a man of my age to put away the pencil and paper? Enough said.

yours truly,

Edward Forde Hickey, Kent August 3rd 2019